STAR TREK®
THE LOST ERA
WELL OF SOULS
2336

Ilsa J. Bick

Based upon STAR TREK
and STAR TREK:
THE NEXT GENERATION®
created by Gene Roddenberry

POCKET BOOKS
New York   London   Toronto   Sydney   Singapore   Farius Prime

This book is a work of fiction. Names, characters, places and incidents are products of the author's imagination or are used fictitiously. Any resemblance to actual events or locales or persons living or dead is entirely coincidental.

An *Original* Publication of POCKET BOOKS

POCKET BOOKS, a division of Simon & Schuster, Inc.
1230 Avenue of the Americas, New York, NY 10020

STAR TREK is a Registered Trademark of Paramount Pictures.

This book is published by Pocket Books, a division of Simon & Schuster, Inc., under exclusive license from Paramount Pictures.

ISBN: 0-7434-6375-7

First Pocket Books printing November 2003

10 9 8 7 6 5 4 3 2 1

POCKET and colophon are registered trademarks of Simon & Schuster, Inc.

Manufactured in the United States of America

For information regarding special discounts for bulk purchases, please contact Simon & Schuster Special Sales at 1-800-456-6798 or business@simonandschuster.com.

This book is for Dean Wesley Smith—editor, writer, mentor, colleague—and for David, with love, always.

HISTORIAN'S NOTE

This story is set in the year 2336, forty-three years after the presumed death of Captain James T. Kirk aboard the *U.S.S. Enterprise*-B in *Star Trek Generations*, and twenty-eight years before the launch of the *Enterprise*-D in "Encounter at Farpoint."

Prologue

Ishep was dreaming, and that should have been a mercy because bad dreams always end. Then Ishep would have awakened and known that this was all in his head.

In his dream, his father, the Night King, wasn't in his tomb deep underground in a labyrinth of tunnels beneath the Red Mountains, and Ishep should have been happy. In his dream, there should have been bright sunlight and grass so green and beautiful his heart hurt—and there was, and it did—and he should have stood with his father by the shores of a deep, clear lake that was clean and still—and he did, because Ishep, who was a bastard, had loved his father more than Prince Nartal, who was First Son and a coward, ever had. But Ishep knew everything was wrong, and it was as if his dream knew that, too. In the next instant, the sky melted, and the lake turned to stone, but Ishep's heart still hurt because his father, the Night King, was dead.

He saw then that his father had no eyes. The worms had eaten them. One worm that was very thick and clotted with black blood oozed from the hole where his father's right eye had been and slithered down his father's cheek, leaving a single, glistening trail like that of a tear. The skin over his father's face was brown and tight as old leather with age and decay, and flaps hung in tatters like torn curtains because the bones of his skull had ripped through as easily as . . . well, as easily as sharp bone slices through wasted skin thinner than paper.

Yet, as Ishep watched, his father moved, shuddered . . . then groaned. The naked white bone of his jaw unhinged, and his mouth dropped open. For a wild moment, Ishep thought that maybe it was all a mistake and his father wasn't dead after all and Prince Nartal hadn't left Ishep behind, lost and alone, in the tombs, but that this was some horrible game *because this is a dream, it* has *to be a dream, I don't want to die down here.* But then his father vomited—no, no, something thick as a man's arm and milky like the bloated belly of a rotted fish bulged and writhed in his father's mouth, like a fat, obscene tongue. The thing spooled out from the dark place inside his father and drooled over his jaw, and Ishep saw the thing's muscles undulate and ripple like waves beneath its too-white scales.

And then it looked at Ishep. Its dead eyes were flat and dull as gray slate. Ishep saw that it had the head of a woman, and all in a rush he understood that he stared into the face of Death itself, into the eyes of Uramtali, Goddess of the Well of Souls, and he knew then that he would die. But he could only watch, in horror, as her skin split open with a loud ripping sound, like cloth being torn in two, and then she didn't have a face anymore: just a skull, and teeth curved and sharp as white knives.

Her voice, in his head: *Are you afraid?*

And Ishep, so terrified his heart pushed in his throat: *Yes, yes!*

Good—her knife-fangs parted, and her mouth gaped open until there was nothing else but the darkness in her throat that was a shaft into which Ishep tripped and began a fall that would last until time itself ceased, and that was forever—*because you should be.*

Screaming, Ishep woke.

The tomb was pitch black. His scream echoed, bounced

off stone, then died. Ishep pushed up on his hands, his blood thumping in his ears. His sandals rasped upon cold stone, and the rock bit into the thin, sensitive skin of his thighs. He listened, but other than the hitching of his breath there was no other sound, not even the faint sizzle of candles guttering—a sound like frying meat—and that was because the candles had burned out. Darkness flowed over him, and when he moved, it was like swimming in thick black water. Although he was cold and stiff from sleeping on stone, his face was hot, and when he brought a hand up to his cheek, he felt the dried salt track of tears.

I'm still here. Moaning, Ishep jammed his fist into his mouth to keep from crying out. *I'm still here and I'm going to die down here and no one will ever find me, no one will know that they've sealed me in by mistake, and my mother, oh, my mother . . .*

His thoughts stuttered to a halt. Something was different, and Ishep seized on this because it gave him something other to do than wait to die of thirst in the tomb of a dead king. The darkness *felt* different, almost as if he'd been moved. Walked in his sleep? Maybe. His father's tomb had two other rooms besides the main burial vault, and he remembered that he'd fallen asleep next to the carved stone edifice of his father's bier. There was treasure all around the reliquary—piles of gem-encrusted goblets and fat yellow discs of gold coin fanning from chests of fine blackwood. But now when he patted the floor, his fingers grazed against icy rock, and nothing else. *Nothing here*—blindly, Ishep crept upon his hands and knees, pausing to sweep his arms in wide arcs—*no treasure, nothing, I must be in one of the other rooms, but which one, where am I, what's happening?*

And then his hands found something smooth and cool: wood. But not a chest—breath hissing through his teeth, Ishep sat back on his heels and ran his fingers up and down—no, this was something tall and slender, with three sides. A pedestal. He stood, his palms following the graceful taper of the wood until he came to the flat, triangular surface, and his fingers slid against something cold and metallic.

There was a soft, perceptible *click*.

Ishep started, gasped, snatched his fingers away as if he'd been burned. He waited, eyes bulging, heart knocking against his ribs.

The darkness began to dissolve. A sharp cry ripped from Ishep's mouth, and he stumbled back as the light bloomed: not like the sudden flare of a torch, but as if the light from one of the world's two moons had lost its way and come here, far underground. The light melted the darkness, and then Ishep saw that the room was bare except for a pedestal of ebony bloodwood. On the dais lay a silver mask.

The mask had no markings and Ishep saw immediately that it would cover his face from his brow to his upper lip. The mask was bathed in a silver glow: a bolt of light that beat down from somewhere high above. Ishep shielded his eyes but couldn't find the source. Then, suddenly, the light intensified, flooding over the dais and spilling to the floor. The light was alive—*like the thing in my dream, coming from my father's mouth!*—and it slithered along the floor in thick tongues that puddled like silver water.

Ishep's mind screamed: *Get out, get out*, run! But his body wouldn't obey, and where was there to run anyway?

Then a voice brushed against his mind: *Come here.*

Ishep's blood iced. What? No, no, he wouldn't! But even as his own mind protested, he felt a firm, steady pressure tugging at his brain, as if something had hooked in fingers of pure steely thought and begun to pull. No—he struggled to break free—he mustn't, he *had* to run, he had to . . .

Come here.

Incredibly, Ishep started forward, his movements as jerky as a puppet whose strings have gotten tangled.

Pick it up. The voice was a whisper, and yet it was so strong. *Put it on.*

"No," Ishep moaned even as he reached for the mask. His fingers slid over the metal, and he was surprised that the mask wasn't cold now but warm as blood.

Do it. Now.

"No," Ishep said, as he slipped the mask onto his face. The metal curled; the edges grasped the skin of his face like greedy, clutching fingers. "No, please!"

A bolt of pain sizzled through his body. Ishep screamed. It was as if someone had poured hot, molten metal into his body. Fire coursed through his veins and licked at his heart; his brain exploded with a sudden white-hot flash that seared his mind.

Now. Turn around. Move.

And then somehow—Ishep didn't know how, because he was burning up, **he was** dying, and there was something crowding into his mind, his body—Ishep was back in the main vault, and he was standing over his father, the dead Night King. The vault was still dark, though Ishep could just make out the hump of his father's body.

Through the roaring in his ears, Ishep heard the rustle of cloth against stone, a sound like the feet of mice skittering over sand. And then his father moved, and his body began to glow.

What was left of Ishep wailed in terror.

The king's mouth opened. Tendrils of something—*the dream, my dream!*—like luminous coils of thick white smoke billowed out, twisting and writhing. The coils mingled; they met; they coalesced and assumed a shape, now a woman, then a serpent, now a naked eyeless skull.

Suddenly, Ishep was aware of movement, a rush of air. Specters pulsed and streamed into the chamber, issuing from the walls like fog rising from a still pond. Ishep recognized the shapes of gods and goddesses, and strange chimeras that were part-beast, part-man, part-woman. They were as amorphous and indistinct as clouds shifting beneath a hot sun. And then the woman-thing, the one that had issued from his father's mouth, gave a great cry and spread its wings and leapt into the mass of roiling shapes. The others closed around the woman-thing the way a man's arms might encircle a lost lover, and in another moment, Ishep saw the woman-thing dissolve; and then, in his mind, Ishep heard the gabble of their voices—or maybe it was their thoughts because he knew there was no sound. Ishep sensed one voice detach itself from the rest, as if it had decided to step aside from a large crowd. The voice was clear and strong and rang through his brain with the clarity of a single, solitary bell.

You are not chosen. The voice-thought—a woman's— paused then walked its spectral thought-fingers over the nooks and crannies of Ishep's mind, as if searching for something. *You are not Night. There is Night within you, but . . .*

The woman's voice-thought trailed away, as if considering what to do next.

Ishep knew, without knowing how he knew, that the voice-thought was talking about the prince, Nartal. Nartal was Night, the prince of a Night King from a line of Night Kings. Nartal had been bred for Night, bred to carry the soul of an Immortal, a *dithparu*.

And then, quite suddenly, Ishep ceased being afraid. Beneath the mask, Ishep felt a strange pressure, like that of hands molding clay, and he knew that he was being kneaded into something new and wholly alien. But he wasn't afraid. Why? How odd . . . Ishep searched his emotions, turning over the secret places of his heart the way a child tips over rocks for bugs. No, he wasn't afraid, and he should have been. Instead of fear, there were other emotions: regret for his mother, though she was moving far away in his thoughts now, growing smaller and more distant, a memory that would soon be lost in the mists of time. There was anger at Prince Nartal, that coward, for slinking away after the rest of the funeral procession had left. But, most of all, there was sadness, and grief. Because Ishep knew that he was dying, and there was nothing he could do but watch his life slip away.

The woman's—Uramtali's—voice-thought again: *Why are you here?*

Ishep said, out loud, "I love my father, and I followed the procession here, and then I hid because I wanted to see an Immortal, a *dithparu*, being born. Only now I don't know the way out because Nartal left and I got lost."

Then, more boldly and with sudden inspiration: "That wasn't supposed to happen, was it? The princes have always stayed behind, because they're supposed to carry a *dithparu* from the Well of Souls, that's what they say."

That's true. Now . . . As Ishep watched, the whirling spirit-shapes bunched, shifted. *We have to think what to do next.* A pause, then: *Maybe you.*

Then, as the thing's thought-fingers wriggled deeper into the crevices of his mind, it was as if its thoughts and Ishep's merged, and then Ishep knew the truth.

They're just spirits, and that's all they are. Ishep grappled after the thought, tried to hang onto it. *They're Immortals, but they need a body, a certain kind of body, a body bred for Night. Only then, for some reason, they have to return here, because this is the place where they live; they can't leave this place on their own. But now Nartal's broken the line and now everything will change. They'll never get out anymore, because only Nartal knew the way out, they don't know the way, because they're spirits and they can't know, and now they're trapped here until time stops, and that's forever . . .*

Something was happening to the spirit-shapes. As Ishep stared, one portion of the mass seemed to bud, then separate itself from the rest. The figure hovered before Ishep, congealing like cooling glass into something recognizable: a snake with the head of a woman that shifted to a skull then back again, as if it couldn't quite make up its mind what it was, or would become. The woman's face, when it was a face, had ridges encircling the brows and tracking down the neck on either side, and the ridges had scales, just as the snake's body did below the woman's waist. The woman's hair was sleek and seemed to have a life of its own, falling in undulating, liquid black waves along its shoulders. Yet the woman's eyes were cold and flat and the color of slate. The woman-snake—now woman, now skull, now vapor—floated before Ishep, and Ishep saw a welter of emotions chase across its ever-changing features before settling into one that Ishep instantly recognized: hunger.

"Uramtali," Ishep whispered, his voice breaking. "Are you Uramtali?"

If you like. Prince Nartal was Night. The woman-snake pulsed and grew and reared above Ishep, her clawed fingers unfurling, spreading. *But you are the son of a Night King and there is Night in you. Just enough.* Then: *Would you like to see your father again?*

Ishep remembered the woman-thing that had joined the other spirit-shapes. Not his father, of course. These spirit-shapes were the Immortals, the *dithparus*. His father's soul was mortal, and so his father was gone, his spirit vanishing along with his last breath.

Still, Ishep said, "Yes."

Good. Are you afraid?

With a languid movement, Ishep shook his head. A strange warm torpor seized him, as if he were very young and been given too many goblets of wine, and suddenly, he was very sleepy.

Good-bye, Mother. Ishep felt his soul streaming away. His knees buckled. *Good-bye.*

Aloud, he said only, "No. I'm not afraid."

In the last instant of his life, Ishep saw something very much like regret flicker in the woman-snake's cold flat eyes.

You should be, she said, gathering herself. *You should be.*
And then Ishep screamed—but not for long.

Dawn ate away the night. In the palace, Nartal hid, waiting until the appointed hour when he would emerge and claim his place as the newly anointed Night King, bearing the soul of an Immortal. Except it was a lie, and it was the beginning of an end so far in the future that neither Nartal nor anyone else could possibly imagine it.

Far beneath the skin of this world, in a place where men from distant planets would not walk for another 6,000 years, the boy who had been Ishep sat. Ishep—the boy—was gone. Only the shell of his body, and the thing that was immortal, remained. Above, the world would spin on its axis, and the two suns would rise and set, but things would change, and very soon, because the world needed the Immortal in its shell to tend to the machines and make the light globes float. But the Immortal Uramtali—the *dithparu*—was trapped. So the world would break, and here was the supreme irony: For all its great powers, the thing was not a mind reader, and only Prince Nartal knew the way out.

Still, maybe it could last until it found another. Maybe.

Chapter 1

If she scanned one more duty roster, Captain Rachel Garrett was certain she would either scream or take her thumbs and pop the eyeballs out of the head of the first unlucky person to set his big toe into her ready room, and probably both.

Oh, we are in a good mood, we are just full of good cheer, aren't we, sweetheart?

"Well, I hate this," Garrett said, talking back to that nagging little voice in her head. She scowled, hunched over yet another ream of scrolling names, and knew, beyond a shadow of a doubt, that she had a migraine coming, a real whopper, and wasn't that just her dumb luck? "And I hate you."

But I'm not the one who wanted to be captain. Nooo, you wanted the glamour, you read about all the Archers and the Aprils and the Pikes and the Kirks and the Harrimans of the universe and how they zipped around in their starships and you decided, girl, you want you one of those. Only no one ever talked about duty rosters and being short an officer because you were stupid enough to let your XO go on R and R and the crew's still being on edge because you were too far away to help Nigel Holmes when he needed you most and everything that's happened since is your fault, it's your fault, it's your . . .

"Go away." Blinking against a lancet of pain skewering

her brain, Garrett pinched the bridge of her nose between her thumb and index finger. "Buzz off."

But the voice had a point, and the very fact that she was arguing with that little piece of herself hunkered somewhere deep in the recesses of what passed as her brain meant that maybe she *should* call it a night, or maybe a day, or . . . what time was it anyway? Frowning, Garrett glanced at her chronometer and then groaned. She'd worked straight through into the beginning of gamma shift. That meant that her new ops, Lieutenant Commander Darya Bat-Levi, was gone, relieved by the next Officer of the Day. Well, working straight through beta shift would explain why she was hungry, tired, sore—Garrett reached around and massaged a muscle, tight as a banjo string, in her neck. If she hadn't eaten or moved her aching butt one millimeter for hours, no wonder she was having an argument with a nasty little voice in her head. Except someone had to do this work, and without a first officer to pick up the slack, there really wasn't anyone else, was there? Not anyone qualified, that is. Oh, she could probably tag one of the bridge officers to step up to the plate. Bat-Levi, maybe, though Garrett didn't like the idea; the woman was on probation, after all. But Thule G'Dok Glemoor, for example: the Naxeran lieutenant was tactical, good head on his shoulders. In fact, he was OOD this very minute; maybe she should loosen the reins, tap Glemoor to . . .

"Don't kid a kidder," Garrett muttered, saying it before that needling little voice started up again. She was no more likely to order one of her bridge officers to step outside the scope of his duties than she was to suddenly sprout a set of Andorian antennae. The plain truth was she had trouble letting go. Not allocating duties: she couldn't captain the ship otherwise. But if there was *extra* work, she did it. Great, when she was a kid and her mom had chores that needed doing. Terrible, now that she was a captain and short an officer, and couldn't even tag ops to take over because Bat-Levi was still on psychiatric probation, and that new psychiatrist, Whatshisname, Tyvan, hadn't given his blessing yet and . . .

She put both hands in the small of her complaining back and arched. "Next time, Garrett, you don't let your first officer go on R and R when you don't have backup. Next time, you tell that Nigel Holmes that he . . ."

She stopped abruptly—talking and stretching. Mercifully, her little voice decided this was one time she didn't require commentary, or a restatement of the obvious: that Nigel Holmes—her former first officer and maybe a little more than just a friend, though she would never, *ever* admit that to anyone, much less herself—was dead and had been very dead for over six months now. Except her subconscious didn't want to let him go, did it? *Nosiree*, she thought, forestalling that little voice. *No, and we both know why, don't we? Samir al-Halak's your first officer now, and yes, he is away on R and R and it was rotten timing, only you're not sure you like Halak very much because he isn't Nigel and can never be Nigel, and so you let him go even when you shouldn't have, and that's because you can't let Nigel alone, can you? That's why you've tightened up around the ship, not trusting the crew to pitch in when you need the help, right? Right?*

"Wrong," she said, out loud. "Wrong, wrong, you are so wrong."

Blinking, she tried focusing on the pulsing red letters that made up the duty roster—stellar magnetometry, this time around, a chuckle a minute—and failed, miserably, because the letters wavered and refused to coalesce into anything recognizable and *that* was because she was ready to burst into tears.

I don't have time for this. She pushed up from her desk. *You idiot, you don't have time for this. Coffee, go get yourself some coffee.*

Trying very hard not to think, she crossed to a small cabinet below her replicator, stooped and pulled out a grinder, her stash of beans. She popped the vacuum lid and inhaled, gratefully. Nothing like the aroma of fresh coffee beans, and nothing like a good cup of fresh-brewed coffee. Garrett didn't trust the mess chef (nothing against the man; she didn't trust anyone to brew a cup just the way she liked it— that damned problem letting go again), and she couldn't stand replicator coffee. Replicator brew tasted . . . well, artificial. Like burnt plastic.

The grinder was whirring so loudly she almost didn't hear the hail shrilling from her companel. Just a cup of coffee— she crossed back to her desk and killed the hail with a vicious jab at her comswitch—just one lousy cup of coffee in peace and quiet, that's all she was asking, and why couldn't they leave her alone? *"Yes?"*

There was an instant's startled silence, and Garrett had time to reflect that she sounded as if she might just order a full spread of photon torpedoes if whoever was calling uttered *one more* word. Then a reedy voice sounded through the speaker. "Uhm . . . ah . . . call for you, Captain."

Great. Garrett blew out, exasperated. Super. Bite off the man's head, why don't you? Clear the decks, folks, the captain's on a rampage. Lieutenant Darco Bulast was a fine communications officer, and however angry she was at herself for the weird twists and turns her mind was taking this evening, or this morning, or whatever the hell time it was, beating up on the rotund little Atrean wasn't fair, or very captainlike, for that matter. "Thank you, Mr. Bulast. From whom?"

Bulast told her, and then there was another moment's silence, only this time it was because Garrett's emotions, now a mix of apprehension and sudden remorse, were doing roller-coaster somersaults and double loop-de-loops for good measure. And this time the only voice inside her head was pure Rachel Garrett: *Oh my God, it's Ven, and I forgot again, oh, that's just great, that is* juuusssst *perfect. . . .*

There'd be hell to pay, no way she could duck it, and

could things get any worse? Could they? Sure, probably, why not, this was her lucky day, right? Quickly, she glanced at her reflection in her blanked desk monitor, and squinted. She didn't like what she saw. Her complexion was pale, as were her lips. Purple shadows brushed the hollows beneath her walnut-brown eyes, and her auburn hair, usually so neat and smooth it looked held in place with electrostatic charge, was in disarray courtesy of her restless fingers pulling, prodding, twirling as she'd perused the duty rosters and other effluvia normally reserved for officers other than captains. Plainly put, she looked as if she'd been stranded on a planetoid for a month with a canteen, a week's worth of survival rations, no blanket, and nothing to read. And then, in the very next instant, she figured to hell with how she looked; she doubted her looks had much to do with how Ven Kaldarren felt about her these days anyway. She said, "I'll take it in here, Mr. Bulast, thank you."

"No problem, Captain," said Bulast, and Garrett heard the relief. "But I . . ."

"Yes, Mr. Bulast?"

"Well, it's the signal, Captain. It's not on a priority channel and it's not scrambled. But it's not registered either."

"You mean that you can't tell which ship it's coming from?"

"That's right. It's as if, well, I guess you could say that whoever's making the call wants a certain degree of anonymity."

"I see." Unregistered ships weren't unheard of, and certainly not registering a ship that wasn't under Federation jurisdiction wasn't a crime. She dredged up what Kaldarren had told her about the xenoarcheological expedition he'd signed up for. Precious little: they weren't talking much these days, even less now that the custody battle for Jason was behind them. Then she gave up the exercise as pointless. Kaldarren could do what he wanted, whenever he wanted. That was a reason they'd divorced, right?

"Thanks for the information, Mr. Bulast. I'll follow up on it. Now put the call through, please."

"Aye, Captain," and then her companel winked to life, revealing the unsmiling face of her ex-husband. And, damn it, the sight of him still took her breath away. She was used to thinking of Betazoid men as being almost androgynous: slender, dark-eyed, smooth-skinned. Ven was unapologetically different. Always had been, and probably that was the attraction. They'd met in 2316, a year after Garrett's graduation from the academy. By then, she was a lieutenant and posted aboard the *Argos*. Ven was part of a Betazoid delegation of xenoarchaeologists the *Argos* had transported to a Federation Archaeology Council symposium on Rigel III. Ven had hulked above the other Betazoids. Standing at a hair under two meters, Ven was broad in the shoulders and muscular; unlike his comrades, he wore his black wavy hair long, and his Betazoid eyes were full and slightly hooded, fringed with a lush set of black lashes. Bedroom eyes: That was the term, and then-Lieutenant Garrett's first thought.

Lust at first sight, Garrett thought now. *A long time ago, before things went south*. They'd divorced in 2333, a year after she'd taken command of the *Enterprise*.

"How are you, Ven?" she asked. Garrett felt the unpleasant jolt in the pit of her stomach she always did when they spoke, as if she expected a reprimand by a superior officer. So different from those first few years, when they couldn't keep their hands off each other. Now she and Kaldarren couldn't stand to be on separate monitors in different rooms several dozen light-years apart.

Kaldarren's head moved in a curt nod. "Fine," he said, barely moving his lips. Kaldarren had all the animation of a piece of stone, and the dark eyes that had once burned for her were hard and flinty. "Jason is fine. My mother's fine. Now that's out of the way, what happened to you?"

"Well, yes," Garrett tried a smile, "I guess I missed you on

Betazed. You're calling from a ship, right? Right. So you and Jase have already left . . ."

"Oh, were you really planning on coming?" Kaldarren's black eyes went wide with mock astonishment. "Forgive me, Rachel, I guess I misinterpreted. When Jason's birthday came and went and we didn't hear from you, I assumed that, after a week, we were free to leave the planet. Or were you planning on surprising us by dropping by in another month?"

Garrett was stung, and then angry. What the hell did Kaldarren know about what she was going through, anyway? They hadn't talked in months, really, and so he didn't have a clue about what it was like to lose a perfectly good officer, a friend, and all because she was stupid enough to . . .

Stop. That damn little voice again, but Garrett held back long enough to swallow the retort pushing against her lips. *Listen to what he's saying. You let them down, again. He's right to be angry.*

"You're right to be angry," she said. It seemed as good a line as any, and the little voice, for once, was dead on. "I said I would come to Betazed, and I didn't. I didn't even call. That was wrong of me, and you're right."

"Yes," said Kaldarren, clearly not mollified. "I *was* angry, and I'm *still* angry. Do you want to know why?"

No. "I have a pretty good idea, but, sure, tell me." *Let her rip; I deserve it.*

"It's not because of me, my feelings, though I doubt very much that they enter into your equations these days. There's nothing between us anymore, and we know that."

Garrett knew that this was where Kaldarren was wrong. Hatred and love: They were intense emotions, and a person didn't waste emotions on anything that was unimportant. So their hatred—and was it hate, or just plain hurt?—was important to him, and maybe to her. Garrett's mind drifted to the words of an ancient poet who'd once written that our worst monsters are the people we've loved the most intensely. Ovid, she thought.

"I'm angry because of what you're doing to our son." Kaldarren's face was taut with emotion, and Garrett saw then that his eyes were sadder than she remembered, more deeply set, the circles beneath them more pronounced, as if Kaldarren wasn't sleeping well. A tracery of fine wrinkles splayed like wings from the corners of his eyes, and the black hair, which he still wore loose, was shot through with silver at the temples. "I'm angry because every time you let him down is one more wound that won't heal, and believe me, I know how much that . . ."

Kaldarren broke off then turned his face from his viewscreen, but not before Garrett saw the pain. How many days and nights had Kaldarren waited for her? Too many, she knew.

"How much that hurts," she said. "How much it hurts to hope, and then have your hopes destroyed and not be able to do a damn thing about it."

"Yes." Kaldarren's voice was a hiss. "Yes. Every time you don't keep your word, I see how Jase suffers. I remember how much I suffered."

She saw that his fists bunched, and though they were too far apart—and she was no telepath—she felt his anger and hurt and frustration.

"You had your own work," said Garrett. There was more defensiveness in her tone than she wanted, and she felt her migraine knife its way into the space behind her eyeballs. "You made sure you weren't around."

"What was I supposed to do? Wait until my wife decided it was convenient for her to happen by my little corner of the galaxy? Sit around in an empty house, hoping that the next call would be from the woman who said she loved me but who could never seem to find the time to actually *be* with me?"

"Please." Garrett closed her eyes. Her brain felt bruised, and she was suddenly nauseated. She'd been standing, but now she sagged into her chair, licked her lips. "Please, Ven."

"Please what? Please pretend that I didn't hurt? Please make believe that we can be civilized about this?"

"No. I know we can't. But we've been over this. What purpose does it serve to keep . . . ?"

"Don't *tell* me what we've been over!" Kaldarren paused, took some deep breaths then continued, his tone more controlled, "If I want to go over it a *thousand* times, you *will* listen. You owe me the courtesy, at least."

"Oh?" She sounded spiteful, even to herself. But she couldn't help it. "I do?"

"Yes. Oh. You do. Because you're doing it again, only this time you're doing it to a little boy who loves you. A little boy who worships his mother, thinks she's the greatest woman alive because she commands a starship." Kaldarren said this with a sort of flourish, a flash of bravura. "The Great Captain Rachel Garrett. Commander of the illustrious *Enterprise*, the flagship of Starfleet."

Garrett felt the heat rise in her neck and, my God, her head was killing her. The lights in her ready room were too damn bright. She narrowed her eyes to cut down on the glare. "I'm not after Jase's worship. I'm not out to be *anyone's* hero."

And that little voice: *Liar, liar, liar.*

"Don't," Kaldarren said. "Don't lie to me, and don't lie to yourself. This is what you've always wanted, Rachel. More than you ever wanted love or family, you've wanted command. Well, now you have it. But you still have responsibilities."

Garrett flared, the blinding jabs of pain in her temples making her even angrier. "I know *that*. Damn you, Ven, you try sitting in this chair day after day, making the really hard decisions and knowing that the lives of your crew . . ."

"Stop." Kaldarren scrubbed away her words with the flat of his hand. "Rachel, to be very frank, I couldn't care less about your duties, or your really hard decisions. They're no more real or harder than the ones I face, every day, as Jason's father. So I don't care about your crew, or your starship. I don't even know if I care about you."

He let that hang in the air between them for a moment. "You'll never understand how that feels: not to know if I care about the woman I held in my arms, who gave birth to my son. But one thing I do know. I do care, *very* deeply, about our son, and I will not let you hurt him. *Nothing* is more important than how you treat your son—not your work, not your ship, not your crew. You simply cannot keep doing this."

"Or?" Garrett stared into Kaldarren's unflinching eyes. She knew there was something he hadn't spoken, a final piece he hadn't divulged. "Or?"

Kaldarren looked away then, as if collecting his thoughts. Or maybe he simply hated what he felt forced to say. "Or I will make sure that you don't see him." He looked back, and those eyes of his locked onto hers and wouldn't let go. "I have full custody."

"Because we both knew that I couldn't take Jase on a starship," said Garrett, a little desperate now, her heart doing a little trip-hammer stutter-step against her ribs. "The only reason you got custody was we *agreed . . .*"

"And," said Kaldarren, talking over her, "and I will go back to court if I have to and make sure that you are not allowed visitation. At. All."

Stunned, Garrett could only stare. "I'm," she said, hating that the words came out in panicked little hesitations, like a subspace transmission awash with interference, "you . . . Ven, you . . . can't . . . *wouldn't.*"

"I can. I would. I *will*. Rachel," said Kaldarren, and the way he said her name, Garrett could almost believe, for a fraction of a second, that he didn't hate her at all but was still, very desperately, in love. "Rachel, you can't keep doing this. Please try to understand. I know you're not a monster. I wouldn't have loved a monster. At least, I don't think I would, though we do seem to bring out the worst in each other. But what you do when you don't keep a promise, *that's* monstrous. That's wrong. It's not even humane. You have to make a choice. You chose against me once, against . . . us."

"I seem to recall that you chose against us, too," she said, relieved that her mouth cooperated. "You filed for divorce, not I."

"Fair enough. But I chose to stop bleeding, Rachel. I chose to bring an end to one type of pain, and I exchanged it for another. Now *you* have to choose: your ship or your family. You can't have both."

"What kind of choice is that? Your ship, or your family," she said, the blood pounding a samba beat in her temples now. She scrubbed her forehead with her right hand, restrained the urge to start cursing, *loudly*. "Christ, Ven, you sound like a character from a cheap holonovel. What exactly am I supposed to do? I can't just drop everything when things become inconvenient. There are some things, *many* things that happen aboard ship that require my presence."

"Such as?"

"Such as now, right *now*. My first officer's away, and I've got no replacement, and I can't tag my new ops, this woman named Bat-Levi, because she's on psychiatric probation and that's because she went a little crazy a while back, but she's supposed to be really sharp even if she *is* a bit off, and . . ."

She paused for breath. Kaldarren didn't need the litany, after all. "Those are all good reasons why I, as captain, can't just leave. Ven, you act like I have a choice. I don't. I can't delegate these things away," she said, sidestepping the fact that, probably, she could, if she were wired just a little bit differently. "What kind of choice is *no* choice?"

"No, Rachel, you *do* have a choice." Kaldarren sighed. "Don't you understand? You *have* a choice. You have *choices.* Your problem is that you simply don't like the ones you have."

He was right, and she knew it. Damn him, but he'd cut right to the heart of things, like he always had, as if he really was reading her mind.

Don't be stupid; it's not the telepathy. The man was married to you for seventeen years. Who better to know how you think?

She said, "I want to talk to Jason. Can I speak with him, please? Try to explain? Please?"

"And how do you propose to explain things, Rachel?" Kaldarren's eyes were large and sad. "What can you possibly say that will make things any better?"

And, much as Garrett hated to admit it, the man had a point.

"Please, Ven," she said again. "Please?"

Chapter 2

"Can we get on with this, please?" asked Lieutenant Commander Darya Bat-Levi. Her voice was strained, but her tone was still polite. "*Please?* I've just gotten off shift. I'm tired, it's late, and while I appreciate you being willing to move my . . . *appointment* around to accommodate my duty schedule, I really would like to get this over with, if it's all the same to you. So can we move things along, please?"

And then she *did* move. A simple thing, crossing her right knee over her left leg. When she did so, there was a small click, the halting choke of a servo as the joint flexed, extended. The whirr and clack of machinery.

Borg. Dr. Yuriel Tyvan felt his stomach clench. *Borg.* The thought was immediate and visceral, like a roundhouse punch to the solar plexus that has you wondering if you'll ever breathe again. Tyvan's mouth went dry, and his heart ramped up, the hairs prickling along the back of his neck. *Borg.*

The Borg were the black maw of a tunnel, a long, dark corridor filled with inchoate sounds and images too chaotic to be called memories: the rippling of the deck beneath his feet and shuddering up his thighs, the high thin screams of the other refugees. Sweat tracking down his neck, soaking the back of his shirt. The acrid smell of his fear. The way his mother had clutched at his arm so tightly her nails ripped into his skin and left marks: a row of tiny crescent moons incised in red. They were the only remnants of his mother Tyvan had left—marks that had healed, and memories that would not.

Now, of course, Tyvan knew that the first powerful jolt, the one that sent him reeling against a bulkhead and a stout, heavy girder crashing down to crush his mother's back, was not a disruptor beam fired from a Borg cube. At the time, his mind gabbled in panic: Somehow the Borg had made it from the Delta Quadrant, tracked them down, and now they were going to die, and if they didn't die, they would be assimilated . . .

Now, after forty-three years, Tyvan knew that an energy ribbon, the Nexus, had destroyed the two ships, the *Lakul* and the *Robert Fox*, carrying the pitiful remnants of his civilization to safety. But he didn't know about the Nexus until long afterward, when he and forty-six of his fellow El-Aurians were safe on the *Enterprise*-B, and his parents were dead.

He appreciated the irony. Here he was on another *Enterprise*. He should have felt safe, but he didn't. Tyvan never felt safe, knowing the Borg were out there, somewhere. Waiting. Biding their time. Machines were patient. Machines didn't know guilt, or fear. Machines could wait—forever, if necessary.

"Please?" asked Bat-Levi again, her tone testy now, and Tyvan blinked back to the present.

Darya Bat-Levi was no Borg. The woman sitting in the overstuffed beige armchair—the chair he reserved for pa-

tients—was in her early thirties, and Tyvan thought she'd
once been beautiful. She wasn't beautiful now. An explosion
and long exposure to theta radiation had taken care of that.
A taut, shiny pink scar ran from her right temple to the
angle of her jaw and trailed down into the hollow of her
throat. The scar was so tight the right corner of Bat-Levi's
mouth pulled down into a lopsided grimace. Tyvan knew
from Bat-Levi's medical files that her hair had once been
black. Most of it still was, except for a wide, silvery-white
swath that ran from just above her right eyebrow and
streaked over her ear like the tail of a dying comet. Her
spine, from thoracic vertebra four on down, was a titanium
implant. And there were the artificial limbs made of titanium alloy and polydermal sheaths: Bat-Levi's legs, and her
left arm and hand, the one whose fingers had no nails.

Her body mass was now sixty-six percent metal, thirty-
four percent everything else, give or take. That's the way
Tyvan figured it. Bat-Levi didn't move like a Borg, or even
look that much like a Borg. She squealed when she walked,
though this meant that she needed to get her servos adjusted. (Tyvan thought she let her servos go on purpose, and
he would get to that, all in good time, and probably tonight.
There was method to his madness, too.) The medical engineers hadn't been able to restore much in the way of sensation, but he knew that Bat-Levi felt pressure, and she felt
pain. She needed pressure sense, or else she couldn't walk,
and she needed to feel pain, or she'd never know to pull her
hand out of a fire. Her skin was pink, not a sickly grayish-
white; she had a soul and emotions. Her mind—imprisoned
in the body Tyvan was sure she cherished—was her own.
Tyvan knew that Darya Bat-Levi didn't have the foggiest idea
who the Borg were, or even that they existed. Few in the
Alpha Quadrant did. Yet.

"Sorry," said Tyvan. His fear had made his underarms
damp with sweat, and perspiration crawled beneath his col-

lar. "My mind wandered a bit there. The hour, I guess. I apologize."

"If you'd like me to come back another time," said Bat-Levi, her tone hopeful. "I know *I'm* tired and . . ."

"No," said Tyvan, cutting her off. He watched her face settle into an expression just shy of sullen resentment. "I'm with you right now. This is your time."

"My time." Bat-Levi mouthed the words as if they tasted bad. Her scar rippled as she clenched her jaw. "I hate when you psychiatrists couch things as matters of choice when there are none. Like I asked for this, like I came to you and said I really wanted to spend time in here."

"No one's forcing you to talk about anything, Darya."

"Oh, no?" That tiny snick again, as she readjusted her spine, as if some bit of metal had snapped back into place "I have to be here, don't I? Five sessions, that's the number, right? That's as many sessions as you need to write up a report, recommend whether or not I can stay active. You and Starfleet and the Vulcan shrinks . . . you all agreed. A precondition to my coming back to duty: Keep an eye on the crazy woman. Doesn't matter that I do my job just fine. You're all just worried that I'm still crazy."

"I don't know if the Vulcans think you're crazy. I didn't speak with your physician."

"But you read his report."

"Skimmed, actually: All doctors, even erudite Vulcan psychiatrists, tend to write summaries that verge on the incomprehensible. Anyway, *crazy* isn't a word we use to describe patients anymore."

"And Starfleet?"

"I don't recall they used the word *crazy*, either. Someone—I believe it was Captain Nash—mentioned that you were troubled. Other than that, he said very nice things. But you know all this, Darya. You have the same access to your personnel files that I do. Besides, no one would have allowed you to return to duty if they thought you couldn't handle it. Captain Garrett's put you at ops. You think she would have done that if she thought you were crazy?" (Actually, Tyvan had no idea how Garrett felt. The captain avoided him like the plague.)

"Whatever." Bat-Levi held herself ramrod straight, and Tyvan wasn't sure if this was because her spine was less flexible, or she was really that defensive. Looking at the way her black eyes flashed—a veritable semaphore of hostility—Tyvan decided on the latter.

"You want to talk about how angry you are, in general?" asked Tyvan. He shifted in his chair, and he caught the squeal of leather. "Or how frightened you are?"

Bat-Levi jerked, and a servo clattered. "I'm not scared. I'm not scared of anything."

"Really?"

"Really."

"Okay," said Tyvan, and laced his fingers across his middle. The silence stretched for several minutes. An antique wind-up clock, with a brass disc pendulum, ticked, tocked, ticked. (He had a regulation chronometer that would ding at the end of their session, but he kept the clock because the face was circular and the sweep of the hands, round and round, was a reminder that life and the psyche were circular because the important things came up again and again.) Tyvan never took his eyes from Bat-Levi; Bat-Levi seemed to find something fascinating on the carpet. Finally, Bat-Levi looked up. "*What?*"

"I was looking at your hand," said Tyvan, deciding to go for broke. Besides, he was being truthful. "The artificial one."

He saw her flinch—and there was that squeal of servos again—then resist the temptation to hide the hand. "What about it?" she asked.

"No nails. How come they forgot to give you nails?"

A red flush bloomed along the underside of her jaw. "I . . . I don't know. I never asked. Then, once I noticed, I decided it wasn't important."

"Oh. Well, that was an oversight. Makes it that much harder for people not to stare." Tyvan blinked once, very slowly. (His therapy supervisor once said Tyvan reminded him of a lizard drowsing on a rock.) "You'd think they'd want to avoid that."

"Avoid what?"

"People staring."

"*That?* I don't care. People are going to stare anyway, don't you think? Nails, no nails, what are nails when you look the way I do?"

"Well," Tyvan's eyes moved over her body as if taking inventory, "now that you mention it, nails aren't that big a deal. Of course, I guess you were counting on that."

Bat-Levi's jaw spasmed, pulling the scar along the right side of her face even tighter. It shone pink like the smooth skin of a naked rat. "I don't know what you mean."

Tyvan pinned her with a look. "I don't buy that."

"Oh?"

"Yeah, oh, I don't buy that." He shifted his lanky frame (he was so thin, sitting for long made his tailbone ache) and ran a hand through cinnamon-colored hair that he knew needed a trim. "Look, you're a smart woman. You've sat with shrinks before, right?"

Bat-Levi pushed air out between her lips in a dismissive snort. "More than my share: first on Starbase 32 when they tried talking me into reconstructive surgery, then on Meir III at my parents' place, and again on Vulcan. Want to know something?"

"What?"

"I liked the Vulcans best. They're so logical, and they can be very passionate in their logic. But they know how to keep things in perspective, and I have to be honest here. Meditation and Healing Disciplines have helped more than all the cathartic theatrics you other psychiatrists seem to want."

"Actually," said Tyvan, "I don't want you to dissolve into a puddle of elemental protoplasm." He stopped, worried that this sounded too defensive and thought that, maybe, he was. She'd spent a lot of time with psychiatrists; that was clear. He tried another tack. "You think you've figured me out."

"Sure." Bat-Levi smirked, easy to do given the way the right side of her mouth curled. "Lull the patient into thinking you're really not paying attention, that things are going along fine, then *snap!* You'll be all over me like a Darwellian long-tongue slurping up an unsuspecting fly."

"I'm not paying attention?" asked Tyvan, knowing that he hadn't been, not earlier.

"No, I said you just *looked* like you weren't. You're very good at it. You looked a million kilometers away. But, you see, *I* know that you're just waiting, watching for a chink in my armor." She reached down with her artificial hand and gave one of her artificial legs a good thump. She clunked. "In my case, that's apt."

Tyvan took a moment before he replied. "Wow, you are good."

Bat-Levi's twisted smirk of triumph evaporated. "What do you mean?"

"I mean that I started out asking you about your nails and your prosthetics, and now we're talking about how good or not good I am at my job, and whether I measure up to other shrinks you've known. You're very good at ducking."

"I don't know what you're talking about," Bat-Levi said, and Tyvan could tell she was lying. Her face was too stony. On the other hand, maybe that was easy for her. All that scarring must make facial expressions difficult.

Tyvan kept his tone mild. "Don't be stupid, Darya. If you're going to be stupid, you can leave. We both have better things to do."

Her black eyes widened and then shone with bright, un-shed tears, and he saw he'd hit the mark. "You're right," she said, her voice dripping with bitterness. "I'm so stupid. So, okay, you want to talk about my nails, the way I look, my guilt, sure fine, go ahead, fine, make your point."

He paused. Then: "I never said anything about guilt, Darya."

She swallowed so hard he heard it. "Yes, you did," she said, but her voice was smaller, a little timid. "Yes, you did. I heard you. You did." She flared. "Anyway, so I'm feeling guilty. This is a surprise? It's all over my profile. *Yes*, I feel guilty. *Yes*, I get depressed, and, *yes*, I've wanted to die. I've tried to die, and then when the Vulcans wouldn't let me, I stopped trying. I decided that God meant for me to live and remember, so I'm alive and I *do* remember and I feel the guilt every single day of my life. And that's the way it should be. That's justice. There, is that what you want?"

Tyvan was sure that if looks could kill, he'd have been in his casket. "It's not a question of what I want, Darya, though you're right. I'm not surprised. You love your guilt. You'll hang onto guilt until the day you die."

He saw the first slight flicker of uncertainty in her eyes. "What are you talking about?" she asked.

"I mean that guilt is a wonderful thing. It's so expected. We assume that someone who survives or has, perhaps, been indirectly responsible for the death of a loved one ought to feel guilty for being alive."

"Oh, but I'm sure you see it differently."

Tyvan heard the sarcasm and knew that he'd struck a nerve. "That's right. I think that guilt is a wonderful weapon. Guilt is like a mantle you use to cloak yourself from contact with other people. Guilt is armor, just like your body there; and guilt, just like your body, lulls everyone into assuming that guilt explains everything, so they leave you alone. What's the expression? Walking on eggshells, pussyfooting around. Guilt is a marvelous way of making sure that no one sees inside your soul, or knows the truth. And you've gone one better."

"And how is that?" she asked, her tone not sarcastic now. She sounded like a scared little girl.

Tyvan leaned forward, careful not to crowd her. "Darya, you've let yourself stay this way so you can keep everyone else at bay. You know how, way back, on Earth, they used to condemn people who'd committed certain horrible crimes to death?"

Bat-Levi moved her head in a squealing, miniscule nod. "Capital punishment. That was abolished after the Bell Riots, three hundred years ago."

"Right. I've studied that period in Earth's history, and particularly the history of capital punishment."

"Why? That's so gruesome."

"Not if you don't understand the concept. We El-Aurians never practiced capital punishment. Killing someone as the ultimate punishment? Yes, I suppose there's some justice to it: an eye for an eye, that sort of thing."

Bat-Levi shook her head. "No, that's wrong. See, I'm Jewish and . . . well, culturally, really, but my uncle is a rabbi. He said that even the old rabbis, from way back, understood that a literal interpretation of that law helped no one. Taking out eyes, chopping off hands: The old joke was the ancient Middle East must have been filled with one-eyed cripples."

"And how did they resolve the issue? I thought that the orthodox of your many religions were pretty rigid about these things."

"Rigidity isn't confined to Earth. But, to answer your question, the rabbis got together and decided on how to compensate people for loss, damages, things like that. So instead of losing your eye, you might pay what that eye was worth. There were only a few crimes that merited the death penalty. Murder was one of them, but all that finally died out on Earth centuries ago."

Good, good, keep her talking, keep her working with you. "You have any theories on that?"

"On why capital punishment went away?" Bat-Levi thought. "I guess because dying isn't the most awful thing that can happen to a person. Personally, I think . . ."

"What?"

Bat-Levi gave him a frank look. "I think that the minute right *before* you die, when you know that this is it and there's no going back, that's got to be the worst."

"Really? You think that knowing you're about to die is worse than death, than not existing anymore?"

"Not if you believe in some religions. You have to take an afterlife on faith."

"Do you believe in an afterlife?"

Bat-Levi hesitated for an instant. "No, not in the Biblical sense, if that's what you're driving at. On the other hand, Jews don't really believe in a heaven or hell."

"What do they believe?"

"I can't speak for every Jew, but I do know that devout Jews believe that your soul is really just a piece of God. You're renting it for a little while, that's all. In the end, when you die, your soul goes back to God. I guess you'd call it a kind of Oversoul."

"So, no hell? No condemnation for eternity?" Tyvan sat back and laced his fingers over his middle, but he was acutely aware that their time, for this session anyway, was running out, and he wanted her back, like this, willing to work *with* him. "So how do people pay for their sins, in that religion?"

Bat-Levi gave a queer half-smile. "I guess it depends on your definition, doesn't it? On what constitutes payment? Can I ask where this is going?"

"I was just thinking. We were talking about your nails, and then your body, and *you* mentioned guilt, and I . . ."

Tyvan shrugged and shook his head in a *you-got-me* gesture. "Well, I was just wondering how you were paying, that's all."

"Paying."

"Right. For your brother Joshua," he said, as if she needed additional information.

Bat-Levi made a tiny sound—a clicking noise in the back of her throat that Tyvan knew was not a servo but the sound a person would make when she's trying not to cry. He waited her out. The clock ticked, tocked.

Finally, Bat-Levi cleared her throat. "You have an idea about that."

"Well, yes, as a matter of fact, I do. You see, I think you're right. I think that dying isn't the worst punishment sometimes. You said it yourself: It's that awful, terrible instant before, when you *know* and you're more frightened than you thought you could ever be and still be alive. Don't you humans have the expression *scared to death?* Except this is just plain scared. Pure, unadulterated, searing terror: imagining the possibilities, facing that everything you ever believed in may be a lie and that there's simply nothing but blackness, darkness. Something you can't even compare to sleep because at least when you sleep, you dream."

"What does that have to do with me? *I'm* not going to die."

"But you've tried."

"I mean I'm not *now*. Trying, that is."

"No?"

"No, I'm sitting right here. I'm alive. I'm back at work. I'm living."

"Precisely. You're alive, Darya, but that's not the same as living. You're alive, but that's because you've condemned yourself to life."

"No," said Bat-Levi, swallowing hard, "no, I don't want to hear this."

Tyvan pushed on, knowing that time was running out but not wanting to lose the moment. *Careful, careful, not too fast, give her space, give her time.* "Your brother is dead, and you're going to make sure everyone knows that you were responsible. You want people to look at you and see a monster. Only you're hiding in there . . ."

"I'm not a coward," said Bat-Levi. She clenched her fists, and Tyvan was reasonably sure that her left hand—the one without nails—could probably rip his heart right out. "I am *not* a coward. Suicide is the coward's way. I'm alive."

"And you think that makes you brave? You think that parading around your guilt is bravery? No, Darya, no, it takes more bravery to dare to be happy again, to leave your guilt behind. It's braver to *live* than simply be alive."

Bat-Levi's laugh was bitter, almost a snarl. "You're like all the other doctors, shaking their heads and *tsk-tsk*ing over poor, benighted Darya Bat-Levi. Such a beautiful woman, and *now* look at her."

"This has nothing to do with beauty. This has to do with parading your inner ugliness. I'm not suggesting that you run out and change. I want you to understand your choices. So let's look at the facts. You refused evacuation to Starfleet Medical. You refused every single reconstructive surgery, every offer of synthetic skin grafts. Ten years have passed, and even though better, more lifelike prostheses are available, you have those." He indicated her artificial legs and left arm. "You limp, and you don't need to. You have scars you don't need to keep. You wrap yourself in guilt you don't require, because it's easier."

"Don't tell me what I need!" The words erupted from Bat-Levi's throat in a hoarse shout. Spit frothed at the corners of her mouth, and the cords bulged in her neck. "Do you think I *want* to live like this? Do you think I *enjoy* looking like a freak? *Do* you?"

"Yes, Darya," Tyvan began, but then there was a soft ding as their session time ran out, and his heart sank.

Bat-Levi heard the sound, too. "That's it." She jerked herself from her chair, pushing back on the cushions until she tottered to her feet, her prosthetics protesting. She stood, swayed, pulled her body around for the door. "I'm done, I'm out of here."

"Darya." Tyvan was on his feet, cursing himself for his timing which was rotten, rotten, he should have paid closer attention to the time, what an idiot! "Darya, wait, I don't want you to leave like this . . ."

"But I do." Bat-Levi glanced back, her face contorted into a mask of rage and grief. "I do, and I will. It's my life, Doctor, and I will do with it as I please. Oh, don't worry, I'll be back, but when it's my time and not a second before. For now, write whatever you have to, say whatever you want, but I've put in my time, and there's no regulation in the universe that says I have to sit here one second more."

"Darya, *please*," Tyvan said, but she had turned aside and was through the door. Her servos squealed, the door hissed, and then she was gone.

Tyvan let out his breath in an explosive sigh. "Great," he said to the air, to no one in particular. Sinking back into his chair, he propped the points of his elbows upon his knees and held his forehead with both hands. "Good job, Tyvan, you idiot, bravo. That was perfect timing, just perfect."

He sat then and listened to the ticking of his clock and thought long and hard about life and cycles and time.

Chapter 3

Perfect timing. Commander Samir al-Halak dragged his forearm across his face, mopping away sweat with the sleeve of a camel-colored tunic that was open at his throat and showed off the olive color of his skin. *Just perfect. Somebody, please,*

*tell me, what was I thinking when I detoured to Farius Prime?
I could've been swimming in Lake Cataria. Ani and I could
be making love, right now, in the grass under a cool night sky.
So what in God's name was I thinking?*

Halak hadn't wanted to come to Farius Prime at all. His
plan had been to spend his R and R with his lover, Anisar
Batra; their plan had been to leave *Enterprise* together and
go to Betazed. He and Batra had planned the trip for weeks;
she'd coordinated her leave with *Enterprise*'s other paleoge-
neticist, and he'd gone to Garrett with his request for R and
R a good month before. Their plan had *not* included a detour to the Maltabra City bazaar on Farius Prime, and the
plan most certainly had not involved coming to Maltabra in
high summer, when the weather was more miserable than
usual and the air so humid Halak felt as if he were pushing
through soggy gauze curtains. That the plan had changed—
that he'd snuck off the ship early and that Batra had, *somehow,* tracked him to Farius Prime and was dogging his heels
at this very moment—just made Halak hate everything
about Farius Prime more than he already did.

The central bazaar of Maltabra City stretched for two
kilometers in every direction, so there was no way around it:
precisely what the city's planners had in mind. The bazaar
was always packed, and the air heavy with the mingled aro-
mas of sweat, mint tea, rancid broiled kabobs that had sat for
so long under a hot afternoon sun that the vendor had more
bluebottle flies and Terellian swarmmogs than customers.
An occasional breeze carried a metallic odor of salt and wet
aluminum from the Galldean Sea, six kilometers due east.
There was the overlapping babble of humans and humanoids and assorted aliens all shouting in different lan-
guages and at the top of their lungs; the whispered
exchanges of drug dealers looking to score; the pleas of their
clientele, desperate for a hit of that planet's prime commod-
ity, red ice. And there were colors: the brilliant turquoise sky

and the searing white of sand and stone so bright Halak
blinked back tears, and the customers, who ran the gamut of
the "naturals"—Orions in their native green and the sky-
blue of the Andorians—to more ambitious (and audacious)
body dyes, fur, or scales.

Halak dodged around a Katangan merchant haggling
with a jade-green Orion man about the cost of a liter of
alpha-currant nectar—*"But at that price, you're asking me to
take food from my children's mouths, no, no, what do you take
me for?"*—and planted his right foot squarely into a stack of
beaten copper pans spread on an indigo blanket. The pans
belonged to a wizened Bilanan woman (from the northern
continent, so she had seven facial knobs, not four) wrapped
in a blood-red caftan with gold embroidery. The stack collapsed with a resounding crash, and Halak staggered, felt his
ankle twist, and then a bolt of pain rocket to his knee.

"Here now!" the Bilanan said, outraged. Even her facial
knobs quivered. "There's people trying to make an honest
living!"

"Sorry," said Halak, not really meaning it but just wanting
to make the woman be quiet. Digging into a leather pouch
he wore around his waist, he tossed the Bilanan a few coins.
"That covers it, right?"

"Don't you think that makes everything all rosy," said the
woman, snatching up the coins. Reeling in a leather cord
that dangled around her neck, she dragged a pouch from
some nether region of her caftan, dropped in the coins,
closed the purse tight by tugging at the cord with her teeth,
and let the pouch fall back into the folds of her garment—
and so quickly the money was gone before Halak blinked.
"Don't you go thinking . . ."

Halak didn't stay to hear the rest. Hobbling away from the
woman, he elbowed his way deeper into the crowd, his right
ankle complaining with every step.

Behind, he heard Batra say, "Samir, you're limping."

"It's nothing."

"But don't you think you ought to take it easy?"

"No," said Halak, throwing the word over his shoulder. "I *don't* think. And right now I don't want to know what *you* think either."

Instantly, he was overcome with remorse. He stopped, turned, and looked down at his companion. "I'm sorry. It's just that I didn't ask you to come, I didn't *want* . . ."

"Well, that's just too bad," said Batra, her voice sounding a little watery. "That's just too damned bad. How *dare* you treat me that way? Only cowards bully."

Halak bit back a reply. She was right, and, not for the first time, he marveled that she was the only woman he knew who could make him feel as if he were about ten years old. It wasn't that she was very imposing. Anisar Batra was a tiny woman, with a long shock of shimmering raven-black hair that she wore up when she was aboard ship, and almond-shaped eyes the color of chocolate. Normally, those eyes held nothing but love. (Sometimes she got a little annoyed with him, and then they seemed to shoot phaser beams, set to kill. All right, maybe that was when she was a lot annoyed. What she saw in him was anyone's guess. Halak knew he wasn't particularly handsome or tall. In fact, he had the compact build of a well-muscled wrestler, something that came in handy when a man had a temper, and Halak *had* a temper. On the other hand, they'd been lovers for six months, and Halak didn't intimidate her in the slightest. It was one of the things he loved about her.)

But he didn't want to fight with her, and Halak saw that her eyes were liquid with unshed tears of surprise and hurt. But she was good and blistered, too; her copper-colored skin was turning a shade the near side of maroon.

"I'm sorry," he said again, chastened. "It's just that you don't understand."

"Don't I? Well then," Batra said, folding her arms over an

emerald-green, short-sleeved choli that showed off her trim waist and a sparkling garnet tucked in her navel, "maybe you'll just explain it to me."

"There's nothing to explain."

Batra gave a breathy laugh that wasn't really a laugh at all. "Oh, no? Let me refresh your memory, *Commander*. What *I* recall was that *we*—emphasis on the *we*—made plans to take our R and R *together*," she said this very distinctly, as if she were speaking Vulcan to a Klingon tourist who hadn't the foggiest. "As I recall, we had no intention of setting one toe on Farius Prime, much less traipsing around a dusty bazaar, under a hot sun. We said Lake Cataria. Betazed? That ring a bell?"

"I'm not stupid, Ani." Halak scooped a hand through his crop of close-cut black curls and blew out. "I was going to meet you on Betazed sooner or later."

Batra arched one black eyebrow, her left. "Emphasis on later, I'm sure. We were supposed to leave together. We were supposed to be having that serious talk two people who supposedly love each other usually have when they're trying to decide if they can stand each other's company for the long haul."

"I can stand your company, Ani." Halak's lips twitched, and he tried not to smile. (*God, no, then he'd get a lecture about how he wasn't taking her seriously.*) "You're just a pain in the neck."

She didn't smile. "Yes, I am your particular little pain, and you wouldn't have it any other way. So you want to explain why you've been looking to ditch me ever since I showed up at Starbase 5?"

"Because I wasn't expecting you. And how did you find me, anyway? I didn't leave word where I was going."

"Woman's intuition."

Halak barked a laugh that sounded as if he'd cracked a dry branch over his knee. "Farius Prime is the *first* place a woman thinks about? Come on, Ani, that's no answer, and you know it. How did you find out?"

Batra licked her lips, and for an instant, it crossed Halak's mind that she might be getting ready to lie.

"Well, I just *did*," she said, tersely. She mopped her forehead with the back of one hand. "Look, it's too hot to stand here, arguing. What difference does it make, anyway, and especially now? I'm here, I'm hot, I'm thirsty, and my mouth has so much sand my teeth are getting a nice buff and shine. I think it's high time we get someplace cool, and I buy you a drink. Don't you agree?"

"No." His ankle was killing him. "I don't want a drink. I just want to . . ."

"Good," said Batra, linking her arm through his. She pulled him toward the nearest café. "I'm parched."

They made Halak check his phaser at the door. Batra's eyebrows headed for her hairline when she saw the weapon.

"Personal carry. No regulation against that." Halak gave a half-shrug. "You never know."

She didn't reply. They ordered then drank in silence, and Halak had almost finished with his second Saurian brandy when Batra said, "Penny for your thoughts."

Halak shook his head. "They're not worth that much."

"Samir, are we going to talk about it?"

Halak lifted his glass to his lips. "No."

"Are you like this all the time, or do you practice a lot when you're alone?"

"Actually, I save it all up for you," said Halak, and then drained the rest of his drink. He craned his neck, peering around Batra for the waitress.

"Probably because I'm the only one aboard patient enough to put up with you."

"No, you're the only one aboard *lucky* enough." Halak's eyes swept the café. The interior was very dark and close, smelling of mint tea, sugary roasted almonds, and the sour tang of Trakian ale. Halak spotted one of the café's wait-

resses: an Atrean, dressed in a tight weave of hip-hugging
silver mesh that began below her bejeweled navel and
ended at a spot barely brazing the underside of her but-
tocks; silver strappy sandals that threaded up to mid-calf;
a mane of silver hair that coiled in strategic swaths over
her breasts; and very little else. Halak whistled, and when
she looked his way, he pointed to his glass and held up a
finger.

"You really need another?" asked Batra.

"You're not going to let us leave until we talk. I'm apt to
get dry."

"Uh-huh," said Batra. She sipped at a tall glass of iced
Molov mint tea. "Well, we could talk about your leaving *Enterprise* without me. Or we could talk about why we're on a
planet with no redeeming virtues."

Halak snorted, a humorless exhalation through his nose.
"I don't like either of those topics."

"Well, I . . ." Batra began but stopped when the Atrean
expertly tacked a napkin to the table with a fresh glass of
brandy and retrieved Halak's empty. The woman lingered a
moment longer, bending so that her hair had to adjust by
curling and rethreading itself, like a mat of snakes, to keep
her breasts covered up. Even so, Halak got a good glimpse
before the Atrean straightened, flashed a tiny smile to Halak,
and turned on her heel, her long shank of hair flaring to reveal the small of her naked back. Halak's head swiveled to
watch her go.

"Well, I want to know," said Batra, reaching across and
taking Halak by the chin. She pulled his head around but
let her fingers linger over the raised ridge of a thin white scar
that skittered over his left jaw. "And I want us to make it to
Betazed in one piece."

Halak grabbed her hand and pressed his lips to her fingers. "We'll make it. We would have made it faster if you
hadn't followed me."

Batra retrieved her hand. "But I have and we're here. You want to talk about that?"

Halak took a sip of the strong orange liquor, swallowed, and inhaled through his teeth against the burn. "Ani, if I had wanted to tell you, I would have. I know that we've been together now for some time . . ."

"Six months. Half a year."

"Half a year. But in every relationship there has to be privacy. Even telepaths have places in their minds they keep locked."

"Everyone has a right to privacy. But there's a difference between privacy and secrets. The way I see it, this is about you keeping secrets."

"What secrets are you referring to, Ani?"

"You want me to make a list?"

Halak gave a mirthless laugh. "That many? We only have a week's leave."

"Okay, then how about you and I? Where do we go from here?"

Halak reached across the table and took her hands in his. "I know where *I'm* going—to Betazed with the woman I love. Now, as I recall, I asked you a question about two weeks ago. It was the same question I asked you several months ago. Both times, you said you wanted to think. Well, you've thought and I've waited. You want to tell me now?"

Even through the haze, Halak saw the color rise in Batra's cheeks. "No," she said. Her eyes drifted to the table. "Or, maybe . . . I don't know. It's so sudden. When you asked the first time, we'd only known each other two months."

"Ten weeks." Halak gave her hands a squeeze. "Four weeks longer than I needed to know for sure. But I didn't want you to think I was an impulsive guy."

"Oh, never that." Her eyes still didn't meet his. "No, I know you're not impulsive, Samir. You may be opinionated, and you're lucky Captain Garrett . . ."

"Let's not talk about Garrett, all right?" Halak softened the admonition by running the fingers of his right hand along the back of her left. "We're off duty, Lieutenant. Your hair is down, the choli's on, and I'm sitting across from the most beautiful woman in the quadrant. *Enterprise* is far away, and I'd like to keep it there, if you don't mind. This is supposed to be *our* time."

"And that's precisely my point," said Batra, freeing her hand. "This was . . . this *is* our time. And yet we're here, on Farius Prime, where no one in his right mind goes, not if he wants to stay out of trouble. But that's your problem, isn't it? That you're always in trouble?"

"That's the rumor," he said. It was as close a reference to his previous posting on the *Barker*—and the fact that he hadn't been transferred to *Enterprise* under the best of circumstances—as she'd ever come. He'd given her the official version, but no one—not Garrett, or Batra, or anyone else on board—knew the whole story. Halak kept his face impassive. "You have a question?"

"No," she said, her teeth nipping at a corner of her lower lip. "Well, yes. I know you've told me about that Ryn mission, right before you were transferred. . . ."

"And?" he prompted when she hesitated.

"And I know it's not the whole truth. Don't bother to deny it; I'm not really asking you to tell me right now. But that's just an example."

Halak reached a hand to the scar along his jaw: a souvenir of that particularly disastrous mission. "An example of what?"

"Of how you approach things. You tell the truth, but only to a certain point. I feel it," she bunched a fist over her heart, "right here."

"You have something specific in mind?"

"Yes, I do. Why are we here?" Batra tapped a nail upon their table with a tiny click. "And why didn't you want me with you?"

Halak blew out. "Damn, but you're persistent."

"Yes. So answer the question."

"All right." Halak took a pull of his drink, liking the way it burned a track down to his stomach before spreading out along his belly like fingers of liquid fire. "I'll tell you what. I answer your question and you answer mine. Deal?"

She hesitated for a fraction of a second. "Okay. You first."

He put his hands on the table and laced his fingers together. "I'm here to see an old friend. Her name is Dalal. Dalal took care of me on Vendrak IV."

"Where you were born. This was after your parents died?"

"Exactly."

"Is she one of your relatives?"

"No. Just an old family friend. Actually, she used to work for my father."

"As what?"

Halak shrugged. "Housekeeper, secretary, nanny . . . you name it. My mother died first . . . you know that, of course. From Denebian fever."

"I know. But you never really talked about how that happened."

"How does anyone get Denebian fever?" Halak put both hands around his drink but didn't lift his glass. "Not enough food, terrible living conditions. We didn't have it all that great, not until my father found steady work. But she got sick before he could and then she died. I was ten."

Batra's eyes were full of sympathy. "That's so awful."

Halak tried a smile that didn't quite work. "Yeah, I guess you could say that." (Of course, he couldn't really describe to her what it *was* like to watch his mother shrivel away bit by bit. And what she said to his father when she thought Halak couldn't hear: *I'll never see my children grow up . . .*)

He closed down the memory. "After that, my father . . . he was never the same. For one thing, he just didn't have a lot of time for me. At first, I thought it was because of my mother, but he'd never really been there. Always gone on business. A . . . what's the old saying?" Halak snapped his fingers. "A fly by night. That's it."

Batra's brows met in a frown. "Fly by night?"

"Yeah, it's an old nautical expression. This big sail," Halak held his arms apart, gestured with his hands, "and you could rig it and forget it. But what it really means is someone who's only interested in a quick profit. That was my father. Always some scheme. Except nothing panned out, not until . . ." His voice trailed away.

"Until what?"

"Oh." Halak blinked, refocused. "Until he got involved in some business . . . I was too young to know exactly what."

"And then?"

"A couple of things. One, he was gone for long, long stretches of time. Longer than before, but by that time, Dalal was there and she made sure I had food, clothes on my back. She even worked at trying to get me to go to school."

"How did she do?"

"*Well*, except school." Halak sighed, finger-combed his hair. "I was a pain in the ass. Always in trouble. I started stealing. Little things at first—you know, food, I was always good at stealing food, maybe because I always felt hungry, even when I had plenty to eat."

"I don't think a kid forgets going hungry."

"No, but I think I did it to get back at my father. See, he took up with another woman not long after Dalal came to live with us, and this woman moved in. I never liked her much, and not just because she wasn't my mother. You know, she tried to get me to call her Mom, must have been a hundred times. A thousand. I never could, and looking back on it, I think she did her best to make me like her. But I didn't. Sort of a willful type of hate, if you know what I mean. Dalal didn't like her either, but I never knew if that wasn't just jealousy."

"And you weren't? Jealous, I mean."

Halak ran a meditative finger over his scar. "Probably, though it's only now that I see it. Back then, I was just an angry kid whose mother was dead and whose father was gone all the time but thought this other woman might solve all my problems. Eventually she left my father. Then, when my father died, Dalal took over. I was fourteen."

"How did your father die?"

Halak's fingers teased a corner of his cocktail napkin. The paper tore, and he rolled it into a tight ball. "Business deal gone bad. I really don't know the specifics."

"With all that, I'm amazed you made it into the Academy."

"Makes two of us. But after my parents were gone and there was just Dalal, I think I realized that I had to do something to help myself. I'm not an institutional type of guy, but I also never felt a sense of belonging to a real family, and I guess I figured Starfleet was the place where I could. Find a family, have a sense of belonging somewhere. Anyway, that's where Dalal fits in. I figure I owe her. So, she called," Halak put his hands out in a gesture that encompassed the café, "and I came."

"But she was on Vendrak IV," Batra said slowly, as if she wanted to cement the details of his story in her mind. "And now she's on Farius Prime. That's a long way from Vendrak IV, Samir. How did she get here? Why?"

"Why does anyone come to Farius Prime?" Halak asked rhetorically. "They come for the money. The last I heard, Dalal was on Vendrak IV. I haven't heard from her for years, ever since I left for the Academy. And then, you know, deep space assignments and all that," Halak spread his hands, a *what-can-I-say* gesture. "Time passes."

"So why does she want to see you now?"

"I'm not sure," Halak said, relieved that this, at least, was true. "But I owe her, Ani. Dalal put up with a hell of a lot."

"This still doesn't explain why you had to sneak around."

Halak sighed. "Look, Farius Prime isn't the nicest planet

in the galaxy. I didn't want you exposed to that. I don't want anything to happen to you, Ani."

"I can handle myself."

"I'm not saying you can't. Hell, you're better with a phaser than I am. But that's not the point. Farius Prime is a rough place."

"And how would you know?"

"Know that it's rough?" Halak hiked a shoulder. "How does anyone know anything?"

Batra gave Halak a narrow look. "Stop playing games. You've been here more than once, and don't bother to deny it. I can tell: the way you handle yourself, the fact that you seem to know where you're going. You never once asked for directions."

He felt a little clutch of anxiety in the pit of his gut, and he became aware that his fists were clenched. He forced his fingers to unfurl. *Relax, would you, she doesn't know; none of them know.*

He kept his features matter-of-fact, and opted for the truth—to a point. "Ani, I don't want to fight. I don't want to hurt you, and I don't want you to *be* hurt. This isn't about you handling yourself. It's about being smart, not taking unnecessary risks. Now, whether or not I was right to keep where I was going from you, the fact is I did. On the other hand, you followed me, and I'd love to know how you managed that."

"Is that your question?" she asked. Her voice was taut, and Halak gave her a searching look and knew she was hiding something, but he was damned if he knew what. But that just made two of them doing the same thing to one another.

"No," said Halak, at last, reaching for her hands again. "That's not my question. This is: the same question I asked you twice before."

He felt her hands flinch, but she didn't draw them away, and he felt a flare of hope. He gave her fingers a gentle squeeze.

"Ani," he said, trying to put everything he felt into that one word and wondering if she would ever, *could* ever know how very much he hated keeping secrets from a woman he loved as much as he did her. "Ani, will you marry me? Please?"

Chapter 4

When Ven Kaldarren didn't respond, Garrett leaned in closer to her companel. A little crazy, sure, but maybe, if she could close the physical divide just a little bit, this might be the ticket to bridging the emotional chasm that yawned between them like a black and bottomless pit.

"Please," Garrett said again. "Please, Ven, don't make me beg. You knew I'd want to speak with Jase if you called. If you wanted to humiliate me, you could've done the same thing in a prerecorded message."

"No," he said, and his voice was thick. (With anger? Sadness? She couldn't tell.) "No, I didn't call to humiliate you. You should know me better, Rachel. I would never do that to you. That's a coward's way, and I'm not a coward about most things."

This was true. She was the one who'd always been gone on deep space assignments, the one who was conveniently away, or had somewhere to go if there was a personal problem. How ironic that she could face down phaser blasts, Klingons, and ion storms, but she absolutely withered, *cringed* when it came to dealing with her own emotions, or the feelings of the people she really, truly cared about.

Maybe that's why I'm good at captaining, and crummy at everything else. When you're a captain, there are rules and regulations and nice, safe codes of behavior. Everything's so civilized.

She looked into Ven Kaldarren's ravaged eyes and read

his sorrow and hurt. *But there's nothing civilized about love, nothing.*

"No," she said finally. "You aren't, and . . ." She cleared her throat. "I'm sorry, Ven. That was unfair of me. Please, I would like to speak with Jase. No excuses; I won't ask him to forgive me because he has every right to be angry, too . . ."

"He'll never hate you, Rachel," Kaldarren said. "He loves you. He always will, no matter what happens."

And no matter what you do. Kaldarren hadn't said it, but he might as well have; Garrett read it in his eyes. And did she see something else there? Something about her?

She brought herself sternly. *Don't go there. That's over and done with.*

He broke the silence first. "Let me get him. He . . . I think he'd like to hear from his mother."

Garrett opened her mouth to thank him, but Kaldarren's body swiveled to one side as he turned in his chair, and then he was gone. Staring at the emptiness where her ex-husband had been, Garrett waited, her head throbbing, her heart aching. She tried not to think. Not now. Maybe she would think later, or maybe she wouldn't think at all because there were a lot of things pressing in on her, a lot of responsibilities. For now, though, she had to focus on Jase.

There was a blur of movement on the companel, and she blinked, plastering an automatic smile on her face before she'd even registered that Jase had slid into Kaldarren's empty seat.

"Sweetheart," she said. *Too bright, too chipper, tone it down, you sound like a chipmunk.* "How are you, honey?"

"Fine." Jason had Kaldarren's black hair, though it was much shorter, and the same black eyes, though he had Garrett's paler coloring and the same oval cast to his face that made him look fragile as fine china. "How are you, Mom?"

"I'm okay," she said, lying. "I missed your birthday. I'm sorry. That was wrong."

Jase hiked his shoulders. "S'okay."

"It's not. A boy doesn't have his twelfth birthday every day." *Not so cheery; you can't smooth this over.* "I promised you I'd be there, but I wasn't. That must've made you angry."

"No," said Jase, though his voice broke a little and Garrett couldn't tell if it was from the lie, or that he was growing up. "It made *Dad* angry."

"Oh?"

"Yeah. He didn't say anything," Jase added, as if worried Garrett might think that Kaldarren was goading the boy into taking sides. "He never says anything. He doesn't talk about you much, not even when Nan wants to. He won't. I know because I've heard him tell her to be quiet; that it's not right to talk about you. Then sometimes they get really quiet, and they aren't talking, but they still are, you know? The way the room gets really still and the air is hard, like ice, and I just know that they're *thinking* at each other, real loud."

Garrett could imagine that this was exactly how an argument between two telepaths might seem to someone who couldn't read minds, and she ought to know. *Excluded* was the word that came to her mind, and that was the way she'd felt whenever they visited Ven's mother, as if they and all telepaths were part of a club to which she was denied admittance, maybe for her own good. She'd always nurtured the sneaking suspicion that Ven's mother, an imposing and somewhat imperious woman named Molaranna, made cutting little telepathic jibes about Garrett. To Garrett, the atmosphere always turned frosty whenever she and Ven visited, and sometimes the pauses in the conversations weren't empty at all but felt full of things being said in the air above her head.

She gave Jase a small smile. "But you said Dad was angry. If he didn't tell you, how do you know how he felt?"

That shoulder hike again. "I just do. It's hard to put into words. But Dad's feelings . . . they kind of come off in waves. Like heat shimmers off hot sand, the way you can see them in the air. You know?"

"Sure," said Garrett, remembering those cold pregnant silences. "What about you?"

"What about what?"

Garrett gave him a look. "I mean, how did you feel? When I couldn't . . ." She broke off, and rephrased. "When I *didn't* come for your birthday after I promised I would?"

"It made me sad," Jase said, with the simple, unflinching directness that only children who love their parents have. "You promised, and you didn't show up. You didn't call."

It was on the tip of Garrett's tongue to tell her son about all the things that were going on with her crew, the ship. But she held back. He was a boy. She was the parent. It wasn't Jase's job to comfort her. *No excuses.*

"Yes," she said, "and I'm sorry, and it's not okay. It's never okay to break a promise."

Jase nodded. His eyes fell, and he blinked. "But there was a good reason, right?" he asked his hands. "I mean, you're a captain and all, and so you must have had a lot to do, stuff that's really important."

Oh, yeah, duty rosters are really important. Letting your first officer go on R and R because you'd rather not have him around is really important.

"You're important," said Garrett, and that was the truth. She couldn't bring herself to say that he was more important than her ship; he'd see through that because, after all, she hadn't made the choice to be there for him. But she told him the truth.

"Sure," said Jase, still staring into his hands.

Garrett waited a beat. "Where are you all headed, by the way? I forgot to ask your father."

Jase shook his head. "I don't know. Dad didn't say. We're just," he made a helpless-looking gesture with his hands, "on a ship."

"Are there other scientists on board?"

Jason nodded. "Yeah, one other, and the pilot. He's Nax-eran. And another kid. His name's Pahl. He's Naxeran, too."

"Oh," said Garrett. "Well, that's good. I mean you'll have someone to talk to."

"Yeah," said Jase, without much conviction. "It would be okay if we stayed home, though."

Home, as in Betazed, Garrett translated silently. Betazed was home for Jase. She could count on one hand the num-ber of times he'd visited her family on Earth. That was okay, though; she didn't much enjoy seeing her family either.

"Are you getting tired of going off with your dad?"

"Only a little." Jase looked wary. "Why?"

"How many expeditions does this make this year?"

"This is only the third." That same defensive tone again. "It's not so bad."

Garrett let it go. She didn't have a better alternative any-way, though maybe she ought to talk to Kaldarren about not agreeing to so many trips. Uprooting Jase and traipsing across the galaxy at every turn couldn't be any better for him than following her to every starbase. In fact, when she thought about it, Kaldarren's dragging Jase with him wherever he went wasn't all that much different from packing a family aboard a starship—not that anyone did that, of course. Whether you were on a starship or a science transport, space was dangerous.

"Okay," she said. She paused, at a loss to know what to say next. "Did you get some nice things for your birthday?"

Jase's face lit up. "Yeah. I got this really cool easel and some new paints from Dad and Nan. You should see . . ."

Garrett listened as her son rattled on about his painting, and she felt a tug at her heart. Jase was so sensitive, she knew. He was more like his father. Kaldarren's work was xenoarchaeology, but what he loved was art. Jase had the same soul, the same ability to appreciate and create beauty, and these were abilities she lacked. Oh, she liked art, all right. But make something? Hell—Garrett almost shook her head—she'd been working on the same piece of bargello embroidery for the past three years.

"I'd like to see your work," she said, when Jase paused for breath. Her keen eyes picked up how much color there was in his cheeks, how his eyes sparkled with excitement.

Oh, my son, you're going to be an artist someday, I can feel it, and one day when you're grown and not my little boy anymore, you'll have your first show and I'll be there. I promise.

The shrill edge of a hail sliced into her thoughts. "Wait, Jase," she said. Muting the audio so Jase couldn't hear, she punched up another channel. "Yes, Mr. Bulast?"

"I'm sorry, Captain," said Bulast, still sounding a little shell-shocked, "but you asked to be notified when astrocartography wanted to steal some power from the deflector array for their long-range mapping, and it would have gone all right, but engineering's having fits because of some problems with circuit overloads and . . ."

Yet another thing a first officer would have attended to. Garrett suppressed a sigh. "All right, thank you. Give me a minute, Mr. Bulast. Tell engineering I'll be right down."

"Aye, Captain." Bulast signed off.

"You have to go," said Jase, when she'd turned back and switched on the audio.

Garrett nodded. "I'm sorry, Jase. There's something I have to take care of down in engineering. Honestly, they're like kids, and they need me to . . ." She heard what she was doing, stopped herself. "I'm sorry, Jase. I just . . . I have to go."

Jase's eyes were solemn. They looked very black and much too large for his face. "Okay. When will I see you, Mom?"

"Soon. I don't know when," she said, truthfully. "Soon, I hope. When you and Dad get back."

"Okay."

"Can I speak with your father?"

"I . . ." Jase's eyes flicked to somewhere off-screen, and then it came to Garrett that Kaldarren must be there, just out of sight. Then Jase looked back at her. "He's busy right now." Jase's hand moved forward to break the connection. "Bye, Mom."

"Bye-bye, sweetie." Then she had a thought. "Jase, wait . . ." But she was too late. Her companel winked, and went black.

Damn. Garrett stared at the empty screen. How bad had this day been? *Let me count the ways.* No first officer on board; duty rosters out the wazoo; a justifiably pissed-off ex-husband; her son and his father headed off for God-knows-where; and a headache that was leaking out of her ears.

Enough. The light was too damned bright, and she'd had enough badness for one day. She just wanted to be alone, a couple of minutes. Just. Alone.

"Lights, out," she said. And then Garrett sat, alone, in the dark.

Chapter 5

She hated being in the dark, in every sense of the word.

Batra and Halak arrived in the Kohol District well after the sun had slid behind blocky monoliths of apartments and tenement complexes. Most of the alleys were already dark—the better to hide the filth—and they moved in and out of slices of thick shadow and fading sunlight. The air was chilly, perhaps because the buildings were tall and blocked out what little sun might have warmed the streets and alleys, and smelled very bad. Instead of the scent of mint tea and spiced kabobs of the bazaar Batra caught the fetid odor of human waste, boiled garbage, and something else. Cautiously, she sniffed, cringed. Copper, or iron. And a rotted, sickly-sweet smell she associated with gangrene. The smell was strong enough to leave a taste, and she turned aside and spat.

The sounds were different here. If the bazaar swirled with life, the ghetto teemed with shadows: people rustling in and out of doorways, their backs hunched, their shawls or cloaks drawn up to hide their faces. She listened, hard, but she heard very little conversation. A few whispered exchanges, the slithering of bodies sliding along walls, the slip of footsteps against slick stone. The walkways were cluttered with mounds of things that looked like clothes, though Batra didn't trust herself to take a closer look. Although Halak still had her by the hand, she picked her way through green muck and skirted gray pools of water. Her open-toed sandals squelched through gluey mounds of water-logged paper—*paper, they still use paper here*—and she winced, her teeth showing in a grimace, as she felt something wet and sticky ooze between her toes.

"Are you all right?" Halak asked, sparing her a quick glance that bounced away to scan the area immediately around them.

"Sure," she said, giving his hand a little squeeze. "It's just . . . I didn't expect it to be this bad. You're sure she lives here?"

"Gemini Street. A few more blocks, I think, and then to the left."

"Any idea why?"

"Why she lives here? I'm not sure. Last thing I heard, she was living on the south side of town, near the bazaar. I didn't realize she'd moved until that message of hers. It doesn't make any sense. She knew she could contact me if she needed help." He sounded worried. "I can't imagine she lives here because she likes it."

Batra had opened her mouth to reply when a low rumble shook the ground and panes of glass set in windows rattled. The ground twitched beneath her feet, and she saw ripples dance in a pool of gray water in the center of a pitted, rubble-strewn road that she was sure no vehicle had used in years. Then she heard the muted roar of an engine, and understood.

"Spaceport?"

Halak nodded. "There's the central hub to the south, where we came in. Then there's another, smaller transit center round about here about five kilometers to the east, near the Galldean Sea. Mainly private vessels."

"Here?" Batra couldn't disguise her surprise. "What for?"

"Drugs. Red ice, mainly." Halak pulled her closer, and they started walked again. "It makes good business sense. Funnel the drugs in and out of the areas where your customer base is, though I would suspect that most of the people here get the stuff cut and diluted by a good half, if not more."

Batra dodged a dead warden rat, its body so bloated with gas that all six of its legs bristled like the quills of a spiny urchin. "Red ice?"

"Genetically modified heroin. Amazing, when you think about it. There are so many other drugs you can manufacture that are cleaner, easier. Anyway, red ice is heroin that's produced by crossing Asian poppies with the hallucinogen extracted from Morolovov gapsum plants from Deneb V. Only the powder's not white or brown, like heroin from poppies. It's orange. But the nickname came from what happens after you use the stuff for a long time."

Batra wasn't sure she wanted to know, but she asked anyway. "What happens?"

Halak bobbed his head toward a slumped figure just ahead. The figure—and it looked like a Caldorian to Batra, because of the facial hair and claws—sagged against a metal railing along stone steps of an apartment complex. As they came alongside the still figure, Batra saw that the Caldorian—Batra could never be sure what sex a Caldorian was because of all that fur—didn't seem to register that they were even there. Its facial fur was copper-colored with tiny black spots, and she saw thick tufts of orange hair covering its knuckles and arms. But the fur over its chest was matted and black. Shiny. As they passed, she caught that metallic odor again, the one she'd smelled earlier but couldn't identify: like crushed, wet aluminum, or slicked rust. And then it came to her. "Blood," she said.

"That's right. It's called red ice because, eventually, it reacts with blood. Or rather, iron: any humanoid with hemoglobin based on iron is affected. I don't know the precise pathway . . . this way," he gestured left, and Batra saw a corroded plaque affixed to a wall that said *meni Stre*. Gemini Street was like the alleys they'd passed: narrow and close. Batra heard the sound of water dribbling into sewers and pattering on stone.

"But the result is the same, regardless," said Halak. "Use red ice long enough, and your tissues begin to break down, you start to hemorrhage. Ironic, isn't it? An addict spends his life giving away what little money he can beg, borrow, or steal to get this stuff, and then it ends up eating him alive. You don't know how sad . . ."

His voice died and then, in the next instant, Batra heard it, too: the rapid patter of footsteps, just behind. Coming fast.

Batra whirled right. There was a blur of motion, and then Halak was jerking her to his left, fast, his right hand whipping round to the small of his back for his phaser.

Then she saw another one coming in from the left, too late. *More than one!* "Samir!"

Halak turned but not fast enough. Three men hit him at once: one from each side, and the last barreling into Halak's midsection dead-on. The force of the impact sent his body careening into Batra. Off-balance, she slammed against a brick wall. She crumpled, the wind knocked out of her. As she sagged into a pool of filth, she was aware of hands on her, grappling with her choli, at her waist, running up and down her body.

Searching. She struggled to remain conscious. Her lungs felt like they were on fire, and she couldn't get her breath. *They're searching for credits, whatever they can find. . . .*

Dimly, she heard Halak's harsh grunts as he wrestled with their attackers. There was a thud, the sound of fists hitting flesh, and then a gasp of shock, though she didn't think it was Halak. Someone backpedaled into the wall to her left, and she twisted, saw that one of their assailants was tangled in his own robes, his hands flailing.

Clawing hands scrabbled over her waist, tugged at her pouch. The cloth bit into her side, and then there was a ripping sound, and she felt her pouch give.

Anger replaced shock. "No!" she cried. Surging up, she grabbed at the wrist before it could snatch itself away. She was focused only on that, on getting that hand. Snagging it, she hauled herself around until she saw an expanse of grimy, filthy skin. She opened her mouth and then clamped down hard. Whatever was attached to the hand—man, alien, she didn't care—screamed. Batra's mouth filled with the acrid taste of sweat, dirt, and a warm spurt of fluid that tasted like scummy pond water. Then there was a rush of air, and her attacker brought his fist crashing into the side of her head. The right side of her face exploded with pain, and she screamed and lost her grip. The force of the blow sent her spinning, and she smacked into the wall just behind hard enough that the point of her chin banged into stone. Her teeth clicked, and there was another flash of pain, then the brackish salty taste of blood in her mouth. She'd bitten her tongue. Batra groaned; her vision blacked, seemed to contract.

Still, she heard Halak grappling with their assailants, the sounds of the fists on his body. Her eyelids fluttered. There was a flash of something shiny, and at first she thought it was at a trick of the light until she remembered—her mind moving so slowly it was like a computer with faulty chips—that the alley was dark and there was no light this far into the Kohol District.

"Knife," she croaked. She coughed, turned to her side, felt muck clinging to her cheek, her hair. "Knife . . . Samir . . . knife, *knife!*"

The flash arced up, then down. Halak turned aside, to the right, only just in time to avoid having the knife bury itself in his neck. He screamed.

No, no, no! Batra rolled, sat up. She swung her head around and tried to focus. She saw that one of the men—and they were men, she saw now, though their faces were shrouded by cloaks, and the light in the alley was too dim—was behind Halak, pinning Halak's arms back through the crooks of his elbows. The one Halak had sent flying was staggering to his feet, clawing his way up the wall he'd hit. The last held a knife that was black and slick with Halak's blood.

"You shouldn't be here," she heard the man say. The man thrust his face toward Halak. "You shouldn't have come here."

"Let her go," Batra heard the pain in Halak's voice. He was gasping. "Please, she's not part . . . she doesn't know. Just let her *go.*"

No one was paying attention to her. Because Batra was on the ground and because Halak's arms were pulled back so tightly that the slits in Halak's tunic had parted, she saw what Halak had been reaching for, behind his back. What the men didn't see.

Without stopping to think if she could reach it, she did. Springing forward, she snatched the phaser from Halak's belt, thumbed it to stun. She was already rolling, crouching in an attack stance, before the man with the knife realized what she'd done.

Batra spotted, and fired. Her aim was true. The phaser beam lanced through the dim light of the alley, catching the one with the knife full in the chest. He jerked back, his arms flying wide. She heard the clatter of the knife on stone. The man staggered, then crumpled. Batra's nostrils twitched with the acrid odor of singed cloth.

Seizing the moment, Halak yanked his right arm free, spun to his left, and straight-armed his attacker under his chin with the heel of his right hand. There was an audible thunk of teeth, and the assailant's head snapped back. Reaching up, Halak grabbed the man's head between his hands and then brought his right knee up as he forced the man's head down. There was a sickening crack as Halak drove his knee into the man's face. The man went down in a heap and didn't move.

Batra heard movement to her left and she pivoted on her heels: just in time to see the third attacker angle his way into a side alley and disappear.

For a minute, the only sound was their harsh, labored breathing. Phaser still in her hand, Batra collapsed into a huddle, her head aching, her ears still ringing. Her mouth tasted sour, and she worked her tongue, dislodging a clot that she spat to one side.

From her left, she heard Halak's groan. She looked over. Halak had sagged to the pavement and lay on his stomach. A dark bloom of color stained the left arm of his tunic.

"Samir!" She crawled over on hands and knees to his side. Tucking the phaser into her waistband, she touched his arm with tentative fingers. They came away wet and black.

"Oh my God." Carefully, Batra rolled the sleeve of his tunic up until she saw the wound: easily a six- to seven-centimeter slash along his left bicep, from which blood flowed but didn't pulse.

"I don't think it hit an artery," she said. She was aware of how filthy her hands were, and she tried wiping them clean on her pantaloons: a hopeless task. "We need to get you to a doctor, and . . ."

Her eyes dropped to a spot on his right side. Her breath sizzled between her teeth. "Oh, no."

There was another stain on his tunic, further down, along his right side. At first, she thought it was merely blood from his arm, but then she saw the stain grow before her eyes.

"Oh, no," she said again, "oh, no, no." With trembling

fingers, she tugged up his tunic until she found the wound. Her heart iced with fear. The knife had sliced into Halak's side, arcing down from the edge of his rib cage to the small of his back. She guessed that he must have turned, trying to deflect the blow with his arm, and only been partially successful. If he hadn't turned, the knife would have stabbed down into the exposed angle of his neck made by his collarbone and shoulder blade: a lethal wound.

But this wound, my God, it looked bad, and they were far from anyone who might help them and . . . *Stop*. Batra gnawed on her lower lip, forcing her galloping thoughts to slow, shoving down the scream that balled into the back of her throat. She couldn't help if she panicked.

Gently, she probed the wound. As soon as she peeled the edges apart, Halak moaned.

"No," he said, his voice barely audible. His face had gone so pale his eyes looked like sunken, dark pits in a field of dusky chalk. "No, leave it, leave it, stop . . ."

"Quiet," Batra said. "I have to see how bad."

Halak subsided into silence. The small muscles along his jaw jerked and quivered as she moved her fingers over the wound. She breathed out. The wound wasn't gaping, probably because the knife was sharp. Her eyes roved the fabric of the tunic. Its edges were not frayed, so the knife hadn't been serrated. That was good, and in that, he'd been lucky. A serrated edge would have snagged on the way out, ripping and tearing at Halak's flesh and causing more damage.

Think, think, what's there? Her mind worked over what she knew. She remembered enough basic anatomy—comparative xenozoology had been a required course for her undergraduate work—and the most vulnerable organ in the path of the knife would have been Halak's right kidney. She didn't think the knife had gone in that deeply, but it was sharp enough to slice through fabric without fraying the edges. It couldn't have been a stiletto either, because the wound was a slash not a puncture. *Probably curved.* Her eyes ran over the wound track. *And very sharp.*

She paused, her fingers poised over Halak's skin. "I've got to pull the edges apart and see how deep."

"Go," said Halak. His voice came out as more of a grunt, and shiny beads of perspiration sprouted along his forehead and trickled in rivulets down his cheeks. "But hu . . . hurry. Not sure I can . . . stay . . . stay *conscious* . . . we've got . . . we've got. . . ." He broke off, panting, unable to finish.

"I know. We've got to get off the street," said Batra. She licked her lips. "Hang on."

She eased the cut edges of his skin apart. They came away with a slight, moist, sucking sound. As if a stopper had been pulled, dark red blood gushered out and spilled down along Halak's side to soak into the waistband of his trousers. But, as Batra watched, the flow diminished to a thick, steady stream. Not pulsing, so no arteries had been cut. Batra's careful eyes inspected the wound. There was a thin ridge of fat, stained orange, just beneath Halak's skin, and she saw where the knife had sliced through muscle. She couldn't tell, but she didn't think the knife had hit his kidney or gone into his abdomen.

"How . . . how bad?" Halak whispered.

"Bad," said Batra. She rolled his tunic back over the wound. "Not as bad as it could be. But we'll need a doctor to know for sure and . . ."

"No. No doctor. Dalal . . . not that . . . *far.* . . ."

"Dalal?" Batra was astonished. "Samir, you need to see a doctor!"

"No," said Halak. His throat worked in a painful swallow. "No, it's not that bad. We need to get to Dalal and then get . . . get out . . . out of here."

Batra opened her mouth to protest but didn't. She didn't have a prayer of getting out of the district alone. If they'd looked like victims for the coyotes before, now she'd have to fend off the vultures. Her alert eyes darted up and down the alley then up to scour the face of the tenements. All the windows were closed, their shutters drawn, or polarizing filters—*why would you need polarizing filters in a dark alley?*—dialed to maximum opaqueness.

No one peeping out to see what all the fuss is about. Probably because in a place like this, no one hears a thing.

Then her ears pricked. She listened, hard, and heard the sound again: a slight scraping, like the edge of a box being dragged on gravel.

Behind, and to the left. Barely breathing, she eased out the phaser tucked in her waistband with her right hand.

The sound came again.

The muscles of her haunches tensed, ready to spring. Batra pivoted, slowly, the phaser up, ready. . . .

A wave of relief flowed through her limbs, leaving her weak and shaking. The man she'd put down with her phaser blast was starting to come around. She watched as his head moved feebly from side to side, and then, as his right leg flexed, bent at the knee, and then extended, the mystery of the gravel noise was solved: his shoe, scudding along stone.

Quickly, her eyes shifted to the one Halak had knocked out. He lay, unmoving, twins gouts of blood streaming from his nostrils.

Well, if one was coming around, it was high time for her and Halak to get gone. Batra swiped up her discarded pouch from where the third one had dropped it and tucked the phaser inside. As she turned, she caught a glint of metal in the gutter alongside the man's body. The knife. Quickly, she scuttled over, plucking the gored blade from a slurry of gray mud and stagnant water. She wiped the blade clean on his pantaloons then tucked it into her waistband.

Halak was still hunched, almost doubled over. She dropped to a crouch alongside. "Samir," she said, her tone urgent, "we have to go. Can you stand?"

He nodded. She moved around to his right side, planted

her left shoulder into his right armpit, and helped him to his feet. He sagged; his tunic was clammy with sweat, and her skin crawled at the sticky feel of fresh blood oozing from the wound in his side.

"Samir," she said, working to keep her voice calm, "Samir, which way? How far?"

For a moment, she thought he'd passed out, and she had to repeat the question twice before he answered. Then his eyelids fluttered.

"That way," he managed to say, lifting his chin in the general direction in which they'd been heading. "Halfway down . . . on the le . . . left." He stammered out the number of the tenement.

They headed out, Batra staggering under Halak's weight that seemed to grow heavier with every step. *Please.* Her breath came in gasps, and she had a hard time keeping her footing on the slick stones. She wasn't a religious woman, but she found herself offering up a prayer to whatever god might be watching over them now. *Please, just let Halak live and please, just get us to this woman Dalal, and then we'll do the rest, that's all I ask.*

She had no idea what that rest would be. At the moment, she didn't think it mattered.

Chapter 6

Staring into the blank screen that had held his mother's face moments before, Jase Garrett wasn't sure what to do next. Part of him wanted to scream. Sure, he'd met a couple of her crew and they were nice, but maybe that was because he was the captain's kid. But when his mother started getting all reasonable, when she acted so grown-up and like she had to go take care of all these adults who were acting like kids, he just wanted to haul off and yell and scream and stamp his feet: I'm *more important! I don't care what you have to do, I don't care how important you are because you should love me* more *than you love them, because* I'm *your kid, not* them!

He didn't say any of that, of course, and his mother wasn't a telepath, like his dad and his Nan, the one on Betazed. So that was kind of a relief because that meant he could scream in his head as much as he wanted and not have to worry about making his mother upset. But he meant what he'd said to her now. His dad was really angry, because his dad was really sad, just like him, and so part of him wanted to cry, too. Jase drew in a deep, tremulous breath, and felt that peculiar, itchy sting in his nose that warned him he'd do just that if he weren't careful. He was twelve, nearly a man, and men didn't cry, or miss their mothers. He had to be brave and pretend that these little things like his mother missing his birthday, or not calling for weeks, sometimes months at a time didn't matter. The way his dad pretended. So crying wouldn't be good for anybody. He lived with his dad now, all the time, and he didn't want to make it hard for his dad because then his dad might not let him come with him on digs and stuff. His dad *needed* him to be brave. . . .

"It's hard," said Ven Kaldarren. His tone was gentle. "Sometimes being brave is acknowledging that you're not."

Jase looked over at his father, who was still standing just off to one side, opposite the viewscreen so Jase's mother hadn't been able to see him. "What?"

"Being brave isn't all it's cracked up to be."

"I don't understand." Jase balled a fist against one eye and scrubbed hard, but his fist came away wet. "Is that what happened with you and Mom?"

"How do you mean?"

"I mean, did you decide that you couldn't be brave anymore?"

"In what way?"

Jase chewed on the inside of his lower lip. Words were so hard sometimes. He wished he could just *think* what he wanted, pretend that there was an invisible link between his brain and his father's mind, the way a computer downloaded information.

"Well, waiting, I guess," said Jase, and then it was as if an invisible spigot in his mind had turned on and the words came pouring out, like water. "Waiting for Mom to come home, I mean. It was, like, you could keep pretending that having her around didn't matter, and so that's how you were playing at being brave when what was really braver was being able to tell her that you couldn't wait around anymore. It was braver to tell her you were sad and angry than it was to keep pretending it didn't matter that she loved Starfleet more than she loved you."

Jase saw Kaldarren's eyes change and turn inward, as if his father were staring into a deep well somewhere inside. Jase felt a hitch in his chest.

"Sorry," said Jase, quickly, wanting to make things better. He was so stupid. No wonder his parents got divorced, with such a dumb kid. Jase knew: He was the reason they fought. Before they divorced, they fought all the time over him, and after, they'd fought over where he was supposed to live. Not that it made any sense: There was no place on his mom's ship for a kid. But Jase didn't understand why his mom fought so hard about having him go live with her family on Earth instead of his dad's on Betazed. She didn't even *like* her family. Well—Jase picked at a cuticle on his thumb— she didn't like her *mother.* Actually, neither did Jase. Every time his mom's mom looked at him, he figured he'd done something wrong, because her mouth was always so pinched and tight, like she'd been sucking lemons.

A shadow crossed Kaldarren's face. "Sorry. What are you sorry about?"

Jase hunched one shoulder. "I dunno. Stupid stuff."

"No, stop that. You're not stupid." Kaldarren walked over

to the boy and put his hand on Jase's shoulder. Jase felt his father's hand tremble a little, and he wondered if maybe his father would cry after all.

"You're not stupid," said Kaldarren, his voice firm even if his hand was not. "Don't ever say that about yourself. And don't apologize for how you feel. Your feelings are yours, Jase, and they're as important as anyone else's. Your mother's, mine," he ran his thumb along the soft down on Jase's cheek, "just as important. Both of us want what's best for you."

"If that's true," said Jase, "then why did you and Mom divorce? If you and Mom care so much about me, why aren't you still married?" It was a question that had no answer. Jase knew it, but he asked anyway.

To his credit, Kaldarren didn't try to provide a definitive answer. "We just aren't, Jase. Things do change, and I know that sounds trite, but it's true. It's like growing up and realizing that you like a certain vegetable you hated when you were a child. Things change. People change. In the best of all possible worlds, people should be able to change and adapt to each other. That's what marriage is supposed to be about."

"Then how come you didn't?"

Kaldarren inhaled a deep breath then let it out in a long sigh. "I wish I knew. I guess the best answer I can come up with is that, somewhere along the way, your mother and I lost sight of each other. You know that old Earth saying, out of sight, out of mind? It's supposed to mean that when something's not right in front of you all the time, you tend to forget about it. In a marriage, even when two people are apart, they should still be able to hold a picture of the other person in their head, so that the other person is always in sight, someone to be aware of and know is there."

"So who lost sight of who?"

"Whom," Kaldarren corrected, absently, then moved his hand to riffle his son's black hair. "Sorry. Parents can be pretty annoying."

Especially when all your problems are because of their problems. Quickly, Jase clamped down on that thought; he didn't think his dad would read his mind, but he wasn't quite sure. There had been times on Betazed, before the divorce, when he'd heard his dad's voice in his head, only faintly like a dying echo. (Like the time Jase had come downstairs because he was certain his parents were fighting, only he found them sitting in the dark, at the kitchen table, the air alive with silent shouts in that terrible, black stillness. And the way Jase had peered around the doorjamb, his panicked thoughts—*no, no, no, no, this is my fault, they wouldn't fight if it weren't for me!*—tumbling like rocks down a mountain in an avalanche. Only then his father had peered through the gloom, as if he'd known Jase was there, and Jase remembered hearing his father's voice in his head, quite distinctly: *No, son, don't do that to yourself; this isn't your fault.*)

Now, Jase shrugged. "Sometimes."

Kaldarren's left eyebrow twitched with skepticism. "Well, anyway, I guess you'd say we lost sight of each other. I don't know who did it first, but the point is that it happened, and we've tried to learn from it and not lose sight of you. That's why I was angry with your mother just now, because I think she slipped a little."

She slipped a lot, thought Jase. A *lot* a lot.

Kaldarren cocked his head to one side and fixed Jase with those eyes of his. "And I'm working hard to make sure that doesn't happen again," he continued. "But I'm sorry we've hurt you. I'm sorry for all the times you've been hurt and for all the times to come, in life, when you *will* be hurt, by us or someone else. But I can't pad the world's corners for you, Jase. I wish I could, but I can't. But we'll . . . I'll do my best not to let that happen again, but . . . I'm sorry, son."

"Yeah," said Jase, his lips wobbling. Now the tears did come. "Me, too."

* * *

You hypocrite. Kaldarren stared at his reflection in the blank viewscreen, and he saw his lips curl with self-loathing. *You're a damned hypocrite.*

Ven Kaldarren sat, alone. His son had left: to go for a walk, Jase said. Kaldarren let him escape. The ship (no name, no registry, the better to disappear with, my dear) was small, but Jase liked walking, and he'd done a lot of it when they lived on Betazed. Kaldarren remembered that when he and Rachel fought, Jason would leave and circle around a small lake close by the house. Kaldarren knew this lake—more of a large pond, really—and it had very blue water, alive with skating water bugs and fish that leapt after insects flitting over the water. In the center of the lake was an island carpeted with katarian emerald grass and feathered with tall rushes and frilled tassels. There were also trees on this very tiny island—Betazoid weeping willows, and strombolian firs that vibrated in the wind and produced a clear, clean melody, like bells.

Kaldarren suspected Jase enjoyed the lake because of a pair of flanarian birds that had staked out the island. The flanarians were a little like Earth's Canadian geese, except their feathers were cobalt-blue, their faces starkly white like bald eagles, and their feet a bright ibis-orange. Flanarian birds, like geese and Vulcan *mah-tor-pahlahs*, mated for life, and this particular pair produced a new brood every year. Kaldarren had often sat on shore and watched as the parents tended their troublesome young, circling around in the water to pick up a straggler, or waiting for any that lagged behind.

"No one left behind," Kaldarren whispered now. He sighed and felt his heart twist with remorse. "I'm sorry, Jase."

Touching the boy while the air had been so charged with emotion had been a mistake, and a blessing. He'd felt Jase's hurt flood through him like a sudden gush of scalding water. How sad his son was. Kaldarren's heart tugged with pity. Physical contact always enhanced his telepathic abilities, and he knew what Jase did not: The boy's empathic abilities were getting stronger. Eerie, sometimes, how on the mark the boy was, could be. What Jase had said to his mother, about Kaldarren's anger and sorrow—it was uncannily accurate.

Have to watch that. He's still just a little boy, and it's up to me to protect him.

The thought made his stomach sour. What a self-serving hypocrite he was. If protecting Jase was his first priority, what was he doing with the boy on *this* ship?

No. Kaldarren walled off those thoughts, practiced a mental exercise of visualizing an airlock, in vacuum, and then shoving his secret thoughts in there: Telepathic Privacy 101. He couldn't afford to think about these things around Jase. Jase might not be a telepath (or was he, could he be?), but Kaldarren worried that his secrets might leak around the edges for his son to pick up.

Or Rachel. She used to be very good at reading you, once, and you encouraged that, didn't you? Much more intimate that way. Of course, such intimacy was normal between mates, and more so when one of them was a telepath, as if close proximity revealed new talents the nontelepathic partner had never been aware of. (How else to explain how long-term mates could finish each other's sentences?) But seeing Garrett, even at a remove, always upset him. So many memories and feelings, and things past tangled with things in the present, like some crazy spider's web. He wanted to hate her, just *hate* her, because pure, unadulterated hate would be so much simpler.

But you didn't catch her in bed with another man. She was faithful in her way. You just figured out she was more in love with a thing than with you.

And even if he *had* found her with a lover, would things have been different? Maybe: The idea of her body in another man's arms made him ill. Yes, he'd hate her if that had happened, but he would love her still and so he did now.

She was the only woman whose neck he'd love to break and whose lips he longed to press to his.

So why had he called? Just to torture himself? Her? Kaldarren rejected both, but he wondered all the same. Maybe it had been a mistake to call—*look what* that *stirred up, threatening to drag her back to court*—and, at the same time, he thought that perhaps he'd called because he *wanted* her to ask questions, maybe even stop him from following the course he was now. Rachel Garrett's common sense was a universal constant, like the speed of light, and he could always count on her honesty in this, if not in everything else. (Except her emotions: She'd never been very good at staring her own emotions in the face, but Kaldarren allowed that everyone had a blind spot.) She was—what was that Earth expression?—sharp as a tack when it came to flaying an argument apart bit by bit. So maybe he'd called because he wanted her to talk him out of it; maybe he was hoping she'd ask why he was aboard an unregistered ship and just where was he going anyway. . . .

Absolutely not. He gave his brain an irritated little slap. *You hypocrite. And just what would you have said if she asked, hmmm? You wouldn't have told the truth. Jase was right there, and the most you would have done was sidestep the issue, but Jase would know you were lying, and then he'd wonder why.*

Truth to tell, Kaldarren wondered that himself—why? Why risk his reputation on something like this? For that matter, why risk his life? (No, he wasn't really risking his life; he was being a little melodramatic, and that was because he was so stressed, all this secrecy, the little fact that they were—he was—about to come perilously close to breaking the law.)

So, why risk it? And why risk his *son?* What was he trying to prove, and to whom? That Garrett wasn't the only one who went boldly off where only fools dared to go?

Ah, Rachel, I don't know, and it's too late. Kaldarren's head sagged, and he rested the back of his head against his chair. He was so tired: of thinking, of disappointment. Better to think positively, he knew, and it was normal to have second thoughts, but he'd always known that his intuition was as strong a gift as telepathy.

And I'm committed, or maybe I should be committed, I don't know. But it's one of those irrevocable steps in life, like finding your lover in bed with someone else, or saying the word divorce. Too late to turn back now.

And how complicated life had suddenly become.

Chapter 7

"You were lucky," said Dalal, dipping a cloth into a basin of warm water and some sort of disinfectant. She was a tiny woman, swathed in a cream-colored chador. She had nut-brown skin and sharp black eyes set in a nest of wrinkles so deep they seemed etched with a diamond-edged stylus. Now, those eyes glittered at Batra, and the skin around Dalal's mouth puckered into a scowl so the lines around her mouth knifed into her skin. "Both of you. Lucky to get away without new red necklaces, you catch my meaning."

"Yes, I know," said Batra. She knelt alongside a low divan in a back room of Dalal's tiny apartment. Every now and again, the floor shivered as another ship departed the spaceport, and Batra heard the tinkle and clatter of glass and pottery as vibrations shuddered up her legs. The room was spare. Besides the divan, there was a low round wooden table, on which Dalal had placed a metal container of medical supplies, and two chairs: one in which Dalal sat as rigidly as if the chair were made of steel instead of some kind of wood, and a frayed, overstuffed armchair that was so old the middle sagged.

"What," Batra had to form the words carefully because of the swelling in her mouth and along her jaw, "what about Samir?"

"What about him? You can see for yourself, can't you? You've got eyes." The old woman's fierce face was almost displeased, and Batra thought Dalal was just itching to give her and Halak a good tongue-lashing. Dalal was out of luck, though; Halak was unconscious. He'd passed out as Batra had hauled him up the last two steps onto a landing on the tenement's third floor. Too late, she'd discovered when she'd pushed her way into the building that the lift was broken. So they'd been forced to climb, and the pain had done him in.

They'd stretched him out on his stomach, so Dalal would have an easier time tending to his wounds. Now Batra looked at his half-naked body. He looked as defenseless as a little boy. Dalal had cut his tunic away before going to work, and Batra picked out familiar scars. In the past, she hadn't thought much about them, but in light of what had happened and what he'd told her, those scars took on new meaning.

Probably a story behind every one.

Batra turned her gaze to the old woman. "He's been unconscious for nearly an hour."

"Better for me." Dalal harrumphed, sponging away the last bit of Halak's dried blood from his back. Dalal had already bandaged Halak's left arm; a white bandage was twisted around his bicep, and Batra saw that an irregular rust-colored flower of blood, black around the edges, had bloomed on the bandage.

Dalal wrung water and disinfectant out from the cloth. The liquid in the white-enameled basin had turned a deep copper, and she motioned at Batra. "There, go empty that and refill it. You know where the kettle is."

Pushing to her feet, Batra retrieved the basin and then turned aside and went down the hall, toward the front of the apartment, turning right into a small kitchen that didn't have a replicator but did have a tiny stove and round tandoor oven whose interior was ceramic tile.

My God, what's going on here? Batra leaned against the metal rim of Dalal's sink and stared dully at the water—colored copper because of Halak's blood. *I don't understand any of this.*

Her muscles ached, and a twinge of pain flitted along the left side of her mouth. She had a bruise there, she knew. When she'd washed her hands in Dalal's miniscule bathroom, she'd inspected a fist-sized, purple-black bruise staining her right cheek down to the angle of her jaw. Her tongue was sore but not too deeply cut; Dalal had already examined it, then ordered her to rinse out with warm water and some sort of medicinal salt that made the inside of Batra's mouth feel as if it had caught on fire. Clearly, the old woman knew a few things about medicine.

Batra swirled the dirty water into a sink and then tipped out hot water that Dalal had boiled in a kettle into the basin. Steam billowed up in clouds, and Batra leaned forward, letting the moist warm air caress her battered face. The steam was soothing. She was aware, all too keenly, of how close a call they'd had, and she still wasn't sure if she'd heard Halak correctly. What had he said?

Let her go. She's not part of . . . she doesn't know.

Know what? Batra felt the metal basin warm under her fingers. *This wasn't just a robbery; we were targeted, and Samir knows why.*

And was this the man who'd asked to marry her? What she'd said was that marriages weren't made in Starfleet so they should wait, but she'd lied. (She was such a liar; she knew exactly why she wanted to put him off.) She knew now what she *should've* said: *Before, or after the funeral, darling?*

Batra felt a ball of hysterical laughter bubble up in her throat, and she swallowed back, hard. Who was she to chastise him, anyway? She wasn't telling him the whole truth; she didn't have the guts to tell him what Stern had said.

(Batra had known the instant the ship's chief medical officer Dr. Stern had come into the room. *I'm afraid the news isn't good, Lieutenant. About you having children, I mean.*)

Secrets. Batra scooped up the basin. There were too many secrets: hers, his. She padded noiselessly down the hall on a thin carpet of an exotic kilin design, practically the only sign of luxury in the otherwise drab and dingy little apartment. Batra's feet were bare; Dalal had taken Batra's ruined sandals and promised others before they left. The carpet was soft against her battered soles and Batra paused a moment, enjoying the sensation.

Ahead, in the back room, she heard Dalal's voice, low but very clear: ". . . might as well take out an advert, the two of you traipsing around like that. Why'd you bring her?"

Then, Halak, his voice weak: "She followed me. I don't know how."

Batra froze.

Dalal again: "You trust her?"

"To a certain point." A pause. "I don't know what she would do."

Do? Batra's fingers tightened around the basin. *Do about what?*

"What does she know?" Halak must've responded with some gesture because Dalal continued, her voice angry, "That's no answer, boy. They *knew* where to find you."

"What do you want me to say, Dalal? Ani knows what they all know. As for finding me . . . all they had to do was check the passenger manifest."

"Which they wouldn't *know* to check less'n they were tipped off somehow."

"And you don't think they keep tabs on you?"

"None of your lip. They've no cause to bother me."

"Just your being alive is reason enough to . . ." Halak's voice dropped, and Batra strained to hear. She caught the last part. ". . . anyway, if not for Ani . . ."

"You'd be dead." Dalal made an impatient, old woman sound. "Your Starfleet's made you careless, coming here the way you did. Where are your wits?"

"Dalal, I *came*." Halak sounded very weary. "You called. I came. So why don't you finish bandaging me up and then . . ."

Batra heard a rustle of clothing, a slight grunt as Dalal got to her feet. "Where *is* that girl with the water?" Dalal's voice was coming closer to the hall, and Batra heard the *shush* of the woman's slippers. "She should . . ."

Quickly, Batra covered the last few meters to the room just as Dalal shuffled into the hall. "Sorry," she said, giving the old woman a tight smile, and the basin. "I waited until it had cooled down a little. It was scalding hot."

She made a show of peering around the woman's shoulders. "Is he awake yet?"

"Just now," said Dalal, with an abrupt jerk of her head. Her lips were set in a thin, suspicious line, and Batra saw the woman's black gaze drift to Batra's bare feet.

"Oh, good," said Batra, hurrying past. She crossed to Halak's side and dropped to her knees. Her hands reached for his left, and their fingers laced. "How are you?"

Halak was still on his stomach, the cloth Dalal used to clean him draped over his skin, covering the wound. His color was off; he looked ashen and worn. But when he saw Batra, his lips curled into a tired smile. "I should ask the same of you," he said. "You look terrible."

"Thanks," said Batra, knowing he was right. Her long black hair was matted with blood and mud. Her new pantaloons were ruined. She knew she'd never get them clean, and she wasn't really sure she would ever wear them again even if she could. Long scratches scored the skin of her waist, where one of the men had fumbled for her pouch; from his nails, she guessed.

"No," said Halak. "Thank *you*. If it hadn't been for you . . ."

"Samir." She felt tears sting the back of her eyelids. Her

resolve not to question him crumbled. "Samir, who were those men? You acted as if you knew them."

"No," he said, and his voice carried conviction. "I've never seen them before in my life."

Her heart sank. She watched his face to see if there was anything that gave away the lie but saw nothing. Or, maybe, technically, he was telling the truth—he'd never seen *them*.

"But I heard you," she said. "Why else would they attack us?"

"Money."

"No, that's too simple. You rob someone, you don't stick around to bully them. And they *talked* to you, I heard . . ."

Dalal cut in. "That's enough of that." She squared the basin on the small side table then opened the metal box containing bandages and other medical supplies. "We have enough to worry about without you plaguing him with unnecessary questions."

"Unneces—"

"Ani." Halak squeezed her hand. "Dalal's just a crabby old woman used to bossing people around."

"Crabby." Dalal's withered fingers stirred the box's contents then plucked out a selection of antimicrobial packs and pressure rolls. "Can't see that my bossing you around did you any good."

"Of course, it did. I'm in Starfleet, aren't I?"

"Exactly what I said." Dalal's eyes drilled Batra. "You going to help, or just sit there?"

"Of course, I'll help," said Batra. Did the old woman think a little blood bothered her? "Tell me what you want me to do."

Dalal directed her to open three of the antimicrobial packs and to stand ready with a pressure roll. Halak's skin flinched when Dalal removed the wet cloth from his back. The old woman had packed the wound with coagulant gauze, and she fished this out now, teasing an end free then pulling out the long bloody ribbon.

"It's bad," she said, by way of commentary. "I can't see that it cut any deeper than the muscle, but I'm no doctor. You'll need a good one, though, to piece this skin back together. Use those fancy autosutures they've got. Muscle's cut clean through, and that'll take special equipment. You get this taken care of when you get back to your ship."

"What about a hospital here?" Batra asked. She saw that Halak's features had twisted, and his skin jumped with every pull of the gauze ribbon. A tear leaked from the corner of his left eye. He pressed his forehead into the divan, burying his face, and said nothing.

"Wouldn't be good for him," said Dalal, in a tone that said the matter was closed. Dalal sprayed a dermal anesthetic over the wound, and then together they laid the three antimicrobial pads along Halak's left flank. Then Dalal had Batra help Halak sit up so she could pass the pressure roll around Halak's middle.

"That should keep you," said Dalal, binding the pressure roll in place with an autoseal. "That anesthetic spray will last about five hours. After that, it's going to hurt like the dickens. And don't make too many sudden moves, or else you'll rip that right open again."

"I'll remember that," said Halak. His face had more color, but there were dark smudges under his eyes, like bruises. When he moved, he splinted his left side, not moving the muscles much. Gingerly, he reached around and worked a kink in his left shoulder with his right palm. "I don't suppose you have any clothes."

"No trousers your size, but I'll wash what you've got, and I might have another tunic you can use," said Dalal. She turned and seemed to really see Batra for the first time. "I'll probably have something for you, too. No fancy britches or chadors, though."

"Whatever you have is fine."

"Well then, get yourself cleaned up. You know where the

bathroom is." Dalal made that harrumphing, old-woman sound again. "Frankly, I'm surprised you weren't jumped long before. That costume practically screams *tourist*. Wouldn't survive long here, I can tell you that."

Batra felt the color rise in her cheeks. "Dalal," Halak began.

"No, Samir, it's all right," said Batra. Pushing to her feet, she squared her shoulders and glared down at the little woman. "You're right, Dalal. My clothes do scream *tourist*, but that's what I am, and I'm not ashamed of that. I serve in Starfleet, and I'm not ashamed of that either. I'm not an addict. I don't live in a slum. I haven't known the type of poverty that exists here, but I'll tell you something: simply surviving is nothing to be proud of. You survive, Dalal, but you lock your door and screen your windows. Your neighbors all survive, but not one of them came to help us. Survival isn't so hard, you know. It's being compassionate that is. It's remembering that those are people dying out there—human or not—and helping someone takes more courage than hiding or simply surviving. Frankly, this planet's the ass end of the galaxy, and you can keep it."

She stopped talking, not because she didn't have more to say but because she knew she'd said too much. She was breathing hard, and the heat in her neck let her know that her color must be close to mahogany.

Dalal didn't say anything. She sat, her hands folded, her wrinkled visage as still as cut stone.

It was Halak who broke the silence. "Well, Dalal?"

There was another beat-pause, and then Dalal snorted, a horsey sound. "Got a mouth on her. Bring you nothing but trouble, Samir, mark my word."

She rose, pulling herself to her full height of one and a third meters, meaning the crown of her head just brushed Batra's chin. Tilting her head back, she pinned Batra with another of those glares.

"Get washed up," she said. "I'll bring you clothes. Then I

expect the two of you are hungry. I know I am. Anyway, it'll be safer for you to leave well after dark. Won't attract as much attention that way." And with that, Dalal shuffled out.

Batra expelled her breath in a laugh. "Was that a test? I feel like I just passed a test."

"Probably," Halak said.

When she stepped out of the shower, Batra saw that Dalal had left her a pile of clothes: a V-necked copper-colored tunic, a pair of off-white pyjama pants with button ankle cuffs, and black, thick-soled slippers. The shower made her feel almost human again, and the clothes gave her a lift. She dressed, knotted her long hair, still wet, into a thick, black braid, and followed her nose.

The meal was simple: fresh-baked khbouz markouk done in Dalal's tandoor; whipped minted yogurt with chunks of crisp, fresh-cut Morellian cucumber; piping hot Kalo root stew; and cinnamon-spiced Yridian tea. She and Dalal sat cross-legged on a brightly colored linen cloth spread upon the floor before the divan, their backs propped by firm orange and rust-colored bolsters while Halak reclined on the divan, his back and left side supported by large, fluffy pillows. He ate from a smaller plate she'd prepared and placed upon the small round table, within easy reach.

A transport rumbled overhead. The building shook. They ate in silence for several minutes, using their fingers.

"Well," said Halak. He tore off a bit of thin, brown-speckled khbouz markouk and used it to spoon up a mouthful of stew. "I don't know when I've had a better meal, Dalal."

Dalal grunted. She folded a piece of bread into her mouth and chewed. "Replicator food. It's a wonder you have any meat left on you, boy. Anyway, I suspect that anything tastes good after being cooped up in a can, warping from planet to planet."

"You're a fine cook, and you know it." Halak grinned over the old woman over the rim of a gray ceramic mug. He made a great show of inhaling his tea's aroma before tipping the mug to his lips. He took in a mouthful, rolled the tea around his tongue, and then swallowed. "Now, speaking of being cooped up, Dalal, we were on our way for a week's R and R: rest and relaxation. Actually, we should be on our way now," he softened this with a smile, "but you called me, and I've come. Granted, I've gotten here more flamboyantly than I expected. Now, tell me what's going on."

Dalal's face got a pinched, displeased look Batra was getting to know well. For an instant, Dalal's eyes slid to Batra's face then back to Halak's, but Batra could almost see the wheels turning, the old woman debating just how much she should, or could, say.

"It's about Arava," said Dalal then. "She's gotten herself in very deep, Samir."

Batra saw Halak go rigid. He replaced his mug upon the small round table next to his plate then leaned upon his right elbow and laced his fingers. "I thought she agreed to go off-world."

"She had. She did. Then she came back. She," that quick glance at Batra again, "she changed her mind."

"What changed it?" Halak's voice was very low and steady, but Batra heard a trace of menace simmering just beneath. "Why didn't she stay gone?"

"I don't know." Dalal's eyes shut tight, as if closing off sights only she saw, then clicked open. "She's taken over where Baatin left off. It's the boy, I think. They're controlling her through the boy."

"You mean she's working for Qadir?" Halak's voice notched up. "She's working for the *Qatala*?"

Dalal nodded. Halak was silent, and then cut the air with a sharp, violent curse.

Batra leaned forward. "Samir?"

Halak ignored her. "Dalal, I *told* her."

"We all did," Dalal quailed. She wrung her hands: the

first time Batra had seen the woman cowed at all. "I'm sorry, Samir. Maybe I should have called you sooner."

"How long?"

"I'm not . . ."

"Dalal," Halak's eyes blazed, "how . . . *long*?"

"Three years." Dalal wouldn't meet Halak's gaze. "Two, that it's been worse."

Halak looked stunned. "Three *years? Years?* Dalal, I don't understand. The last time we spoke, *you* said . . ."

"I know," said Dalal, in a miserable sort of way that made Batra feel sorry for her. "I hoped that she would . . ." She broke off, threw up her hands in a hopeless gesture. "I lied."

"As you lied about where you were living," said Halak. "Why did you move here? Was it because of the Qatala?"

Dalal hesitated, nibbling her lower lip, then nodded. "I . . . They forced me. At first, I think they wanted to make Arava behave, but now they don't need me. They leave me alone. Still, after all that happened, Halak, I . . . I couldn't take blood money anymore, not theirs and not the Syndicate's either. But I couldn't leave, not with Arava working both ends against the middle and not showing any signs of wanting to leave. Now, I don't know if it's that she *won't* leave, or *can't.*"

Batra couldn't take being in the dark another moment. "Hello," she said, loudly. Dalal and Halak both looked at her as if they'd forgotten she was there. *Figures.* "What is going on, please? Who is Baatin? Who is Arava? And what the hell is the Qatala?"

Halak exhaled hugely. "You wouldn't understand," he said, going to rake his right hand through his hair but wincing as the sudden movement pulled at his bandages.

"Oh, no," said Batra. "We're not going there again. Listen, Samir, I'm in this pretty deep, wouldn't you say? Now I'm not asking you for a blow-by-blow, but I've been mugged, my boyfriend's gotten himself knifed, my best clothes have been trashed, my mouth hurts, and I'm likely to miss my connection to Betazed. Now I think I'm entitled to some explanation, don't you?"

Halak looked from Batra, to Dalal who moved her shoulders in an almost imperceptible shrug, and then back again.

"All right," he said. He sagged back against a pillow as if he were suddenly tired of everything, and talked to the ceiling. "Here's the long and the short of it: Arava, Baatin, and I go way back. We lived together after Baatin's mother died, and Arava's mother left her. Dalal took care of us all, under one roof. My father did not object. He wasn't around much to object."

"And this was on Vendrak IV."

"That's right. They're the closest things to a brother and sister I have . . . had. Baatin's dead. He died several years ago . . . no," he said as Batra opened her mouth, "I can't tell you how he died, so don't ask. Let's just say, he fell in with the wrong crowd."

"You don't trust me."

Halak made an impatient noise. "It's not a question of trust. It's that you don't need to know. I said before, some things are private, Ani."

"You mean secret."

"Secret, private," Halak rested his left wrist on his forehead and rolled his head aside until his face was in profile, "call it whatever you want. If that means I'm keeping secrets, then so be it."

Batra's gaze slid to Dalal. Dalal was staring at some spot on her lap. *No help there.*

Batra returned her attention to Halak. "All right," she said. "I don't like it, but all right. We'll play it your way. So what about them? And what about this," she frowned over the word, "this Qatala?"

"You have to understand how things work here on Farius Prime." Halak spoke as if reciting from a well-memorized text. "You can look it up; Starfleet's got records. But the gist is, Farius Prime is a good place for business—*illegal* business."

"You mean drugs, like that red ice."

"And more. Syndicate's just a fancy word for crime families. One's the Orion Syndicate. I don't know much about it. Like I said, I've only visited Dalal here a few times since I left Vendrak IV."

Actually, Batra wasn't sure Halak had said that at all. Quickly, she cast her mind back over what Halak had told her, and she was pretty sure that he'd mentioned only that Dalal lived on the south side of town the last he'd *heard*. Had she caught Halak in another lie? And then, come to think of it, Halak had *just* said something about the last time he and Dalal had talked, and the way he'd said it made *that* sound like it had happened recently, not years ago. What was going on here? Was it *her* time sense that was all jumbled? But before she could ask, Halak was talking again.

"The other crime syndicate is the Asfar Qatala. It's big, really big. Lot of people, lots of money, and you can bet their tentacles reach into some pretty high places. Some Federation governments, for sure, though they're careful, don't get caught out. The cover is legit. Mahfouz Qadir deals in the acquisition and sale of archaeological artifacts, antiquities, art. All that lets Qadir use ships to run things covertly."

"Things like red ice?"

"Whatever will bring Qadir the best price and more power. Anyway, somehow or other, Baatin got involved in their operations, in the Qatala's. I don't know how."

"But what does this have to do with you? If this Baatin was involved, but he's dead, and Arava . . . even if she's involved, why is this *your* problem?"

Dalal answered. "You heard him. Like brother and sister. Blood's thick."

"But Samir *hasn't* been involved." Batra turned to Halak. "You *left*. You got on with your life. Baatin and Arava, they went on with theirs. You all made choices. Sounds like they made some bad ones. Why is *any* of this *your* problem?"

Halak shook his head. "You don't understand. When you've got nothing left, Ani, you help the people who stuck by you. I can't explain it any better."

Batra tried a different tack. "So what does Arava need?"

"To come to her senses, for one," said Halak, but he looked at Dalal. "Dalal?"

"She might listen to you," Dalal said, her gnarled fingers picking at her chabor. "She won't listen to me, or maybe she can't, I don't know. But I don't leave without her."

"Why won't Arava leave?" asked Batra. "Is she being held prisoner?"

"Only if you count living in the lap of luxury a prison. She's making a lot of money, and she's very rich, and I'm afraid . . ." Dalal broke off, shook her head.

"Of what?" Batra asked. "What are you afraid of, Dalal?"

For the first time, Dalal looked Batra in the eye, and Batra saw pain, fear. And love.

"I'm afraid she'll die," Dalal said, simply. "I'm afraid they'll kill her."

Chapter 8

Jase's shoes clapped against metal, a hollow sound. The ship was small, with only four decks and a large cargo bay. Their quarters were gray, and the recycling system couldn't keep up, so the air got musty and left a taste like thick fur on Jase's tongue. Since the ship didn't have a name or a registry number, they called it just *the ship*. It couldn't go very fast either, just warp three or something, and they'd already been in space ten days from the time they'd transferred at a rendezvous point from a transport vessel to the ship. (The transport was the second one they'd taken; the first one they'd caught on Betazed had dropped them after thirty light years on Beta Calara III, and then they'd met up with the others— Pahl and his uncle—and then they met up with *another* ship . . . Jase couldn't keep everything straight, and all this changing and switching was very odd, too, like maybe people were worried that someone might follow them, or something.)

There were five of them aboard: Jase and his father; the stocky, muscular man named Su Chen-Mai; and two Naxerans, the pilot Lam Leahru-Mar and his nephew, Pahl. Pahl was Jase's age and it was good to have someone around to talk to, probably because Pahl didn't really want to be there either.

The ship belonged to Chen-Mai. His dad said that Chen-Mai came from Guangzhou on Earth and was an old friend from his graduate school days at the Tarkava Institute on B'Utu Aura. Jase allowed that might be true (why would his father lie?), except Chen-Mai and his father didn't act like two guys who liked each other very much. The air always got thick around Chen-Mai.

No, sticky. Standing by a viewing port, Jase looked at stars smeared to long rainbows by the ship's warp bubble. Just like the air got heavy and angry, almost green-black, around his parents—it was the best description Jase had of their feelings crackling back and forth—the air got *sticky* around Chen-Mai. The air felt—no, *was* bad.

Jase rested his forehead against the portal. The tensor-treated glass was cool and that was good because his face was hot from crying. He didn't like this ship. He didn't like Chen-Mai, and his father was lying, and there was something very, very wrong.

He heard a small scuffling sound out of his right ear and in another moment, Pahl came alongside. Jase didn't turn to look at his friend because he thought his eyes might be red, and he didn't want Pahl to know he'd been crying. He wasn't sure how he felt about Pahl being there at that precise moment, but Jase didn't want to be rude. It wasn't as if either of them had a lot of other friends to be around. So Jase didn't do anything except make a sound in the back of his throat, a sort of grunt.

"That's okay," said Pahl. Pahl's voice was soft and whispery, as if he always had laryngitis. "Not talking, I mean. Is it okay if I stand here?"

Jase made another sound that Pahl seemed to take as assent. At least, he didn't leave. For a good long time—long enough for Jase's forehead to cool and his eyes to stop burning—they stood together, in silence, staring out at streaky, smudgy stars. Crying always left Jase feeling wrung out, like an old used rag, and the stars whizzing by were hypnotic and made him sleepy. Jase had almost forgotten Pahl was there until Pahl said, "You think we'll get there soon?"

Jase scrubbed his forehead against the portal in a weary shake of his head. "I don't know. Dad hasn't said."

"Neither has Uncle Lam," said Pahl. "I think it's going to be soon, though. Today. Just a feeling." He paused. "Talking to your mother is hard, isn't it?"

"Yes," said Jase, not really surprised that Pahl knew. (For not the first time, Jase wondered if maybe Pahl was a telepath, like *his* dad. Jase had asked Kaldarren about it once, and his dad had only said that he didn't know and wouldn't go prying into another person's mind, not unless there was a very good reason, or he'd been invited. If Pahl was a telepath—though this was highly unlikely because there was no record of any Naxeran having telepathic capabilities—his skills would develop in their own good time. Anyway, his dad said, a good telepath never barged in when he hadn't been invited.)

Jase looked at his friend. The Naxeran boy regarded him with a solemn, appraising look, and his face was very still except for his frills that quivered slightly as if Pahl were a type of cat who'd sniffed out trouble. All Naxerans had frills: pileated appendages that ran four to a side and were arranged horizontally on either side of their nose, just exactly like a cat's whiskers. Except Jase had to be careful never to say *whiskers*. Naxerans were very sensitive about their looks, though Jase couldn't understand why. After all, the galaxy was filled with all types, and it wasn't as if Pahl had the antennae of an Andorian, or something. But the Naxerans were very particular about their frills and didn't like it at all when anyone called their frills anything but.

Pahl asked, "Does your mom make you sad?"

"Sometimes. Angry, too. Like I want to break something."

"You're not angry now."

"No."

Pahl turned away to stare out the portal again. "I had a dream about *my* mother."

"Again?"

Pahl nodded. Jase saw that he was paler than usual, which was saying something for a Naxeran. All Naxerans had skin that was very dark, like ebony. But Pahl's coloring was closer to milk chocolate. Jase thought that was probably because Pahl's mother had been a Weyrie. Weyries were a special kind of Naxeran. Jase didn't really understand the particulars, but he knew that Weyries' skin was snow-white and their eyes a deep blue, like ancient Antarctic ice, instead of gold like other Naxerans.

Pahl closed his eyes, ice-blue as a Weyrie's, as if staring at some inner vision. "If I *have* to dream, why can't they be good ones?"

Jase didn't know what to say. (Naxerans didn't dream. They weren't supposed to sleep either. Except Pahl did both. He didn't sleep long, only two or three hours at most. Long enough for him to dream, though.)

"You know what Uncle Lam says?" Pahl's eyes were still shut tight. "He says I'm a freak. He says it's because of my mother that I dream. Uncle Lam says all Weyries are crazy and that my mother was a Weyrie and that's the reason I am the way I am and look the way I do. He says that no one on Naxera understands the Weyries at all. He says that the Weyries are all mistakes and throwbacks. So whenever I tell him I dream, he gives me this look, as if he's worried that I'll go crazy, like my mother.

"Do you know," Pahl's face swiveled toward Jase, and his blue eyes were wide and swam with a bright shine of pain, "he said that I was lucky not to know my mother. He said it was a good thing she jumped off that cliff and drowned when I was only three, so I wouldn't have to know anything about her. I don't understand that." A solitary tear slid down Pahl's cheek, and his frills shuddered.

Jase felt a lump at the back of his throat. Pahl's distress was so obvious, Jase forgot his own and he desperately wanted to make his friend feel better. "Tell me your dream. Was it the cliff again?"

Pahl nodded. "Only this time, the water was different. Instead of it being green, the way it is on Naxera, the water was silver. Like it was night and there were two moons, only the moons were in the water, so the water was silver."

"*Two* moons?" Jase frowned. "But Naxera's only got one, and it never gets dark, anyway, not with two stars, and all."

"Except at Braque-Efram when Pica eclipses both the Brother Stars. I know," said Pahl. "That was what was so strange."

The ship gave a little jolt, and the lights flickered then flared back to life. *Dropped out of warp.* Jase spared a glance out the portal and saw that the stars had returned to normal. *Pahl was right. Must be nearly there.* "Was the place somewhere on Naxera?"

"I don't think so. This place was a large lake, not a sea, and it was," Pahl's ice-blue eyes squinted, looking into the memory, "it was like the lake was in a bowl made by a circle of mountains. It wasn't like a real place that I know."

"But your mother jumped in the sea." They'd talked about Pahl's dreams enough and Pahl had told Jase how his mother died, so Jase felt comfortable talking about it.

"I know." Pahl scratched at the frills feathering his right cheek. "But it was my mother in the dream, all right. Only here's the strange part, the one that wasn't like all the other dreams. One minute I was at the bottom of the cliff, looking up at her, and even though it was night—night, Jase, like where there are lots and lots of stars, so it wasn't Naxera—I could see her face. She was very sad. I could see it in her eyes and the way she looked down at me. She reached out her hand and then, all of a sudden, I was up there with her, on the cliff. There was a very strong wind, but it was cold and full of light, almost like clouds swirling around us. There were voices, too, very strange, singing in a language I didn't understand, or maybe I just couldn't hear them well enough. It was like they were talking to me, calling. Wanting to get inside."

"Inside. Like in your brain?"

"Yes." Pahl's silken whisper again. "Like they wanted to slip inside, look through my eyes."

A flash, like silver lightening zig-zagging against a dark sky, or a jagged white crack streaking through black glass, sparked in Jase's mind, and then he saw them, the images from Pahl's dream. Just for an instant, but they were there: luminous, white, shifting into bizarre shapes, and a woman, a man with the body of a lizard? snake? and the wings of a bat.

Looking through Pahl's eyes. Jase's mouth went dry. The longer Pahl talked in that queer whispery voice, the more Jase felt his mind slipping away a little bit, as if part of what made him Jason Garrett was gone and something of what made up who Pahl was had wriggled its way into his mind. He couldn't explain it any better than that; he barely knew how to find the words to describe it. But Pahl's words—his thoughts, what he'd seen (*seeing through Pahl's eyes*)—seemed to snake their way into Jase's brain so that Jase felt dizzy, a little unreal. Frightened. He felt his fear like a cold finger tracing its way down his spine, and he shivered.

"And then," said Pahl, his whispery voice lilting in a singsong chant, like a lullaby, "my mother took my hand. She turned to me and held out her hand, and I reached for her. I touched her, and her skin was cold like stone, and I looked into her face, and she was crying, but they were tears of blood."

"Blood?" Jase's voice was hushed. "*Blood?*"

"Yes," said Pahl. "And I should have been scared. But I wasn't, and then I couldn't pull away either, and it seemed to me that all those cold white cloud-things had circled round us, tighter and tighter, like a rope, and suddenly I couldn't breathe. Jase, I knew I was going to die."

"Pahl . . ."

"No!" Pahl's voice came in an urgent whisper. "I need to finish. I need to say this."

Pahl stopped and, turning away, put his forehead upon the viewing portal. Jase looked down and saw the surface of a planet slide into view: gray, pocked by meteor strikes. No trees, no water. Cold. Lifeless.

"Pahl," he began, "Pahl, maybe you need to stop, maybe you need . . ."

"My mother," whispered Pahl, "she took my hand, and then . . . then she jumped."

Mind spinning, Jase focused on Pahl's breath steaming, condensing against the tensor-glass, and then evanescing. *Like the ice cloud-creatures, like the woman with the wings of a bat and the body of a snake.*

"She jumped," Pahl said, "and then we were falling through the air, only it wasn't air, I knew then. It was something thick and black and evil. But we fell through it, tumbling and falling, like the way you read about birds shot down from the sky. Then we hit the silver water, and then I was under the water, and I held my breath. I held my breath for as long as I could, and I remember I looked up and saw the underside of the water, bright and silver, and I knew that I needed to get away. I knew that as much as I wanted to be with my mother, I needed air. Only I couldn't get away. She was in the water, and she dragged me down, down, down like a stone. And when I looked over at her, her skin seemed to peel away, little by little, until I saw bone and her teeth and . . ."

"Pahl," said Jase, not able to bear hearing this anymore. Below, on the planet, he saw a ring of ruddy-colored mountains—*not gray, but red like old blood*—and then saw a wide, black chasm gaping like a huge mouth. A crater? Jase's mind snagged on the thought, the way a drowning man grasps a slim branch that can't possibly support his weight. *Maybe a dried-up sea, or a meteor strike* . . . Jase felt his mind spiraling, as if he were caught in a black whirlpool, being dragged deeper and deeper.

"Pahl," said Jase. He brought his hands to his head, felt his fingers dig into his scalp. "Pahl, don't. Stop."

"But you see, I *couldn't*," Pahl rasped, his voice ragged, "I *couldn't* stop her, and I couldn't get away, and then I knew I couldn't hold my breath anymore. So I opened my mouth and all my air rushed out in silver bubbles that burst in front of my face, and then the water, so cold and dark, filled my mouth and gushed down my throat, and I was dying, I knew I was dying. . . ."

"Stop!" Crying out, Jase ducked his head, screwed his eyes shut. He was choking, drowning, he was going to die. . . . "Pahl, stop, please, let me go, *let me go!*"

With an effort that was almost physical, Jase wrenched his mind free, not even knowing that this was what he did. Dimly, he heard Pahl's tortured cry. But there was nothing Jase could do for his friend at that instant. He felt a great ripping and tearing in his mind, as if his brain were made of fabric and had been held, too tightly, between fingers as unyielding as steel, and so had simply shredded in two.

Reeling, Jase slammed back against an exposed conduit. The metal bit into his side, and Jase arched, cried out again as pain shivered down into his pelvis. But the pain was good, because then he had something to focus on instead of the throbbing in his head, the sense of something alien slithering into his mind. Jase's knees folded and his back slid down the bulkhead until he felt metal beneath his thighs and knew he sat on the deck. Jase gulped air. His head spun with vertigo, and he blinked away the blackness edging his vision. After a few moments, when his breathing had slowed and he felt better, Jase let his head fall back against the bulkhead. He looked over at his friend.

Pahl had slumped to the corridor alongside Jase. His face had gone ashen, and his ice-blue eyes were so dark they looked like sapphires.

"Pahl," said Jase. His brain hurt. A line of sweat beaded his upper lip. He swiped at it with the back of his hand. "Pahl, are you all right?"

"Yes. I'm sorry. I don't know what . . ." Pahl closed his eyes. His frills trembled. "I'm sorry."

Jase swallowed back a wave of nausea. "What was that? What happened?"

"I don't know, I don't know . . ."

"That was awful."

"I know, I'm sorry, I don't know . . ."

"Your dream, what happened just now . . ."

"No, no, that's just it. It's no *dream*; it's *not* a dream. Jase, Jase, my mother *killed* me, she killed me, and I . . ."

"No, Pahl," said Jase, putting up his hands as if to ward off something physical. "No, don't say it, if you say it . . ." *It comes* true.

"And I was glad." Pahl's voice came out as a tortured, anguished whisper. "I was *glad*."

Chapter 9

Batra pressed close to Halak as they slipped in and out of shadows inked along Tajora Street by large, blocky warehouses. Tajora Street was a curling boulevard that ran around the northeast corner of Maltabra City and along the Galldean Sea for nearly three kilometers. She glanced at the illuminated dial of her chronometer: an hour shy of midnight. They'd left Dalal's two hours before, slipping down a rear stairwell and out into a back alley. The alley ran diagonally northwest, and when they finally reached the end, they'd had to circle back, heading for the north end of Tajora Street. Halak said that Arava's apartment, like Tajora Street, was in Qatala territory, almost dead center.

Batra's nerves were a jangle of exhaustion and adrenaline-pumped fear. So far they'd been lucky. They hadn't run into any of Qadir's men, not that Batra had the faintest idea what those men might look like anyway. Knowing what she did now, she suspected that their three attackers had been Qatala, though she couldn't be sure and she wasn't going to ask Halak now. There'd be plenty of time for questions if they got to Betazed.

Batra's grip tightened around Halak's hand as he limped, splinting his right side. No. When *we get to Betazed. Stay positive.*

They headed south, keeping the sea on their left. Now and then the alleys and streets echoed with the low growl of a ship taking off from the spaceport to the north. Farius Prime had two moons, though neither was up, and so the sea was just a black wavering expanse: a sense of movement punctuated by the slap of water against concrete and metal posts, and the single solitary moan of a foghorn a kilometer from shore, perched on the end of a rocky quay. The smell was all wrong, though. Not salty: Batra sniffed a sea breeze whistling down the canyons formed by the warehouses that ran east to west, and recoiled. The sea had a nasty, sour, metallic odor, like old clotted blood and boiled fish.

The street was so quiet, the sounds of their footsteps scraping concrete sounded like rocks over sandpaper. The day's heat had gone, though Batra felt residual warmth leaking through the soles of the slippers Dalal had given her. Squares of light speckled the monoliths of apartment buildings to her right; to her left, lining the piers were warehouses, their fronts bathed in fans of reddish-orange light from floodlights that perched above large cargo doors. When Batra raised her eyes to look overhead, the night sky wasn't black but glowed a burnt orange color: reflected glare from the lights clustered at the city's center and diffused by smog and mist rising from the chill sea.

Dark, and yet not dark at all. Batra shivered. Either way, a lot of things could happen, even in a darkness that wasn't.

Halak must have thought she was cold because his right arm slipped around her shoulders. "Not too much farther."

"It's not that," murmured Batra. "It's just . . . I wish this was over with already."

He tightened his grip. "I'm sorry I got you into this, Ani. I didn't know . . ."

"No." Abruptly, Batra stepped out of his embrace but kept her voice low. "No, that's just it, Samir. You *did* know. A man doesn't bring an unregistered phaser along, slink off a ship . . . you knew there'd be trouble, and you knew what type of people you were dealing with. And don't tell me otherwise, please. I may be naïve, I may have lived in more luxury than you . . ."

"Dalal didn't mean . . ."

"This isn't about Dalal!" Batra paused then resumed in a tense whisper. "It's not even about Farius Prime. It's about us, Samir; it's about a man I'm in love with and *thought* I knew."

They faced one another. The light from a nearby warehouse was behind Halak, and his face was in shadow. Batra couldn't read his expression, though she caught the glint of his eyes. His voice came out of the darkness. "What do you want to know, Ani?"

Such simple words: yet behind them were volumes left unspoken. And what *did* she want? For him to clear up all the discrepancies she'd caught at Dalal's? To tell her why the hell people were trying to kill them? To explain how he could know, in such detail, a place as awful as this? Batra was so close she heard Halak's quiet breathing, and she knew that if she put out a hand, she would feel the strong beat of his heart. Yes, here was the man she loved and was willing to sacrifice her career for, and what did she want?

"I don't know," she said, finally. "Everything. And nothing. Because I'm afraid, Samir, I'm *afraid* to know."

Now Batra let Halak pull her close with his good arm. Sighing, she rested her left cheek against his breast. She heard the thud of his heart; the feel of his arm and his familiar scent comforted her. "But even though I'm afraid, I *need* to know. Whatever you've done, I can handle it."

"You can't know that, Ani. That sounds good, but you can't predict something like that. Sometimes love isn't enough."

"Enough for what, Samir? Forgiveness?"

"No, acceptance. There's a big difference between acceptance and forgiveness."

"Samir, I can accept a lot. I can forgive you almost anything."

"There are conditions to everything, Ani, even love."

"Samir," she said. She slid her arms about his waist, felt the bulky roll of his bandage beneath his tunic. "Samir, please, what's going on? Are you in trouble? *Have* you been?"

He laughed: a hopeless sound. "Trouble's what I'm trying to avoid. Ani, if I thought it would help . . ."

His voice cut off. Puzzled, she pulled away and opened her mouth, but Halak put up a warning finger. Batra concentrated. Because she had turned back to Halak, the sea was off to her right, and she was conscious of the water lapping against stone, and then the call of the foghorn, a long lowing like an animal. Then, as the foghorn's groan sighed away, she heard it: the clap of shoes upon stone.

From her left. Batra jerked her head around to scan the walk directly across Tajora Street. She spotted two figures: one tall and broad, the other in what looked like a hooded cloak, and much shorter. Coming straight for them.

Halak eased her to one side—out of the line of fire, she realized—and then she saw his hand hover at the small of his back, over his phaser. He said nothing, and his face was still in shadow, but Batra could feel how alert he'd become. How focused.

"If I tell you to run," he said then, his voice very soft, "don't argue and don't stop to help. Just do what I say."

Batra never did get a chance to ask Halak just exactly *where* she was supposed to run because the two figures crossed into a slant of light, their faces flickering briefly, and Batra heard Halak's breath catch.

"Arava?" he whispered, starting forward. "*Arava?*"

Endangering Batra had been the last thing Halak wanted. Even when the knife had ripped into his side and pain shot through every fiber, what he'd thought about was keeping Batra safe. When he folded her into his arms, he marveled at how tiny she really was, how fragile her bones: like a bird. And then she'd shivered—perhaps from cold but maybe from fear, too—and he felt his resolve harden. No matter what the cost, or how things fell with Arava, he'd keep her safe.

Now, he watched as two figures melted out of the darkness and hurried across Tajora Street. On the alert, he shifted his weight to the balls of his feet. His eyes darted into the shadows. No one else there. Still, if Arava was working for Qadir, he didn't know how much she could be trusted.

He stood his ground as she approached on the run, her cloak snapping, her footfalls crisp, staccato counterpoints to the loping, heavier strides of the larger figure which Halak saw now was a huge, blue-skinned Bolian male.

"Are you out of your *mind*?" Arava kept her hood up so her features were in total darkness, and Halak got more of an impression of her face than a good look. "What in God's name are you doing?"

"Hello, Arava," said Halak. His tone was calm, but he was conscious of his phaser against his back, as if the weapon had gotten white-hot and branded his skin. "Good to see you, too." A quick glance told Halak that the Bolian had two weapons, one on either hip. "Nice toy. Is he new?"

"My bodyguard," Arava said fiercely, "not a toy. You know that, Samir, and you still haven't answered my question."

"How did you know I was here?"

"Maybe the question should be, who doesn't?" Arava gave a laugh that wasn't. "I was practically the last person to hear." A jerk of the head toward Batra: "Who's she?"

Halak put a hand on Batra's shoulder before she could answer. "She's a friend, Arava. She's from my ship."

"Can she be trusted?"

"This does seem to be the topic of the day," Batra broke in. She shook off Halak's hand. "Since I'm here and I'm with Samir, the question's moot."

"I trust her," Halak said. "That should be enough for you, Arava."

He was keenly aware of how vulnerable they were, out in

the open like this. "I think we should continue this inside somewhere, don't you?"

The Bolian spoke for the first time, his voice surprisingly high for such a large man. "He's right."

"Okay," said Arava. She jerked her head to the right. "Over there."

She started for a nearby warehouse, a blocky structure with no windows that squatted at the near side of a pier lined with identical warehouses. Following after, Halak darted looks up and down the street. The street seemed empty. He wondered, briefly, how Arava had known exactly where to intercept them, and then it occurred to him that Qadir's men must have monitored their progress as soon as he and Batra had turned onto Tajora. Dalal was right; he was getting soft. Likely they'd been followed before, perhaps as they'd left Dalal's apartment.

And the men who attacked them? Strictly speaking, he'd told the truth. He hadn't recognized them, and hadn't a clue who they worked for. Qadir, or the Orion Syndicate? Maybe if he had a few moments alone with Arava, he'd ask her what she knew, or had heard.

God, Ani. He owed her more than his life. Yes, there were family matters to consider: his loyalty to Dalal, for one. As for Baatin . . . Halak's heart twisted with pain. He'd bear the guilt for Baatin for the rest of his life, and he wanted to make things right by Arava, but not if it meant endangering Batra more than he already had.

Arava keyed a combination on a magnetic lock, verified her identity via retinal scan, and ushered them inside a small side door set well away from the street. She had the Bolian—who she called Matsaro—stand guard outside then led the way into the building.

"Lights," said Arava. "Half."

Instantly, the interior of the warehouse was suffused with a dusky yellow light. The space was twice the size of a standard cargo bay and three times as high. The warehouse was packed with crates and containers stacked floor to ceiling in long precise rows running from the entrance to a larger set of doors at the very end. Halak browsed the containers for markings, or an indication of destination or origin, and found none. Understandable: Making things appear and disappear was Qadir's stock and trade. He was sure some of the crates were legitimate, but most probably weren't.

"Well," said Arava, shrugging out of her cloak and tossing it onto a nearby barrel. Her face was a smooth oval, and her hair—a golden, honey blonde—spilled about her shoulders. "The prodigal son returns. Your timing stinks. What, did you think Qadir would just forget?"

Halak heard Batra's sudden intake of breath. "Actually, I didn't pick the time," said Halak, choosing not to address what Qadir might, or might not forget. "Dalal contacted me. Said I had to talk some sense into you."

"Sense." Arava gave that nonlaugh again. She hugged her arms to her chest, as if she were cold. With her blonde hair and large, brown-black eyes, she looked very small to Halak, almost like a child. But there was a hard edge to her now, a cynicism and bitterness he didn't remember. The Arava he'd left behind had been a young, fresh-faced woman. He saw now the changes that time—and tragedy—had inscribed on her features. A tracery of tiny lines fanned from the corners of her eyes and her face was white and pinched, with a furrow chiseled into either side of her nose, as if she never really found anything to smile about.

"Dalal doesn't know what she's talking about," said Arava, crossly. "She's meddling in things that aren't her concern."

"Really? She's concerned enough about you to stay on this godforsaken planet."

"That's her choice."

"Come on, Arava. Dalal's known you since you were old enough to spit."

Arava gave Halak a narrow look. "I'm *fine*."

"If you're with Qadir, you aren't."

"I know what I'm doing."

"I won't remind you who that sounds like."

That stung, as he'd meant it to. Halak saw a flash of pain crease her brow. "That wasn't fair," she said.

"I don't care about what's fair. I care about what's right. I care about living, and I care about you. Life isn't fair, Arava. I'm just trying to help you stay alive, so we can have debates about how unfair life is when we're old and gray."

"I was born old. You, of all people, ought to know that."

"You're saying that the people who love you ought to look the other way? Let you choose a path that can only end very badly?"

"I know the risks."

"Do you?" Halak erased the distance between them until he stood just centimeters away. He didn't touch her, though he wanted to. *Arava, Arava, please listen to me. . . .* "Do you really?"

Arava swallowed, a loud liquid sound in the sudden silence. Her eyes were bright, but her voice was firm. "I know what I'm doing. Dalal's concern won't change a thing. The risks have always been there, they're not going to go away. And until I finish, no place I run will be far enough. As for risk," she lifted her chin in the direction of his left arm, "you're the one who ought to be worried. The way you're holding yourself, looks to me like they cut you up pretty good."

"They did all right. We did better."

"Yeah? You think so? Let me tell you something, Samir. You walked away because you had Lady Luck on your side, nothing more and nothing less. Next time, maybe, you won't be so lucky. Maybe Lady Luck'll take a hike."

"No, she won't," said Batra. "Not a chance in hell."

Halak flashed her a tight, grateful smile before turning back to Arava. "Luck, no luck . . . you know what I think? I think I was *meant* to walk away. Even out of uniform, my being in Starfleet has certain advantages. Kill me, and Qadir attracts too much attention. Scaring me off serves just fine. I think this, us meeting and *contact* with Starfleet"—he used his hand to indicate the space between them—"this is what Qadir wants to avoid."

"*You?*" Arava made a derisive sound. "You're too obvious. He's worried about the ones he *can't* see."

"And how many of those are there?"

Alarm flickered across Arava's face, and her eyes narrowed: a warning. "Don't ask stupid questions, Samir."

"I'm sorry." Halak spread his hands in a placating gesture then lightly placed them on her shoulders. She was thinner than he remembered; the humps of her bones dug into his palms. "Look, I didn't come all this way to fight with you."

"Then what did you come for?" Arava shot back. She twisted away. "I don't need lectures, Samir. I made my choice. I just need more time, that's all."

"Time?"

Arava's eyes flicked to Batra and back to Halak. She arched her eyebrows. The question was there: *Is it safe?* Halak moved his head fractionally, side to side.

"Right." Arava made a small sound in the back of her throat. Sighing, she scooped a hand through her golden hair. "Baatin was in deep, you know that. I've"—that quick sidelong glance to Batra again—"I've taken over where he left off, that's all. It shouldn't be much longer."

This was what Halak had been afraid of. Baatin had been smart, careful. Trusted. And he was still just as dead. "Do you know how much longer?"

Arava chose her words with care. "I've done some . . . negotiating. Depending upon what the higher-ups say, maybe as soon as next week, the week after. There's a glitch, though. I'm not the only one who's . . . interested. But I can tell you that something's up. There are new people in the organization, and there's talk."

"Talk?"

"Of men from the Orion Syndicate infiltrating the rank and file, working their way up. The problem is, no one knows exactly who."

"You think it's true?"

Arava hesitated then nodded. "There have been intercepts of some shipments. Others disappear before they reach their destination. Qadir thinks there's a mole, maybe more than one. I've already been questioned, twice."

"How close do you think he is?"

Arava considered. "Let me put it this way: I hear he's getting a telepath next."

"Then you're running out of time."

"Maybe. I told the . . . contact, and she's working on it." Arava dragged in a deep breath. "Just a little longer, though. That's all I need."

"I can't believe that you couldn't leave now. Don't you have enough to . . . ?"

"Not quite yet. Look, I've worked long and hard to get where I am, and I'm not going to cash out now. I want to take as large a piece of Qadir with me as I can."

"Baatin tried that."

"And failed. Yes, I *know*," said Arava, bitterly. "You think I don't think about Baatin every damn day? Probably more than you ever will."

"No," said Halak, feeling a crush of guilt. "But this isn't a contest." He blew out, frustrated. "All right then. You've made up your mind. I'll leave you alone."

Arava jerked her head in a curt nod. "That's what I want. Do you think you can get Dalal . . . ?"

"She's not going to budge a millimeter until you're off-world."

"Stubborn old mule." A tiny smile flitted over Arava's lips. "Remember the time I brought home that Vulcan *sehlat*? I thought Dalal was going to have a heart attack."

"Yes, and I remember how set she was on getting rid of it, and how you cried all night until she gave in." Halak grinned. "Damn thing nearly took my finger off the first time I tried petting it."

"That's because you didn't smell right. It was just being territorial." Arava's expression softened. She walked to Halak, reached up, and cupped his face in her hands. "A lot of memories. When I'm out of here, Samir, I promise . . ."

"Sure," said Halak, kissing Arava on the forehead. Then he saw Batra standing off to one side. Her face was pale; her lips were set. Halak was seized by an urge to tell her everything, right there—and discarded the impulse as suicidal. He could never tell her. He could never tell anyone.

But it's not what you think. He tried to say this with his eyes. *Ani, it's not what you're thinking.* But Batra's expression was unreadable.

Halak looked back down at Arava. "Sure," he said again. "Sure."

He tried to make certain that his smile made it to his eyes. Later, he was pretty sure it didn't.

Chapter 10

Pressed against the slick stones of an apartment building across the street, the woman watched and waited. She'd seen them meet: Arava with her Bolian bodyguard, the commander, and a small woman with long black hair she didn't recognize but who seemed to be with Halak. From a distance, she couldn't tell if the woman was a local. She tended to doubt it. Something about the way the woman carried herself suggested a life that hadn't been conditioned by deprivation, or the everyday struggle for simple survival. Another Starfleet? More than likely: She'd have to run a check when she had a moment, figure out the likely candidates aboard *Enterprise*.

She glanced over her shoulder every few moments, though she'd set up proximity alarms (silent, so only she would know, via a microtransceiver tucked in her right ear, if someone got within twenty meters). She was certain she hadn't been followed, but operatives didn't stay alive on Farius Prime for long if they weren't cautious. (Two of her immediate predecessors had met ignominious ends: one with a knife wound through the heart in what was, putatively, a barroom brawl, and the other who'd been reduced to an oily smudge with a submolecular pattern disruptor. The weapon was illegal as sin, and very efficient.) She'd hung well back, letting the tracking device she'd slipped into the clasp of Arava's cloak do the work for her.

All the while she waited for Halak to reemerge, the question kept bouncing around her brain: What was he doing here? It wasn't as if coming to Farius Prime was illegal; it wasn't a proscribed or quarantined world. But Farius Prime was the type of planet most people were happy to see receding in the distance.

And the point was Halak *was* here, and he was making contact with Arava. She fretted. Trouble there. She'd worked hard to make things come off with Arava; they were at a very delicate stage in their negotiations; and now if Halak interfered . . . A lot of work, a lot of *time*—a lot of *money* greasing the appropriate palms—it would all be for nothing if Halak screwed up the works.

She considered, briefly, that Halak might be one of her own. There had been rumors floating around about that Ryn mission, the one before he transferred to *Enterprise*. Eight months of down time might be an appropriate period for someone to go to ground. But she couldn't believe he'd been deployed to the same theater without someone giving her a head's up, not when things were this delicate.

The Bolian, Matsaro, worried her, too. She knew the man by reputation, of course. A Qatala man for years, but she had her ear to the ground, and there were rumors that the Bolian wanted more than Qadir was willing to give. Except when she'd told Arava, Arava shrugged her off, and that made her uneasy. Arava was too damned sure of herself, not willing to listen to reason, and she put too much store in her being the only way, after Baatin was dead, of anyone getting into the Qatala.

Well, times had changed, and she'd recruited another source. No sense putting all her eggs in Arava's basket.

She breathed a little easier when, after a half hour, Halak and the small woman emerged. There was a brief exchange, and then Arava went one way; the Bolian, Halak, and the woman went another. Matsaro was probably escorting Halak off-world. She hoped so. She didn't need the complications.

She checked the time. Good: over three hours before she and Arava were scheduled to make contact. Time enough for her to get some answers.

A half hour later, she was in her tiny apartment, keying in her authorization code to open a secured channel.

Her CO answered right away, prompting her to wonder if the woman ever slept. "Batanides."

Then, when she recognized her caller, SI Commander Marta Batanides's piercing blue eyes narrowed with concern. "Burke. You're on an emergency channel, and a day early. What's wrong, Lieutenant?"

"Plenty," said Starfleet Intelligence Special Agent Laura Burke, her tone clipped and urgent. "Why the hell didn't you tell me about Halak?"

Chapter 11

What the hell was *that?*

The pain was so intense and yet so fleeting that Ven Kaldarren's mind barely had time to register that the sensation *was* pain until it had flowed through and over him, the way a wall of water rushes toward shore. Kaldarren's vision blacked, and the space behind his eyes blazed with a searing, brilliant mind-image: something that was white, swirling, luminous. Something on the edge of becoming.

And then, just as quickly, the mind-image was gone. So was the pain. Kaldarren felt the pain ebb and retreat, emptying out like a wave scouring sand. Even as it left him, Kaldarren scrambled after the mind-image, trying vainly to grab hold of something as insubstantial as thought.

What was that? *Who* are *you?* Kaldarren opened his mind—carefully (he'd almost had his head blown off, after all)—and waited. *Tell me, please. Don't be afraid.*

Nothing.

He wasn't altogether surprised. The contact had felt inadvertent and inchoate, like half-formed thoughts leaking around and over the edges of an alien mind, rather than something directed or exploratory. He couldn't even tell if the mind-image had originated on the ship, or from the surface of the planet about which they'd slipped into orbit thirty minutes ago.

(Where are the boys?)

Mind still aching from the ferocity of the contact, Kaldarren grappled with residual sensations left from the mind-image, trying to put a name to the face, as it were. He couldn't, though there was something almost familiar about the contact, as if he'd known the mind behind the thought. But the mind-image was fading fast, thinning like a cloud dissipating under a hot sun. In the next moment, it was gone.

A voice rasped across his consciousness, like nails biting into sandpaper. ". . . you *listening?*"

"Yes." Blinking, Kaldarren looked down on the sullen, angry features that belonged to Su Chen-Mai, and reality leaked back little by little. Kaldarren was aware now of the ship, its bridge, and that he'd come to the bridge of their small vessel a half hour after Jase had left their quarters.

Chen-Mai, hands on hips, glared up at him. Lam Leahru-Mar, the Naxeran, sat in the pilot's chair, his frills trembling with anxiety. Like their quarters below deck, the bridge was very small, with barely enough room for a pilot and copilot, but that was because Chen-Mai was a smuggler and smugglers didn't waste precious cargo space.

"Yes, of course, I'm listening," Kaldarren lied.

"Then what do you think? You picking up anything, or what?" Chen-Mai rapped. He was a square man, with a moon-shaped face and narrow eyes, and he was very bald. He wasn't tall but muscular and stocky, and when he became agitated—something that happened often enough— his sallow cheeks mottled with red splotches that made him look as if he'd just come in from the cold.

"I don't think anything," said Kaldarren. Best not to mention what he'd experienced until he understood what it meant: whether the image was thought-residua imprinted upon the planet from its long-dead inhabitants, or the true touch of an alien mind that was still very much alive.

"I don't think that I'll know anything until we get down to the surface. I've told you before, Chen-Mai, my abilities are limited by distance." Kaldarren didn't volunteer that who or whatever had touched his mind was much more powerful. "I think that our most pressing concern has got to be the Cardassians."

Leahru-Mar made a nervous click in the back of his throat. "He's right about that. How do we know your information's good?"

"It's good," said Chen-Mai, his tone curt. "Their patrols come through here every fourteen days. As long as you did your job and kept them from seeing us, then we've got that long to find the portal."

Despite his anxiety, Leahru-Mar's ebony features turned peevish. "I did my job. We're alive, aren't we? No Cardassians shooting at us. Besides, it wasn't all that hard to hide the ship. We're small, and this is a binary star system. The primary went supernova, and the neutron star that's left is accreting matter and gas from the brown star's heliosphere, and . . ."

"English." Chen-Mai glowered. (He might have been born under the sign of the monkey, but he complained like a goat.) "In English."

Leahru-Mar opened his mouth then seemed to reconsider whatever it was he'd been about to say. Instead, he punched up a display on the bridge's viewscreen. A grid display wavered into focus, showing a privileged view of the binary system: The neutron star, embedded within a large nebula, was coded yellow. The slightly larger brown star, with its larger orbit, was orange.

"It's pretty basic. You have a nebula left over from the time when this binary's primary star went supernova. All that ionized gas and plasma makes it tough for anyone to see us, though it also works the other way. It makes it hard for *us* to see *them*. The distance between the two stars is point-zero-three AU, so the orbits are fast. About three solar days, give or take. Again, that works to our advantage because the close proximity means that those plasma streamers," Leahru-Mar brought up twin red whorls spiraling from the orange-colored brown star toward the neutron star, "are highly volatile. Plus, this isn't your usual neutron star. It's a magnetar; it's generating an intense magnetic field because the spin is so fast. So, for want of a better description, the whole place is one big magnetic *and* radioactive sink. Again, this works to our advantage because not only are signals subtended by the magnetic field, but the area's ion-saturated because the neutron star's stealing matter from the brown star. In turn, those accretion plasma streamers make for a very strong stellar wind."

"Meaning that the surface of the planet is one big ion storm," said Chen-Mai, satisfied with his own acumen. "We'll be almost invisible."

Leahru-Mar gave a nod of agreement. "That's right," he said, with all the enthusiasm of a parent whose toddler's taken his first step. "To a cursory scan, that is. Anyone looking hard will see us, but only through a tremendous amount of distortion. They may not even know what they're seeing."

"There's no reason anyone *should* be looking for us," said Chen-Mai. "The Cardassians abandoned this site years ago and it's outside their borders. There's the biosphere they left behind, but it's automated. Perfect for us. Otherwise, we'd have to spend the entire time on the ship."

"That begs an important question, though," said Kaldarren, who was not as cowed as the Naxeran when it came to dealing with Chen-Mai. Kaldarren wondered whether or not Chen-Mai had chosen Mar because the Naxeran was a member of the weaker Leahru clan instead of the dominant G'Doks. Having someone to bully around would, Kaldarren reflected, be consonant with Chen-Mai's personality style. "Why leave a biosphere active if you aren't planning to come back?"

"Self-explanatory, isn't it? Because there's something valuable down there."

"Meaning they *could* come back," said Mar. His nose crinkled, and he nervously groomed his frills with the back of his right hand. "Maybe before we expect them to."

"Not going to happen. Starting now, we've got fourteen days, and if everything goes the way it should," Chen-Mai's lips tugged into something approximating a smug grin, "we'll find it and cash in."

A big *if*, Kaldarren thought. Actually, a lot of *ifs: if* this was the right binary star system; *if* these were the correct ruins; *if* these ruins were Hebitian; *if* the ancient Hebitians, a civilization the Cardassians claimed as their ancestors, were telepaths; and all those *ifs* begging a larger question.

Kaldarren turned aside, staring down at the long-dead planet spread below their ship. The planet looked like a flawed, red-gray agate marble, though his keen eyes picked out surface details as their ship skimmed over them in its orbit: the stippled ridges of mountains that were a curious rust color; a large irregular trough scooped out of the surface that had been a lake, or an inland sea.

The bigger question: If the Hebitians had lived here, how had they gotten to the planet to begin with?

Kaldarren reviewed what he knew. According to the Cardassians, they claimed descent from an ancient civilization, the Hebitians. Hebitian ruins found on Cardassia Prime testified that the Hebitians had developed a rich, highly evolved culture. The burial tombs the Hebitians had left behind brimmed with tremendous wealth, and it was from the plunder of those tombs that the Cardassians had built up their formidable military and financed their missions of conquest.

But another fact: There wasn't a shred of evidence to suggest that the Hebitians were a spacefaring race, and nothing in any of the ancient Hebitian texts discovered so far suggested that the Hebitians had left the planet, ever. Until now.

Their orbit had brought them over a dried ocean bed, and Kaldarren could just make out the sheer drop-off of a continental shelf. Down there, once, there had been water, and on that water, ships had scudded from one shore to the next. Some of the ships had sunk, and if he only had time enough, Kaldarren might walk the trenches and submerged mountains, now laid bare to the naked eye, and wander into wrecks no living person had glimpsed for thousands, perhaps tens of thousands of years.

Kaldarren felt the familiar tingle of excitement the prospect of a new discovery always brought. When Chen-Mai had originally contacted him with writings that the man claimed were ancient Cardassian, Kaldarren had been dismissive. Only after he'd studied the writings himself was he convinced that there might be some truth behind the legends that the Hebitians were telepaths and that they had developed a fabulous technology: a psionic intradimensional portal capable of allowing the Hebitians to move about the galaxy with nothing more substantial than thought.

Which was why Chen-Mai needed Kaldarren. Chen-Mai's motives were pure and simple: profit. He was, he'd explained, acting at the behest of an employer who was very wealthy and would pay very well for the technology. Even if the technology turned out not to exist, the discovery of another Cardassian tomb, and the riches that were surely within, would be more than ample return for the investment.

Failure was not an option. Neither was getting caught by the Cardassians. The region wasn't technically Cardassian; it was in dispute. Still, the Cardassians were very touchy about these things and would view any ship in the region, exclusive of pre-arranged Starfleet contacts, as a violation—and a provocation.

So why am I here? Why have I come to this godforsaken place where I'm just as likely to get shot by a Cardassian as find anything? They were questions Kaldarren had asked himself many times over, and ones to which he had yet to discover a satisfactory answer. He didn't need the money. Money wasn't a consideration on any Federation world. It was true that he needed resources that were hard to come by; all researchers competed for better ships, more personnel. That was why the Federation Science Council expected fairly detailed proposals.

Was it the challenge? Certainly there was that. But if Kaldarren were honest with himself, he would admit that he craved the prestige. He could picture the envy of his colleagues, the adulation and publicity he'd garner if he, Ven Kaldarren, were the author of the find of the century. (That Chen-Mai's employer might not allow Kaldarren to publicize, much less publish and present, his findings had never occurred to him.)

But was he so callow that all he wanted was notoriety? No, there was more to it than that, and Kaldarren thought he'd hit upon it just a little while ago. There was Rachel Garrett. And why? Jase's respect? To prove to his son that he, Kaldarren, was just as important as his mother? Maybe.

Or maybe it just has to do with Rachel. Just . . . Rachel. How long before that pain, and his desire for her, went away?

There was no answer for that particular question. He didn't expect one—yet. Soon, though: He suspected he needed to know, and very soon. He couldn't keep on this way, taking these kinds of risks. It wasn't good for Jase—or him.

"I have a question," he said, out loud. Kaldarren looked over at Chen-Mai. "If we don't find the portal . . ."

Chen-Mai didn't even let him finish the sentence. "Then you'd better hope the Cardassians do catch us, because you won't like the alternative. Neither will your boy."

Failure is not an option. Kaldarren let a moment go by. "Well then," he said, "I guess I'd better not fail."

"No." Chen-Mai didn't so much as crack a smile. "I guess you'd better not."

Chapter 12

This had better work. Halak watched as the carpet of light that was Maltabra City slid away beneath the aircar. *This had damn well better work.*

He was on edge, maybe because the Bolian was driving. But there was *something* wrong, something *more*. Halak could feel it.

"Matsaro will take you to the shuttle," Arava had said. She'd plucked up her cloak and slid it about her shoulders. Her fingers worked the clasp: a jevonite dragon with ruby eyes and golden scales that was Qadir's personal emblem.

(Halak hadn't wanted to question her too closely on how she'd come by the piece. He wasn't sure he wanted to know. Qadir only gave baubles and expensive trinkets to potential conquests. Or intimates.)

Arava said, "I've hidden the shuttle there, in a valley near the old Tsoran mine. Everyone moved out of the hills long ago, ever since the mines dried up. I checked, and there are no expeditions registered for that area. So you won't run into anyone, and vice versa. You shouldn't have any trouble."

"We have passage off Farius Prime," said Batra. Halak had heard the strain in Batra's voice, and he'd taken her hand. But her fingers were cold, and she hadn't spared him a glance.

Arava had shaken her head. "I want you to use the shuttle to get off-world. It's got a fake registry. No one will know it's you. Avoid the spaceport at all costs. I'm pretty sure Qadir's men are watching out for you."

"But you said yourself that our being in Starfleet . . ."

"Will only get you so far." Arava's tone was firm. "You have no reason to trust me, I know. You don't know me. But you have to trust me on this."

Batra had gone very pale. "I'm not sure I have a choice. I guess if Halak trusts you, I have to."

"Fair enough. The reality is that even if Qadir isn't looking for Samir, the Orion Syndicate would be just as happy to get their hands on him." Arava had turned a grim smile on Halak. "You're more valuable than you know. A lot of information in that brain of yours."

"What about you?" Halak said. He'd given up hope of

having her leave with them. Halak comforted himself with the reality that she'd stayed alive and moved up the ranks in Qadir's organization for years now.

"When I'm ready, you'll know," she'd said. "There'll be plenty of noise, and you can bet that everyone in the damn quadrant will hear it."

Now, dead ahead, Halak saw the city's perimeter beacons winking. In a few more moments, they would be out of the city proper, and that much closer to getting off the planet. Everything had gone according to plan. The Bolian had gotten them off without a hitch; they weren't being followed; and in a few seconds, they'd be beyond the precincts of the city proper. But Halak just couldn't shake the feeling that he'd missed something.

But what was it? Halak worried the feeling like a dog nosing an old bone. Halak had glanced at the Bolian's onboard systems and seen that the proximity alarm was on. So no one could sneak up on them from behind, and they weren't being followed.

The Bolian said, "Something on your mind?"

"What?" Halak realized then that he was practically breathing down the Bolian's neck. "No," he said, watching as the Bolian keyed in the aircar's transponder to signal to the perimeter automated sentries that their aircar was leaving the city's immediate vicinity. "Uh, how much longer?"

"About another twenty minutes." The Bolian's blue eyes flicked to Halak and then back to his instruments. "Sit back, will you? You're making me nervous."

"Sure," said Halak. The aircar's onboard computer pinged with a recognition signal and he listened as the city computer noted the date and time. "You've been where we're going?"

"Once or twice. It's a valley along the far western flank of the range. There's nothing out there but a bunch of rocks,

WELL OF SOULS   115

okay? No way anyone can sneak up on us either. The valley's too well hidden. So relax. Arava told me to take care of you, and I'll take care of you."

"Right. Sorry." Watching the black landscape skimming below, Halak sighed. A muscle complained along his right side, and he shifted, wincing. Other than getting himself knifed, he wasn't sure exactly what he'd accomplished.

Or lost. His eyes slid to Batra who sat on his right. The Bolian had left the interior lights off in the aircar, and the only light came from the green and yellow glow of instruments and sensors in the front. So Batra was a shadow, like an old daguerreotype: all dark profile, though he caught the glint of reflected light in her eyes. He wanted to say something, but he couldn't. There was no soundproof barrier between them and the Bolian, so he wasn't free to talk. Halak chewed the inside of his cheek. He wasn't sure what he could say—or reveal—anyway.

No one must know. Turning aside, Halak rested his forehead upon the cool glass of the aircar's passenger window and closed his eyes. Lies layered upon other lies, and no way to see his way clear. And now there was Batra, who'd seen and heard too much already. He'd have to think of something he could tell her.

Unless it was already too late for that. Halak's stomach churned with anxiety. Batra had said nothing after they'd left Arava. There had been no time for talk, no privacy for it either. A blessing, and a curse: He had time to think out what he wanted, or thought it safe to tell her. But, with every passing moment, he felt her edging further away, the unspoken breach between them widening. But, if he told her everything, he'd lose her. Halak had no illusions about that. And if he didn't, he'd likely lose her anyway. He had to worry about what might get her killed, too.

Arava was right. Starfleet was a buffer, but not even Starfleet could, or would, protect either of them forever.

He leaned forward. "What about patrols?"

The Bolian didn't look around. The glow from the instruments made his blue skin look yellow. "None from the city out this far," said the Bolian, as a single soft ping sounded as the aircar chimed the quarter-hour. "The shuttle's computer has a preprogrammed flight path input that will take you out of Farius Prime's space and keep you well away from regularly scheduled transport corridors. The shuttle's transponder signal registers as Vulcan. Plenty of Vulcan merchant ships in and out of here all the time."

"Oh?" Somehow the image of Vulcans running illegal arms or drugs didn't square with Halak.

"There are plenty of legit Vulcans doing business here. Anyway, Arava thought it was better that the ship show as Vulcan. You're less likely to be shot at, for one."

"That's comforting. What about communications?"

"Keep your channels closed until you're a good parsec out of Farius Prime's space. Then you can use communications. Not before: There's a Syndicate listening post on the second moon, and the Qatala maintains a perimeter relay system. More than likely, they won't be interested in you, but I wouldn't take any chances." The Bolian paused. "Any idea where you're headed?"

Halak hesitated. There was something about what the Bolian had just said that bothered him. Or maybe it was something the Bolian had done. Something about a heading . . . The feeling he'd had earlier—that there was something not quite right—bubbled to the surface of his mind. But he still didn't know. . . .

As for where they were going, his next move depended on Batra. But he had no illusions: They weren't going to Betazed. More than likely, Batra wouldn't want to have anything more to do with him. But they'd still have to get in touch with *Enterprise*. (He'd think of some way to explain how they came to have a Vulcan shuttle later.)

None of this was the Bolian's concern, so Halak said, in an offhand way, "Not yet. Betazed, maybe."

"Mmm." The Bolian's fingers crawled over the altitude controls and Halak felt the pit of his stomach drop as the Bolian decelerated. He watched over the Bolian's shoulder as the aircar's sensors detailed the cleft of a narrow valley, and then the shuttle itself.

He saw immediately that the Bolian had been right. The valley was isolated, and there were no passes or trails. Halak saw that the valley was really a couloir, surrounded by eskers and moraines—rocks and boulders pushed into piles by a glacier as it had advanced and then retreated. Plenty of cover for anyone wanting to ambush them, but the sensors showed all clear.

"Any way someone could mask a signature?" he asked the Bolian. "Hide their ship, maybe? How about the magnetic fields around these mountains?"

"Magnetic fields are there; they almost always are, even around these extinct volcanoes. But if you're talking a cloak, I doubt it."

"Mmmm." Halak didn't see anything out of the ordinary. But he wanted to be sure. He'd had enough surprises for one day. "Scan for life signs, would you?"

"Did that already. Not a living breathing soul around for fifty kilometers. That is, unless you count the Katangan mountain lions and a couple herds of caprinated rams."

"Great. So do it again," said Halak.

"Whatever you say." The Bolian hiked his shoulders and activated the aircar's sensors.

One glance confirmed that the Bolian was correct: no one else there. The Bolian swung his head around. "Okay?"

"Just about. Don't land right away. I want to do a flyby, go north about two kilometers," Halak tapped the sensor grid, "to that talus out there, and then circle back from the east."

"What for? You just saw. The sensors . . ."

"I know what I saw. Humor me, okay? When you come back around, I want you to angle the aircar so I get a good look at the shuttle."

He felt Batra touch his elbow. "Samir?"

He twisted his head to look back at her. "I just want to be sure."

"But Arava . . ."

"I know what she said. But things haven't exactly gone according to plan now, have they? I just want to be sure," he said again, reaching for her face. Her cheek was as still and cool as marble under his fingers. "I want to keep you as safe as I can."

"Suit yourself," said the Bolian.

In another moment, Halak felt their speed pick up again, and he watched as they lifted out of the valley. The Bolian circled and as he came in from the east, he flicked on a set of floodlights. Peering out the windscreen, Halak saw the steep slope of rocks and debris fanning around the base of a craggy peak that was the talus. The surrounding mountains were void of vegetation, and as they dipped back to the couloir, he saw scree and weathered arroyos where erosion had sluiced away soil to reveal bare red rock. In another second, he spotted their shuttle squatting on the surface.

"Satisfied?" asked the Bolian.

"Yes," said Halak. "You can set us down now."

In another minute, the aircar had ridden a vertical column of compressed air to the surface. The Bolian killed the engine but left a pair of headlamps on that illuminated the shuttle in a wash of silver light. He then popped the driver's side gullwing door before unfolding his lanky frame; Halak did the same with the rear passenger door. Sliding out, he turned and reached back to take Batra by the hand.

"Let's go," he said.

But Batra didn't take his hand. Instead she looked past

Halak, over his shoulder. "Samir," she said, her voice strangled. Her eyes were wide and dark. "Samir."

The way she said his name, he knew even before he turned. In the same instant, he heard the soft ping of the aircar's chronometer, and then it hit him: the thing he couldn't put his finger on. *That damn ping.*

Halak exhaled, very slowly, but his mind raced, riffling through his options. He had to gamble now that the Bolian didn't know about his phaser. His brain leapt back to his meeting with Arava. He didn't think the fact that he had a phaser had come up while the Bolian was around, but he couldn't remember. He had to play this exactly right. Halak inched around: halfway, to his left, keeping his phaser hand—and his phaser—hidden from view.

The Bolian leveled a weapon at his chest. With an almost dispassionate eye, Halak saw that the weapon was a Breen pulse gun. Breen pulse guns were illegal in Federation space because they had no safety, and only one setting: kill.

Halak waited a full three seconds before speaking. "You know, I had a hunch. Things were just going too smoothly. I'm rusty, though. I missed it until just now. You keyed in an exit code when you left the city limits. But, see, *not* keying in the code would've made sense, if you were trying to get someone out and didn't want anyone to know. But Arava said that Qadir's men were out looking for me, and so if you keyed in a code and you're one of Arava's men—and by extension, Qadir's—then that means Qadir ought to have sent someone after us. But he didn't because Qadir knows all about this already, doesn't he?" Halak shook his head in wonderment. "You're working for Qadir, not Arava. I missed it."

"Bad luck for you. Back away from the car, please. Hands in the air where I can see them."

Halak made a half move to comply but stopped. "What's going to happen to Arava?"

"Not up to me. For what it's worth, my bet is that Qadir

will take a good long time deciding. Then again, you won't be in any position to worry about anything in a few more minutes. I said, back away."

"Why didn't you kill us earlier? No, wait, I know. The residual weapons discharge would show up on scan, and I'll bet Arava will run an interior scan on this aircar as soon as you get back. If it shows up that a weapon was fired . . ."

"Then bad luck for me." The Bolian nodded. "She'd know something happened. For right now, it's better that she not know."

Halak's belly tightened. "What are you going to do to her?"

The Bolian made a face. "I told you. I don't know what they have planned. Not my department."

"No, I suppose not. Just killing us."

"That's right. Come on now, back away."

Halak still didn't move. "And I guess the other problem for you is that Arava expects this shuttle to be gone. A corpse can't fly. Oh, but the computer's got a preprogrammed flight path. Damn," Halak feigned incredulity, though he wondered how he'd been so stupid, "you gave me *two* clues, and I missed that one, too. And I'll lay odds that something really bad's going to happen to the engines right outside of Farius Prime space."

"Let's just say you'll have a really bad accident."

"Right, because the unexplained disappearance of two Starfleet officers would draw too much attention to Farius Prime. But if our ship explodes a nice distance away, that solves a lot of problems. Only you can't leave us alive until that happens."

"Because you might get smart all of a sudden and figure it all out, find how I rigged the explosive, and keep yourself from blowing up—more bad luck, but for me this time. My employers don't like mistakes. But you want to know the real reason I didn't kill you before now?" The Bolian's lips split in a wide grin. "I didn't want to have to carry you. You'd be amazed how heavy dead people are. So much easier if you just walk into the shuttle, and we do it in there. Now," the Bolian waggled his pulse gun once, "away from the door. Bring her, too."

"She's not part of this," said Halak, knowing this wouldn't do them any good. His hand crept by painful millimeters toward his phaser. "She doesn't know anything."

"She knows *you*. Too bad for her." The Bolian gestured with the pulse gun. "And that phaser you've got? Don't think about it. Hands in the air where I can see them, *now*."

Halak's shoulders slumped. He lifted his hands, palms-out, in an attitude of surrender.

The Bolian moved a step closer. "Which side?"

"The right." Halak's last chance, he knew: He could make a grab for the pulse gun when the Bolian got closer.

The Bolian jammed the muzzle of his weapon against Halak's left temple. "You make one move, you even sneeze, I'll burn you right now."

Halak felt that last burst of hope drain away. He stood very still as the Bolian patted around his waist until he found the phaser.

"Thank you." The Bolian jerked the phaser free and stepped back. "Now move two steps to your right, please. Not a step more."

Halak did as he was told. Stone squealed beneath his slippers. The Bolian flicked the pulse gun at Batra. "Out of the car."

Batra slid from her seat and stood, hands up. The Bolian gestured with his weapon. "That pouch: Unsnap it, then open it and shake out you've got in there. Once it's empty, toss it on the ground in front of you and then step back."

Slowly, Batra reached her hands around to the small of her back. There was a tiny click, and the straps of her pouch fell away from her waist. Batra gathered the straps in her left hand.

"Open it and empty it, I said."

Batra did as she was told. A credit chip and identification pattered to the ground. Then she let the pouch slip from her fingers. The pouch whispered against gravel and scree.

"Back up," said the Bolian. "Over there, to the right, next to him." He waited until Batra had moved into position; then he dropped to his haunches and, keeping his weapon trained on them, stirred the pouch's contents with his free hand. "That's all?"

"Yes," said Batra. Her voice was tight. "That's all."

The Bolian pushed to his feet. His knees crackled, and Halak had an absurd thought. He hadn't known that Bolians got chondromalasia.

"Okay. Move," said the Bolian. "Toward the shuttle."

They started for the shuttle, Halak first. The going was treacherous. The couloir's floor was studded with rock, and slurries of scree made the footing slippery. His slippers were soft and flexible, not made for climbing, the jagged edges of rocks biting the sensitive undersides of his feet, and he winced, staggered. His balance was off, too, because the Bolian made them keep their hands up and visible. Behind, he could hear Batra shuffling and sliding over rocks, with the Bolian carefully picking his way a short distance behind.

Suddenly, there was a sliding noise as Batra lost her balance, and then the sound of rock scraping against rock. Batra gave a single sharp cry. Halak jerked around in time to see her tumble to her knees. He moved toward her.

"Stop," said the Bolian. "She can get up on her own."

"Please," said Halak, "let me help her."

"Absolutely not. Stand clear."

"Sorry," said Batra. Halak heard tears edging her voice. Her face was turned back over her shoulder toward the Bolian, and Halak couldn't see her expression. Her left hand clutched her left foot. "But I twisted my ankle. I don't think I can stand."

"Get up," said the Bolian. He twitched the pulse gun. "Now."

Her sobs tearing from her throat, Batra made some feeble scrambling motions. "I *can't*."

"Let me go to her," Halak repeated.

"No." The Bolian watched as Batra rolled onto her right side and then got most of her weight onto her right knee. "Come on."

"Almost," said Batra. She was panting. "Almost there," she said, trying to balance on her right foot. But she slid, and spilled onto the rocks again.

Halak clenched his fists in frustration. "For God's sake!"

"Stay where you are," said the Bolian. "Keep your hands up where I can see them!" Cursing, he scrambled over the rocks until he was standing over Batra. Bending at the waist, he reached across his body with his left hand and grabbed Batra's left bicep.

"I *said*," he seethed, hauling her upright, his feet slithering on rocks, "stand *up* . . ."

Suddenly, Batra exploded in motion. Surging up, she brought her right arm whipping around, and Halak caught the flash of something long and metallic.

The knife. His mouth gaped in astonishment. The knife she'd taken from the men that afternoon.

And then he remembered: She'd tucked it into her waistband.

With a wild screeching howl, Batra jammed the knife into the Bolian's left flank. The Bolian arched and screamed. The sudden movement threw them both off-balance on the rocks, and Batra, still howling, had the knife in her hand, and as the Bolian lurched backward, she threw her weight forward, driving the knife in deeper. Halak saw them stagger and nearly fall, and then he saw the Bolian's face twist with rage and pain, his right hand jerk. The hand with the pulse gun.

"Ani!" Halak shouted. It was as if he'd been in suspended animation and suddenly snapped back to life. He sprang forward, his hands outstretched, trying to get there in time. "Ani, Ani, the gun, the gun, *look out for the gun!*"

The Bolian fired. There was a flash, a sizzle. A sweet smell that reminded Halak of burnt pork.

Batra shrieked—once.

"Oh God, no! What have you *done?*" Halak was rocketing toward the Bolian, even as Batra's body sagged to the rocks. *"What have you done? What have you done, what have you done!?"*

Halak slammed into the Bolian. Matsaro's breath whooshed from his lungs, and Halak's momentum lifted the Bolian from Batra's body and brought him crashing down onto his back. Halak heard a ripping sound, and his mind registered, dimly, that his back wound had torn open again. Pain rippled like liquid fire down into his hips and up to his right arm, and in another instant, Halak felt a warm stream of his own blood drizzling down his skin, pooling at his waist.

But then the moment passed, and Halak barely felt his own body. It was as if that single bright point of grief—that instant when Batra had screamed and Halak had known that she was truly, irrevocably dead—had burned his brain clean, searing into his consciousness until his mind boiled with a single, awful purpose: vengeance.

Beneath him, Halak felt the Bolian twitch, then heave as the knife was driven in up to the hilt. He heard a hitch in the Bolian's breathing and the harsh rasp of the Bolian's breath in his ear, and he was dimly aware that the Bolian still had his pulse gun clenched in his right hand and was struggling to bring his arm around.

Halak's fingers scrabbled over an edge of sharp stone, and then his right hand closed around the rock. Rolling atop the Bolian, he straddled the Bolian's chest, planting his knees on either side of the Bolian's head.

"No, no, *no!*" Halak screamed and brought the rock smashing down. The impact of rock against hard bone shivered up Halak's arms; there was the sound that a ripe melon makes when it's been thrown against a wall, and Halak felt the Bolian's body jerk and flop beneath his body like a beached fish slapping against a dock.

"No, no!" Clutching the rock, he raised both hands above his head and brought the rock down again and again. "No, no, oh God, *no, no . . .*"

Halak kept on long after the Bolian had stopped twitching. He kept on until the sound the rock made as it crushed through skull and flesh and tore through brain became soft and wet, and he kept on until his arms burned with fatigue, and the rock was so slippery that Halak couldn't hold on anymore, and the rock slid from his fingers.

Halak slumped over the Bolian's body. His breath jerked in quick, sharp paroxysms, and his hands were slick with the Bolian's blood. His own blood oozed along his skin and pattered to the thirsty earth, like a slow, steady rain.

And then—he wasn't sure when, or how—Halak was hunched over Batra. She lay on her back, her arms outstretched. There was a ragged burned patch over her left breast where the blast from the pulse gun had seared her skin, ripped into her chest, and ruptured her heart, and in the light from the headlamps that tanned the darkness he could see that her eyes were open and her lips peeled back from her teeth in a death rictus.

"Ani," he said brokenly, reaching for her face. This time, her skin wasn't cool. It was icy, the warmth leeching away under his fingers even as he knelt beside her.

"Oh, Ani, Ani, Ani." Halak gathered Batra's limp body into his arms. He folded her to his breast and dipped his face into her hair. He inhaled the scent of jasmine and lemon, the scent that was his beloved Ani. He wept, alone, under an alien sky.

Then he carried her to the shuttle. The shuttle was small—only big enough for two—and there was no place for him to lay her out properly. In the end, he settled for detaching a restraining harness from one of the shuttle's two chairs and strapping her body in place along the deck, looping the harness around her legs and chest and buckling the harness to a plate that ran the length of the shuttle's starboard side.

He stood over Matsaro for a few minutes. The Bolian didn't have a head anymore: just a misshapen, pulpy mass of smashed bone and flesh and blood. Stooping, Halak pulled the pulse-gun from Matsaro's dead fingers and stuck it into his damp, bloody waistband, and he retrieved his phaser. Then, grabbing fistfuls of the Bolian's shirt, Halak hauled him back along the rocks and then hoisted the Bolian into the aircar. The Bolian slithered along the length of the front seat, his body twisted and his left hip jutting up, so that what was left of Matsaro's head hung down, out of sight.

Halak was seized with a sudden wave of dizziness, and then nausea. He slumped against the side of the aircar, turned his head to one side, and vomited. When he was through, he clung to the cool metal of the aircar, fighting to stay conscious.

Lost a lot of blood. Halak ran his tongue over his lips, but his lips were numb and didn't feel right. His legs were wobbly, and his vision was narrowing to a single point. *Lost a lot of blood, that's all, and . . . oh my God, oh my God, Ani, Ani . . .*

He couldn't lose consciousness. Halak's brain moved slowly, and he felt sluggish, stupid. He had to stay conscious. He shook his head from side to side, and it felt as if his face was as gluey as molten taffy, his movements slow and languid. Slowly, he reached in and punched in a new heading. He heard a click, then a whine as the aircar's engine caught.

Stay focused—Halak programmed the aircar's speed and angle of descent—*one thing at a time.*

On an afterthought, he tossed in his phaser and the pulse-gun, heard them clatter against something metallic and disappear into the well in front of the driver's seat. Best not to have them on him. Then, reaching up with both hands, he forced the doors of the aircar down and shut. The movement made the pain in his side much worse.

"Please," he panted, pushing down hard on the door until he heard the lock engage. "Please, please, please, God, please."

Staggering back, he watched as the aircar shivered, then rose on its column of compressed air. The aircar turned, and Halak felt air puff against his face, and a chill rippled through his sweat-slicked skin. The aircar turned a lazy circle and then began its climb, heading east. The aircar's lights dwindled then winked out.

They might not find the body for a long time, if ever. Halak turned and began to trudge back to the shuttle. Every step made his stomach lurch and heave. He didn't know how long it would take the aircar to sink, but with the speed at which the aircar would slam into the sea, there might not be much left to sink anyway. Probably not much of a body left either. That would be good for Arava and give her some time to get away.

Inside the shuttle, he found a flashlight. Then, he went back out and crawled along on his hands and knees, feeling and looking for the explosive. He found it, finally, nestled at the very back of the port nacelle, attached to the outside of the hull and rigged to detonate as soon as anything other than short-range communications was accessed. They would have disintegrated the instant they hailed *Enterprise*.

It took him an hour to reach hailing distance. During the flight, he hadn't looked at Batra's body, because he had to work hard on the simple act of flying the shuttle. That, and staying conscious. He'd figured out how to bypass the pre-programmed flight path not because he needed to—the computer lockout was programmed to drop as soon as the shuttle's sensors told the computer that the ship was out of Farius Prime's space—but because it gave him something to do. He felt drained, dull. Empty. Dead.

Halak opened a channel. "*Enterprise,*" he said, slurring the word, "*Enterprise,* this is Halak. *Enterprise,* this is an emergency hail, this is . . ."

His gaze fell on Batra's body, and then it was as if he peered through a pane of flawed glass.

She never answered. Grief balled in his throat, and it was as if a giant fist had reached in, taken hold of his heart, and squeezed. *She never really answered the question, and now she never can. Never will.*

"*Enterprise,*" Halak said again. Tears crawled along his cheeks, but he didn't care if they knew he was weeping. "*Enterprise.*"

Chapter 13

"Captain, I'm busy," Marta Batanides protested. Her coiffed pillow of brown hair was showing the strain; errant tendrils feathered her neck. "I don't have time to argue with you about this."

Captain Rachel Garrett gave a short bark of derisive laughter, though none of this was funny in the slightest. She was so angry the muscles in her neck were taut as Vulcan lute strings, and her shoulders hurt. She knew she'd pay for this later—a migraine to beat the band for sure. Just as soon as she had the time and luxury to have one.

Thank God, she was in her ready room (where she seemed to be spending an inordinate amount of time these days, tending to business). When the Vulcan warpshuttle had come alongside *Enterprise* an hour ago, Garrett had such a heated exchange with the Starfleet Intelligence officer onboard—a Lieutenant Laura Burke—the *Enterprise's* bridge hummed with tension. After that, she decided that it was better to do battle with Starfleet Intelligence in private, with the gloves off: *mano a mano*, as it were.

"You don't have time? Gee, that's too bad. I suggest you make it, Marta." Unlike Commander Batanides, Garrett didn't take refuge behind formalities. The two women had known each other—albeit briefly—when Garrett had been on a layover on Starbase Earhart in 2327. Garrett had been heading back to the *Carthage*, where she was XO. Batanides was fresh out of the Academy. Batanides was a striking woman then—a lean brunette with a long neck and wide, almost oval-shaped blue eyes—and Garrett had seen nothing in the face that stared out of her companel to change her opinion. The two women had struck up a casual friendship; Garrett wasn't there long enough for more than a few drinks in the bar. Garrett remembered Batanides as a somewhat anxious young ensign waiting for her first assignment. There were two others from her class, she recalled, close friends that Garrett hadn't met at all, though she'd heard through the grapevine that there'd been a bar fight the day after Garrett shipped out: a couple of Nausicaans and one of Batanides's friends. The friend was unarmed, and so, of course, one of the Nausicaans pulled a knife. Stabbed Batanides's friend in the back, right through the heart, or so Garrett understood. It figured; Nausicaans were never known to worry about little things, such as fair play.

Well, as far as Garrett was concerned, it would be fair play all the way as long as she was in charge of *Enterprise*: everything on the up and up, and out front, something Starfleet Intelligence wasn't exactly famous for.

"Now," Garrett said, taking aim with her right index finger, "either you deal straight with me, or your people are going to hang in space a long, long time, and I mean it, Marta. I'll take this as high as it needs to go. I am not going along with this until I understand why the hell they're here in the first place. They show up *unannounced*, *no* advance warning, *no* contact from Starfleet Command, nothing. I don't get a single communiqué; no one's on the horn to me. Last time I checked, our communications systems were working just fine. So I'll just chalk it up to an oversight on your part. But you want cooperation from this moment forward? Then you damn well ask me for it. Now, on whose authority is Burke here?"

To her credit, Batanides sat through Garrett's diatribe without a squeak of protest, though Garrett could tell by the way that Batanides's lips thinned until her mouth disappeared that the woman was not pleased.

"Burke has authorization from Starfleet Intelligence," said Batanides.

"Meaning you. Sorry, Marta, not good enough." Garrett wagged her head from side to side. "That's not the way things run on my ship. *I* call the shots, not Starfleet Intelligence, and in case you haven't noticed, *Commander,* you don't outrank me. The way I see it, you're asking for a favor I don't have to grant. Okay, fine. You want me to do you a favor? Then you goddamned make the time and tell me why the hell Starfleet Intelligence is so interested in Halak—*my* first officer, might I add—or I send your people packing."

"Captain, don't force me to . . ."

"To what?" Garrett interrupted. Batanides didn't know, but Garrett didn't respond well to threats, and was just as likely to come out swinging if Batanides so much as twitched. "Go to a higher-up? Great. Do it. The more higher-ups involved, the better."

"*Why* are you being so antagonistic?"

Maybe because I got to be the lucky one to give notification to Anisar Batra's mother. Maybe because these are my *people.* "Let's just say I don't like people who make their living working in the shadows. I prefer things straight on. I like to know whom I'm dealing with. Now I know there's good and valuable work that SI docs," Garrett said, not believing a word but knowing she had to give Batanides something, "and I understand that intelligence operatives have their place. I'm not naïve, and I'm not particularly pugilistic."

(*Oh, really?*)

"Really," Garrett said, as much to Batanides as that little voice in her head. "But, you know, my plate's a little full right now. In case you haven't noticed, one of my officers is dead, and my XO is being held pending an inquiry. I don't need your people running around on my ship. Starfleet Intelligence comes aboard, I have a whole new set of headaches, and I sure as hell don't have time to baby-sit your people."

"No one's asking you to," said Batanides. "All I'm asking is that they pursue their own investigation and sit in on the inquiry."

"Why? And into *what*?" Garrett jabbed the point of her index finger into her desk. "Damn it, Marta, you're presuming a lot. I've been on the up and up with you. I filed my report, and I'll hold an inquiry, thanks. Everything will be by the book. Presuming there's sufficient evidence to press specific charges—and that's putting the cart before the horse, you know, because we haven't had the damn inquiry—I'll remand Commander Halak to Starfleet Command for further disciplinary action, *if* it's needed. You can get a crack at him then. What's so important about the inquiry that you people want in?"

Batanides's tongue flicked over her lips. "Look, Captain, you're asking the impossible. I can only say that we're interested in Commander Halak's story."

"Story?" There was something about the way Batanides said the word that made Garrett uneasy. "Are you saying you don't believe my first officer?"

"I said we were interested."

"May I ask why?"

Batanides blew out, backhanded a wisp of hair fluttering

along her cheek. "Captain, I *can't*. Please understand my position. Most of what you want is classified."

"At what level?"

"Need to know."

"And you don't think I need to know."

"No, you don't," said Batanides, with such bluntness that Garrett blinked. "I'm sorry, but if the gloves are off here . . ."

"Please," Garrett held up her hands, palms out, "don't pull punches on my account. The gloves are off and . . .?"

"And the simple truth is, Captain, you and your crew are unimportant. You are not part of the bigger picture."

Ouch. Well, at least the woman got to the point. "Bigger picture."

Batanides dragged in a deep breath. Exhaled. "Lieutenant Laura Burke is part of an ongoing covert investigation into certain aspects of, shall we say, *government* on Farius Prime."

"Government." Garrett chewed the word. "A euphemism for?"

"The Asfar Qatala and Orion Syndicate."

"Organized crime. Okay." Garrett spread her hands, hiked her shoulders. "So what? What about them? It's not like they're some sort of secret."

"But it's not every day that a Starfleet officer chooses to go to a place where organized crime substitutes for law and order."

Garrett had known that; in fact, she had a couple questions of her own about Halak's choices. Still, she shook her head. "It's not a proscribed world. Commander Halak didn't break any rules." She decided not to add that she thought Halak's judgment stunk. *Need to know, Marta.*

"We're aware of that aspect of the case. But he might be."

"Be what? Involved? Halak?" Garrett had a sudden inspiration. "Does this have anything to do with that flap over the Ryns eight months back, before he transferred here?"

"Possibly. I'm sorry," Batanides said quickly, in answer to

Garrett's grunt of exasperation. "That's all I can say. Really. Try to understand *my* position. Just how covert would anything be if I, or any other intelligence operative, had to explain every nuance, every move?"

She had a point; Garrett gave her that. "And the Vulcan?"

"Lieutenant Sivek, yes. We have enlisted the cooperation of Vulcan's security agency, V'Shar. Sivek's on loan."

"Why is Vulcan interested?"

"Same reason as the Andorians, the Threllians, the Pythagos Clans. They're all Federation worlds, and the Federation, as a whole, is more than a little concerned about red ice."

"Red ice." Garrett searched her memory. "A genetically altered opiate."

"Right. At first, it showed up on a colony or two, none of them Federation. It may seem cold and calculated, but the Federation has enough to worry about. Playing the universe's policeman means your resources get stretched, so you pick and choose what to worry about."

Garrett knew it wasn't fair, but she said it anyway. "So as long as red ice killed other people—non-Federation worlds, of course—then it was okay?"

"I'll just let that pass," said Batanides dryly. "Two years ago, red ice started popping up on Federation colonies. The remote ones, mainly, as if whoever distributing it knew that bypassing busier worlds would keep them in business longer. The Federation wants to stop the spread of the drug; they've asked for our help."

"Fair enough. What does this have to do with my first officer?"

"We just want to listen to what he has to say. He's been on Farius Prime; for whatever reason, he became a target. We want to know why. Other Starfleet officers have been to the planet and left without incident. Now Burke and Lieutenant Sivek are trained investigators and excellent intelligence officers. I . . . *we'd* like you to give them access to Commander Halak's ship."

Ah, the royal we. "For what purpose?"

"First, a complete and thorough search. Then the inquiry, and it's more than likely we'll want to ask Commander Halak some questions. Maybe have a few revelations of our own. Then, depending on what we . . . *you* find, we go from there."

"We."

"Yes, Captain, we. We will consult with one another; *we*, in conjunction with other Starfleet officers, will decide what to do."

"Just how much weight will *my* opinion have?"

For the first time, Batanides smiled. "Don't you think that depends on what we find, Captain?"

And, with that, Garrett had to be satisfied. After Batanides rang off, Garrett punched up the bridge, and gave the appropriate orders at which point Bulast informed her that Dr. Stern wanted to see her in sickbay. Now.

"Actually," said Bulast, "the way she said *now* . . ."

"Meant *yesterday.*" Garrett sighed. Stern was probably the only person aboard she let boss her around—to a point. "I got it. Tell her I'll be right down."

Great. Garrett ducked out of her ready room, bypassing the bridge, and scuttled down the hall toward a turbolift. The doors swished open; they hissed closed; and, as if on cue, Garrett's migraine thumped to life. *This is just turning out to be another great day in a string of great days.*

The *Enterprise*'s chief medical officer, Jo Stern, eyed her captain as Garrett stepped into Stern's office in sickbay. "You look like hell," Stern said.

"Thanks," said Garrett, dropping into a chair across Stern's desk. She winced, blinked against the overhead lights. "You always keep it so damn bright in here?"

"Headache?" Stern depressed a control and the clear soundproof glass door to her office hummed shut.

"Worse." Propping her elbows on Stern's desk, Garrett washed her face with her hands. "Migraine."

Stern commanded the lights to half. "Want something for it?"

"No."

"Good, I'll have some, too." Stern pushed back from her desk and crossed to a thermos she kept filled with hot coffee for precisely these occasions. She siphoned out two gray stoneware mugs' worth and popped the top of a container of chilled cream. "Too early for a drink, so coffee will have to do. Lucky for you, caffeine does wonders for migraines. That's cream and two sugars, right?"

"Yeah. Thanks," Garrett said, accepting the mug of steaming coffee from her friend. Stern's brew was nearly as good as her own. Garrett inhaled, blew then sipped. She sighed, this time with pleasure. "You don't know how good this tastes."

"Bet I do," said Stern, sliding behind her desk again. She eyed Garrett through the steam rising from her own mug. "You ready to talk about that call from Ven yet?"

Stern was an old friend and knew about Garrett's divorce and the agony Garrett felt over her and Jase having to live apart. Still, Garrett wasn't really in the mood to rehash it all. So, instead, Garrett sipped, swallowed. "Not really. Thanks, though."

"Suit yourself."

"Anyway, that's old news. A lot's happened since then." (The call had come a few days ago, but Garrett felt like she'd aged twenty years.) Garrett cradled her mug in both hands, enjoying the warmth that came through the stoneware. "So what's on your mind, Jo? You gave Bulast the impression that this was some sort of emergency."

"In a way."

"Halak?"

"You could say that."

"How is he?"

"He looks like hell, too." Stern had a smoky voice that always reminded Garrett of dim bars. This was apt: Stern, like Garrett, took her bourbon neat. "But I'd say it's a toss-up who looks worse, you or him. Of course, Halak's got a lot of reasons. On the other hand, so do you. Other than the reasons we all know, like worrying about crew morale, having to make notification to next of kin, and whipping your acting first officer into shape . . . how is Bat-Levi doing, by the way?"

"She's good," said Garrett. "She was good at ops, and she's good at being the XO. But I have to admit, I was a little concerned at first."

"You mean, because of her looks."

"Sure. But I was thinking more about her mental stability."

"Another good reason for us to have a psychiatrist aboard this time out," said Stern. "Anyway, the Vulcans have vouched for her. So has Starfleet Medical. Still, she's a strange duck, though she's damned sharp, I'll give her that. But that's why you look like hell? Worrying about Darya Bat-Levi?"

"No. Starfleet Intelligence."

Stern groaned. "An oxymoron if ever there was one."

"That's a really old joke."

"About what you can expect from a really old wreck." Stern was fifty-one, ten years Garrett's senior, and there wasn't a thread of gray anywhere in the shock of wheat-colored hair that she habitually wore pulled back from her face in a tight ponytail that brushed the nape of her neck. A woman of strong opinions and acerbic wit, Stern was lean and wiry, with a square face and wide mouth. She wasn't beautiful and knew it; she didn't mourn that either. She had what she called her man's hands: large, capable, adept at manipulating a laser scalpel. "So what do they want?"

Garrett filled Stern in on her conversation with Bat-anides. "So we're to cooperate with Lieutenants Burke and Sivek, no matter what. I don't get it, frankly. What could Halak know that could possibly interest them?"

Stern looked thoughtful. "It might be nothing more complicated than what Batanides told you. Maybe they just want to debrief him, hear what he saw or heard."

"Then why search the shuttle? We already did that anyway."

Stern made a face and drank from her mug. "You got me on that. So there's another agenda. You get any clue about what's between the lines?"

"Something about the Orion Syndicate and some other crime family, the Asfar Qatala, and red ice."

"Red ice?" Stern ran a blunt finger around her mug's rim. Her nails were flat-cut. "That's bad business. And they think Halak's involved?"

"How could he be? Anyway, it's Starfleet Intelligence's time to waste." Garrett gave a dismissive wave of her hand. "So what's going on with Halak?"

"Well, I think you can hold your inquiry in a couple of days. We have to wait for your two SI types to finish with their little dance anyway, right?" When Garrett nodded, Stern continued, "You know he might feel better if his captain visited."

"*This* is why you called? Wondering why I haven't been mopping my first officer's feverish brow?"

"Partly."

Garrett ducked her head over her coffee. "I've been busy."

"That's crap, Rachel," Stern said mildly. "Sure, you've been busy. Hell, we've all been busy. But he's your goddamned XO."

Garrett felt a wave of heat rise in her neck. "I know that."

"And?"

"And nothing," said Garrett. She picked up her mug, put it down without tasting, picked it up again. "*What?*"

Stern's face was impassive. "You want me to say it, or are you going to?"

"Say what?" (*Stop playing dumb.*) "Say *what?*"

"Cripes, Rachel, for a smart lady, you can be pretty willfully stupid sometimes, you know that? I'm talking about how you keep beating up this poor guy because he's not Nigel Holmes."

Garrett went rigid. "That's ridiculous."

(*Liar, liar, liar.*)

"Oh, crap," said Stern. "You can tell yourself that if you want to, and since you're the captain, I guess you can do any damned thing you please. But you'd have to be brain-dead not to notice that the two of you aren't exactly chummy."

"Chummy. I've *been* an XO, remember? There's no need for chumminess. It's a job, Jo, just a job."

"With responsibilities and delegation of duties based upon mutual respect and trust." Stern held up her hands in mock surrender. "Hey, don't get on my case; it's in the manual."

"Did it ever occur to you that our lack of chumminess might be mutual?"

"Is it?"

"Yes." She had to admit that Halak was more than competent, and she had developed a grudging fondness for the man, though he could be exasperating the way he argued.

(*So can you.*)

They'd always argued in private, but still. Halak had a savage intensity she found disturbing. Never outright subordinate, but . . . Halak seemed to be watching her. Weighing her against some internal scale, judging her ability to command the respect and loyalty of her crew before deciding whether or not she was worthy of his.

(*Or maybe it's mutual. After all, Halak's no Nigel Holmes.*)

And she missed Nigel. Nigel Holmes had been with Garrett from the moment she took command of the *Enterprise* four years before. She'd trusted Holmes; he'd saved her life on two occasions; and then she'd failed to save his. The *Enterprise* had been too far away from Holmes's shuttle when it came under attack from renegade Klingons, and Nigel had died.

Aloud, she said, "I think we're like two porcupines, Jo.

I'm prickly about Nigel, and Halak's got whatever ghosts he's carting."

"So you haven't made the poor guy's life any easier."

"I think I just said that." Garrett felt the muscles of her jaw and neck tighten. "If you have a point, make it."

"I thought I just did. Even before all this with Batra, it's safe to say that you didn't exactly trust or respect the man. I know, I know," Stern held her palm like a traffic cop signaling a stop, "things aren't looking too good for him right now. Frankly, when I tell you what's on my mind . . ."

"There's more?"

"Don't get snide. All I'm saying is that you might be right not to trust him, but that's not my point. My *point* is that if you treat someone like a visitor you'd just as soon boot out the airlock without a helmet, it shouldn't be a surprise if the guy feels he can't come to you for help, or advice. Answer me this," Stern leaned on her folded forearms, "did you ever, once, invite this guy to have dinner with you? *Once?*"

"What does that . . .?"

"Fine, I'll take that as a *no*. And how often did you and Nigel have dinner? Or coffee? Or just plain talk?"

Too many times to count. "All right, point taken," said Garrett. She toyed with her mug. "I'll admit that it's been very hard since Nigel . . . died. I just can't get used to *not* seeing him on the bridge, that's all. And it's *not* what you're thinking."

"And what am I thinking?"

Garrett drew in a deep breath. "Come on, Jo, we're both grown-ups here. You're thinking love affair, right? Well, you're dead wrong. We were very good friends, and that's it. I was . . . comfortable with him, and it's been a long time since I felt comfortable with a man."

"You mean, anyone who wasn't Ven."

Garrett gave her a frank look. "That's right. Once burned,

twice shy, I guess. I can *work* with men, fine. But talk? *Really* talk? That's another kettle of fish."

Stern shrugged. "I don't doubt that you work with men just fine. I've heard no complaints. Actually, the crew respects you, a lot. We'll get to the crew in a sec. Go on."

"There's nothing more to say. I miss Nigel, and it's my fault things worked out the way they did. He's dead because I made a command decision. I feel like I killed a friend, Jo, and I have to live with that."

"Okay," said Stern, nodding. "Okay. But there's no reason that *Halak* has to live with it. The poor guy didn't do anything but show up, you know? You want to keep beating up on yourself, go right ahead. I wouldn't recommend it, but be my guest. But don't take it out on Halak. He's got enough problems."

"All right, Doc." Garrett exhaled. "Point taken. Now what's this about the crew?"

Stern gave her a searching look, as if weighing whether to drop it and go on, or pursue what they'd been talking about. "A couple of things," she said, evidently deciding on the former. "Just want to put a bug in your ear, that's all. I did morning sick call. It was packed. An awful lot of somatic complaints. You know the drill: fatigue, upset stomachs. Headaches." She eyed Garrett.

Garrett ignored the inference. "And?"

"Crew's pretty shook up. They want to point fingers. Understandable."

"Anyone in particular?"

"More shook up than anyone else? Yeah. Castillo." Sighing, Stern threw her hands up in a *what-can-you-do* gesture. "I don't know, Rachel. Like I said, maybe it's good we've got a psychiatrist aboard this time around."

Garrett's concern was immediate. Castillo was young, she reflected, and he had all the qualities youth possessed: enthusiasm, energy, passion. He was also loyal, and stubborn to a fault.

But she should have known that, no matter what face

Castillo showed her every day, he would feel Batra's loss as keenly as Halak. Batra and Castillo had been an item for several months, and then Halak had shown up, and that was that. Garrett knew what everyone knew. Castillo and Batra were still friends, but on a ship—even one with over 700 souls aboard—privacy was hard to come by, and there had been a few times on the bridge when Garrett sensed the tension between Castillo and Halak. (And now, in light of what Stern had said, Garrett wondered if she hadn't helped that along.)

"He's *that* bad?" asked Garrett.

"Let's just say that he wouldn't mind if Halak went somewhere far away and never came back," said Stern.

"He *told* you this?"

Stern hiked one shoulder. "In not so many words. He talks. I listen. Right now, I'm not inclined to do anything more, but I might."

"Order him to see Tyvan? For what it's worth, whatever he's going through hasn't affected his work. I haven't picked up on anything other than what you'd expect."

"Of course not. You're the captain. Castillo practically worships the ground you walk on, for crying out loud. You think he's going to let you see anything? Anyway, I said I *might* send him to Tyvan. Depends on how things shake out. Actually, I'm hoping he goes on his own. Be good for him to come to that realization instead of being ordered."

"You think this is going to be trouble when Halak returns to duty."

"Yeah," said Stern, and paused. Then: "*If* he returns to duty."

Garrett's eyebrows shot for her hairline. "*If?* He's hurt that badly?"

"Oh, no, it's not that. His arm's much better. He can use it without a lot of difficulty. His side, too, though that cut was pretty damn deep. Three more centimeters to the right, and that knife would have gone into his kidney. He bled like stink. That's why he finally passed out. I had to give him a couple of transfusions just to get his blood pressure off the floor. Amazing, he managed to stay conscious long enough to pilot that shuttle. Chalk it up as one more mystery."

"Mystery." Garrett gave Stern a narrow look. "Referring to?"

"Well, that Ryn business for one."

"Old news, Jo. He was cleared and reassigned." Privately, the fact that Halak *had* transferred always bothered Garrett. She knew it was unfair to judge Halak by that fact (*You've been judging him all along. It's no wonder he's in this mess.*) but if she'd been in command of the *Barker*, she might have done the same thing: request that Halak be reassigned. On the other hand, if Halak had been a good first officer, she'd have fought for him to stay, or tried talking him out of it.

(*And if he'd been Nigel . . .*)

Shut up, she told the voice, *just shut up.*

"And a couple of the *Barker's* crew ended up dead, too," Stern was saying. "Anyway, for what it's worth, Tyvan's done an evaluation. Halak might have opened up with him. If not, then Tyvan will have something to say about that, too."

"Mmmm." Garrett reserved judgment on Dr. Yuriel Tyvan. She didn't know the El-Aurian psychiatrist well. To be honest, she'd deliberately avoided him ever since he'd come aboard during a stopover at Starbase 5. "I'm not sure that Halak will feel he can talk very freely with a psychiatrist who's doing a return-to-duty eval."

"Your paranoia's showing."

"Come on, Jo. This is Starfleet. In the good old days, they used to board people out of the military for psychological reasons. Frankly, I don't see how a psychiatrist can serve two masters: Starfleet *and* the patient. You doctors have a lot of power . . . don't make faces. You know I'm right. Relieving people from duty, making recommendations on retention, or return to duty . . . things haven't changed that much. I'm not sure I blame Halak; *I* wouldn't feel free to spill my guts to a psychiatrist who I know is going to turn around and talk about what I just said with everybody else."

"I don't think Tyvan's like that. Anyway, the idea's worth a try. We both know what deep space can do to people."

"I don't remember that the early starships had any need for a psychiatrist."

"Couldn't prove that by Mac," said Stern. "He's got more than a couple of stories about crazy crewmen."

It took Garrett a moment to place the reference. "Mac. You mean Leonard McCoy? Have you talked to him about Tyvan?"

"Yup. Mac and I go back a ways, you know that. Anyway, I called his office back at Starfleet Medical right before we picked up Tyvan. Know what he said? The scuttlebutt's that Starfleet's thinking about posting families together for deep space exploration."

"Kids on a starship? Families? I don't believe it."

"I don't make up the news. I just report it. It's just a rumor, but the way Mac was talking? I think Tyvan's an experiment. You put families aboard a ship, maybe there won't be so many divorces, separations. People will be happier. . . ."

Something must have changed in Garrett's face because Stern stopped and looked chagrined. "Sorry, Rachel. I have a big mouth."

Garrett shook her head and retrieved her coffee. The mug was cold; a chalky scum oiled the surface. But she held onto the mug just to have something to do with her hands. "Don't worry about it, Jo. I'm past the divorce. Really. Now, what do you want to tell me about Halak? What did you mean *if* he returns to duty?"

Stern looked as if she wanted to say something else but changed her mind. "Okay. It's this: Do you understand, and I mean *precisely*, what Halak was doing on Farius Prime to begin with?"

Garrett frowned. "No. What someone does on R and R is his business. He said he was visiting an old family friend. That's his right. Farius Prime isn't proscribed, so he didn't break any regulations by going. But you do have to question his judgment about taking Batra along."

"No." Stern screwed up her face in a frown of disagreement. "That was an accident, Rachel. Batra was a grown woman who made a choice. A bad one, as it turned out. You can't blame Halak for that. What you *can* blame him for is his not being exactly helpful about filling in the gaps and the discrepancies."

Garrett was alert to the change in Stern's tone. "There's a problem."

"Yeah." Stern laced her fingers together and leaned her forearms on her desk. "Rachel, his story doesn't jibe. Not all of it, anyway."

"Which part?"

"How about a lot of it? Right now, he's sticking to it. He and Batra go to the bazaar, then they see this . . . what's her name . . . this Dalal character. They have dinner. Then they're on their way back to the spaceport when this Bolian and a goon jump them, force them into an aircar, and take them out to God knows where for God knows what. Wherever they're going, there just happens to be a shuttle. Halak doesn't know why or how; it's just there. Then there's a scuffle. The Bolian has a pulse gun; the goon has a knife. Halak gets knifed, but Batra manages to get the knife away from whomever's got Halak and she stabs the Bolian, the one with the pulse gun. Then Batra's killed, and then Halak shoots both the Bolian and the goon. Only . . ."

"Only what?"

"Only there's no ionized residue on Halak's skin. There is on Batra's, around the entry wound. But if Halak pulled the trigger on the Bolian and another goon, then there should be blowback. There isn't."

"Meaning he didn't use the pulse gun."

"Not damned likely. And if there *was* another goon, he remains a mystery because I can't find a trace of *him* anywhere—no blood, no DNA, nothing. On the other hand, the blood on Halak's clothing? Two types, his own and the Bolian's."

"He said that Batra stabbed the Bolian. If Halak struggled with the Bolian, he'd have the Bolian's blood on his clothing. That jibes."

"Rachel, Halak had that Bolian's blood all *over* him—under his nails, in his hair, on his neck. His cheeks, for God's sake. Not to mention bone and stuff that tests out as cerebral cortex. Bolian."

"And from that you infer . . . what?"

"You ever take a good look at blood spatter? Well, I have. Did a bunch of forensics work when I was in training before I decided on going the deep space route. Now, blood oozes. It pools. It flows. And it spurts, but only if the heart's still pumping. What the spatter pattern looks like depends on how the body's positioned; how much you get on you depends on your relationship to the body. Now to get all that blood where it ended up, I figure the Bolian was lying on his back and Halak was on top, maybe straddling him."

"So what are you thinking?"

"That he sure as hell didn't stab the Bolian to death. You don't get Bolian brains under your fingernails if you're stabbing him." Stern shrugged, rubbed her neck with her hand. "Jeez, Rachel, I dunno. All I know is that the evidence suggests that Halak didn't use a pulse gun or a phaser, and he may not have used a knife. The evidence suggests that he bludgeoned the guy to death."

"Could it be that things just happened too quickly? Mixed him up?"

"Sure. In fact, I'd say that would be par for the course. I'm no psychiatrist, but trauma's funny. Either you remember everything—how things smelled and tasted and even what clothes you were wearing—clear as a bell, or it's all a jumble. So I'd be inclined to let it go except for a few other things. That wound, Rachel, the one on Halak's back, and his left arm? They're old."

Garrett was startled. "Old? What you mean?"

"I mean that he was stabbed all right, only it happened earlier and then the wounds dehisced, pulled apart, probably as a result of the fight with the Bolian. By the time I got to them, rudimentary epithelial regeneration had already begun. So I couldn't close them right away. Tissues don't heal as well, more chance of infection. I had to leave the wounds open, let them granulate in a bit, and then close them up. I did the second surgery on his back yesterday. Only when I tested the skin around his wounds, I found evidence of antimicrobial packs."

"What?" Garrett was flabbergasted. "But then that would mean . . ."

"He got knifed much earlier, and someone patched him up. Only the question is who? This Dalal?" Stern leaned in closer. "An interesting question, isn't it? I'll tell you something else. Halak lost a lot of blood, only where is it? There wasn't enough soaked into his clothes, or pooled in that shuttle, to account for the way his intravascular volume was down. So he did his bleeding, only not in the shuttle."

As astonishing as it was for her to think it, Garrett found what she thought even more incredible to say aloud. But she did anyway. "You think he's lying."

Stern hesitated. "God, I hate going that far, especially with a fellow officer, and I happen to like Halak quite a bit. Let's just say I don't think it's so cut and dried, pardon the pun. There was undigested food in Batra's stomach, so she had a meal before she died, and I have no doubt she was shot. Only she was pretty banged up, her jaw especially. But, Rachel, get this: she bruised. Her tongue was lacerated, like she bit herself. Only there were no clots, and the tissue was regenerating. If Halak's correct in his sequence, she died before she had a chance to bruise, and there ought to have been blood clots in her mouth. There weren't. And here's a kicker: There are traces of an antiseptic salt in her mouth. Someone tended to her, too."

Garrett sat very still, her headache forgotten, absorbing the implications of what Stern was saying. If Halak hadn't outright lied, then he was omitting a great deal. But omissions were not, in and of themselves, crimes. Stern hadn't found anything to contradict Halak's assertion that he'd killed in self-defense, and no one on Farius Prime was even admitting to, or advertising that someone had misplaced a Bolian.

"You said there were a few things that didn't jibe," Garrett said. "The wounds, the blood spatter."

Stern ticked the rest off on her fingers. "The amount of blood loss, and Batra's bruises. The stuff in her mouth. And one more thing."

"What's that?"

Stern's eyes zeroed in on Garrett. "Dirt."

Chapter 14

His companel shrilled, and Tyvan jumped.

"Shouldn't you answer that?" asked Bat-Levi.

"Oh, it can wait," Tyvan lied. He knew who it was: Bulast, to remind him that Halak's inquiry, delayed three days while Starfleet Intelligence rummaged around his ship and the commander mended, would begin in fifteen minutes.

"Oh," was all Bat-Levi said, though the skin above her eyebrows furrowed in a slight frown. He read her meaning. Hails weren't things an officer could afford to ignore.

The hail cut the air again.

"One second," said Tyvan. Nothing was more important than being with Bat-Levi right now; he was sure the captain would see it that way. Still, since his chair—black leather, high-backed—squatted in front of his desk, he faced the unenviable task of hoisting himself around in his seat to grope for the audio cutoff: an undignified posture for an officer, he reflected, so it was good he wasn't one to stand on ceremony. Tyvan rummaged around and killed the audio in mid-bleat. "No, I shouldn't answer that," he said, dropping back. "You came by to see me. Something must be wrong."

"Wrong?" said Bat-Levi. The horizontal furrows above her eyebrows deepened, and her eyes narrowed, as if she worried that she'd made a mistake, or thought this was some sort of test. "Why do you say that? This is when I'm scheduled to see you. Session four. You schedule, I come. Simple as that."

So she didn't know. She had no idea. Very interesting. When Bat-Levi had shown up at his office door twenty minutes before, Tyvan had to contain his surprise, especially given the fact that he had to be very *elsewhere* in short order. He'd been about to put her off and ask why she was here, now, didn't she realize what day it was, but then caught a glimpse of the unmistakable shine of unshed tears in her overly bright black eyes. And then he'd understood and he'd kept his mouth shut, let her come into his office, her servos squalling, and get herself settled. She hadn't been angry, thank heaven, or even distantly polite; she'd seemed tired and wrung out, and her movements were slower, as if she carried some greater weight than her prosthetics.

Tyvan decided to handle the issue with as much tact as he could. He didn't want to risk embarrassing her, and then having her shut down. *Please, no, not a repeat of last time, please.*

"Well, Darya," he began, "the reason is . . . today isn't one of your regularly scheduled days."

He saw confusion flicker across her features. "What? It's *not?*"

"No. Your appointment isn't until 1330 tomorrow."
When Bat-Levi didn't respond, Tyvan added, "So I just assumed that you'd come by because something's wrong. Is there something you want to talk about? Halak, perhaps, or Anisar Batra? She was a good friend of yours, wasn't she?"

"Yes," said Bat-Levi, though her voice was faint and the response automatic. Her eyes had a faraway look as if she were taking a mental inventory. Tyvan waited.

"I'm sorry," Bat-Levi said at last. She made a move to get up. "I . . . I don't know why I . . ."

Tyvan waved her back without moving from his seat. "Sit. I have nothing going on right now." (*Well, not much, just a little inquiry and a formal report.*)

She did, again automatically, that confused, surprised look still on her face. They said nothing for a few moments. Tyvan listened to the tick-tock of his clock and prayed, fervently, that Garrett would be satisfied with taking out only a small piece of his hide.

Bat-Levi licked her lips. "Isn't Freud the one who said that there's no such thing as forgetting?"

"Not in so many words, and not about everything. Actually, Talok of Vulcan went one step further. He wrote that normal people can't forget what they already know. All things being equal, if a person forgets something, it's to serve some deeper purpose for the unconscious mind. Why do you ask?"

"Because I'm here, now, when I shouldn't be." Her eyes slid to the floor and then back to his. "And as you've said, I've seen a lot of psychiatrists, so I don't think this is an accident."

"What do you think it is?"

Her gaze was steady, but he heard a slight tremor in her voice. "I think it's one of two things. Either I told myself I had to be here at this time so it would seem more like *your* idea than mine . . ."

"Or?" Tyvan prompted, though he was impressed. She

was right. She had spent a lot of time in the patient's chair, long enough to do a good piece of self-analysis without any help from him.

She lifted her chin, pulling her straighter. Her scar gleamed a bright pink in the overhead lights. "Or I have something really important to tell you, and it can't wait. Or maybe both."

"I agree," said Tyvan. His manner was still calm, but inside he felt a shock of excitement. "Where would you like to start?"

He saw from the look in her eyes that she was still debating about whether or not to flee. Then she reeled in a deep and tremulous breath then let it out, as if steeling herself. "Look, I'll be honest with you. I owe you an apology for the way I behaved last time."

She paused a half-beat, as if to give Tyvan an opening. Tyvan made no move to agree or disagree.

"I think it's safe to say that I don't like being here," Bat-Levi resumed, "and I don't really enjoy you, per se. I don't mean to be rude, but that's the way it is. I know that I don't have to like you. It's not your job to have me like you."

"As I recall, a teacher once told me that if patients liked me, I wasn't doing my job," said Tyvan, and he meant that. Patients became anxious when a psychiatrist confronted them with the need for change. No one liked change, and the people who wanted to avoid *change* avoided *him*, and in the close quarters of a ship, other people, not his patients, avoided him by association. (Of course, this meant that when he did his job well, he was lonely a great deal. How many people who'd confided their deepest fears and wildest fantasies had paled when he walked into a room? More than he could count: He knew that instant of wild animal panic that sparked in a patient's eyes too well. It didn't matter if the encounter was on the street, in a shuttle terminal, aboard ship; a patient's reactions were, usually, the same. That flicker of surprise followed by fear that was replaced by an uneasy civility: *How are you, Doctor? Good to see you.* Smiles that were all teeth and too wide, gestures that were too animated. They were all lying, of course. No one was happy to see him outside the office.)

As if reading his thoughts, Bat-Levi said, "Then I'd think you'd be a pretty lonely man. Ships are roomier than they used to be but not *that* roomy."

"Maybe," said Tyvan, not wanting to stray too far. His problems were his problems, not hers. "Is this about Anisar Batra?"

"Yes and no. I've been thinking about what you said: about guilt and responsibility. I'll be honest about Ani. She was my friend, and I can't imagine how Halak's going to be able to look at himself in the mirror again. Halak's got to live with this now every day of his life. I'll bet that not a day has gone by when he hasn't rehashed everything in his mind, wondered where he went wrong, what he could have done differently." Bat-Levi moved her head from side to side, the movement stuttering as if her neck were made of gears that weren't meshing properly. The right corner of her mouth was taut, twisting her mouth into a grimace. "Every morning he's alive is another morning she isn't."

"Do you think he got her killed?"

"Yes, I do. He may not have meant it to happen . . . no, that's stupid; I *know* he didn't want anything like that to happen to Ani. But it did, and he's got to feel some responsibility."

Tyvan shook his head. "That's not what I asked. *Feeling* responsible isn't the same as *being* responsible. I asked if he got her killed. You said he did. So you must think he could have done something to prevent it."

"That's like arguing about how many angels can dance on the head on a pin. He could have sent her away."

"But Batra was an adult. Don't you think that was up to her to make a choice?"

"Adults don't always know the answers. You don't expose the people you love to danger, and if you see danger and don't do something about it, then it's only right, it's only just that you should live with your guilt every day of your life. I know it isn't fair, but life isn't fair. You do something like that, you should pay."

"Even if what happened was an accident?"

Bat-Levi made an irritable gesture with her good hand: a flick of the wrist. "A lot of the things that people call accidents can be prevented, and Halak should've known. Farius Prime isn't exactly sugar and spice. What the hell was he thinking? He was careless, and now," her voice thickened and her eyes welled, "now Ani's dead."

"I imagine Halak feels pretty terrible."

"I wouldn't know about that."

"Have you asked him?"

Bat-Levi wet her lips. "No. Halak, he's hard to get to know. Like there's this hard shell all around him, and you know he'd like you to break through only . . ."

"Only what?" Tyvan prompted when she didn't continue.

"Nothing." And then her watery gaze jerked away.

Tyvan decided to risk it. "I think you just lied to me."

Bat-Levi's eyes arced back, and Tyvan saw that they sparked with anger. The small muscles of her cheeks danced. A single tear tracked down the scar over her right cheek, but she made no move to wipe it away. Tyvan waited.

"I hate you," said Bat-Levi. Her chin quivered, and another tear slid to join the first. "You know, I really hate you."

Tyvan nodded.

Bat-Levi drew in a shuddery breath, used her good hand to smear away tears. "Well, you got me, didn't you?"

"What did I get, Darya?"

"I'm talking about Halak, but . . . I'm talking about me. That's it, isn't it?" she asked then continued, without waiting for a reply, "That's why I came a day early. This is all about me, my armor, my guilt. This is all about Joshua."

Her eyes tracked left, to the floor. Neither of them spoke for a few seconds. The clock ticked.

"Well," said Bat-Levi, and then she looked Tyvan full in the face. "What do you want to know?"

"Whatever you'll tell me," said Tyvan, simply.

Chapter 15

Bat-Levi's day hadn't started well. She'd tumbled into bed at 0200, tumbled out at 0530, and gulped sour replicator coffee before dashing off to meet Joshua at the slip where the *Lion* was docked. And now the generator was acting up, and her nose itched. Absently, Bat-Levi brought up her left hand to give her nose a good scratch and was rewarded with the solid thud of her gloved hand colliding with her helmet. She cursed, silently. If Joshua weren't in such a hurry to get underway, she wouldn't be in this pickle. She'd never gotten used to EVAs, even though they were required at the Academy because, dollars to doughnuts, put her in a tin can, turn on the air, and she was guaranteed to have to scratch *something*, every single time.

Bat-Levi blew out, her hair fluttering away from her forehead, but an errant strand glued itself to her sweaty cheek. She wiggled her mouth, trying to dislodge it. Instead, she only succeeded in getting the hair lodged under her tongue. *Damn.* She tried spitting out. The hair stayed put. Her own fault: She'd been in such a rush she hadn't secured her hair before ducking into her suit. And she was practically drowning in sweat. She was always so damned hot in her suit, no matter how low she cranked the temp. She made some *pfft-pfft* spitting sounds.

"What's that?" Joshua's voice was tinny inside her helmet. "What's going on down there?"

"Nothing." A finger of sweat crawled down Bat-Levi's back. Hair plastered her tongue. "I'm fine."

"You sound grumpy."

"Well, I am grumpy," she said, talking around hair. She gave up trying to spit it out. "You and your stupid generator."

"Hey, this is your baby, too."

"*My* baby." In vacuum and weightless—and thank goodness for that, because among the many other things she hated about EVAs was how robotic the suits made her feel—Bat-Levi grabbed a handhold and pulled herself over to the panel behind which lay the influx particle siphon of their emissions generator. "I have news for you, Jock-o. While you've been hatching your latest scheme, I've been sweating it out at the Academy. You didn't even come to my graduation."

"I was busy." Bat-Levi heard the *blip-bleep-blat* of controls being keyed in. Joshua was at the helm of their ship, the *Lion*, while she went below deck, suited up, and cracked the magnetic airlock and hatch of a vacuum containment pod bolted to the ship's belly. "Besides, I knew I'd see you sooner or later." More bleats. "Anyway, what could be better than spending time with your baby brother, huh?"

"Baby brother, my eye. By a whole two minutes, Jock-o."

"Hey, two minutes can be an eternity, like *now*. Are you going to get in behind that panel and tweak that intermix ratio, or are we going to hang out here all day, watching Starbase 32 doing a nice pirouette, way out in the middle of nowhere?"

"Coming," said Bat-Levi. Joshua didn't know about Devlin Connolly, and so he couldn't know that she'd given up a week's leave on Pacifica with Dev to work with Joshua. But Joshua was the one going full bore after the Cochrane Medal. Joshua had drawn up the specs for a self-replicating nanoparticle emissions generator. The theory was hers, using vacuum energy as fuel. (The Heisenberg Uncertainty Principle implied that even under conditions where all sources of energy—whether from matter, heat, or light—were removed, random electromagnetic oscillations remained. The most straightforward example of vacuum energy was the

Casimir effect. Two metal plates, in close enough proximity, would come together because, as the plates blocked light energy from getting in between, vacuum energy pushed the plates together. Bat-Levi reasoned that if this negative energy, a limitless power source, could be harnessed into an electromagnetic bottle, it could substitute for the present-day warp drives. The energy to power the ship would come from space itself.)

Joshua made the intuitive leap his twin sister hadn't: If energy could be removed from space, could this same process open up fissures in space itself, creating gateways to other dimensional spacetime membranes and allow the ship to jump through the openings, like traversing wormholes?

So their generator: a Casimir sink, on a much larger scale. The generator itself was housed in the vacuum pod in an attempt to keep the ambient conditions as close to the vacuum of space as possible (though not as cold). The glitch was that they still had to use present-day technology simply to move the ship around and to power the initial conversion reaction necessary to siphon away vacuum energy. Hence, the problem: The *Lion* was equipped with a warp drive, and the tricky part was keeping the intermix ratio of deuterons and antideuterons stable in the face of an influx of additional vacuum energy.

Bat-Levi manipulated a set of Kelly bolts securing a metal panel over the injectors that controlled the nanoparticle plasma stream. The panel floated free, and she peered inside. The plasma was a dark cobalt blue and flowed like liquid, the way fire behaves in weightlessness.

Joshua's voice came again. "Well?"

"Hang on," said Bat-Levi. An array of prismatic grids, arranged in two series, deflected the plasma stream, funneling errant particles back toward their central nodal injector point. Each grid functioned independently, and she saw now that one wasn't self-correcting quickly enough, creating uncontrolled power surges. Bat-Levi pulled a prismatic spanner from her waist and fiddled with the grid's alignment. "How's that?"

"Not good enough. I'm still reading a five percent flux in the energy dispersal pattern. That just won't cut it, Darya. You know we've got to maintain an even pattern of energy dispersion, or else we'll rip out chunks of subspace."

"Heck." Bat-Levi recalibrated her spanner and tried again. "Jock-o, have you ever considered giving this a little more time? The last simulator run, the generator did that little runaway surge, and this grid is just not cutting it."

"Yeah, but only for three-point-four-seven seconds."

"*Yeah*, and plenty long enough for our port nacelle to linearly accelerate twice as fast as the one to starboard."

"And I got it back under control. I know; I'm hearing you."

"And?" Bat-Levi paused, a Kelly bolt between her fingers.

"*And* I don't want to wait. Darya, you're shipping out on the *Wheedon* in two weeks. We won't get another chance, not unless you stay put."

Bat-Levi shook her head then realized Joshua couldn't see her. "Sorry, Jock-o, I'm not putting off my vacation, even for you."

"You have something better to do?"

Yes. Bat-Levi felt a twinge of guilt. "Let's just say that I have other plans. Look," she talked at the canopy over the pod, a habit she noticed all people in suits had: talking up into thin air, "you can do this without me, Jock-o. We'll play around with the ship today, but if it's not optimal, then you put it off. Run the test flight when she reads steady across the board."

"No. You're part of this, Darya. I want you with me."

Bat-Levi decided not to argue. She checked the ratio of the influx of nanoparticles across the series of prismatic grids. The ratio fluctuated—enough so that Bat-Levi knew she'd have to make manual adjustments along the way. Not good. Maybe she should play with this longer, and to hell with Joshua's impatience. But she was cooking in this damn suit, and she knew she couldn't make the thing perfect.

Working as quickly as her gloved fingers allowed, Bat-Levi bolted the panel back into place. Then she clambered into a small airlock, waited for the lock to repressurize, and scrambled out of the vacuum pod. Battening down the magnetic hatch located amidships, she keyed in her coded combination, waited for the iris to constrict and seal. Then she popped her top. There was an audible hiss, then the relatively cool, dry air of the shuttle hit her face, and she blew out a great breath of relief. Then she pulled the hair out of her mouth and gave her nose a good scratch.

She spared a peak at the generator through a portal adjacent to the magnetically sealed hatch. All the generator's indicators were green; the flow of nanoparticles appeared stable.

After she peeled out of her suit and stowed it next to Joshua's, she pattered up the gangway amidships to the upper deck. Joshua's back hunched over the shuttle's main control console. Bat-Levi squeezed her way forward to an auxiliary monitoring station. The *Lion* was a modified four-passenger shuttle, twelve meters stem to stern and six meters at its beam. With all that extra equipment crammed onto the main deck, the fit was tight.

Joshua looked over as she dropped into her seat. "Ask you something?"

Bat-Levi brought the readings on the nanoparticle emissions generator on-line. Her eyes narrowed as she studied the stability of the particle stream. That damn burp . . . She fiddled with an injector aperture and changed the collision angle by a tenth of a nanometer. "Fire away. What's on your mind?"

"You."

Bat-Levi didn't look up from her readings. By God, this generator was fickle. "Yeah?"

"Yeah. You met someone." Not a question.

That got her attention. She looked up and swiveled

around to face him. For some reason, she felt a wave of embarrassment, as if her twin brother had caught her in a lie.
She and Joshua were more than two peas in a pod; her father
joked that they were probably as close to being telepaths as
nontelepaths got. Yet, close as they were, she hadn't told
Joshua about Devlin. She wasn't sure why. Privacy, maybe:
Her love life was none of her brother's concern. But the truth
was that she felt, vaguely, like she was betraying Joshua.

Bat-Levi looked into the face she knew almost better than
her own. "Yes."

Joshua gave a contemplative nod. "I thought so. You
haven't been all here, you know? You've been a million kilometers away ever since you showed up two days ago."

Bat-Levi felt heat in her cheeks. "I hadn't imagined it was
that noticeable."

"I know you, kiddo. So what's his name?"

"Devlin Connolly." Just saying the name caused a little
tingle of excitement—and longing—to course through her.
"Same year as me. He's shipping out on the *Kallman*. We'd
planned to take a week together before then."

"I figured. There's something," Joshua stirred the air between them with one hand, "in the middle."

"I was planning on telling you."

"Darya," said Joshua, his face serious. His hair was even
darker than hers and very curly. He finger-combed a handful
back from his high, smooth forehead. "You don't owe me
any explanations."

"Well, we don't usually keep secrets, and . . ."

Joshua eyed her askance. "Speak for yourself. There are
some pretty nice women I met at the Cochrane."

"Really?" Bat-Levi's curiosity was piqued. She wondered
what her parents, dynamic propulsions experts on the
Cochrane's faculty, thought about Joshua's paramours.
"What did Mom and Dad . . . ?"

"I don't share everything. So, do you love him?"

"I think so." Bat-Levi nodded, relieved to tell someone. "Yes."

Joshua reached over and covered her right hand with his left. "It's okay, Darya. Really. It's good you met someone."

"Yeah?" Bat-Levi felt like crying. "You'll probably hate him."

"Probably. Actually, it's more likely Mom will. You know what she thinks about Starfleet . . ." Joshua caught himself, gave a rueful grin. "Sorry."

"That's okay." Bat-Levi swiped the wet from her eyes. "And it's not as if there aren't problems. You know, being posted to different ships, trying to coordinate leaves." An Academy truism: Most relationships didn't survive longer than the first six months after graduation. Bat-Levi wondered if other couples believed they would be the exceptions. She knew that she and Devlin did.

"I can imagine." Joshua gave her fingers a squeeze. "Well, we pull this off, not only won't Mom and Dad have *anything* to complain about, we'll get the Cochrane, and *you'll* have to beat the offers down with a stick."

"We'll see," said Bat-Levi. "Don't jinx it."

"Fair enough." He squeezed her hand one final time. "Time to put on a show for the folks on 32, then let you catch up with your boyfriend."

"Some show." Bat-Levi gave a shaky laugh. She waved her hand in the general direction of Starbase 32. Squares of yellow light studded the windows of the blue and gray station, and the shape always reminded her of a slowly spinning child's top. Starbase 32 hung, by itself, on the fringes of the Federation. The nearest inhabited planet was thirty light-years away. "This region of space is just about as deserted as you can get."

Joshua pulled up their preflight checklist. "Well, that way, if the generator fails, we won't take out so many planets at the same time now, will we?"

"That's not funny, Jock-o." *Because if we don't do this*

right, half the ship gets sucked into an interphasic whirlpool.
Bat-Levi's gaze strayed back to the prismatic grid flow indicator on her console. The flow had stabilized, and there were
no further indications of trouble. Still, she wished Joshua
would run just a few more simulations. *That damn flow
never has settled down.* She checked the power couplings on
their nacelles and, in an afterthought, the explosive bolts to
the nacelles. Just in case.

She stole a peek at her younger brother and saw, with a
sudden bittersweet pang, how much more grown-up he
seemed. Funny, how she'd left for the Academy and he'd been
just a boy. Now they were both breaking out, finding their way
in the universe—and probably away from each other.

Her thoughts floated to Devlin Connolly, only this time
she felt a little sad. Like she was acknowledging the death of
something. Later, she would know: a prophetic thought.

The generator had been online for a half hour into
the test flight when Bat-Levi said, "I don't like the looks of
this."

"Mmmm?"

"The transdimensional rift off the port quarter doesn't
seem stable. Here," she funneled the information to his control display. "Take a look."

Her auxiliary console was to Joshua's left and behind, so
she couldn't get a good look at his face as he bent over the
readings. "That doesn't look too bad," he said. "The variance
in rift integrity isn't even statistically significant. The simula-
tion proved a tiny variance isn't important."

But just how tiny is tiny? "Look, if this were an *antimatter*
injector, you wouldn't tolerate a variance of even a . . . no,
don't shake your head at me, Joshua. Listen, no machine is
perfect, and that includes our generator. Now, this thing is
taking more vacuum energy from port than starboard. We
both know that the dimensional rifts *must* be bilateral and

equal. Otherwise, we'll create an imbalance in the ambient vacuum energy and . . ."

"And create an energy sink that will theoretically collapse adjacent dimensional branes in a cascade," said Joshua, his tone a caricature of a displeased schoolteacher, "thereby causing an imbalance in linear acceleration over different areas of the ship. Darya, I designed the simulations, remember?"

"I'm just *saying*."

"I hear you." Turning aside, Joshua shook his head. "Honestly, you're in Starfleet? Didn't one of your heroes once say that risk was your business?"

"James Kirk. He was right. He took risks. But he wasn't stupid."

"Neither am I." Joshua's hands moved over his controls. "I'm going to open up a jump-point. Hang on."

Facing forward and staring out at the winking docking lights of Starbase 32, Bat-Levi braced herself. What would crossing the threshold of a jump-point feel like? Bat-Levi didn't know. She'd never been through an actual wormhole, though they'd done simulator runs of gravimetric distortions to warp bubbles caused by an intermix imbalance. Then the effect had been as violent as it was spectacular: a sensation of tripping and the ship lurching then careening through space, out of control. Now she expected the same. Maybe something just as violent, like being thrown from her seat, or a jolt, a quiver running through the ship and shivering up her legs. Something.

Only there was nothing. One moment, she was staring at the gray and blue top that was Starbase 32. The next, she wasn't.

Space crinkled. Not a fold exactly, but the stars suddenly puckered into a cone. There was not the usual smearing of stars into rainbows that she associated with warp drive. The stars simply glimmered, winked. Flashed off. She felt a slight jerk, but the feeling was more internal than external, as if her body had pushed through a pane of clear, semi-liquid gelatin. And then Starbase 32 was gone. So were the stars.

"Joshua?" Bat-Levi had to say his name twice because her throat was so dry. "Where?"

Her brother's body was still as death. "We're inside."

"Inside," she said the word as if she didn't understand it. This hadn't been on the simulations. "You mean, inside a *rift*?"

Joshua pulled his face around, his eyes bright with excitement. "We're inside a jump tunnel."

My God. "Are we *moving*?"

"The computer says so. How's our influx?"

"Vacuum energy influx is constant," said Bat-Levi, grateful for something to do. "So is our jump bubble. But where are we . . . ?"

"Going? Haven't a clue. I programmed in a five second jump, so we ought to be coming out soon."

"But the stars," Bat-Levi began, and then her eyes widened. "Joshua."

Joshua's head snapped forward. The stars were back. Starbase 32 wasn't.

Bat-Levi released a breath she hadn't known she held. "Where are we?"

"Computer says . . ." Jason's fingers scurried over his console. "Computer says that we're twelve-point-five-seven parsecs distant from our previous position."

"Oh, my God," said Bat-Levi. Her eyes darted to her instruments. The generator flux was reading steady, the dimensional rift bubble over the ship stable. "That was *it*?"

Joshua was laughing now. "You were expecting something else?"

"Well, *yes*," she said, but she was smiling. "You did it, Jock-o."

"Yeah," said Joshua, finger-combing his hair again and again, "yeah. We did." He let out a sudden whoop. "By God, Darya! By God!"

They grinned at one another like maniacs for a full thirty seconds before Bat-Levi said, "Hey, can you get us back?"

"Hey," said Joshua, still smiling as he plotted their return and re-initiated, "after that, a piece of cake. A piece of . . ."

Suddenly, the ship lurched, as if some huge foot had kicked them from behind. Bat-Levi slammed forward, her hand shooting out to keep her face from smacking into her console. Her gaze raked over her controls. "Joshua, the pod's magnetic containment field . . ."

"It's breaking down. I see it." Joshua's fingers flew over his command console. "Hang on, hang on. Shutting down."

Damn, I didn't check the field; I didn't double-check it! Bat-Levi felt another lurch. Heard a low groan of metal and then the computer chattering a warning about hull structural integrity. "I read pockets of subspace opening up, Joshua! Off the port quarter, same place I picked up that instability before! And now there's a second pocket, off the starboard bow!"

"We're not shutting down. I'm taking the computer offline, switching to manual . . . negative. Generator's still online. Damn it, the intake's frozen!"

"Now abeam to starboard, another pocket," said Bat-Levi, her voice shrill.

A split-second later, the computer chimed in. "*Warning: subspace variance at point-seven . . .*"

"Shut up!" Bat-Levi jabbed the audio off. "Joshua, that pocket's increasing in size exponentially! And there are two more, one off the starboard quarter, one dead astern!"

"I see them, I see them. It's an energy surge in the particle stream, siphoning off vacuum energy at unequal rates. That means adjacent brancs are collapsing, because of electromagnetic pressure on the opposite side of the energy sink. Darya," Joshua spared her a quick glance, "are you *sure* you adjusted those grids?"

"Yes, yes, of course, I'm sure!" She'd told him, she'd *told* him. "I did the best I could. I told you, they weren't stable, and I've been twiddling with them . . ."

She broke off. *Get a hold of yourself.* She had to think. They didn't have much time. The ship yawed drunkenly, and her seat spun around, almost throwing her to the deck. She heard a long, low grinding sound and knew that stress on the hull was increasing.

Think. Bat-Levi's brain clicked into overdrive. As more pockets of subspace opened around the ship, the ship itself would continue to linearly accelerate, but at different rates and in different directions. Just like a starship that had lost one or both of its nacelles: Parts of the ship would travel at different rates, with pieces of the ship slipping past others, or going off in entirely new directions.

If they couldn't shut down the generator, they would break apart.

On a starship, in a runaway, there was only one option. Jettison the core and worry about how you got home later.

The *Lion* shuddered. Spun to port. An alarm sounded; their inertial dampers were failing.

"Joshua, we have to blow the pod," she said urgently, trying not to think what a sudden explosive influx of energy would do to the surrounding spacetime. "We *have* to!"

"Darya, I know, I know, but . . ."

The blood iced in her veins as she read his look. "Oh, no." Quickly, she scanned her readouts. "Oh, no, no, no, no . . ."

"The explosive bolts are frozen," said Joshua. His face was white as salt. "No way to blow them automatically."

The ship rocked as if slapped by a giant hand. Bat-Levi thought fast. There were pockets of subspace opening all around them, which meant that the generator was still siphoning vacuum energy. If she could just get a stable jump-point, re-initialize the computer and have it reverse course and get back, or *closer* to Starbase 32, they could abandon ship.

Her fingers were a blur over her console. "I'm re-routing auxiliary power to the generator."

"Darya, no! You're going to *increase* . . ."

"Don't you see? It's the only way," she said, not bothering to turn around. She punched in their return coordinates. "If I just reopen a jump point where we had before . . ."

There was high metallic scream. A sensation of something ripping apart, like a piece of cloth pulled in opposite directions at its weakest point. "There goes the hull, there goes the hull!" Joshua shouted.

"Hang on, hang on!" Bat-Levi grabbed her console with both hands. "Jump point opening . . . *now!*"

This time, she saw it: a jagged hole in space that dilated, gaped like a huge mouth . . . and then sucked them in.

Suddenly, she couldn't breathe. She tried taking a breath and couldn't. Her chest felt as if she were flattening, elongating; her heart slowing, her limbs spooling out like long threads . . .

Passing through a dimensional shift. Her brain was sluggish, ticking through the problem like the old gears of a grandfather's clock. The ship must be caught in different dimensions; that was why her body felt like putty, and was this what it felt like to exist in a two-dimensional plane . . . ?

And then it was as if her mind, held in place by some invisible tether, snapped back into her body. She was aware that her lungs burned, and she inhaled a lungful of air and let it out in a moan.

The ship groaned with her. In an instant, she knew. The generator was still engaged. A shrill alarm undulated through the shuttle, and the emergency lights had turned burnt amber, dying her skin muddy orange. They were functioning on auxiliary power only, but the ship was still bucking and heaving. She realized then that she was sprawled on the deck, and her chin ached, and when she brought her hand, her fingers came away red with her blood.

"Joshua," she choked, spat out a gob of blood-tinged saliva. Her mouth tasted like warm salt. She propped herself up on her arms. "Joshua?"

He wasn't in his pilot's chair. Bat-Levi clawed her way over to the command console and hauled herself upright.

Starbase 32 was there, dead ahead.

She brought her fist down on the companel. "Starbase 32, Starbase 32, request emergency beam-out! I repeat, request emergency beam-out! We have a runaway! Starbase 32, do you copy?"

There was a sizzle of static, a sputter, and then Bat-Levi caught fragments of words: . . . *n't . . . good lock . . . gravi . . . distor . . . evacuate . . .* Then a wash of interference.

Starbase 32 couldn't get a lock. The shuttle staggered, and Bat-Levi grabbed hold of the command console to keep from hurtling to the deck. They had to get out, she and Joshua had to evacuate, they had to get *out!*

Bat-Levi spun on her heel. "Joshua, we have to go, *now!* Josh . . . !"

Her voice died in her throat. The hatch to below-decks was open.

No! No! He's trying to take the generator offline . . .

"But there's no time," she whispered, and then she was shouting again, to no one, "there's no time, no time . . . !"

Somehow she stumbled below deck. Her eyes flicked to the rack where they stowed their environmental suits. Her stomach bottomed out. Joshua's was missing.

He's in the pod. Bat-Levi's mind raced. *He's in the* pod. She had to stop him. She'd drag him out by force; she'd knock him unconscious, if she had to, but she had to stop him before the ship broke apart. Grabbing her own suit, Bat-Levi dashed to the magnetically sealed hatch that led to the pod. Through the portal alongside, she could see Joshua's suited figured hovering over the generator.

"Joshua!" she screamed, bringing her fist down on the

portal, even though she knew the sound wouldn't carry in vacuum. Maybe the movement would get his attention. "Joshua, *stop!*"

Joshua didn't look up. Quickly, she pulled on her suit. Kneeling, with her helmet tucked under her left arm, she keyed in her combination to open the magnetic lock.

But nothing happened. She punched in the code again. Her eye caught movement, and she watched as Joshua glided away from the generator and then Bat-Levi understood. They hadn't been able to blow the pod free because the explosive bolts had frozen. So Joshua was arming them himself. Joshua was going to blow the pod clear . . . *from the inside.*

"No, *no!*" Bat-Levi screamed. She brought her fists down again and again, hammering on the portal. "Joshua, no, stop, *stop!*"

Whether it was the vibration, or some premonition, Joshua looked up. She saw the horror on his face through his faceplate, and then he waved his hand the way a person does when he wants you to go away, and she saw his mouth moving, the words he was shouting: *No, no, Darya, go back, get out, get away!*

"*Damn* you!" Bat-Levi clawed her way to a computer com. She punched the audio to life, and the computer, silent for so long, urped, "*. . . ull breach imminent in twenty-five-point-nine seconds. Recommend immediate emergency evacua. . . .*"

"Computer!" Bat-Levi shouted. "Magnetic seal to vacuum pod, emergency override!"

"*Emergency override command acknowledged. Magnetic hatch disengaged.*"

At her feet, the hatch began to dilate. Bat-Levi jumped down into the airlock, her fingers flying over the controls. As she jammed her helmet over her head and toggled the seals shut, she heard two things. One was that maddeningly calm voice of the computer telling her that the explosive bolts to the vacuum pod were engaged, and they had three seconds to detonation.

The other was her brother's anguished scream: "No, Darya, *no!*"

And then the bolts ignited. And blew.

Bat-Levi was *aware* of the light more than she actually *saw* it: a white-hot flare that seared her retinas. Then she was aware of her body impacting something solid, and her brain exploded with pain. There was a sensation of being flung back and of something—the ship, or maybe it was the pod— blowing free, disintegrating into a halo of debris. Bat-Levi was standing, and then, suddenly, she wasn't standing on anything anymore, because the airlock was gone and she was standing on empty space and the stars spread like diamonds beneath her feet and then the strange shape of Starbase 32, upended like a child's top, wheeled in her vision.

And then she saw nothing. Felt nothing. Because there was nothing left.

Chapter 16

"You understand now, right?" Bat-Levi's voice was thick. Her streaming eyes focused on Tyvan. "You understand why I'm . . . why things are the way they are."

Tyvan debated then said, "I understand that what happened to you was a horrible thing. And I understand how you feel that you're to blame."

"I should have double-checked that grid. But I wasn't on task. I just wanted to get the hell out of there, get on with my," she gave a bleak laugh, "my damned love life."

"Right. But Joshua was in a hurry, too. But," he said, cutting her off when he saw her open her mouth, "but you've already made up your mind about that. We could argue all day, and I'll bet other doctors have done just that. So I don't think it's worth rehashing. I don't see the point in trying to talk you out of guilt you so clearly want to hang onto. But I'll tell you what I'm more interested in."

Bat-Levi's lips had thinned, and Tyvan knew this was not how she expected things to go. She'd told her story, and it was horrific, but he also knew that she'd told it before. The words had a rehearsed quality; the story was a neat, tidy package, and Joshua's death would be the first thing that any psychiatrist, him included, would've latched onto—because it was so *obvious*.

"And what's that?" she asked, her voice flat.

"Did you keep your date with Devlin Connolly?"

Bat-Levi blinked. "What? That's what you want to know?" An undercurrent of fury churned in her voice. "*That?*"

"Yes."

"What kind of question is that?"

"I thought it was a good one. After all, Devlin Connolly was your lover . . ."

"Was," she said, "*was.*"

"So it stands to reason you'd have contacted him again."

"Unbelievable." Bat-Levi grasped the arms of her chair, and Tyvan saw the fabric pucker as her fingers dug in. "Un. Be. Lievable. Doctor, take a good, hard look. I wasn't exactly in any shape to go to Pacifica."

Tyvan's eyes traveled over her body, her disfigured features as if seeing them for the first time. "Well, no, but we've already established that this is the body you wanted. I don't see what one has to do with the other. So, did you send for him? I'm sure Devlin . . ."

"No," she interrupted. All the color had bled from her face now—*Borg*, thought Tyvan, *just like the Borg*—and this made her scar stand out so pink and taut, it rippled like a worm. "I didn't send for him."

"Ever?"

"Ever." Her jaw thrust out, as if daring him to take a swing. "*Ever.*"

"Did he call? Did he want to see you?"

For the first time, he saw uncertainty. Then her eyes grew hooded. "Yes, he called—about a week after. He wanted to know why I wouldn't let them evacuate me to Starfleet Medical."

"It's a good question. Did you tell him why?"

She seemed to find something fascinating at the tips of her boots. "We didn't speak. There was nothing to say."

"Nothing to say? Darya, I thought you said that you and Devlin . . ."

Bat-Levi threw him a sharp, defiant look. "That was *before.*"

"But how did the accident change anything? I would've thought you'd need . . . *want* Devlin more than ever. He called, so he was willing."

Tyvan saw that Bat-Levi's index finger had stolen to the cuticle of her right thumb. He watched as her nail tore at the skin. "I didn't need his help."

"Why not?"

She shook her head with a short, irritable gesture. A bubble of red blood welled up along her right thumbnail, but if it hurt, she gave no indication. "Because I didn't want him to see me like this. Why would any man want," she held up her artificial hand, "this?"

"You don't seem to have had a lot of faith in Devlin."

Bat-Levi exhaled something like a laugh. "It doesn't take faith to know what's repulsive."

"Sure. Appearance is the first thing by which anyone is judged. But you'd think that a man who'd met all kinds of aliens—and some of them pretty ugly by human standards— would look a little deeper into the woman he loved."

"Well, I didn't bother to find out."

"I guess I'm interested in that."

"And I guess I'm not. Look at me, Doctor. What man would want this, what man could love someone who looks like this?"

"I don't know, Darya," said Tyvan gently. "I don't know why you never bothered to find out. Then again, I don't know why you wanted to hurt Devlin Connolly either."

"*Hurt* him . . ."

"But that happens. We all lash out at the people we care about, and you're furious with yourself, sure. And you're furious with Joshua for going ahead with something you knew he shouldn't have. Except you can't get at him. You can't tell Joshua how angry you are, how much he's made everyone suffer. So you turn that anger on yourself, and you throw love back into the faces of people who care about you."

"*Care* about me," Bat-Levi bristled. There was blood all over her thumbnail now. "*Care* about me? There's no one who cares about *me*. I'm a cog in a machine. No, no, I'm a *machine* within a machine. I do my job; I'm alive because everyone says I ought to be grateful *to* be. But they don't know what it's like."

"Yes, you've made sure of that. I'll bet it takes a lot of energy, keeping that armor in place."

Then, just as Bat-Levi opened her mouth to reply, Tyvan's office door chimed. Tyvan felt a quick flash of irritation. *Why* was someone bothering him? He was with a *patient*; he shouldn't be interrupted. Then he glanced at his chronometer and knew exactly why. Halak's inquiry had convened twenty minutes ago.

Bat-Levi was already pushing her way to her feet, the servos in her knees squealing a protest. "I don't know why I keep doing this to myself. I'm gone. I came a day early, we talked about some things, and now I'm gone. There's no regulation that says I have to sit here and let you goad me."

The chime sounded again. "Doctor?" A man's voice, followed by a knock. "Dr. Tyvan?"

"Just a moment," Tyvan called, exasperated. *Never rains*

but it pours. "Darya, I think that it's valuable for us to look at the *way* you're thinking and . . ."

"No." Bat-Levi cut him off. "No. I *don't* think it's valuable. I stayed here way too long. I don't know why I listen to you, but I'm not interested in finding out why. I don't have a choice about seeing you. My orders are to report. Well, I reported—a day early, but I did it, and that's session number four, Doc. One more, and then you get to write your precious report. But for now," she made an offhand gesture to the door, "it sounds like you don't have a choice either."

Before he could say anything more, she wheeled about, with an alacrity that surprised him. The door hissed to one side and Bat-Levi barreled through.

"Whoa!" said Ensign Richard Castillo, jumping to one side. He put his hands up, palms out "Sorry, Ma'am. I . . ."

"It's fine, Ensign," said Bat-Levi. She pushed past, heading down the corridor. "I was just leaving."

"Sure," said Castillo, to her rapidly retreating back. "Ma'am."

Bat-Levi didn't reply. Tyvan heard the thud of her prosthetic legs fade as she rounded the bend of the corridor, and disappeared.

Castillo turned his puzzled gaze to Tyvan. "Sorry, sir. Honestly, I didn't know. But you didn't answer your hails, and Captain Garrett called the bridge and she's pretty steamed . . ."

"It's fine, Ensign," said Tyvan, echoing Bat-Levi, but more kindly. "Please let the captain know I'm on my way."

"Well," said Castillo, looking apologetic, "that's just it. My orders are to escort you down, sir. Ah, see, the captain . . ."

"I understand," said Tyvan. "So, the captain's hot?"

"Uh." Castillo looked startled, and, too late, Tyvan considered that "hot" might have different connotations to a young man. "Well, yessir, you could say that." A quick smile that flitted on and off, like a light. Castillo had unusually blue eyes set off beneath a full head of light brown curls. If not for an angular jaw, he would have looked almost cherubic.

"Scorching?" asked Tyvan, annoyed that Garrett thought he needed a babysitter. On the other hand, he hadn't given her much choice. She'd probably give him a good dressing down in private. "Or just steamed?"

"Think supernova," said Castillo. He hesitated, and Tyvan saw a twinkle of mischief in the ensign's face. "I think Lieutenant Bulast said the channel melted. Sir."

"Well, that sounds unpleasant."

"Judging by Lieutenant Bulast's face, I think so." Castillo seemed to want to say something more.

"Yes, Ensign? Something else on your mind?"

"Yes, sir." Castillo squared his shoulders. "Two things, actually."

Tyvan folded his arms. "Fire away. We psychiatrists don't bite, and if Captain Garrett's *that* angry, a minute more won't make any difference."

"Well, uh, I don't know you very well, sir, you just having come aboard and all and . . ."

"You have a point, Ensign?"

Castillo straightened a bit, as if Tyvan had chastised him for slouching. "Yessir. Look, you're not an Academy grad. I understand that, and I've heard that, uh, having people . . . doctors who are civilians come in, well, I know that civilians do things differently. I know that, you know, medicine isn't the military."

"It's clear you haven't spent much time with surgeons," said Tyvan, with a wry smile. "Or some hardcore nurses. You object to my being late, Ensign?"

"No, sir. That's for you and the captain to square. It's just that, you know, the captain, she's steamed. But, *because* of you, Lieutenant Bulast's gotten an earful, and that's not right."

Now *this* was a surprise. *Not as eager to please as he looks, taking on a superior officer like that.* "You've got a good point. Tell you what: I'll talk to Captain Garrett, let her know it was my fault, all right?" *Just as soon as she's done chewing me out.*

Castillo's head moved in a short nod. "Thank you, sir. I was kind of hoping you might do that. Lieutenant Bulast . . . well, he's feeling kind of low anyway."

"Why is that?"

The young ensign moved his shoulders in a negligent shrug. "Could be because of Lieutenant Batra."

Tyvan's eyebrows arched. "They were that close?"

"They spent time together and . . ." Castillo fidgeted, looked away.

"I see," said Tyvan, though he really didn't. His thoughts were already wandering ahead to the inquiry, and Garrett. Garrett would really let him have it afterward, and an angry Garrett was trouble he didn't need. He didn't have to be a psychiatrist or a Listener to know that she wasn't exactly thrilled with his being posted aboard the *Enterprise.*

Tyvan made a move to gather his materials when he saw that Castillo was still fidgeting. "Something else, Ensign?"

"Uh," Castillo took a deep breath, "yes. I was wondering. Could I . . . could we . . ."

Tyvan decided that letting Castillo stew wouldn't help. "You want to schedule some time, Ensign?"

"Yes, sir." Castillo looked relieved, though his neck was mottled with red blotches.

More surprises. "Certainly. Now's not a good time, though. How about we schedule something as soon as I'm done? All right?"

"Yeah, of course, you're right. Sorry," said Castillo, and Tyvan was relieved that Castillo had dropped the "sir." Rank always made him uncomfortable. "We should go."

"Right." Medical boards and inquiries—Tyvan felt a quick spark of disgust—he understood why the military had them, but boarding people out of the military because they might have certain physical or mental problems smacked too much of the twenty-first century, as if medicine hadn't progressed in three centuries and most illnesses weren't remediable by accommodation, medication, or intervention.

"Well, let's get going, Ensign," said Tyvan, with more enthusiasm than he felt. "That way, you won't get blistered by the captain, either."

Castillo bobbed his head then stepped out of the way, allowing Tyvan to go first. In the turbolift, Castillo stood behind and slightly off to the left, his hands clasped behind his back. Neither spoke. Instead they stood, staring at a strip of metal above the turbolift doors.

In the silence, broken only by the whirr of the turbolift, Tyvan's thoughts drifted to Bat-Levi. He'd taken a risk, again. But it was either break through her armor, or sit back and take the path of least resistance and do nothing.

The turbolift dinged, and the computer announced their deck. The doors parted.

But Bat-Levi was right about one thing, thought Tyvan as he walked the corridor to the conference room. She didn't need to do anything but report. Well, he understood her reactions. Patients were so resistant to change. But change was necessary for a patient to break out of old self-destructive patterns, and that was his mission: to break down resistance.

Resistance—Tyvan heard the mechanical voices of thousands of drones in his head, a single voice that was many, and one he would never forget—*is futile.*

The realization hit him like a thunderbolt. But then he was at the conference room doors and Garrett was waiting, and Tyvan would have to think about what this meant about *him* later. But, he thought, as the doors hissed apart, how odd that he hadn't seen the irony.

Chapter 17

As it happened, Garrett let Tyvan have it in public.

"My apologies, Captain," he said, walking rapidly to a vacant chair at Stern's left elbow. He registered that, besides Garrett, Stern, and a lieutenant recording the proceedings, there were two strangers: a blonde-haired, brown-eyed female lieutenant sitting directly across from Garrett, and to the blonde's left, a moderately tall though somewhat stocky Vulcan male dressed in the gray and black uniform of the V'Shar, the Vulcan security agency. The blonde would be the Starfleet Intelligence agent, Laura Burke, and the Vulcan's name was Sivek, if Tyvan remembered correctly.

Stern murmured something he didn't catch. Sliding into his chair, Tyvan bobbed his head at Garrett, who was to Stern's right. It hit him at the last second that he probably shouldn't have sat down until Garrett gave him some indication. *Bravo, Tyvan.* "I was detained by a patient."

"I see." Garrett's dark brown eyes were hard. "And do you always refuse to answer hails when you're with a patient, Doctor?"

"Well," said Tyvan, trying to defuse the situation with a small smile, "I don't like to interrupt the flow of a patient's session." He almost winced.

"I see," said Garrett again, her tone indicating that she *didn't* see at all. "Well, let me put it to you this way, *Commander.* You're a Starfleet officer who just *happens* to be a doctor, not the other way around. You wear a uniform. You are given orders, and unless there's a pretty damn good reason for you to disobey—and offhand, I can't think of very many—then you obey them. I can appreciate that you felt you had important work to do. Someone's bleeding to death, you might be late. But you're a psychiatrist, and none of your patients are likely to bleed to death."

Tyvan could have mentioned suicidal or homicidal patients, but thought he ought to just sit and listen. It was, he reflected, what shrinks supposedly did best.

"So," said Garrett, "until you can prove to me that a psychiatric session is equivalent to a life-or-death situation, then there is *nothing* more important than your duties to this ship—not a patient, not this," Garrett churned the air with her hand, "*flow* of a session, nothing. When I have you hailed, I expect you to answer. You don't ignore a hail because then you're ignoring me, and I get, well, a little *unreasonable* when a member of my crew doesn't follow an order. So this is your first and *only* warning. You read me, mister?"

Tyvan was numb with embarrassment and shock. Only aboard a couple of weeks, and already he'd managed to alienate the captain. But she was right. *This is a mistake. I have no business being here, I can't function here.* For not the first time, he wondered how Stern did it. Doctors needed autonomy; he required a system to be flexible to the needs of his patients. But that's not what the military was about. So it was either play by the rules, or think up creative ways around them.

All he said was, "Absolutely, Captain." The temperature in the conference room was cool, but Tyvan felt an uncharacteristic heat traveling up his face and realized that he was blushing to the roots of his hair, like an errant schoolboy who'd been caught blowing spitballs. "It won't happen again."

"No, it won't because the next time will be your last," said Garrett. She turned away, swiveling her chair toward a blank-faced lieutenant who sat across and to her right, making recordings of the proceedings. "Strike all that from the record, please."

Stern took advantage of the momentary lull to lean toward him and murmur, "Nice move. See me after."

Tyvan didn't reply. Instead, he played with his padd, scrolled to his reports, and thought, right. Nice move.

"All right." Garrett leaned her forearms on the conference table and laced her fingers together. "Where were we?"

Stern spoke up. "Commander Halak's toxicological analysis, Captain."

Garrett made a *go-on* motion with her hand. Stern consulted her padd. "As I said, there was nothing, Captain. Commander Halak was clean across the board. No drugs, nothing illegal. Clean as a whistle." Stern threw a pointed glance at Lieutenant Burke. "If Commander Halak was involved with red ice, or this Asfar whatchamacallit, it wasn't as a user."

"Qatala." Burke favored Stern with a frosty brown stare. "The Asfar Qatala."

"Right." Stern grunted, returned her gaze to Garrett. "Like I said, not involved."

"With red ice," Burke added.

"That's enough." Garrett rapped her knuckles on the table. God, she didn't like this woman. "You've made your point, Burke."

Burke sat back without a word of protest. Garrett suppressed a sigh. Not fair to be angry: Garrett might hate what Burke did for a living, but Burke was doing her job, and Halak had plenty to explain. Garrett *still* didn't understand what had happened, but then again, she hadn't confronted Halak herself either.

Stern had argued. "You're the captain, for crying out loud. More importantly, you're *his* captain. Talk to him, Rachel. He's a decent man, and I'll bet there's some explanation for this. I have to admit I don't have a clue what that might be."

"That's because there isn't," Garrett had said. "Jo, you're the one with the evidence. He's lying, and he thinks he can get away with it."

"And you're not interested *why*? *You've* never lied when you've been in a jam?"

Garrett knew what her friend was referring to, and she inwardly cursed that she'd ever told Jo Stern about what had happened on that night long ago, when she was eighteen and scared to death.

Instead, she'd said, "Don't start. The situations aren't the least bit similar."

Stern had thrown up her hands in disgust. "Jeez, there it is again. The truth is you don't *want* to hear Halak's story. You've already made up your mind about him."

And was that true? If Garrett had gone to Halak as his captain—no, his *friend*, as she would have done for Nigel— would they even be sitting here now? Probably not, and the realization made her feel petty and small. Maybe Stern was right.

No. Garrett felt her heart harden. Halak was Halak, a man with a history and his own baggage and questions dogging his heels, and he'd taken what trust she'd had—precious little— and betrayed it by getting one of her officers killed and then concocting an outlandish story that leaked worse than a sieve.

And Starfleet Intelligence? Garrett's eyes went to Burke and then Sivek. Wild cards. Still, Garrett felt a premonitory thrill up and down her spine: They had something.

Garrett said, "Burke, is there anything you'd like to ask before we move on?"

As Garrett expected, Burke moved her sleek, groomed head from side to side. Garrett doubted that one blonde curl was ever out of place. The woman was more placid than a Vulcan—or a viper waiting for a chance to pounce.

"No, thank you, Captain, not at this time," she said, her voice as polished as very smooth glass, "though I am curious. Dr. Stern, so far your report focuses on the nothings: no drugs, etc. But Commander Halak was severely wounded. That's a *something*."

Clever girl, Garrett thought. A statement begging a response.

"Thanks, I was getting there," said Stern, her tone dry. Whatever she felt about Starfleet Intelligence, being intimidated didn't seem to be one of Stern's problems. She plucked up her padd. "But, in my line of work, it's customary to list the things that are normal, too. Just so everyone knows you checked."

Reading from her padd, Stern began with Halak's knife wounds. She described the pattern of the wounds and the type of blade that was likely responsible. "The wound to the arm was likely defensive," said Stern, illustrating by bringing her own left arm up at an angle and across her face. "First of all, it's a slash, not a stab. Still, it's a gaping wound because of the direction the blade was moving at the time of contact, moving across Langer's lines. These are elastic fibers in the dermis. Slash along the lines, and the wound is narrow and slitlike. Slash across, as in Halak's case, and you've got a large gaping wound. The second point is that the slash has a beveled margin. It's easier if I show you."

Pushing back from her seat, Stern crossed to the viewscreen mounted in the left wall of the conference room and had the computer bring up images scanned during her examination of Halak. A color image that was clearly the wound to Halak's left bicep wavered into focus. The image must have been scanned almost immediately after Halak was beamed aboard; Garrett saw how the skin was so pale the hair along Halak's forearm looked like corkscrews against white paper. The wound itself was fleshy and filled with blackish-purple blood clots.

"First of all, the weapon was single-edged. You can tell because one end of the stab wound, here," said Stern, using her finger to illustrate, "where the stab wound starts, is pointed. The other end is blunt, and there's a divot that got taken out of his arm when the knife was withdrawn. So his assailant comes at him; Halak throws up his arm to take the hit, and the assailant stabs him with a downward slashing motion, like this." Stern illustrated.

"That squares with what Halak said," Garrett offered.

Stern was nodding. "Yeah, so far so good. They're jumped. This other guy—and he's right-handed, by the way—rushes Halak, and Halak deflects the first blow. But here's what doesn't jibe. The first wound is a clean slash. Down, in, out. The second, the one on Halak's right flank, isn't so clean."

Stern called up another image and this time Garrett saw from the knobs of Halak's spine and the curve of his right hip that the image had been scanned as the commander lay on his stomach. She also saw, immediately, how different this wound was from the first. The stab wound was larger and very long, easily ten to twelve centimeters. The wound wasn't gaping, but it wasn't a line either. It was very deep, and the wound almost looked like a V, with the point jutting toward Halak's spine.

"Now, that's not a straight slash because the knife changed direction," said Stern. "Part of it you can explain because of where he's been stabbed, right? Unless you're unconscious, lying down, not resisting, or being held very tightly, a slash that long and in that particular place isn't going to be straight. That V, though, that's caused by movement, probably by Halak twisting to get away. See? You can tell where the cut changes direction and the skin is torn. Now what's wrong with this scenario?"

Garrett's forehead furrowed. "I'm not sure I see anything wrong. That's what Halak said happened." She saw Tyvan and Stern exchange glances, and Stern give the other doctor a slight nod. "Dr. Tyvan?" asked Garrett.

"I think Dr. Stern is suggesting he left out a few things, Captain. If I'm hearing this correctly, there are several problems with Halak's account. First of all, unless he's behind you, a right-handed assailant can't stab you on your right side. If he's coming at you from the front, or slashes around at your back, then the wound will be on the left, just like the wound on Halak's left forearm."

"So he got behind Halak," said Garrett.

"Yes, but the question is: how?"

"Distracted? He managed to get away, but the guy jumped him? You know," said Garrett, stroking her chin between thumb and index finger, "it could work just the way Halak said if the Bolian puts a pulse gun to Batra's head. That would make Halak stop whatever he was doing and leave plenty of time for his assailant to get around behind him. Then, for whatever reason, Halak is stabbed; in the confusion, Batra elbows the Bolian, gets away, makes a grab for the knife . . ." She trailed to a halt, shook her head. "That doesn't feel right."

"Because it probably isn't." Tyvan looked over at Stern. "No wounds on Batra's hands, are there?" When Stern shook her head, he turned back to Garrett. "So it's unlikely she made a grab for a weapon that way. She'd have gotten cut. But this begs the question. Where are the defensive wounds on Commander Halak? If I were being stabbed from behind, I'd do something about it. But the wound is far too deep and far too regular, even with that divot, unless Halak was standing still. And the only way for that to happen would be if he were held from behind, with his arms pulled back and out of the way."

"You see what I'm driving at, Captain," said Stern. "There had to be more than just the Bolian and this other guy. Or he was knifed at a different time. I say the knifing happened first."

Quickly, Stern went through what Garrett already knew: Halak's blood loss, the fact that the wounds were a good six hours older than the time frame Halak had given, the traces of antimicrobial packs on Halak's skin, traces of Bolian blood and brain matter under Halak's nails, and the absence of ionized residue from the pulse gun or a phaser on Halak's hands or clothing.

"But Batra fired a phaser, not a pulse gun," said Stern.

"There was evidence of mitochondrial disruption in the cells of her right hand consonant with phased energy exposure."

Garrett gave Stern a weary look. "And I take it that Halak didn't check a phaser out of the weapons locker."

"Nope, and nothing in the shuttle. Had to be his personal carry and then either he ditched it, or it got left behind. There's no regulation against that, though."

"Anything else?" When Stern shook her head, Garrett looked at Burke. "Questions?"

Burke made a pass motion with her hand. Garrett directed her attention back to Stern. "What else about Batra, other than evidence of there being a phaser involved?"

Stern summarized what she'd already told Garrett. "Then there's the dirt."

"Dirt?" Tyvan echoed.

"Dirt," Stern repeated. "Look, I don't have any doubt that most of what Halak said is true. Really," she added in response to a skeptical snort from Burke. "I believe that he was attacked; I believe that he defended himself. I believe that a Bolian killed Batra. All that squares with the evidence. But the time course is off. The sequence is wrong. I didn't start to put it all together until I began comparing what I found on Halak with what I found on Batra. Just like Halak, Batra had Bolian blood on her hands, under her nails, on her clothes, in her hair, and the blood spatter's consistent with her stabbing the Bolian. Then the Bolian shoots her at point blank range. The impact knocks Batra off her feet onto her back, but she's dead before she hits the ground. Death was virtually instantaneous. The lieutenant's heart stopped pumping. No blood flow, no bleeding.

"But here's the kicker: the dirt. The dirt on her clothes, especially on her back, doesn't look much like what you'd find in a city. And there's dirt on her jaw—actually, minute fragments embedded in tissue. But it's not the *same* dirt."

"I'm not following," said Tyvan.

"Look, we know she was hit because of that bruise on her jaw and those bite marks on her tongue. But I assumed *someone* hit her, because Halak said they were jumped. Made sense. But that's wrong. She had abrasions on her jaw, and there was dirt in the wound. Only it wasn't dirt. It was brick."

Burke stirred. "But why couldn't she have been hit by a fist?"

"Because the lieutenant's skin was torn. Her skin had come into contact with something sharp, jagged, and hard. Someone hits you across the face with his fist your skin's not going to tear, not unless what he's wearing, like a ring, catches on skin. And there should be marks that look like fingers, or a fist. There should be prints. Now, I found nothing that smacks of fingers or an imprint from a ring, and there were no prints. There were, however, latent prints on her clothing. The Bolian's easy to spot; their ridge patterns are species-specific, can't confuse them. And Halak's. Hers. But that's it."

Tyvan sat up. "No fourth person. Halak said there was another man."

Stern's eyebrows arched. "See the problem? Halak says there was another guy when Batra was killed, and I just showed you that in order for Halak to get cut the way he did, there had to be at least two more: one to hold him, the other to take care of Batra. Only where are they? And somehow Batra got the knife only no one noticed? No one tried to grab her? Unless something happened much earlier than he says and then the brick . . ."

Tyvan finished for her. "Comes from the city. Meaning they were attacked, first, in the city."

Stern took aim with a forefinger. "Bingo. There's no mistake. Brick's very porous. It crumbles. This stuff is cheap, so I'm guessing some slum on Farius Prime. But there's no brick anywhere on her clothing, just her skin. So Batra got herself cleaned up. Probably changed her clothes. That's why the dirt on her clothes is different from what's embedded in her jaw. She didn't get hit. She *slammed* into a brick wall. But the dirt on her clothes was a mixture of quartz and mica, some decomposed organic matter . . ."

"That would still be consistent with a city," said Tyvan.

"There was also a fair amount of bentonite. That's volcanic ash. And there were high levels of triuridium."

"Farius Prime's got triuridium mines."

"That's right, except those mines have been closed a good long time. It's why that Asfar-whatsa got so powerful to begin with, because the mines dried up. So if the mines aren't active, that means there are no workers bringing the stuff back into the city. There's nothing being released in the air; there's been no volcanic activity on that planet for centuries. So the only place you're going to find volcanic ash and triuridium . . ."

"Is at the mines," said Garrett. She was past anger now. She'd sat through Stern's dissertation, knowing where it led but still not wanting to believe it. *I may not like him much, but maybe that's my fault, and he's still my XO.* Now, she felt only a creeping weariness, as if an enormous weight had settled on her shoulders. "So there were two separate events."

"That's how I see it, Captain."

"Me, too." Garrett scrubbed her face with her hands. Then she rolled her eyes toward Tyvan. "You have *anything* germane? Anything to explain this?"

But it was Burke who answered, flashing Garrett a smile that was infuriating because it was so disingenuous, and just a little too smug. "Captain, there's nothing a *psychiatrist* can say. Nothing at all."

Tyvan stiffened, but Garrett didn't reply. Instead, she reached for companel before her on the conference room table. "Security, get Halak in here. Now."

Chapter 18

"Well, Commander?" Garrett asked, not sure that she didn't want to shake Halak until his teeth rattled. "Can you shed some light here?"

There was a pause, as if it had taken time for Garrett's question to register. Then Halak moved his head fractionally in a weary negative. "I can't explain it, Captain. I've told you what happened. I loved Ani, and I wouldn't have done anything to harm her. I simply don't know what else you want me to say."

"The truth would be a good start."

"Captain, I've *told* you the truth," said Halak. His voice was hoarse. "I received a message from an old family friend. I detoured to Farius Prime to see her. I admit I should have reported that change in my itinerary. I didn't, mainly because I had no intention of staying on Farius Prime for long. Ani followed me. I don't know how she figured out where I was going; I didn't tell her. But she ended up on the passenger transport from Starbase 5, and there was nothing for it but have her tag along."

"Stop." Garrett hacked the air with the side of her hand. "Stop right there, Halak. I don't want to hear this again. That's not what we're interested in, and you know it."

"Captain." Halak ran a hand through black hair that was greasy and matted, like lumps of cooked tar. "Captain, I don't know how to resolve the discrepancies. I don't know how the dirt that you say shouldn't have been there got there. Dirt is dirt, and I don't know. The simple truth is that we were attacked. She was killed and there's nothing I can do about it. I don't know what you want from me."

She heard the genuine undercurrent of pain, and Halak looked awful. His eyes were dull, their whites etched with a tracery of thin, red lines. The lids were swollen and the skin beneath his eyes looked smudged, puffy, and bruised. The olive cast to his skin had turned sallow, and his features were pinched and sharp as if he'd lost weight. When he walked, he favored his right side, and it was obvious he was still in pain. And he was grieving: no faking there.

But it was a grief Burke wanted to exploit. Garrett cast a swift glance at the Starfleet Intelligence officer. The lieutenant was all attention, her brown eyes sparkling and bright. She looked like a Perettian glare-hawk just itching for its chance to swoop down and strike. Well, if Halak couldn't do better, she'd have her chance. Garrett wouldn't have any alternative.

Damn Halak, why was he sticking to that story? Impatience gnawed at Garrett's gut like the sharp beak of hunger. Didn't he realize that he was throwing everything away—his career, the shreds of what little trust she had in him? *Work with me.* She tried willing the thought into the gulf between them. *Help us help you before it's too late and it's out of my hands.* Later, she would be surprised that, yes, she *did* want to help.

"Halak." She edged her voice with the imperiousness of a command. "That's not good enough. I don't know what the real story is, but it's somewhere between the lines. I'm going to make this extremely easy for you, Commander. Either you address these discrepancies here and now, or I have no choice but to remand you over to Starfleet Command for a more formal inquiry, and probable disciplinary action."

Burke spoke. "Captain, if you would *please* let me . . ."

"Stow it, Burke." Garrett didn't even glance her way. "If Halak goes anywhere, I talk to Starfleet Command first."

"That's not what . . ."

Livid, Garrett swung her head around and glared. "What part of *shut up* don't you understand, Burke?"

Burke's cheeks flared red, and Garrett felt a vicious stab of satisfaction. "I understand perfectly, Captain, but . . ."

"Obviously, you don't. Be. Quiet. When I want to hear

from you, I'll ask. If you can't comply, then you leave and I'll take my chances with Starfleet. Got it?"

Without waiting for Burke's reply, Garrett spun her chair back toward Halak and pinned him with a hard look. "Now, Commander, I want the truth. This is an inquiry. You are under oath as a Starfleet officer and a member of my crew. Don't make me recommend you be charged with perjury. Now, on your word, as an officer in Starfleet and a member of my crew, *my first officer*, what the hell happened?"

Garrett saw the indecision flash in Halak's eyes, and then understanding. His tongue flicked out to moisten his lips, and his Adam's apple bobbled as he swallowed, hard. She waited.

"All right. But, Captain, please understand that whatever I left out," his eyes darted away, but not before Garrett read his shame, "I did it to protect innocent people. I did it. . . ."

"You let me be the judge of whether you acted wisely, or not," said Garrett. "Go on."

Using the back of his hand, Halak swiped at perspiration beaded on his forehead. Garrett saw sweat trickle down his left temple. "I have to start from the time we hit the market." When Garrett waved for him to continue, he said, "Ani and I had a talk, in a café. She wanted to know more about my past, who I was there to see. I told her about Dalal. Dalal was a woman who worked for my father."

Briefly, he sketched in the details of his childhood on Vendrak IV. "When my father died, Dalal took over. She made sure I buckled down, and it's because of her that I ended up in Starfleet. Like I told Ani, I owe Dalal a lot. Why Dalal ended up on Farius Prime, I don't know. But when she called, I came."

"And then?"

"And then, on our way to her apartment, we were jumped." Halak closed his eyes, spoke through teeth that were clenched tight. "Yes, I lied. Three men—I'd never seen them before—attacked us. One of them grabbed Ani.

She fought, bit him on the hand, and he knocked her against a wall. I didn't see all of it because the other two had gone for me."

In a monotone, Halak recounted how he'd been stabbed. "And then Ani grabbed my phaser and she shot one of them. The one with the knife."

"A phaser." Garrett's voice was thick. "So you *did* have a phaser."

"Yes. My own weapon."

"Do we have it registered?"

"No."

Garrett closed her eyes for a brief instant. "*Halak,*" she said, exasperated. A finger of pain dragged across her right temple, and she knew a headache was on its way.

She flicked a finger—a signal for Halak to continue—and then she listened with a growing sense of unreality as Halak told about stumbling up to Dalal's apartment with Batra, and how Dalal had patched him up, given them a change of clothes, and fed them. When Halak paused, Garrett said, "And why did Dalal want to see you?"

Halak looked at his hands. "You know, after all that, she didn't say. Maybe just to check up on me. I don't know." His eyes drifted back to Garrett's. "Anyway, we talked. I tried to get her to leave Farius Prime. She wouldn't. In the end, because we'd missed our return transport, Dalal offered to set us up with someone she knew. Dalal lives on Gemini Street, not far from the spaceport. So we, Ani and I, went to meet up with this fellow, name of Matsaro."

"The Bolian."

"That's right. Obviously, he knew we weren't natives and he said that his shuttle wasn't registered and that he'd stowed it in one of those old abandoned mines in the Katanga Mountains. I didn't like it, but I wanted to get Ani off the planet and I knew I had to get better medical attention than Dalal was able to give. So we went with him. I had my phaser. Ani had the knife. We went by aircar. There was a shuttle waiting, just like he said. But then, at the last second, he turned around and demanded credits. When he found out we didn't have any—our credits had been stolen—he threatened to kill us. He had a pulse gun, and he took my phaser. Then he started marching us over the rocks toward one of the old mine entrances. I think he figured to hide our bodies there. Anyway, there was a lot of loose rock, and the going was rough. Ani fell, twisted her ankle."

"And?" Garrett asked.

Halak raised his face, but Garrett saw that he was far away, looking at the memory. "He wouldn't let me help her. When she couldn't get up, the Bolian reached down, and that's when Ani," his voice broke, "that's when she stabbed him."

"He didn't know she still had the knife."

Halak's face was a study in misery. "That's right. And then, before I could get there, he shot her." A single tear rolled down his right cheek. "There wasn't anything I could do, Captain."

The room was silent for several moments. Then Garrett cleared her throat. "What happened next?"

Halak tore his gaze away from the memory and looked straight at her and said in a voice as flat and matter-of-fact as if they were discussing a duty roster, "I killed him. I grabbed a rock and I smashed his skull. I beat him until he didn't have much of anything left you could call a head. Then I put him back into his aircar and programmed it to crash into the Galldean Sea. I tossed the pulse gun and my phaser in there, too. And then I put Batra in the shuttle and . . . well, you know the rest."

Garrett nodded, digesting what she'd heard. If Halak was to be believed, he'd killed in self-defense. His story certainly explained the discrepancies Stern had found. "But why didn't you come forward with this earlier, Commander?"

"Because, Captain, I was worried about Dalal, about implicating her in any way."

Garrett spread her hands. "But how would she figure in?"

"I guess I wasn't thinking clearly," said Halak. "I guess I panicked."

That struck a false chord in Garrett. She frowned. Halak was impulsive, and he was passionate. But Halak didn't panic. With a sudden pang of dismay, she realized that she'd believed him—until that moment.

"Captain." It was Burke, again. "Captain, *please*, may I say something?"

Garrett didn't see how she could refuse now. "Does it have direct bearing on what Halak's just told us?"

"Yes, ma'am."

"Proceed." Then, as Burke opened her mouth, Garrett added, "You take one detour into hypotheticals without convincing me you need to go there, and I'm shutting you down, Lieutenant."

Burke's voice was smooth as velvet. "Understood, Captain. I'm just going to deal with facts."

She swiveled her chair toward Halak. "You say you went to see a woman named Dalal?"

Halak's black eyes were wary. "Yes."

"On Gemini Street?"

"That's right. I said that before."

"Yes, I know, and that's what puzzles me, Commander." Burke inclined her head toward Sivek; the Vulcan hadn't said one word thus far. "Puzzles *us*, actually. You see, we checked out the name and the address you provided. Commander," Burke used his title almost regretfully, "there is no such woman. There isn't now, and there never has been."

Garrett started. "What?"

Alarmed, Halak sat bolt upright. "What are you talking about?"

Burke was unruffled. "Precisely what I just said, Commander. There is no Dalal. She's a story you made up to cover your real motive for visiting Farius Prime."

"No," said Halak, half-rising from his seat, "no! That's not true!"

Burke looked at Halak askance. "You really aren't in a position to be telling me about truth, Commander."

"Burke! No, Halak." Garrett put out a hand as if to restrain her first officer even though she couldn't touch him. "Sit. Down. Now."

"But, Captain . . ."

"Am I speaking Klingon?" Garrett flared. "I said, sit down and be quiet, mister!"

She flashed an angry look at Burke. "Burke, I warned you. I won't have you inciting my officers. If this is a crazy theory . . ."

Sivek interrupted, but he did it so smoothly, his interruption sounded as if it had been by invitation. "It's not theory, Captain. I have verified Lieutenant Burke's information through the V'Shar. Dalal does not now, nor has she ever existed. She is a convenient, though necessary, fabrication."

"That's *crap!*" Stern said. "You heard the man! I *told* you I found evidence that he'd been patched up! What, you think Halak bandaged *himself?*"

"Doctor," said Sivek, and if Garrett hadn't known better, she'd have thought the Vulcan purred. "The fact that Commander Halak's wounds were tended to is not in dispute. It's obvious that they were. But it does not logically follow that the person who treated Commander Halak was in fact the woman he claims."

"And you have a different theory?" asked Garrett.

"We do," said Burke. "Captain, I think that if you'll allow me some free rein here, a little leeway, I'll be able to shed some light on any nagging issues that remain."

"Go. Make it good, Burke."

Burke scraped back her chair and stood. Crossing her arms, she approached Halak. "Commander, I just told you that this woman Dalal doesn't exist. We checked it out."

"Then they did something to her," said Halak. The color

in his face had drained away until his eyes looked painted on. "They did something."

"They, Commander? What *they* are you referring to?"

Halak made a nondescript move of his hand. "I don't know. Just an expression. But she lived there. She was *there*."

"Perhaps." Burke injected just enough skepticism into her tone so it was clear she didn't believe a word. "But let's leave Dalal aside for a second, all right? I want to focus on something else, something earlier in your career. Let's talk about the Ryns, Commander."

"The Ryns?" Halak's voice registered his surprise, and Garrett saw his eyes shutter, his face close, like containment doors slamming down during a warp core breach. "What do the Ryns have to do with anything?"

"A great deal, I think. After your Ryn mission, you were removed from the *Barker*, weren't you?"

"No," said Halak. "I *requested* a transfer. Captain Connors agreed with my reasons."

"And those were?"

"Captain Connors understood that some of the crew might look at me differently."

"And why would that be?"

Halak flushed a deep crimson. "I think it's all in the record, Lieutenant."

"Yes. Why don't tell us again anyway?"

"Because of my actions in the space around Ryn III, two of my crewmates died. If you've read my record, then you know that a formal inquiry was held and I was cleared of any culpability. Still, I was the first officer. Those men died on my watch. I would have died, too, but I didn't. I knew that it would be hard for some of the crew to work well with me, given the circumstances."

"Pardon me for seeming flip or naïve," said Burke, "but if you were cleared, Commander, why did you think you had to leave? People *do* die in the course of their duties. It's always regrettable when this happens, but still their deaths weren't your fault." She paused, probably for effect. "Were they?"

Halak's jaw firmed. "No. But just because I know that *intellectually* doesn't mean that others might not view it that way. I had my reasons for wanting a transfer. Captain Connors agreed with them."

"Well, *we* don't know what they were. Why don't you tell us?"

Garrett said, "This is going somewhere, Burke." Not asking.

"Yes, Captain, it is."

"Well, instead of beating around the bush, why don't you tie it up for me?"

"Of course, Captain. The tie-in is this: red ice."

"Red ice?" Garrett scowled. "I'm not following you, Lieutenant."

"Captain, we all know that both the Orion Syndicate and the Asfar Qatala are vying for control of distribution of red ice. We know that both crime syndicates are based on Farius Prime. It is also a fact that Commander Halak's ostensible mission to Ryn III was to make contact with a middleman for the Orion Syndicate."

"Captain," said Halak.

Garrett held up a hand to stop him. "Burke, you're not telling me something I don't already know. This is a command concern. I knew about this when Halak requested a transfer; I knew about his mission to Ryn III, and I knew he'd been asked to investigate red ice distribution. So just what, exactly, are you suggesting? That Commander Halak's previous encounter with the Ryns explains this? Ties in?"

Burke clasped her hands together. "Yes. Commander Halak's primary goal was not to visit some old family friend. She's another lie in a string of lies. But red ice is real, and I believe that Commander Halak did his job on Ryn III very well. I believe that he made contact with the Orion Syndicate on Ryn III; that he made a deal. . . ."

Halak was up and out of his seat. "That's not true!" He brought his fist down on the table. "That is *not* true!"

Burke talked over him. "And that Commander Halak's involvement became known to the Asfar Qatala, and they moved to eliminate the competition."

"That's a *lie!* I've made my report," Halak said. "I had nothing more to do with the Syndicate once I left Ryn III! Whatever you think you've found, it's all a lie! It's a *plant* and . . . !" His mouth clamped shut, as if he'd realized he made a mistake.

"A plant?" Burke leveled her brown gaze. "How do you know I've *found* anything, Commander?"

"I . . . I don't know. I just said that. I don't have any idea what you're talking about."

"Halak," said Garrett. She didn't know where this was going, but she knew, instinctively, there was more here than Halak was at liberty to say. Or defend against. No matter what his guilt—no matter if she believed in him or not—she had to keep him from making things worse. "Halak, stop."

"Commander," said Tyvan. "Listen to the captain. You need . . ."

"Don't tell me what I need!" Halak's face contorted with fury. "You're not the one she's accusing. You don't *know* what I need!"

"Well, I *do* know!" Garrett's voice was like the snap of a whip. "Settle down, mister! That's an order!"

"Captain," Halak began. He stopped, closed his eyes. He gripped the edge of the table so hard, his knuckles turned white. "Captain, *please*. You're going to sit there and listen to her lies?"

"As opposed to yours? Have you given us any choice, Halak?"

Halak opened his mouth. Shut it. His legs folded, and he dropped back into his seat.

After a moment's silence, Garrett said, "Burke, you've got proof?"

Burke had watched the exchange without comment. "Yes."

Garrett heard Halak's sharp intake of breath. She kept her attention focused on Burke. "You can produce it?"

"Yes."

"Any objection if we let Halak tell his side of things?"

Burke spread her hands. "Absolutely none."

"Good." Garrett turned to Halak. "Let's hear it, Commander. The ball's in your court."

She added a silent emendation: Play it wisely.

Chapter 19

"There's the perimeter beacon dead ahead," Halak said. He was in the front seat, passenger's side, and pointed through a spray of sleet pattering against the landskimmer's windscreen.

"I see it," said Strong, who was driving. He ratcheted up the landskimmer's speed another twenty kilometers. The tiny craft shivered as the engine kicked in.

Halak heard the Doppler rise and fall of the beacon, and then their craft's ping of acknowledgement. The beacon was a blur as they whizzed past. On instinct, he glanced up, scanning the underbellies of a layer of gunmetal gray clouds. No air patrols. Yet.

As if reading his thoughts, Strong said, "Now they come after us. Soon as they figure out the skimmer's stolen."

"Well, I think we outran them," said Thex, his blue antennae wiggling with agitation. Using his forearm to swab away condensation that had fogged the chilled glass of the rear windscreen, Thex squinted. "I don't see anyone."

"Don't count them out." Halak's teeth grated. The squeaky sound of fabric on glass set them on edge. "How much further, Strong?"

"Twenty kilometers, Commander."

"That's pretty far."

"It was the best I could do. I didn't want the city sensor grid picking up on our re-entry trail."

"I know, I know." Halak fidgeted. Watched as the scenery scrolled beneath them. Once away from the coast, the terrain on Ryn III turned arid, the vegetation brown and sparse, dotting craggy hills scored by arroyos.

Halak dug his nails into a week's worth of beard glazing his jaw and jowls and gave himself a good scratch. His nails rasped over stubble. Good God, but he'd be glad to get back to the *Barker*. First thing he'd do was stand under a steaming hot shower—*real* water—for a half hour (he didn't care if he used up his allotment for the week) and then a shave. (Starfleet Intelligence thought they had to look the part of mercenaries down on their luck. So, the ratty clothing, the beards—all except Thex, whose cheeks were baby-smooth.)

He was antsy. Halak never *had* liked landskimmers. In the air, he could turn and fight. Air was like space: three-dimensional. Traveling a scant seven meters above the surface, with no room to really maneuver, made him anxious. Halak dug into his beard again, for want of anything better to do. "Just feels too far away. You've got a fix on the shuttle?"

"Shuttle telemetry's coming in loud and clear. Lucky I didn't crack her up, getting her out of parked lunar orbit and piloting via remote. She landed okay, though."

"Good," said Halak, knowing their situation was anything but. Having the unmarked, unregistered shuttle touch down without incident was about the only bright spot. He blew out a breath. He was sweating like a pig, partly from heat, the rest from nerves. He shrugged out of his khaki-colored jacket. Beneath the jacket, he wore Marassian wool pants and a throck-haired shirt: local civilian dress. They'd arrived in the middle of the local spring. The weather was like San Francisco in winter—brisk, cold, with a strong wind coming in off the water and smacking you in the face like an icy fist, and gushers of sleety rain that got dumped by heavy gray clouds every afternoon. But the landskimmer was small, warm, and close with the overripe odor of men's sweat. Rivulets of perspiration dribbled from Halak's armpits and crawled over his ribs. Reaching forward, Halak fiddled with a vent, angling cool air into his face.

Strong said, "Setting the shuttle down at the edge of town was too risky."

"Yeah," said Halak, without enthusiasm. He felt moisture evanescing from his neck, and his shoulders jerked with an involuntary shiver. He sopped the back of his neck with his sleeve. "Still too far away."

"We'll make it."

Thex piped up from the back seat. "What I wouldn't give for an emergency beam-out to the *Barker*, sir."

Halak grunted an assent. "No cavalry this time around. We're on our own until we clear Ryn space."

"Plausible deniability," said Strong, making it sound like something obscene. He depressed the throttle, trying to get more speed out of the skimmer. The vehicle lurched and shuddered. "Hope Starfleet Intelligence is happy."

"Ease off before we come apart," said Halak.

"Aye, sir," Strong said. He sucked air then let it out in a long exhalation. "Sorry. It's just, well, damn it, it seems *stupid* to have taken this many risks and come away with so little. Waste of time, putting our necks on the line. Felt really close, you know? Like we're so close to getting something useful on the Syndicate, then our cover gets blown."

Halak didn't respond. Strong was right. Ten days wasted, and nothing to show. Hell, they'd be lucky to get off the planet. The ostensible mission had been as deceptively simple as it had been dangerous. Ryn III was one of the Asfar Qatala's distribution hubs for red ice. The Orion Syndicate was also involved, but Starfleet was still amassing intel on them. Red ice was a secondary concern. The primary goal was to get information on how the Syndicate was currently set up, how it's network functioned, who controlled what. Follow the money. So, their mission: Pose as independent mercenaries, vie for a piece of the distribution pie, make contact with an operative in the Orion Syndicate. Get the information, and then get the heck off the planet.

The rationale for a trio was also deceptively simple. Three people were, in theory, harder to keep track of than two. If one of them were suspected of being an SI plant, this would take the focus off the other two. At least, that's what Starfleet Intelligence explained to Thex and Strong. Regrettably, this might lead to one of them being *eliminated*— SI-speak for *very dead*. But no one had forced Thex and Strong to volunteer. What SI didn't bother explaining was that it was also easier for one of them to peel off from the other two and do another mission—the *real* mission—on the side, without the other two being involved. That's the rationale that SI—and specifically Commander Marta Batanides—had offered about why Halak, in particular, should volunteer.

Halak didn't want the mission. He also couldn't refuse, not when Batanides did an end-around and asked him, again, in front of Captain Connors—not without arousing suspicion. Not without making someone want to take a much closer look at Samir al-Halak, maybe pick apart his past just a teensy bit more. So Halak was stuck. On the one hand, he couldn't risk SI nosing around more than Batanides, maybe, already had. On the other, he couldn't risk anyone from the Qatala—or the Syndicate—drawing a bead. True, he'd been a much younger man when he'd had any dealings with either organization. A boy, really: The last time he'd been on Farius Prime he'd been clean-shaven and about ten kilos lighter. Still.

Angling the landskimmer into a narrow valley formed by the cleft of two deep arroyos, Strong said, "I still don't understand how that happened, sir. The only time all three of us have been in the same room was when we were each trying to outbid the other. We took different rooms, never crossed paths. Secured channels on our communicators so we didn't even have to meet. Doesn't make sense they could have figured out who we are, you ask me. Hey, Thex," Strong angled his head up, talking to the roof, "how did you say they made us?"

"All I know is we were set up for a meet today with the Syndicate representatives. So I'm at the bar, waiting."

Halak half-turned. "And?"

"Two men—a Ryn and a Naiad—were gossiping with a waitress about how they'd heard there were Starfleet people nosing around about the Syndicate. The waitress dismissed it. Said they didn't know what they were talking about, that *she'd* heard the Syndicate hadn't made the Starfleet people at all, but the *Qatala* had. Said there were three of them and that a Qatala man, one of the old-timers, recognized one of them."

Halak felt his stomach bottom out. *Damn, damn.* Someone had recognized him. That was the only explanation. And he'd been so *close* . . .

"Couldn't be one of us," said Strong. His brows mated over the bridge of his nose. "We haven't had anything to do with the Qatala, just the Syndicate guys. Unless Starfleet Intelligence decided to keep an eye on us, and one of them got made. They do that, you know: spies spying on spies. Anyway, it couldn't have been us, Thex. You heard wrong."

"My hearing was perfect," said Thex. "*Is* perfect."

No. Halak chewed on the soft inner flesh of his cheek. Thex hadn't been wrong; he just didn't know. Neither did Strong. None of this was about red ice. Marta Batanides had been very clear about Halak's real mission, one that even Connors didn't know because if something went wrong, only Halak—and not Starfleet—would take the fall.

This was all about the Cardassians.

The facts. The Cardassians had been on a massive expansion kick for the last decade, from their failed attempt to claim Legara IV in 2327 and their annexation of Bajor in '28 to their current wrangling with the Klingon Empire for Raknal V. They'd been expanding, flexing their muscles by conquering smaller, non-Federation worlds nudging the border. There was every reason to believe that the Cardassians wouldn't stop there. But, in order to take on the Federation, the Cardassians needed more and better weapons.

Fact: The Breen made weapons. Good weapons, advanced weapons, such as type-3 disruptors. SI operatives had reports of Breen weapons turning up on Ryn III, probably bound for Cardassia. No one knew for sure.

Fact: well, a rumor, really. The buzz was that the Breen had developed cloaking technology superior to the Klingons. Bad enough. But there were also rumors swirling around that the Breen had succeeded in testing out prototypes of a new weapon designed to dissipate focused phased energy. The upshot? More energy discharge per volley, with greater range and less dissipated radiant energy than current Starfleet technology. Translation: more bang for the buck, and without a lot of spare change.

Fact: The Breen hated dealing with other species, period. The Breen were nonaligned. They were secretive, isolated. Duplicitous. Betazoids couldn't get a read on them, and the Breen shielded their bodies in refrigerated encounter suits that duplicated the ambient conditions of their frozen waste of a homeworld. One might have been tempted to call them cold-blooded but for the belief that the Breen didn't have a drop of blood, of any color or description, flowing in their nonexistent veins.

Fact: Profit was profit. If the Breen were going to get at Cardassian wealth, they'd need a middleman.

And that's where the Syndicate came in. The likely scenario was that the Syndicate provided the Breen with runners and pilots who would do the work, for a very hefty fee, of ferrying weapons bound for Cardassia. In turn, the Syndicate would make sure that any dealings were the Breen were one step removed.

And that's where Halak came in. Pose as a freelancer. Make contact with a dealer who needed a ship to transport Breen materiel into Cardassian space. Figure out to whom the dealer reported—the Syndicate, or the Qatala—and then get a read on the weapons distribution hierarchy.

Yet, somehow, *someone* had made Halak. He'd thought Farius Prime was far enough away from Ryn III, but it seemed he'd been wrong.

So who? He cast his mind over the possibilities. The Ryn weapons dealer he discarded on the spot. Halak had funneled data on the weapons dealer back to Starfleet Intelligence on a secured channel and discovered that the man was a native, had never left the planet.

"Well," he said finally, "what matters now is that we get off the planet and back to the *Barker* without the Ryn fleet on our tail. Then we regroup and figure out what went wrong."

In a few minutes, Strong banked the landskimmer right, and angled into a narrow canyon between high sheer cliffs to which low clumps of scrub clung. Halak scanned the jagged, rocky ridges but saw no one. Then Halak spotted the shuttle, a class two—capacity of four passengers; max speed, warp two. Fast enough. Ryn scouts could only make warp one-point-five. Quickly, his eyes ran over the exterior, looking for signs of damage. There were none.

"All right, go." Signaling for Strong to kill the engine, Halak snapped open his side of the landskimmer and scrambled out. "Go, go, let's go."

They piled into the shuttle, Halak dropping into the pilot's chair, and Strong into the seat next to him. Thex took over monitoring their onboard systems. After a cursory check, Halak punched the shuttle's engines.

In a few moments, Ryn III had fallen away beneath them. Halak was never so happy to see the backside of a planet before in his life. Then, two minutes later, as they passed Ryn III's near moon and went to warp, Thex said, "Something here, Commander."

Hell. "What? A scout?"

Strong shook his head. "Nothing on external scan. No sign of pursuit."

"That's not it," said Thex. He looked up, his sky-blue features pulled in a frown. "I'm getting a signal."

"Signal?" asked Halak. *Barker's too far away. They don't even know we're off-world yet.* "Is it a hail?"

"No, sir, that's just it. It's," Thex's fingers played over his console, "sir, it's coming from *us*."

"What?" Halak spun around in his chair. "Say again?"

"*Us.* It's like *we're* sending out a signal." Thex's eyes, baby blue like his skin, widened. "A homing beacon."

"They must have found the ship," said Strong, the color draining from his face like water from a leaky bucket. His voice was high and tight. "Someone must have found the ship parked around the moon, planted a homing beacon."

"But who?" asked Thex. "Why not board it? That doesn't make sense."

"Worry about what makes sense later," Halak rapped. "First, we shut it down. Thex, can you jam it?"

"Trying, sir," said Thex. He gritted his teeth as if a physical effort on his part would, magically, push his commands through. After a moment, he shook his head. His antennae knotted, unfurled. Kinked. "Negative. I can't. It's not routed through our communications system. In fact, I'm not sure where . . ."

"The engines," said Halak suddenly. *That's what I would do; make it inaccessible.* "Check the engines, the power couplings."

Thex's brow crinkled even as he moved to comply. "The engines? I don't . . . got it. Left nacelle, main power coupling. It's a subspace transponder, Commander, tied into the antimatter injector. No way to disable it without dropping out of warp."

"Probably programmed to *activate* when we went to warp."

"That might explain why we didn't detect it when Lieutenant Strong brought the shuttle in from its lunar stationary orbit. She came in on quarter-impulse."

"But who? Thex, can you get a read on . . .?"

"Sir!" It was Strong. "Two unidentified scouts, closing fast!"

Halak whirled around in his chair. "Where?"

"Off the port bow, sir!" Strong's head jerked up. "Sir, they must have used the same trick."

"Hiding behind the moon," said Halak. "Are they Ryn?"

"Negative. They're way too fast. Coming in at warp five!"

"Thex, what are their weapons?"

"I'm reading type-1 disruptors. We outgun them, sir."

"Raising shields," said Halak. He jabbed at his console, and their shields clicked into place. *And, thank God, they didn't deactivate them.* "Strong, how much longer before we're out of the Ryn system?"

"Five minutes, ten seconds."

"Thex, what about that homing beacon?"

The yellow glare coming from the Andorian's console had turned his skin a sickly shade of green. "Sorry, sir. No way to kill it."

"Without killing us," Halak said. "Cut warp drive, and

we're sitting ducks. All right, everyone hang on. Let's see if I can shake them loose."

The starfield outside the shuttle whirled in a dizzying spiral as Halak banked left and then began what, in an atmosphere, would have been a steep, coiling Immelmann turn.

"They're turning," Strong reported. "Matching course and speed. They just raised their shields."

"Come on," Halak muttered, dropping the shuttle and banking hard right, "come on, come on, cut *loose!*"

"Still with us!"

"Something here, Commander!" It was Thex. "I'm reading fluctuation in one of those ship's warp nacelles. There's been a minute power drop, but it looks like it's increasing. He's going to have to drop out of warp, or else the engine . . ."

"Sir!" Strong sang out. "They're powering up weapons! Locking on!"

"Taking evasive maneuvers!" Halak spun the shuttle to port and pushed the vessel into a steep dive. "Hang on!"

"Too late!" Strong shouted.

A second later, the shuttle lurched. Halak cursed and fought with the controls. "Report!"

"Hit to starboard. They missed the nacelle but got a piece of the aft hull. Shields down to eighty-five percent," said Thex.

"Shall I return fire?" asked Strong, his finger hovering over the targeting computer.

Halak shook his head in a curt negative. "We aren't here to fight, Strong. We keep up this speed, we'll cross into neutral space. With any luck, they'll drop back and . . ."

"Firing again!" shouted Thex.

The shuttle shuddered. Thex checked the damage. "Clipped our starboard nacelle. She's holding!"

"What about shields?"

"Eighty percent!"

"Commander," Strong gripped the edges of his console, "at least let me return fire, try to scare them off!"

"Negative, negative that!" Halak was thinking fast. He couldn't take a chance that these were unmarked Ryn scouts. "Our orders are not to engage . . ."

"They just jumped speed!" Thex called out. "Now at warp six! They're gaining!"

"What?" Halak's heart did a stutter-step. Gaining, it couldn't be. "Thex, are you sure?"

"Oh, hell." Strong's face was shiny with sweat. "Commander, they can't be Ryn, they *can't!* Ryn scouts don't go that fast! They have to be Syndicate!"

"Well, whoever they are, they're getting a lock," Thex warned. "Commander! Whatever you're going to do, do it fast!"

"All right!" Halak snapped. "Strong, *one* shot! Target the vessel with the faulty antimatter injector. See if you can knock it out of commission and get the other vessel to drop back."

Strong bared his teeth in a determined grimace. His fingers danced over his targeting controls. "Aye! Targeting port nacelle of the closest ship. Firing . . . now!"

There was a momentary flicker of the overhead lights, and Halak imagined he heard the dance and sizzle of the phaser blast licking across space.

"We hit him, we hit him!" Thex's voice ramped up with excitement. "Direct hit, port nacelle. His shields are down to sixty percent. I'm reading fluctuations in the engine, worse than before, the injector's . . . *Sir!*" Thex's stricken gaze found Halak. "Sir, his warp bubble's collapsing!"

"Oh, God, he's going to go," Strong said, instinctively straight-arming the edges of his console. "He's got a runaway, he's going to go, he's going to *go!*"

"What about the other ship?" Halak demanded. "Are they close enough, can they help?"

"They're closing in, looks like they might be trying to help, but I don't think they're going to make it!"

"Thex, are we within transporter range?"

"Negative, sir!"

"Do we have time to reach them?"

"Only if you go now, sir, right *now*!"

"What?" Strong was flabbergasted. "Commander?"

Halak ignored him. "All right! Thex, try to raise them, get them to stand down!"

Strong was at his elbow. "Commander, you can't, we'll get too close, we'll be . . ."

"As you *were*, Lieutenant! I'll only bring us around once they acknowledge . . ."

"Too late!" Thex reported. "She's breaking up, she's breaking up!"

Halak had only begun his turn, but it was in time for the space before them to flare white, then red, then yellow as the atmosphere within the smaller ship ignited and bloomed in a fiery shower. A wave front of debris and explosive gases rippled out in ever-widening spheres. Their shuttle shook in the explosive backwash.

There was an instant's silence in the shuttle. Then, Strong said, without being prompted, "No damage."

Halak swallowed his disgust with the lieutenant. He'd deal with Strong later. "Thex, what about that other ship?"

"She was too close, Commander," said Thex. "The explosive backwash knocked out her shields. Her port engine's damaged, and her inertial dampers are gone. I read environmental systems failure and . . ."

Halak heard the dismay in the Andorian's voice. "What is it, Lieutenant?"

"Imminent cascade reaction in their remaining engine. I estimate two minutes to critical. Their explosive bolts must be frozen, or they'd have blown it clear by now."

"How many?"

Thex squinted at his readings. "Two life-forms."

"Ryn?"

"I can't tell. Too much background radiation from that other ship."

Halak closed his eyes. "Did they get off a distress signal?" *Please, yes, yes.*

There was a pause. Then Thex shook his head. "Even if they had, they're too far out. There's no way anyone would reach them in time."

"Lifeboat?"

"Not that I can see, sir."

"Damn," Halak muttered. "All right, hail them, Thex."

Strong gaped. "You're not going *back* for them?"

Halak turned on him. "Of course I'm going back for them. They need our help. I gave you an order, Mr. Thex."

"Aye sir." Swallowing, Thex hesitated, looked at Strong.

"You have a problem, mister?" asked Halak.

"No, sir, it's just," Thex wet his lips, "well . . ."

"Of *course*, there's a problem!" Strong hissed. "They *fired* on us! We don't know who they are, what they want!"

"Objection noted!" said Halak in a voice that dared Strong to contradict him. "Anything else?" When Strong said nothing, Halak jerked his head in an abrupt nod. "Good. Now, hail them, Thex!"

"Hailing. No response. They haven't abandoned ship."

"How much longer before we're in range to beam them aboard?"

"Another twenty seconds. Estimate engine overload in thirty seconds."

"Cutting it too damned close," Strong murmured blackly. "Too close."

"Stow it, Strong! Thex, tell them to prepare to be beamed aboard."

Thex sent off the request. "They received our signal, Commander. No response."

"You're too close," said Strong, his voice beginning to rise, "they're going to blow, and you're bringing us in too close!"

"Try again, Thex." Then Halak heard Thex gasp. "What is it?"

"Commander, there's an energy surge!"

"I knew it. They were playing dead, they're powering up weapons!" Strong's hand flashed over his firing controls. "Firing phasers!"

"No!" Halak shouted. He moved to override Strong's phaser controls, too late. "No, Strong, *stop!*"

Their phasers sizzled. Horrified, Halak watched as the blast caught the scout amidships and knifed through the hull, shredding it like tissue paper.

"What are you *doing?*" Halak screamed. For a wild, insane moment, he wanted to punch Strong in the jaw. "They weren't targeting us!"

Strong's eyes bulged. "I'm s-sorry. I thought they'd laid a trap, I thought they were playing dead, I thought . . ."

"Commander!" It was Thex. "There she goes!"

"Damn!" Halak whirled around in time to see the shuttle go in two successive bursts. Frantically, he wrenched the shuttle about, trying to outrun the aftershocks. "Damn, damn!"

"Shock waves!" Thex cried.

The first shock wave caught them astern, the concussive force rippling over the ship and shaking them as if they were the grip of a giant hand. Alarms screamed. Strong smacked hard against his console and rebounded to the deck with a cry of pain. Something behind Halak shorted; he heard a yelp from Thex, and there was a smell of singed wire and ozone and burnt flesh. Another shock wave slammed them amidships. Halak fought for control, but the ship bucked, heaved, yawed, and then the ship banked sharply left, their gravity cut out for an instant, and Halak went flying. He crashed to the deck, the force of the impact knocking the wind out of him.

For an instant, he simply stopped breathing. The ship

was spinning, and he felt his body flatten out against the starboard bulkhead. He knew, instantly: Their inertial dampers were gone. They were spiraling out of control

Through a haze of pain, he heard the computer intone a warning. "*Warning. Hull shear stress approaching tolerance limits. Warning . . .*"

Abandon ship. Halak shook his vision clear. *We've got to abandon ship.*

But he couldn't move. His chest felt as if it was on fire, and he struggled, tried to get his burning lungs to pull in air. Finally, he drank in a great, wheezing gulp.

"Argh!" he cried. His neck arched, and he felt the muscles of his chest spasm. He labored to pull in another breath. "Strong, *Strong!*"

The centrifugal force that had him plastered to the deck made it almost impossible for him to move his head. Achingly, inch by agonizing inch, he fought against the invisible hand that pinned him in place and pulled his head around until he was looking aft, toward the command console. He saw two things. Strong was sprawled in the space between the pilot and copilot chairs. And Thex was lying, facedown, on the deck, to his left and just out of reach. The Andorian wasn't moving.

"Strong!" Halak wheezed. "Strong, we're spinning counterclockwise. Shut down the starboard thrusters! Throttle up on the port thruster, break the spin!"

In an agony of suspense, Halak watched as Strong clawed his way up the back of his chair. It was like watching someone doing ballet in molasses. Strong fumbled at the controls.

"Shutting down starboard thrusters! Port thruster, engaged. *Now!*"

Halak felt the ship quake. There was a shriek of protest from the computer. The bulkhead vibrated, and Halak felt the shudders running up and down his spine.

Suddenly, the pressure from the invisible hand on his chest lessened. Weakened. Was gone. Gasping, Halak sagged to the deck. For a moment, all he heard was the sobbing of his own breath.

Then, the computer shrilled: *"Warning. Environmental systems failure. Hull stress has exceeded maximum tolerance levels. Hull breach imminent in three-point . . ."*

"Kill that thing, Strong." Halak let his head fall back for an instant. He knew how much time they had. Not much.

"Thex." Halak groped at the Andorian's neck for a pulse. He felt it: faint, thready. Reaching around, Halak heaved Thex over. Halak's breath sizzled through his teeth. An ugly black rose of burnt cloth and skin blossomed on the Andorian's chest.

"Strong, we have to get out! Get off a distress call to the *Barker!*"

The lieutenant's chest heaved, and Halak saw that Strong's face was slicked with blood gushing from a laceration in the man's scalp. *"Strong!"*

"I'm okay," said Strong, his voice hitching with pain. "I'm okay, I'm okay. There," his fingers crawled over the controls, "done. Sending out a general distress. There goes life support." Strong wiped blood from his eyes. Blinked. "Hull stress . . ."

"Forget that!" The ship shimmied, and Halak staggered, clutching at a bulkhead for balance. He clawed his way to the equipment locker, slammed his fist down, and broke the seal. The locker sighed open. Reaching in, Halak dragged out an environmental suit. "Help me!"

"But, Commander," Strong was holding his head and blood leaked around his fingers, "there's no time!"

"Did you *hear* me, Lieutenant? Get over here and *help* me!"

Clamping his mouth shut, Strong said nothing more. Together, they shoved the inert Andorian into an environmental suit.

"All right, slap on a compressive and suit up!" Halak ordered, jamming on Thex's helmet. He eased the Andorian to the deck. "Go, *go!*"

Jamming the white rectangle of a compressive bandage on his scalp, Strong shrugged into his suit. Halak fought with his suit, pawing clumsily at the legs, the arms; he was still dizzy and off-balance, and he could tell from the way the ship bucked, the groan of metal, that it couldn't last much longer.

Without being told, Strong hooked his hands under Thex's right arm, and Halak took the left. They dragged the Andorian upright.

"All right," Halak rasped. His own breaths were loud in his ears. Looking over, he saw Strong's grim, blood-streaked face staring at him from behind his faceplate. Halak read the look. They'd be lucky if anyone heard in time.

Eight hours of air. Halak activated the emergency transport. *Then we suffocate.*

The ship around him shimmered, dissolved, broke apart. The deck fell away from beneath his feet. And then there was blackness. The ship was gone.

Chapter 20

"And the next thing I knew we were floating in space," said Halak. He'd omitted anything to do with his real mission, or his concerns about having been recognized by Qadir's men. He was under orders not to divulge the truth of that Ryn mission to anyone, up to and including his captain. And, of course, SI knew nothing about his past. But the remainder of his story was true; his coal-black eyes had never left Burke's face, and his voice rang with conviction. "No lifeboat. We clipped our suits together. But we were stranded, not even sure if our suit's distress beacons would make it to the *Barker*."

"So your situation was desperate," said Burke, flatly. Throughout Halak's recitation, her brown, appraising gaze betrayed no emotion save a faint derision.

"You could say that," Halak said, without irony. "Thex died two hours after the ship disintegrated. We bled what was left of Thex's air into our systems."

Halak looked over at Garrett, his tone becoming a little defiant as if deflecting a perceived criticism. "Thex wouldn't need it, and Strong's suit was leaking, probably damaged in the beam-out."

Mutely, Garrett nodded. She was shaken. She knew the story from reading Halak's official reports as well as her private talk with Captain Connors. Connors hadn't faulted Halak, and neither did she. Thex hadn't needed air. Halak and Strong had. These were the cold, simple equations of life and death in space.

Halak was telling the truth. Her gut told her so. His recitation was too fluid; everything hung together. Garrett's quick glance around at her officers—Tyvan, Stern, even the lieutenant making recordings—confirmed they believed him, too. So why was Burke quizzing Halak? How did this relate to Batra? Farius Prime?

"Why not simply switch out Lieutenant Thex's seals for Strong's?" asked Burke, as if she found Halak's decision distasteful. "Bleeding air is a bit dramatic."

"Dramatic." Halak's expression revealed what he thought: Here was an officer with a desk job. No matter if he switched seals or bled air, Thex was just as dead. "You think switching out seals isn't dramatic? One slip up, and you're dead. But, yeah, I thought about it. I discarded it."

"Why?"

"I didn't want to compromise Strong's systems more than they already were. His wasn't a simple seal failure. If it'd been that easy, we'd have rigged a stricture above the leak. So we bled the air, and I gave Strong the lion's share. Then we dialed down oxygen, trying to conserve as long as possible. The problem was my repurification system was damaged, and I started building up carbon dioxide."

"Ugly," Stern murmured. "Carbon dioxide poisoning isn't pleasant."

"Plus, we had other problems. I didn't want us to be too far from where our shuttle exploded. *Barker* would be looking for a debris field. But the hell of it was that staying close meant we were at risk from the debris field itself, and radiation. Local space was lousy with it. Add in ambient gamma radiation from the Ryn sun, and I figured that if we didn't suffocate, we'd cook."

"Why not phase your suits' electrostatic charges into a force field?" Burke asked in that same bland, faintly judgmental tone. "That would have bought you some time."

"Sure. We thought of that. But our priority was contact with the *Barker*. Phasing electrostatic fields would have drained our suits' battery packs, made our carrier waves much weaker. With all that radiation, I wasn't sure our distress beacons would pierce the interference locally, much less make it to the *Barker*. We elected to phase our carrier waves, instead. A gamble, but it was the only choice, really."

"But you won," said Burke. "The *Barker* caught your boosted signal."

Halak shrugged irritably. "If you call losing crewmates *winning*. I don't."

"Yes, that's right. I forgot. Strong's air ran out before *Barker* got there."

"That's right."

"And yours didn't."

"No."

"That must have been unpleasant, listening to your crewmate suffocate."

Halak's expression was stony. "Very. Especially when he cracked the seal on his helmet."

Dear Lord. Garrett closed her eyes. She'd seen what happened to the human body under sudden decompression in a vacuum.

Halak continued, his black eyes burning with contempt. "Ever been there, Lieutenant? The guy's out of air. He can't breathe. He's got this insane idea that if he can just twist that helmet loose he'll be able to. Even hanging in space, vacuum all around, he thinks that. It's not logical." Halak's dark eyes raked over Sivek's expressionless features before returning to Burke. "But it happens."

Sivek's only reaction was to blink. Burke didn't acknowledge the reproach. "And you didn't try to stop him."

"Goddamn you." Anger flooded Halak's features, turning his sallow olive skin a copper color. "Of course, I did. But he straight-armed me. I don't know what type of deep-space experience you *haven't* had, Lieutenant, but when you're weightless and someone gives you a push, unless you've got a thruster pack there's no way you're going to change course real fast."

"So he unclipped you. In the middle of suffocating to death, where the only thing on his mind was getting air, he still had the presence of mind to make sure you couldn't stop him."

"No, he didn't unclip me. He pushed, and then he cracked the seal, but when he did that, his systems shut down. After that, I had to rephase my carrier wave with Thex's. Somehow I did it, though I honestly don't remember much. I was pretty far gone. *Barke*r showed up when I had about a half hour of air left. At least that's what the doc told me. I had passed out. Next thing I knew, I was in sickbay."

"And that's all."

Garrett spoke, her voice hard. "There has to be more, Lieutenant?"

"Much," said Burke. "I have proof that nearly everything Commander Halak just told us is a lie. No," she held up her hand when Halak opened his mouth to protest, "that's unfair. Lieutenants Thex and Strong *did* die, just not the way Halak tells it."

"Proof?"

Burke bobbed her neat blonde curls. "Absolutely," she said, steepling her fingers like a professor making an important point she doesn't want her students to forget. "Captain, autopsy results on Lieutenant Thex indicate that his wounds were not that severe. And Strong's tissues do not indicate characteristic changes you would expect to see in severe hypoxia. Thex should've lived. He didn't. Strong wasn't suffocating, but he died, too."

Garrett struggled to keep her disgust for Burke under wraps, and failed. "Are you suggesting, seriously, that Halak stole Thex's air? That he murdered a member of his crew? Maybe both of them?"

"Yes, Captain."

Garrett's tone was deadly. "How? What's more, why?"

"My scenario runs like this: Thex was unconscious. It wouldn't take much for Halak to convince Strong that Thex was dead. Then, under the pretext of sharing Thex's air with Strong, Halak cracked the seals on Strong's helmet. Halak had never intended for either of his crewmates to survive."

"Captain," said Halak, his voice strangled. "Captain."

Burke pushed on. "Then he bled Thex's air into his suit."

"Well, that's dumb. Why not take both?" asked Stern.

"Because then he couldn't be half-dead, could he? That might raise too many eyebrows."

"That's the how," said Garrett. She made a shushing motion with her hand at Halak, who subsided. "Now, what's the why?"

The edges of Burke's lips flirted with a smile, as if she knew that Garrett's not letting Halak interrupt meant that she'd scored points. "Commander Halak's situation was desperate, but for reasons quite different from what he's presented."

"But there was an inquiry, Burke. Halak was cleared."

"Corruption breeds powerful allies, Captain."

"Corruption." Garrett's eyes narrowed. "What are you talking about?"

Sivek stirred. "If I may?" At Garrett's nod, the Vulcan stood and approached the conference room viewscreen.

"I had the opportunity to download a series of encrypted computer records that verify everything Lieutenant Burke alleges."

"Encrypted? From where?"

"From Commander Halak's personal log."

Garrett's eyes widened. "You took it upon yourself to break into Commander Halak's personal log? On whose authority?"

"*I* gave Sivek the go-ahead, Captain," said Burke.

Garrett felt her blood pressure rising. "Without consulting *me*?"

"Captain, Starfleet Intelligence's mandate supercedes command prerogatives in matters of security," said Burke. "But I did clear it with Commander Batanides, if that's any consolation."

"It's not," said Garrett, though she knew that Batanides owed her no explanations and didn't need to ask her permission. "I should've been told."

"Point taken," said Sivek. His sleek black coif gleamed like the skin of a well-oiled seal. "And what is done is done. In any event, embedded within Commander Halak's personal logs were encrypted entries that confirm and augment computer records retrieved from the shuttle Commander Halak appropriated on Farius Prime."

"Whoa, whoa, wait a minute," said Garrett. "We searched that shuttle. Are you telling me that you found things we didn't? How? *Where*?"

"Intelligence operatives are trained to look for that which has been overlooked," said Sivek. He had the computer display a star chart on the conference room's viewscreen. "I have to apologize, Captain. These will necessarily be crude because they've not been completely analyzed. In addition, I'm not at liberty to reveal the entire contents of the files we uncovered. This might be a little confusing, or you might find there to be leaps in logic. That can't be helped."

"Thanks," said Garrett. "I'll try to bear up."

"First, from Commander Halak's personal logs: this is a map of sectors seventeen through nineteen."

Garrett's expert eyes scanned the chart. "Ryn space."

"Precisely. Stardate markers indicate that was recorded nine months ago. Now, here," the Vulcan indicated a yellow-coded star system, "is the Ryn system: the Ryn sun, Ryn III, and its two moons. And here, these green ellipses, you see the range of Ryn scout vessels, their patrol routes, and the orbital paths of planetary security systems."

"What are those other points?" asked Garrett. She pointed at five red, inverted triangles. "Are those satellites?"

"No. Those are drop-off points: distribution nodes, if you will."

"For?"

"Red ice. Extrapolating back from vessels commandeered at various Federation security checkpoints, these coordinates match with our projected points of origin."

"So you're saying those smugglers originated in Ryn space at those precise coordinates." Garrett saw where this was going. Almost peripherally, she noted that Halak hadn't uttered a word of protest since the Vulcan had begun. "And the records you retrieved from the shuttle Halak got on Farius Prime?"

"As I've said, I can't reveal everything. Here is, however, a representative sample. Computer, display File Sivek Exhibit 7-A."

The image on the viewscreen dissolved into soft focus to be replaced by a graphical display of what Garrett saw at once was not a star system but an entire sector. She picked out markers that could only be ships scattered in and around various star systems and nebulae. At first she didn't recognize the region of space, but then she spotted a marker for Starbase 129 and she knew exactly what she was looking at. "That's the Federation border with Cardassian space. Starbase 129 is a listening post."

Her eyes swiveled to Sivek. "Those records are classified. Command level."

"More than classified, Captain. They're top secret, property of Starfleet Intelligence, available only to select command personnel such as yourself." Sivek let that hang in the air a moment then proceeded. "Computer, start animation.

"Here," said Sivek, as markers denoting Cardassian ships advanced and retreated, "is what Starfleet has gathered so far on Cardassian movements in the area. As you can see, they have sufficient ships to maintain fairly tight surveillance of their border, with the exception of this area here."

He tapped the viewscreen with his finger. "Grid 28. The Cardassians are rather sparse there, perhaps because there's a nebula. Hard to get accurate readings."

Garrett didn't offer her opinion that if she were in command of the Cardassian patrols, she'd double her patrols, not decrease them. A nebula was a good place for a smuggler— or anyone—to hide. She knew from experience: when she'd been the *Carthage*'s XO and nearly flattened her shuttle against a Cardassian *Akril*-class ship.

"Those are Cardassian patrols," said Garrett. "So?"

"Isn't it obvious, Captain?" Burke asked.

"No. I see two unrelated findings: Ryn space and Cardassian space. One data set you *allege* was in Halak's possession, though just how you knew to look is a little vague. Just how *did* you know? Never mind," she waved off Burke's reply before the SI officer opened her mouth, "I'll bet you're just dying to tell me. And the other set of data is from a stolen shuttle that wasn't Halak's to begin with. What am I supposed to find that's so damned obvious?"

"Simply this, Captain. Starfleet Intelligence believes that

Commander Halak did his job on Ryn very well. He infiltrated the Syndicate's ranks; he even figured out their red ice distribution network. But he wasn't about to share this with Starfleet. Instead, he was going to share it with the Syndicate's rival, the Asfar Qatala." Her dark brown eyes pegged Halak. "Because Halak's working for Mahfouz Qadir. In fact, Halak's family has been involved with the Qatala for years. Halak's father worked for Qadir, as did his brother. But Halak wants to go one better. He wants to take over. Isn't that right, Commander?"

If the shock waves that rippled through Garrett had been physical, she would have blown apart. As it was, no one said anything. The room was completely silent except for the faint beep-beep-beeping of the computer dutifully recording the proceedings. Halak's color had gone from bronze to ashen, but he said nothing.

It was Garrett who reacted first. "Stop recording," she said to the lieutenant. "Lieutenant Donald, you're excused. You are to go to your quarters and stay there until I, or another officer, instruct you otherwise. Is that clear?"

Lieutenant Donald's face was so chalky every freckle seemed splattered on with a paintbrush. "Yes, ma'am." Without another word, he clicked off the recorder, rose, and hurried from the conference room.

Garrett waited until the door hissed shut. Then, slowly, she eyed Stern, Tyvan, and, lastly, Halak. She said nothing, and all of them, even Halak, met her gaze without flinching. She read the entreaty in Halak's eyes. Then she stood and came around the conference room table until she was nose to nose with Burke. It gave Garrett a vicious thrill of satisfaction when Burke took a step back.

"Talk fast, Lieutenant," Garrett said. "Make it good. No, make it *better*."

"Captain, Halak's lied, *been* lying for years. SI's been watching him for some time."

"And you didn't think to inform his commanding officers?"

"No." She added, hastily, "When we discovered who he really was, we thought it best to use Commander Halak to our advantage."

"*We? Our* advantage? Like we're one big happy family? I don't recall inviting you over for Christmas."

"Captain," Stern began.

Garrett cut her off with an angry gesture. "I don't care who you work for, Burke. Starfleet Intelligence has no right, *no right*, to jeopardize any member of Starfleet, and you can be damned sure I'll be on the horn to Starfleet Command about this, and if I find out that *you* are in any way culpable, I will personally see to it that you are roasted alive."

Two high spots of color burned in Burke's cheeks. "I understand your anger, Captain, and I apologize for my poor choice of words. But I'm only the messenger."

That brought Garrett up short. Burke was right, she knew, but she was so angry it was miracle her head hadn't erupted. *Ease off, girl.* "Apology accepted. Now," she said, with a curt jerk of her head, "I don't suppose you mind filling me in, Burke. Exactly who, or what is Halak?"

Burke's expression was stolid. "Al-Halak is not his last name. *El-Malk* is. He's not an orphan, except technically. His parents *are* dead *now.* But he had a mother and a father, as well as a brother, and they were all very much alive when Halak was born on Deneb V."

Now it was Garrett's turn to blink. "Deneb? Not Vendrak IV? But Deneb's . . ."

"A known hotbed for illegal smugglers, traders of all descriptions. That's right. That's where Halak's father ended up after beating an arms trafficking charge. Mahfouz Qadir was on Deneb at the same time Halak's father showed up. They went into business together, one big happy *crime* family, Captain. And then they went to Farius Prime."

"I find it hard to believe, with that history, that Halak would have been allowed into the Academy."

Sivek spoke. "A masterful forgery, Captain. As I recall, this type of subterfuge isn't exactly unknown. Wasn't there an incident only two years ago where a young man tried to hide the fact that a great-aunt was Cardassian?"

"Yes, but that was discovered."

"Only because the young man's forgeries were poorly made. Think, Captain. It stands to reason that, logically, for every person Starfleet catches, there must be others who slip by simply because their forgeries are more expert."

"Or they have powerful contacts," said Burke. "In fairness to SI, Captain, we didn't know about Halak until after the Ryn incident. There were enough questions about exactly what happened for Starfleet Intelligence to take a good hard look at the commander. After we concluded that his records were a forgery, we started inquiries. We discovered that the commander was and has been lying for a very long time. Sivek?"

Sivek ordered the computer to display another case file. The screen filled with a full frontal and profile shot of a man who looked to be in his mid-forties and who Garrett saw at once had to be Halak's father. There was the same set of the jaw, the same jet-black eyes.

"Najm al Din el-Malk, deceased," said Sivek. "Halak's father changed the family name when they went to Deneb V. Prior to that, records indicate that he was arrested on trafficking charges but released for lack of evidence. Then el-Malk disappeared. Years later, a man named Nu'man al-Halak died when his ship fell into the Deneb sun. How he ended up so close to the sun is a mystery. Nu'man al-Halak was rated an excellent pilot."

"If he burned up, there's no body for DNA comparison," said Garrett. "How do you know they're the same man, or that Halak's related?"

Sivek acknowledged Captain Garrett's point with a nod

of his sleek head. "We don't have definitive proof. There is nothing on either el-Malk, or Nu'man al-Halak in Federation databases. Their records appear to have been erased."

Garrett frowned. "No records at all? That's almost inconceivable. You're talking influence at the highest levels for that to happen."

"That is one conclusion. Interestingly, at the same time that Nu'man al-Halak dies, another individual, much younger, shows up in our records."

Sivek called up another file and Nu'man's face dissolved into the face of a young man with the same cast of his jaw and fierce set to his eyes. "Baatin al-Halak."

"Who is he?"

"Was. He was murdered in a gang-style killing. And he was your commander's older brother."

Despite the bombshell, Garrett's expression was neutral. Out of the corner of her eye, she saw Halak put a hand to his brow. "But, of course, you have no corroborating proof because his DNA isn't on file, am I right?"

Sivek conceded the point with a nod of his head. "My hypothesis, however, is sound. Mahfouz Qadir, Nu'man al-Halak's employer, had Baatin assassinated when Qadir learned that Baatin was dealing with the Orion Syndicate. Baatin must have been alerted. Before he died, he provided his younger brother—your first officer—with false documentation, provided by the Orion Syndicate. That way, no one would ever suspect Halak's connection to Qadir, or Farius Prime."

"And why would the Syndicate be so helpful?"

Burke picked up the thread. "Because the Syndicate knew that Halak would avenge his brother's death, and the Syndicate, as the Qatala's fiercest rivals, was only too happy to oblige. I know that Commander Batanides filled you in on our latest intelligence regarding the Orion Syndicate. Now, what I'm going to show you next, Captain, occurred when Commander Halak and Lieutenant Batra were on Farius Prime."

Burke called up a computer record, and in another instant, an image blurred then cohered on the viewscreen. The scene had clearly been recorded at night; wedges of light fanned doorways to structures that looked to Garrett like warehouses.

She heard Halak straighten in his chair. Sparing him a quick glance, she saw that his eyes were wide, and an expression of dumbfounded amazement played over his features.

She turned back to Burke. "Where is this?"

"Tajora Street, the warehouse district right off the Galldean Sea. Those structures are all Qatala-owned."

"Did you take these?"

"No. I've never been to Farius Prime, Captain. We have our sources, of course. But everything we need to hang Commander Halak is in his records, and right here. Computer, magnify."

The computer complied, and Garrett saw a quartet of figures clustered near the entrance to one of the warehouses. She frowned as she realized that one figure's skin was blue—the Bolian, Matsaro.

"Computer, enhance," said Burke.

The figures wavered into focus. The image was grainy, and there were many shadows cutting across, but the figures were unmistakable. Halak. Batra. A woman, about Batra's age, dressed in a hooded black cloak. And the Bolian.

"Who's the woman?" asked Stern.

"Her name is Arava. She's a highly placed member of the Asfar Qatala. Only she's double-dealing. She's really an Orion Syndicate operative." Burke tapped the viewscreen with a finger. "And that's *your* first officer, Captain. Make no mistake. We have every reason to believe that Halak's plan has been to hide in plain sight, knowing that, eventually, he would come into a position of trust and authority. What's more, he'd have free run of Federation worlds. Armed with this advantage, he went back to Farius Prime: not to help anyone, or visit an old woman who doesn't exist. No, he went back to make contact with Baatin's people—Orion Syndicate operatives like Arava—planted throughout Qadir's organization. Undoubtedly, part of his plan was to map out shipments of red ice, most likely to underprotected Federation outposts, just as he tried, and failed to do in Ryn space. But his aim is to take over the business, taking down Qadir and helping the Orion Syndicate. This is a personal vendetta, Captain, and I'm sorry to say that Starfleet's been his cover."

Burke turned from Garrett to Halak. They locked eyes. "And as for visiting a woman," Burke said, "the only woman Halak came to see was Arava because, you see, Arava was—and *is*—Halak's lover."

Suddenly, Garrett felt her knees buckle. Groping, she found the nearest chair, dropped. She was acutely aware of every sensation at that moment: the tiny pops and crackles of her knees; the friction of her clothing around her wrists, her throat; the way her mouth was drier than sand.

In the silence, Garrett heard Stern's murmured, "Oh, Lord." If Tyvan had any reaction, he kept it to himself.

Then someone said, "That's crazy." Halak. "That's crazy," he said again. His head was in his hands, and his voice was muffled, strangled and he sounded as if he were either on the verge of tears, or a nervous breakdown. His fingers clutched at his hair as if he wanted to yank it out by the roots. "Crazy, you've got it all wrong."

Burke opened her mouth, but Garrett put up a hand. "What did they get wrong, Halak? Which part of the story?"

"So much of it, so much of it."

"But not all of it?"

And then Halak looked up. His eyes were sunken and his face drawn and hollowed out, as if he'd aged a century in the last hour. "Captain," he began, and stopped.

"Halak?"

But Halak was already shaking his head. "I'm sorry, Captain, please forgive me," he said, finally. His black gaze locked on Garrett. "But I respectfully decline to respond as my answers may incriminate me."

Chapter 21

For about the eightieth time, Jase Garrett wondered what the heck he was doing.

Resting, he leaned his weight into the mountain. He was sweating, and he wanted to wipe his face, but being in his suit made that impossible. He'd adjusted his temperature controls twice, but he was still fogging, and it was hard enough to see as it was. The surface was in near-total darkness, the feeble light of the brown star coloring the terrain various shades of gray, rust, and a queer, dull, washed-out bronze that verged on muddy yellow. He flicked his tongue over his upper lip and tasted salt. He squinted, speared the beam of his flash into the slope below. The light picked out slurries of bronze rock and sand-colored debris. Tricky going. He'd have preferred hiking with the light off to free up his hands. He scanned the star-studded sky. The planet's larger moon was near the horizon and the smaller one was higher, but neither cast much light and the steely starlight wasn't bright enough. One misstep, and he'd go tumbling. One thing he didn't want was to get hurt *here*, now, kilometers from help, especially when no one knew where he was. The biosphere, where they'd been living for almost a week and a half, was nestled on the far side of the valley, in a wide cirque. If something happened, he'd lie here for hours before anyone showed. *If* anyone showed before his air ran out.

Smart. He peered back down the mountain. *Really smart*

move, Jase. What had he been thinking? He should've been in his quarters, dutifully studying *something*. Astromechanics. Parallel plane differential calculus. Something. But *nooo*. He was out here, mucking around over red rocks on a dead planet, trying not to get himself killed.

And being tugged—*pulled*—somewhere. He felt it, in his mind. He knew going any further was nuts, totally crazy. But when he thought about turning back, a mosquito whine at the back of his brain started: a mental tug that had led him to stand on a rocky face above a dead lake on a blasted world.

And something really bad had happened here. Jase angled his light behind and back up the mountain. *Maybe explosions, or a war, a really bad war.* Here, the sides of the mountains had fallen away, like orange wax melting under a hot flame. The pass had disappeared and been replaced by a series of chutes that jagged down the mountain, almost as if water had scoured out the rock, leaving deep, wide furrows. The steep mountain chute he'd chosen was littered with rust-colored scree and rubble. There was loose rock and scree everywhere, and that made the going treacherous, like picking his way over a vertical sheet of glare ice.

He'd found a pass incised into the rock about a kilometer northwest of the biosphere. At first, the pass had looked like nothing more than a dried stream, and Jase would have trudged by. But then that mental clarion call tickled his brain and when he got right up to the earth and swept the ground with his flashlight, he saw the faint but unmistakable impressions of footprints worn into the rock. *From the people who used to live here.* Staring at the footprints, Jase had felt a cold finger of dread trail along the knobs of his spine. *Ghosts.* Jase had felt them from orbit and then felt them again, stronger, on the surface. There were ghosts here, ghosts that floated just out of sight, hovered behind the rocks. Lived beneath the ground.

He'd taken the path anyway.

Nerves, he told himself as he trudged along, the beam of

his flashlight punching the semi-darkness. Just nerves. Heck, who wouldn't be a little nervous: stuck on a dead planet, a zillion kilometers from anyone, and cooped up in a biosphere with a guy like Su Chen-Mai?

Jase's eyes darted right and left, scouring the steep mountain terrain. Twice, he could've sworn he was being followed. Twice, he'd ducked into the shadows, nerves jangling. But there'd been no one. Just his imagination: nothing more.

He checked his air. Eight hours left. At the rate he was going, he probably had just enough air to make it a third of the way down before he had to turn around. Again, he considered going back. Again, he discarded the idea. Might as well keep going for as long as he could, see how far he got. Next time (*what was he thinking, there was going to be a next time?*), he'd bring spare air, maybe leave it somewhere so he could change out and get back without having to rush.

He sidestepped, careful to keep his weight angled into the mountain. His feet bit into the earth, and he knew they crunched rock, though he heard nothing but his own breathing because there was no atmosphere to carry the sound. He wished there was something else to focus on but himself: his breathing, the fact that he was sweating so much he felt oily. He was sore, and his thighs trembled with fatigue and a hot burn from muscles that hadn't been used in quite this way for months and months. His knees creaked and screamed with pain from the long downhill trek. His nose itched, and this was guaranteed to drive him crazy. And (*wasn't this just his luck?*) he had to pee. Really bad. Just the thought made his groin clutch.

But there wasn't anything he could do about the sound, his aching muscles, the way his nose itched so much his eyes watered because he was in a stupid environmental suit, a couple four, five kilometers away from the biosphere, under a dead sky littered with the hard, sharp points of millions of stars. There *was* something he could do about having to pee.

He just didn't want to. Not in a suit. No matter how clean everyone (*his mom, his dad, but especially his mom*) said it was, no matter how well the suit grabbed all that stuff and recycled it, or did *whatever*. No way.

He hadn't planned any of this. Oh, he knew that his predicament (the pain in his thighs, the itch in his nose, the need to pee *really bad*) was entirely his own doing. He couldn't even claim that he was just a stupid kid because he wasn't a *total* kid, and even when he had been, he hadn't ever been *stupid*. Like, he shouldn't even have been in the suit. But either he waited until all the adults were gone then steal a suit and sneak out of the biosphere and not tell a soul (not even Pahl) and risk getting grounded for life; or go absolutely-stark-raving-bonkers-bathouse-crazy with boredom. Probably his dad wouldn't ground him for life. Probably.

But he *hated* environmental suits. *Stewing in a tin can, breathing canned air*: That's the way his mom described it, only she *liked* it, go figure. Jase didn't know what a tin can *was*; he had to look it up. After studying a pretty strange painting by a twentieth-century guy who made a fortune painting the same soup can in different colors, Jase figured out two things. Being cooped up in a tin can looked uncomfortable, but the painter had been brilliant.

A couple of years ago, Jase worried that hating environmental suits might keep him out of Starfleet Academy. (That was when he was just a little kid though. Now that he knew he wasn't ever going to the Academy because he was going to be an artist or something, he probably wouldn't need to stick a toe inside an environmental suit.) He knew that sometimes transporters broke down, or shuttles blew apart, and you needed to know how to use a suit. He'd visited his mom enough times while the *Enterprise* was in dock to understand that all sorts of people worked outside, in suits, all the time. He used to stand at one of the dock's observation bays, his face plastered to cool glass, and watch the structural engineers, tiny as ants, crawl over the gray hull of his mom's ship. And the most inane thought: What happens if they have to pee?

Oh, no. At the thought, Jase felt a sharp twinge that bloomed into a full-blown ache in his groin. Again. *Drat.* Screwing up his nose, he hummed something tuneless, just to have something to do instead of thinking how much he had to pee but couldn't. (Well, he *could.* There were buttons and dials and hook-ups, right?)

Of course, right. He wasn't a total moron. Still, gross. Jase tried thinking about sand dunes and deserts and hot red suns. Except his groin complained and his mind wouldn't cooperate and his thoughts kept darting back to glasses of water and full bathtubs and swimming pools and blue, blue oceans.

Walk, Jase. Jase crunched over rock. *Just walk.* As long as he didn't jiggle too much, walking wasn't too bad. But, boy, what a dumb idea, coming out alone. His mom would have a cow if she found out. He didn't know how mothers, or people *had* cows and, truthfully, it was kind of a dumb expression. Probably Pahl would know where the slang came from. The Naxeran knew all these old slang expressions from all over the galaxy, but mainly Earth. Things like *have kittens*, or *stiff as Herbert*, or *he's not operating on all thrusters. Have a cow.*

Thinking about Pahl made him feel bad. Jase had snuck away without telling his friend anything. In fact, he'd avoided the Naxeran all day, since the breakfast they'd had with his own dad and Pahl's uncle. (Su Chen-Mai never ate with them, and that was fine with Jase.) Pahl's uncle and his father talked about their work but in ways that puzzled Jase, as if there was more behind every word they said. He knew that if he concentrated very hard, he'd figure it out. Once, he'd tried: chewing his food, emptying his mind. A meditation trick his dad taught him, something Jase had used in school when he was nervous about a test. Only lately, before they'd come to this place, Jase discovered that instead of his mind getting empty and blank, like a bank of endless white clouds stretched across the sky, he saw pictures. Fragments of pictures, really: colors, a sensation of movement. Nothing he could really describe. And he heard words, only garbled like the way the voices of his parents had been when he'd been small and they had argued.

So he'd tried it that morning at breakfast—to see if he could get at the words bubbling beneath the stream of his dad's conversation. He'd caught something. A picture, very coherent, of a big room made of red stone and a blue sky (*a blue sky in a stone room?*) but then his dad had given him a strange look, as if he knew. Instantly, Jase had clamped down, focusing again on the tart taste of his Maltaran orange juice.

Through it all, Pahl had eaten and chattered about nothing in particular. Jase hadn't told him about what he'd seen in his dad's mind. (If that *was* his dad's mind he touched. Jase wasn't sure.) Pahl was okay, except there was something scary about him. Like there was a yawning black hole and that was Pahl and there was nothing in the hole: no light, and no escape either. (Like when the ship had slid into orbit around the planet, and Jase almost got sucked inside Pahl.)

Not just sucked inside. Jase trudged, swinging the flashlight in a listless, mechanical, to-and-fro arc. Pahl had reached out . . . and *grabbed* his mind, dug in with thought-claws, and then Pahl had hung on, pulling him down into that horrible black nothing in the center of his soul, and Jase had been so scared, he thought he'd just managed to save himself . . .

Jase's left foot came down on a fall of loose scree, and suddenly, Jase was slipping, sliding. His hands flew up; his flashlight spun away. Reeling, Jase lurched right, made a wild grab at a boulder. He missed.

Jase gave a ragged cry. His helmet banged against a boulder and sent him pitching sideways. He hit the ground, his left shoulder crashing into solid rock and Jase screamed. He flipped, cartwheeled head over heels, like an acrobat who's mistimed his roll. His back slammed against the mountain, hard enough to knock the wind from his lungs, and then he was glissading, feet first, out-of-control, skittering down the rocky chute, hurtling down the mountain. Somehow, he rolled right, and then he saw a huge boulder rush at his face. No, not his faceplate, not his faceplate! Screaming, Jase threw his hands up to protect his face, arms crossed, palms out.

That probably saved his life—or, at the very least, his faceplate didn't shatter. Jase felt a hard, bone-shattering jolt in his forearms and then a bolt of pain that rattled his helmet and shivered through his limbs. He felt his body jerk and then fold at his waist, and he came to a sudden stop.

For a moment, he couldn't do anything except focus on breathing. He gulped air. He felt queasy, sick to his stomach. He closed his eyes, working hard not to vomit. Shaken, he clung to the rock, waiting for the dizziness to pass. As he did so, he realized he didn't have to worry about not peeing in his suit—not anymore.

Slowly, Jase pried open his eyes. He lay in an awkward twisted heap, his head down, his waist corkscrewed so that his left hip was pointing up and his right dug into the ground, his body literally folded around a hump of black rock. Maybe a meteor: The surface of the rock was scored with tiny pits. Lucky he hadn't broken his neck. He felt the throb of his blood galloping in his temples, and his brain felt bruised. He was afraid to move. His shoulder hurt; his left hip hurt; his right leg was killing him. Maybe he'd broken something.

He planted his palms against the large boulder and pushed. The movement sent a lightning flash of pain sizzling down his spine. He grimaced, moaned, but kept the pressure up until his body rolled and he lay flat on his back.

It was then that he saw it: to his left. A flash of white. Something moving.

Jase froze. Every muscle went rigid with fear. Sliding his

eyes left, he made out rivulets of small rocks pattering soundlessly along the ground to pool along his left side, like water backing up on the opposite side of a dam.

Someone was coming. Some*thing*. Ghosts, ghosts, those white ghosts! The hairs along the back of his neck stiffened with alarm. Cold sweat glazed his face, his chest, the undersides of his arms. *Have to get away, have to!* But he couldn't move.

Slowly, not wanting to look but knowing he had to, Jase turned his head and looked back up the mountain. He almost cried aloud in relief.

A suited figure was picking its way down the slope.

Environmental suit—Jase watched as the figure bobbed around the rocks—*that's an environmental suit.*

In another moment, Pahl dropped to his knees by Jase's side. Jase saw Pahl's lips moving beneath his frills, but Jase couldn't hear a thing. His comm unit—Jase reached his right hand up and fumbled at his suit for the control—he hadn't activated his comm unit.

He caught Pahl in mid-sentence. ". . . *you hurt?*"

"I'm okay," said Jase, not really knowing if this were true but just so grateful not to be alone, he would have said anything. His shoulder still throbbed, and the back of his head hurt. "That is, I think I'm okay. I don't know. I slipped."

Then he had an awful thought. "What about my suit? Can you see my suit?"

"It looks okay. All your indicators are green. Can you sit up?"

Jase started to nod but stopped as a wave of vertigo left him nauseated. "A little dizzy," Jase said, swallowing back something that tasted sour. He made a face, closed his eyes, and waited for the blackness before his eyes to stop spinning. "I hit my head."

"Did you black out?"

"No. That is, I don't think so." What he didn't tell Pahl

was that he was feeling a little heavy and stupid, the way he did right before he went to sleep. Somehow he knew that was a bad thing because that meant that maybe he had a concussion.

Forcing his eyes open, Jase saw that Pahl's face was creased with concern. "I'll be okay."

Pahl looked doubtful. "You don't look very good."

"I'll be okay," Jase repeated, as if saying it again made it true. "Help me sit up."

Hooking his right arm under Jase's left, Pahl eased his friend upright. Jase winced as the muscles along his spine complained. Pahl steadied Jase as Jase slumped forward, waiting for something bad to happen. When he didn't vomit or pass out, he gave Pahl a weak smile.

"So far so good," he said. "Let's see if I can stand."

The first time he tried to push to his feet, Jase nearly fell. Pahl took most of his weight, and Jase clung to Pahl for support. After a few minutes, Jase felt steady enough to let go. He braced himself against the large boulder he'd collided with and watched as Pahl sidestepped down a short distance to retrieve Jase's flashlight. Jase's head still hurt, and he was reasonably sure he'd had a tremendous bruise on his right shoulder. But he didn't think he'd broken anything, and he wasn't feeling as sick.

"We should go back," he said as Pahl trudged back up the hill, flashlight in hand. Jase had plenty of air but enough adventure for one day.

Pahl nodded then frowned. Pivoting on his heel, he looked down the mountain. Jase saw his friend's gaze flitting across the rock field below. "What is it?"

"I don't know. Something here, though. Like," Pahl's head cocked to one side, as if listening to something very faint, "old voices. You know? Like when there's a big room and it echoes for a long time." Pahl's ice-blue eyes zeroed in on Jase. "You know what I'm talking about."

For a brief instant, Jase had the impulse to lie, to deny the ghosts he sensed hovering in the shadows of this dead planet. Then he thought again about what had happened between them on the shuttle and, instead, he nodded. "I don't really hear them all the time either. They come and go like waves."

Jase wondered why his dad had never mentioned these voices. Then he had an odd thought. Maybe his dad couldn't hear them. Yes, but then why could *he?* He was only half-Betazoid. He wasn't a telepath.

"Can you hear what they're saying? I don't understand them."

"No." Pahl's eyebrows crinkled to a point above the bridge of his nose, and his frills shivered with consternation. "It's like being in a big room with a lot of people all talking at once. But it's stronger here. Actually," Pahl pointed to a mound of boulders forty meters down the mountain and to the right, "right there. I'm going to take a look. You want to come?"

All his common sense told him to stay put, to backtrack his way up the mountain and then down the ruined pass and back to the biosphere. Instead, Jase said, "Sure."

They didn't speak as they made their way down. Jase's head felt mushy, and he had to work hard at the simple act of walking. But he felt that the thought-claws were stronger, too. Ten minutes later, they stood alongside the tumble of nonspecific brown and rust-colored boulders. Jase studied them then looked back up the mountain.

"Up there." Jase pointed at a ragged fringe of overhanging rock. "Landslide." Then he squinted. "Hey, you see that? Two meters up, to the left. That gap."

"It's a hole, like an opening. Cave, maybe." Pahl glanced at Jase. "Let's go."

The boys clambered up the hill, Pahl leading the way. As soon as they were level with the gap, Jase immediately realized that what they'd seen was not a depression, or a hollow caused by rocks falling together, or a true cave. The opening was arched, like a passage in the side of the mountain. Jase edged closer. The opening couldn't be natural.

As if reading his thoughts, Pahl ran his gloved fingers over the rock. "Machine cut. I feel ridges. You wouldn't get that with a phaser."

"But what's weird is that the door is *here*. Usually, a door is something you see from the outside. I mean, if this part of the mountain hadn't sheared away, how would you know it was here?"

"Maybe it was blocked off and you had to know what to look for. Or there might have been an outer door, only it got knocked away."

Jase couldn't see beyond the opening. Then he remembered his flashlight and flicked it on. The blue-white beam speared the inky hollow, and Jase swept the light over the interior of the cave. He could see now that a tunnel led down into the mountain.

"Can you see the end?" asked Pahl.

"No." Taking a few cautious steps forward, Jase angled his light along the walls. He saw then *had* the sense that after three or four meters, the tunnel angled down and curved right. "It feels deep. You know what this reminds me of? Earth. Ancient Egypt. The tombs they used to build for the pharaohs. My dad took me to see them once, about a year ago. A place called the Valley of the Kings."

"Valley of the Kings?"

"Yeah. The Valley of the Kings is a *wadi*, a valley surrounded by high mountains. The mountains have a lot of limestone in them, and that's good because limestone makes for good walls and you can draw on it. The tombs had all these religious pictures and texts on the walls. The entrances," Jase angled his flashlight back to the opening, "they looked just like this one, except they were rectangles, not arches. There was the opening, the entryway into the tomb and then this long shaft."

Jase turned again, watching as the beam from his flashlight was swallowed by darkness, like water disappearing down a pipe. "Sometimes the shafts were ramps, and sometimes there were stairs. The older tombs were really steep and then by the later dynasties, the tunnels got more level. This one looks like it goes down."

"How far?"

"No way of knowing without a tricorder. I mean, if this were Earth, it could be anywhere from fifteen to thirty meters long, and that would just be the first corridor. There's usually more than one, and lots of rooms. I remember that a couple of them had gates and pits and booby traps. They were worried about grave robbers and stuff."

"Then we have to come back," said Pahl. "We have to get tricorders and lights and some extra air packs for our suits so we can come back."

"We don't even know what this is. Maybe it's a big nothing. Or maybe it's an old mineshaft," Jase said, not believing himself for one second.

"We won't know until we explore it." Pahl looked past Jase into the darkness ahead. "It's not a mine. You know that. We were led here. We're *supposed* to be here. Can't you feel it?"

"No," Jase lied. "I just came over the pass. I didn't know there was anything here. It's a coincidence."

Pahl's eyes clouded, and Jase thought that his friend might argue. But Pahl just shrugged. "If that makes you feel better. But I'm coming back."

Jase knew that he would come back, too. But he said only, "Come on. We need to get back to the biosphere before my dad does."

Pahl didn't protest. Jase led the way home, retracing his steps up the steep sides of the mountain and then down into the valley. They didn't speak along the way. From a ridge that ran along the top of the mountains, Jase swept his eyes over the valley floor until he picked out the silver dome of the biosphere. His gaze drifted right, past the ship that squatted on its triangular pad, to the space where his dad usually left their smaller landskimmer. The space was empty. Checking his chronometer, Jase heaved an internal sigh of relief. If his dad and the others stuck to their routine, Jase and Pahl had three hours to spare.

An hour later when they were about a kilometer away and Jase could pick out the triangle of yellow entry lights around the airlock (Jase having discovered that Cardassians liked triangles and rhomboids and diamonds) Pahl said, "We shouldn't tell them."

"No," said Jase.

"And you need to be careful what you think around your father."

Jase stopped and turned back. "My dad wouldn't do that. He respects my privacy. He said one of the most important things about being a telepath is to knock."

"Still. You might," Pahl searched for the word, "leak. I've heard that. Sometimes even when people try very hard not to have their thoughts show, they do, especially if their thoughts are too big for their minds. You know?"

Jase turned away without replying. Pahl was right. Jase knew his dad could pick up on stray thoughts. Gray, he'd have to be gray around his dad.

Jase took a few more steps then thought of something. "Pahl, how did you find me?"

Pahl seemed genuinely perplexed. "I saw you."

But Jase was shaking his head. "You couldn't have. I remember. I looked back up the mountain right before it happened, and there was no one there."

"Well then, I guess I knew you were in trouble because I heard you scream."

Jase thought back to that split second when he knew he would fall. His shrill scream. The silent rocks skittering down the mountain. But it was only after they'd ducked into the biosphere's airlock and were peeling out of their suits—when Jase tugged off his helmet—that Jase knew what was wrong.

I heard you scream. No. Jase stared at his helmet. Pahl couldn't have heard him.

On the mountain, on his back. Staring into Pahl's face. Pahl's lips, moving, but no sound: There had been *no sound*—because Jase's comm unit had been switched *off*.

"Jase?" Pahl was beside him, his suit pooling around his hips. "You okay?"

Your thoughts. You could leak.

"I'm fine." Hooking his helmet onto its peg, Jase thumbed down the locks to hold it in place. "I'm fine. It's nothing, Pahl. It's okay."

And this time he even managed a smile.

Chapter 22

"Look, facts are facts," Castillo said, around mashed potato. (The crew's mess chef was on an Old Earth kick again. Tonight's menu was meat loaf with a tomato-basil glaze, fluffy mashed potatoes swimming in melted butter, green beans with slivered almonds, fresh-baked apple-walnut pie, and strong hot coffee boiled with chicory and finished with a dash of cinnamon, New Orleans-style.)

"Facts?" asked Thule G'Dok Glemoor, his forkful of salad halfway to his mouth. The tactical officer sat at Castillo's left elbow. "What facts? We have only Starfleet Intelligence's word for anything."

Swallowing, Castillo used the side of his fork to chop off another juicy, steaming hunk of meat loaf, spear it, and then cram the bite into his mouth. "If Starfleet Intelligence says they found stuff," he said, his voice muffled by meat loaf, "they found stuff, pure and simple. Anyway, captain's got no choice. They want him; she's got to hand him over, no two ways about it."

"You're suggesting that we simply take their word?"

"You think they make these things up? Not a chance. Besides . . ." Cheeks bulging, Castillo shrugged, swallowed. Hiccupped and then followed that with a gulp of ice water. He placed the flat of his hand against his chest, made a face as whatever he hadn't chewed well went down. "Besides, from what I heard, they've been watching the commander for quite a while, after that Ryn thing . . . you know," he finished, vaguely.

Glemoor's frills twitched as he chewed his lettuce with a contemplative air. "He was cleared. Now, all of a sudden, he isn't. Wasn't." He shook his head, the muscles of his jaw working under his gleaming ebony skin. "I don't understand that."

Focused on cleaning his plate of every last molecule of mashed potato, Castillo grunted. "Boy, I do."

"Oh?" asked Bat-Levi. She sat opposite Glemoor and next to Darco Bulast, who was on her left. After her duty shift was up, she'd thought about skipping dinner and simply grabbing something from a replicator to take back to her quarters. But when she'd clumped her way into the mess, she spied a cluster of crewmen around Castillo, Glemoor, and Anjad Kodell, the ship's Trill engineer. Characteristically, Darco Bulast was also there at his usual spot: diagonally across from and to Castillo's right. If there was one crewmember who enjoyed the mess chef's food more than Castillo, it was the garrulous Atrean; no one could remember the last time he'd missed a meal.

Seeing them all together had started her heart thumping with panic and she'd almost wheeled around and stumped out, but Glemoor called her over. She couldn't refuse, gracefully, and then she thought about Tyvan keeping tabs on her and his report—his damn report—and decided that, hell, she'd show *him*. Hanging onto her guilt: What a load of crap. So, plastering a smile on her face and feeling her scar pull tight as the skin of a drum, she'd come over with her tray, wincing internally at how loud her joints sounded. She just *had* to get them adjusted.

If the others noticed her servos' clatter, they didn't comment, and despite her anxiety, she appreciated Glemoor's gesture. Of all the bridge crew, she felt most at ease with Glemoor and Bulast, whom everyone liked for his cheery good humor. After a few moments, though, Bat-Levi knew something was wrong with Bulast. Rather than join in on the conversation—something Bulast did with as much enthusiasm as he ate—the Atrean slumped over his plate, his attention fixed on his food. She wished she had the courage to nudge him and ask what was wrong but didn't want to pry. She decided that even Bulast could have a bad day.

A bar. Bat-Levi held a cup of steaming coffee in her right hand, the one with fingernails. Next time Command asked for suggestions, she was going to suggest a bar. A *hell of a lot easier to socialize with a drink in your hand.*

Your good *hand.* Her lips turned down in a self-deprecating grimace. Her left hand, the one without nails, she kept tucked down in her lap, out of sight. Her dexterity was fine, but she was still self-conscious, eating in front of other people. Even after all this time.

"And what do you understand?" she asked Castillo.

Castillo's fork clicked against porcelain as he scraped up tomato sauce and mashed potato. "Look, read your history books. This is the way all intelligence agencies operate. They work behind the scenes, gather bits and pieces of the puzzle. Then when they think they've got enough, bam!" He pushed his fork into his mouth and then slid it out, clean. "Done deal by the time they shuttle into town."

Bat-Levi frowned. "Are you saying you mistrusted Commander Halak all along? I don't think that's being particularly fair."

Glemoor spoke up. "Halak had . . . how do you say? A tough row to hoe, yes. Captain Garrett and Nigel Holmes worked together well. They just . . . oh, what is that saying? Commander, it's a sound, meant to signify that two people mesh."

"Click," said Bat-Levi, figuring the Naxeran wouldn't appreciate the irony about asking *her*.

"Yes, thank you." He turned back to Castillo. "I don't think the captain's ever really forgiven herself for what happened to Nigel. You could see it, the way she worked with Halak. Parrying at an arm's length," said Glemoor, whose tactical sense and fondness for fencing made him a formidable opponent. He and the captain fenced often, though she favored saber. "She was cautious. We all were."

Bat-Levi hiked her shoulders. "Holmes was before my time, and Halak's always treated me well. But that doesn't mean Halak has to be everybody's best friend."

Tossing his fork on his plate with a clatter, Castillo sat back and heaved a contented sigh. "Look, I'm not saying that. Of course, everyone's entitled to his privacy. On a ship, you know, you got to have that, what with everybody packed in here together. But you have to admit he hasn't been the easiest kind of guy to get to know."

Bat-Levi replaced her cup very carefully, not because she was afraid of spilling but she wanted to frame her words well. "Ani seemed to find him worth caring about."

Castillo's eyes shuttered, and Bat-Levi saw the color edge over the ensign's collar. Even Bulast shot her a quick glance and frowned. Her heart sank. God, she was an idiot. She'd heard the scuttlebutt about Castillo and Batra, and the interesting triangle Halak's arrival had made. Bat-Levi wanted to kick herself. Just like her to put her foot in her mouth. She compressed her lips into a single thin line. What was she thinking? Better to just do her job and leave the social commentary to somebody else, someone polished, like Glemoor.

"Castillo," she began.

"It's okay." Castillo held up a hand. He cleared his throat and gave her a tight smile that did not show his teeth. "Point taken. It's just, well, he sure as hell picked a funny way of showing he cared, didn't he? About Ani, I mean."

"He couldn't have known what would happen."

Castillo's chin jutted. "Why not? Farius Prime's a rough place."

"The way I heard it, she just showed up," Bat-Levi said, even as her mind screamed at her to be quiet. What was she thinking? "He couldn't control that. Ani was a grown woman, an officer. You can't treat every situation like the military."

"Maybe. But if it had been me?" Castillo snapped his fingers then hooked a thumb over his shoulder. "Off the planet, like that. Ten seconds flat. You protect the people you love, period."

A painful lump swelled in Bat-Levi's throat. *Oh, Joshua.* "That's not always possible, Castillo. No matter how hard you try, sometimes you have to let the people you love take their own risks. You can't control everything, even when you want to. It's like having children."

(Where that came from, she had no idea. She knew as much about raising kids as she did about herding Catabrian warthogs.)

"Eventually, you have to step aside and let kids make mistakes. You just hope that you've taught them well enough they don't do anything terribly foolish, or dangerous. Even then," she gestured with her bad hand without realizing it, "there's nothing you can do but pray for the best."

"Wrong," said Castillo, stubbornly. "No. Absolutely not. We're not talking kids. We're talking relationship. Totally different. The woman I love? Won't happen. Officer, no officer; rank, no rank: The minute I think she's in danger, she's out."

"I think you underestimate most women."

"This isn't about women."

"Then what?" Bat-Levi persisted, wondering why she was going after Castillo. He was young, brash and, yes, a tad chauvinistic. He reminded her of Joshua.

She could almost hear Tyvan's voice: *Maybe that's why you're fighting to change his mind.*

Go away, Tyvan. She clamped down on the psychiatrist's voice. *Just you go away.*

Castillo looked exasperated. "Look, this isn't about what women can, or can't do. I'd expect someone I care about to do the same for me."

"But would you do what she said?"

"Depends."

"But don't you see," Glemoor interrupted, "that's what Bat-Levi is saying. You have a, what you call it, double standard."

Bat-Levi turned to the Naxeran, almost grateful that he'd intervened and yet a little angry, too. She was doing just fine on her own, thanks. *Relax. He's just trying to help. That's what friends do.* Tyvan's thoughts? Her own? Bat-Levi couldn't tell, and that made her mad. That Tyvan was like an infection.

"From what I heard, Batra protected Halak as much as Halak tried to protect her," Glemoor continued. "Anyway, what went on between the two of them is both private, *and* past. There is nothing we can gain by, how do you call it? That game, played with a stuffed skin, players ran around hitting one another and tumbling to the ground. A most puzzling sport."

"Football," said Castillo. "You mean Monday morning quarterbacking."

"Exactly. Yes, thank you."

"Sure, I can agree with that." Castillo pushed his plate away with the flat of one thumb. His fork rattled against porcelain. "My original point was that we don't know Halak very well. We didn't know him then, and we don't know him now. And then we find out he's not who he said he was."

Glemoor stabbed at a slice of pear, nibbled at the port-wine colored flesh. "You are being naïve, Richard. What I don't know is whether your attitude is willful, or calculated to, how do you say it?" Glemoor stared off into space a moment then returned his golden-yellow gaze to Castillo. "Pull my chain?"

"Glemoor, you don't believe SI?" asked Bat-Levi. Privately, she thought the image of the Naxeran eating greens and fruit almost comical. With his long frills and golden eyes, Glemoor looked a little bit like a panther.

"I don't know enough to believe or disbelieve. I *do* know that this would not be the first time an intelligence agency fabricated data to support a hypothesis they were wedded to. Earth history is rife with such examples, from your J. Edgar Hoover to Mars governor Benton Hubbard. And this is not relegated to Earth, you understand. Naxeran history, too—any number of individuals in my own G'Dok clan. Our society is quite stratified. You'd say the Haves, those with less but who still have power, and then the Have-Nots. The G'Dok, the Haves," Glemoor held his hands as if balancing melons, "and the Leahru, those with less, and then at the very, very bottom, off the scale, the Efram. Either you are born to privilege, or you are not, or you are less than someone with none."

"A caste system," said Bat-Levi, who didn't know much about Naxera.

Glemoor nodded, using the knuckles of his right hand to smooth down his frills the way a fastidious man grooms a moustache after taking a sip of tea. Again, Bat-Levi was reminded, involuntarily, of a panther—or a very large, very black cat. "It is that simple, and not simple at all. The Haves, in any society, want to maintain their position. This may include manipulation, or invention."

Castillo gave a fake laugh. "You saying SI's making this up?"

Glemoor's ebony brow creased in a frown. "No, no, not at all. I just find the timing interesting. Things are happening too quickly, no? Usually, things that are quite complex go slowly, one step by one step."

"You mean, a step at a time," Bat-Levi offered.

Glemoor blinked. "I believe I said that. Anyway, my point: If they knew all this before, why not apprehend Halak while he was on Farius Prime, or before? And they're finding computer records that just happen to corroborate their theories they could not have uncovered before? Everything falls into place so neatly, so quickly? You are telling me that no one looked through his private files before now?"

"Maybe they were waiting to see who his contact was. Or maybe they just didn't put two and two together," said Castillo.

Glemoor's frills shivered with surprise. "They implicated Commander Halak in murder but merely bided their time, waiting to gather evidence, yet placing that same commander in a position where, potentially, more deaths would follow? How does that strike you as a strategy?"

"I'm sure *I* don't know," said Castillo. He scooped his hair back in a short, irritated gesture. "You're the tactician, you tell me."

"Well, and I *will* tell you. It makes no sense, tactically or otherwise. You do not leave an enemy behind the front lines and hope you catch him in the act."

"What about when there are spies whom you know are spies? You know, diplomats, stuff like that?"

"The enemy you know," said Glemoor, his long slender fingers inscribing an imaginary box in the air, "you hem them in, that is the expression, correct? You give them the illusion of freedom while keeping a close watch. What does not follow is to let the enemy inflict more damage before exposing, or eliminating him."

Castillo opened his mouth to reply, but it was the Trill, Anjad Kodell, who spoke first. "That's a very important point, Glemoor."

All eyes swiveled to the chief engineer. Bat-Levi saw that most registered surprise. If Halak had been seen as secretive, Kodell was taciturn, socializing with no one. Worse than she was. At least, she made an effort. It helped that her duties now—as acting first officer—left her no choice. On the other hand, Tyvan was forcing the issue. She wondered if Kodell was required to report to Tyvan. Well, she reasoned, they all were, or would be at some point. That was the psychiatrist's job, after all: doing a mental exam, like a physical only with talk. And what did Kodell talk about? Bat-Levi's eyes strayed over the chief engineer's face. Kodell had chocolate-brown spots sprinkled on the skin of both his temples and down either side of his neck before dipping beneath his collar. Idly, she wondered if the spots continued over his chest, or along his back, and if so, just how far they went. Kodell was thin, though not lanky like Tyvan, or graceful like Glemoor who moved with the ease of the panther he resembled. No, Kodell's face had a chiseled, hollowed look, as if he'd lost a lot of weight and never properly filled out again. His hair was the color of ripened wheat, light and brown. He was a carefully neutral man, yet Bat-Levi saw that his dark brown eyes were closed somehow, as if he sheltered some inner pain.

"What point was that?" she asked.

Kodell regarded her with a mild expression. "Why didn't Starfleet Intelligence act sooner? Maybe their findings have no veracity. But just like you have to move to contain your enemy, people act to contain themselves, the things inside that they perceive to be the enemies they've collected over time."

Castillo blinked. "I don't get your point."

"We all have secrets. There are many things people do when they're desperate, things they do that feel right at the time but which they regret later. Just because something is partly true doesn't mean it is the whole truth. Maybe there are some things about his past Halak felt he couldn't share, or didn't want to."

"Well, that's what I'm *saying*," said Castillo. "He was hiding stuff."

Kodell looked toward Bat-Levi, then back at Castillo, and his lips moved in a small, and she thought, sad, smile. "And so do you, I'm sure. Everyone has secrets. They may have nothing to do with right or wrong, legal, illegal. Maybe, for Halak, the price of letting anyone peek into his past was, simply, too great. But," said Kodell, his gaze now wandering over everyone else, "we're still dancing around the real issue, right? If Starfleet Intelligence is right, Halak's a murderer. I don't think anyone's said anything about that. But why? Why won't we discuss murder?"

Murder: The word hung in the air like a bad odor. Castillo dropped his eyes. Glemoor gave a slow, solemn nod. Bulast, who had finished his food, sat listening, with his elbows propped and fleshy chin cupped in his palms.

Bat-Levi spoke first. "Yes, murder changes everything, doesn't it?"

"Of course," said Kodell. "Murder means passion. Sure, you can kill. We're all trained killers, right? Sometimes our duty is synonymous with death—a last resort, usually, but still there. But murder is different. When there's murder, there's passion."

"And so the question is," said Bat-Levi, "that if Halak's a murderer—if he *did* kill two crewmen—why?"

"There is no *if*," said Glemoor. "We know. He killed that Bolian."

"No," said Kodell. "You see? Even you use the euphemism. He *murdered* the Bolian. The Bolian murdered Batra, and Halak murdered him. But that murder we forgive and even understand."

Castillo cleared his throat. "Look, this hasn't got a thing to do with emotion. What Halak did with the *Barker* crew was cold and calculated and pretty damned ruthless. The way I see it, Halak was afraid he'd be exposed. That's what SI said. They know the facts, so that says something, right?" He looked over at Bulast who was staring at spot on the table just in front of his plate. "Right?"

At Bat-Levi's left elbow, Bulast inhaled and blinked, as if his mind had been a million kilometers away. "I don't know that I have an opinion," he said.

That was a first. Bat-Levi turned in surprise. Bulast always had something to say. Come to think of it, this was the first complete sentence he'd uttered for the entire meal.

"An opinion on Halak?" she prodded. "Or SI?"

Bulast spread his hands in a helpless gesture. "On anything. I don't know about the rest of you, but this is probably the worst thing I can ever remember happening on any ship I've served on. Oh, sure, people *do* shoot at us, and they think they have good reasons: territorial disputes, self-defense. But I can't get past the fact that one of our friends is dead, and another person, a man I might not think of as my closest friend but our XO, might be nothing more than a cold-blooded killer. And none of us caught it. Not the captain, not anyone."

Kodell said, "Bulast, who can know what's true, what we should have caught and didn't? Maybe there was *nothing* to catch. All we have is SI's word. That's it."

"And evidence," said Castillo.

"Yes, with SI providing it all. But I'm not talking about that." Clearly frustrated, Kodell clamped his lips together. "I guess I'm just not making myself clear. Isn't it funny that each of us can *understand* the impulse to kill for revenge or self-defense, but that none of us is willing, for one second, to put ourselves in the shoes of someone who feels cornered, or that he has nothing to lose? Maybe Halak *did* kill those two crewmen. I, for one, don't know. But I am willing to try to put myself in his place and try to understand why his reasons felt like good ones."

"That's because murder's murder," said Castillo.

"No," said Bat-Levi. Instinctively, she understood what Kodell was saying. "Sometimes you kill because you don't have a choice. Or because you don't *think* there's a choice—a no-win scenario. You think you're in the classic *Kobayashi Maru*. But there's always a choice. It's simply that you don't like the choices you have."

Kodell stared at her for a long moment. Then he nodded. "Precisely."

After a few moments, Kodell excused himself. Bat-Levi and Glemoor left a short while later. Castillo lingered a moment with Bulast who sat, chin in hands.

"Hell." Castillo blew out. "You ever hear such crap? Pretty black and white, you ask me."

Bulast's shoulders hunched, fell. "I can understand the point."

"Something wrong?"

"Just thinking."

"About?"

"What Kodell said," the Atrean's eyes slid toward Castillo, "about secrets."

Castillo's lips moved in a quizzical smile. "Secrets?"

"Yes. He's right. Everyone's got secrets." Bulast paused then added, "Even you, Richard."

Castillo's lips parted, and he felt a wave of cold dread flood his chest. *Oh, no.* "Me? What are you talking about, Darco?"

"You know exactly what I'm talking about . . . no," said the Atrean as Castillo opened his mouth. "Don't say it. Don't say anything."

Bulast stood then and slid his tray, the plastic loudly

scouring the tabletop. "I know your secret, Richard. I know, *exactly*, what you did with Ani."

He shouldn't have talked so much. What had gotten into him? Kodell hurried along what seemed to be the interminably long corridor curling from the mess hall to the turbolift. The corridor was more crowded than usual, or so it seemed to Kodell, who spent most of his time in Jefferies tubes, fussing with the warp core, or doing systems' checks in engineering. He preferred machines. Machines didn't talk back. (All right, the computer did, but it never started a conversation. Well, a warning, maybe. That didn't count.) But he *had* talked. What was more, he'd actually enjoyed it.

This won't do. Sweat crawled down his back. *This simply won't do.*

He was a Trill, with secrets. And was it simply that fact alone that accounted for his reluctance to mingle? True, the Trill had *their* secrets, in more ways than one. A lucky point-one-percent of the population carried a secret in their bodies. But then there was everybody else, and then there were Trill like him.

It's eating you up, Anjad. Your jealousy, your hurt, and you say you love me, but I know the truth, I know you really want me dead.

Th'leila, how can you say that? I love you.

No, Anjad. You don't know what you love more: me, or what's inside . . .

No. Kodell forced these thoughts back into the black box in his mind where he kept them. *Stop this.* He wouldn't think about Th'leila, and he wouldn't think about Bok, nor would he think of Th'leila Bok: as they were, together, closer than lovers, and how much he loved and hated them both because Th'leila had been lucky, and he had not, and how Bok—Kodell's heart twisted with grief and longing—how Bok had been his, *his* for a brief, precious moment, joining in the conductance fluid medium of the tank, their thoughts entwining, and Bok had been *his* symbiont, before there ever was a Th'leila.

Th'leila's body, her skin slicked with sweat from their love-making, the long golden river of her hair curling around her breasts, and the way she cried out, arching, reaching for him. "Love me, Anjad, show me how you love me . . ."

Just ahead, Kodell spied three enlisted straddling the entire width of the corridor. Kodell dodged left while clearing his throat, loudly. The enlisted on the far left jumped as if he'd been shot with a phaser. He flinched aside, crowding his two companions who bunched to the right, along the bulkhead.

"Sorry, sir. I didn't see . . ."

"Fine, fine." Kodell just waved a hand and shot past. "Carry on."

Bat-Levi. Kodell strode purposefully for the turbolift. Bat-Levi had gotten him started. But she didn't look anything like Th'leila Bok, a woman with hair as golden as liquid sunlight and deep brown eyes and lips so full he never *could* resist catching the lower one between his teeth when they kissed. So what was it? Why now? Kodell clenched his fists, tight, tight. Why was he plagued by thoughts of Th'leila—and Bok—*now?*

Kodell saw a gaggle of crewmen waiting at the turbolift and suppressed an urge to curse. *Take a Jefferies, get some exercise.* Cooped up in a ship all day, crawling around the Jefferies tubes was a relief. Maybe a little like one of those blind, naked Draken mole rats, but still a relief.

Then he heard a woman calling his name, and his stomach did a little leap of dismay. For one brief instant, petty as the impulse was, Kodell debated. He could pretend he hadn't heard then dart right down the near corridor, jog to a Jefferies tube that would take him all the way to Deck 22, and then jump on a turbolift there.

Ahead, he saw a crewman turn his head and then look at

Kodell, who'd hesitated one millisecond too long. "I think she's calling you, sir," the crewman said, helpfully.

"Yes," said Kodell, knowing he couldn't avoid Bat-Levi now. He gave the crewman a tight smile. "Thank you so much, crewman."

He turned, and watched as Bat-Levi approached. He noticed, as if for the first time, that she was fairly skilled in compensating for her prostheses. Her movements weren't clumsy, though she lurched a little to the left. Probably the right knee joint needed readjusting; nothing five minutes with a tefloflex spanner wouldn't solve. And she had to do something about the noise. Those servos sounded like the high-pitched chirping of a flock of Meprean grackles. Strange she hadn't upgraded. Most people cared about those things. On the other hand—his eyes took in her scar, the way her once-pretty face twisted to one side, that streak of white skittering through her black hair like an errant lightening bolt—Darya Bat-Levi clearly wasn't most people.

"Commander," he said as she came to stand before him. Kodell put his hands behind his back, as if coming to attention but really giving himself a warning not to get too comfortable. He noticed then that when she stood, she kept her left hand—the artificial one—tucked, out of sight, at the small of her back.

"Commander," she said, her tone betraying some surprise at the use of her rank. She gave a tentative smile, and he saw how the right side of her mouth was so tight, smiling pulled her lip down in a grimace. He thought it must be painful.

"I just . . . you left so quickly, I didn't have a chance to tell you." She seemed to flounder for what she wanted to say, and he let her. "I just wanted to let you know that I liked what you said. I don't remember ever hearing you talk so much before and . . . sorry, that didn't come out right."

"No," said Kodell, her obvious chagrin making him warm

to her despite his internal admonitions. "But, if I were insecure, I'd wonder if you were keeping score."

"Well, it's just that I wanted to say that I understand."

Kodell kept his voice neutral. "Understand what?"

"What you said. About passion, and things like that."

"I was just talking." Kodell lifted one shoulder, an off-handed gesture. It was cruel of him; he knew that right away because he saw her surprise, and the way color flooded her cheeks. The scar on her face was so red it looked boiled.

"Oh," she said, her voice small, embarrassed. "I'm sorry. I guess I thought . . . well, in the mess, you . . ." She broke off then made a move to back away. "I just thought. . . ."

Instantly, he was ashamed. There was something touching about her, and she was reaching out, making an effort, and he knew, instinctively, that she did this only rarely. Why hurt her?

Because you're frightened. Not Th'leila's voice this time, but the very special voice that was no voice at all but the thoughts of the symbiont Bok resonating in his soul. *Because she's wounded, she's incomplete, and you know precisely how that feels, but she's brave, and you're a coward.*

"No, please," he said, almost blurting it out. "I'm sorry. That wasn't fair. Please, finish what you were saying."

He saw her indecision. Then she said, "Oh, hell."

"Pardon?"

She shook her head, exhaled a short false laugh. "I never was very good at this."

"Good at what?"

"This," she waved her right hand in the space between them, "small talk. Breaking the ice. I'm horrible, always have been. I do better if I cut to the chase."

"Cut to the . . . ?"

"Yes, it means get to the point. It's an Earth saying, back from the days when they made films."

"Films."

"Yes, like holos, only they were pictures on celluloid, and

the way to keep an audience's attention was to cut from a scene that was all talk to one that was all action, and . . ." At the expression on his face, she laughed outright.

This pleased him. "Something's funny."

Her black eyes sparkled. "You sound like Glemoor. You know, the way he always wants people to explain their idioms."

"I've noticed that. You think he doesn't understand?"

Bat-Levi cocked her head to one side. "No, he knows what he's doing. Remember, he's tactical. I've noticed he always does it when things are really delicate. It's hard to explain, but I think it's a sophisticated kind of negotiation. Idioms imply a shared culture, and so when Glemoor asks someone like Castillo to explain, or for help, he's giving Castillo something. Validation, an advantage that really isn't one."

"So you think he appeals to ego."

"Right. It's a way of giving something to someone that doesn't cost you a thing."

"A good tactic," said Kodell, and they exchanged smiles. She was a head shorter, and the fact that he had to look down moved him, made him feel protective.

What is it about this woman? Aloud, he said, "Well, then, cut to the chase, Commander."

Her face grew serious, and they were so close he saw her eyes flick back and forth, searching his.

"Yes. I just wanted to say that I understand. Completely. What you said about someone being angry enough to want to kill, or feel that murder is the only way. I understand all about that. I understand about passion."

"And pain," said Kodell, and then wondered why he'd said that.

"And pain." She paused. "I think maybe you know about pain, too. Loss."

"And why is that?" He tried to keep his voice light, and didn't know if he succeeded. A high thin whine sounded in his ears, almost like an alarm.

"I just *know*. If that makes sense."

He was very still, though his mind was not. Uncanny, how did she know? For some reason, he was acutely aware of the way his heart thudded in his chest: almost as if his heart had stopped beating and just now remembered to come back to life.

Oh, Th'leila Bok, how much of my life have you stolen? How much did I let you steal?

He cleared his throat. "All this talk about emotion, we'll think you've spent too much time with our ship's psychiatrist." He'd meant it as a joke, but instantly he saw her embarrassment, and he knew he'd stumbled into something. "Commander Bat-Levi, I didn't mean . . ."

"It's okay," she said. She made a move to go. "Anyway, I should . . ."

"No, don't." He almost reached out a hand to stop her but restrained himself at the last instant. "I'm the one who should apologize. Not many people to talk to in engineering, just machines," he was aware that he was starting to babble but plunged on, "and, anyhow I'm out of practice, I made a bad joke. I'm sorry."

"It's okay," she said, her voice tight with mortification. "I forgot. It's a small ship and, of course, everyone must know."

Now he was confused. "Know? Know what?"

"Well, that," and just as quickly she stopped herself. Kodell knew at once he shouldn't pursue the matter. "Nothing. Oh, hell," she sighed, "I always put my foot in it."

"I know this idiom. On Trill, we say, *Uncork week-old fermented* klah." Kodell pulled his features into a comical grimace. "Very unpleasant."

Despite herself, Bat-Levi chucked. "Sounds gruesome."

"Smells. Yes. By the way, congratulations; I hear you're going to be our new first officer."

"Just acting. Until the captain decides what she wants to

do." Bat-Levi gave an inverted smile, something that seemed to come naturally. "I'm not sure it's the way I wanted to make XO, though. Not even sure I want to *be* first officer, but, sometimes, opportunity chooses *you*." She pulled herself up. "I should go; I didn't mean to keep you. But, maybe, we could, I don't know, catch a cup of coffee, or something? Sometime?"

Kodell hesitated for what seemed like a long time but was, really, a fraction of a second. "Yes. Coffee. I'd like that," and he meant it.

And then he did something that was, for him, totally out of character, almost insane. "Do you mind if I make a little suggestion?"

Coffee, and then offering to help with her servos—"*I couldn't help noticing that they need adjusting. Why don't you stop by engineering when you've got time?*"—like it was no big deal. Bat-Levi hummed as the turbolift shot up to Deck 12, and the doors sighed open. So, why did it *feel* like such a big deal?

Because it is, honey. It is.

Just you wait, Tyvan. Just you wait. She stumped toward her quarters. She couldn't wait to see the look on his face when she told him. She was even more surprised that the thought—her wanting to tell Tyvan *anything*—didn't make her angry. Not one bit.

Bat-Levi burst out laughing. And that felt good, too.

Chapter 23

Marta Batanides stopped speaking, and for a good ten seconds, the bridge was so quiet the staccato bleeps of the ship's systems cracked like pistol shots. Even Stern, who stood to the left of Garrett's command chair, was speechless.

Although Batanides had come through on audio, Garrett stood before her chair, hands clasped behind her back, her stance formal. "I want to lodge a formal protest."

"Certainly." Batanides's voice was just as formal. "I'll see that Admiral Stout is informed. Anything else?"

"You mean besides the fact that I don't want you taking Commander Halak off the ship without representation, and unaccompanied? That regulations *demand* a command-level inquiry with his captain in attendance? That I *protest* your authorizing the removal of one of *my* officers from *my* ship, yet you haven't filed a *single* charge?" Garrett shook her head even though Batanides couldn't see her. "No."

"Objections noted," said Batanides.

"What about Starfleet Command? My personal report to Admiral Stout?"

"Admiral Stout has authorized *me* to inform *you* that he is aware of your objections and they've been duly noted."

"And?"

"And nothing. Facts are facts, Captain. You are hereby ordered to remand Commander Halak to Lieutenant Burke. Your former first officer," Batanides paused as if to underscore Halak's status, "will not be *un*accompanied. Lieutenant Burke and a representative of the Vulcan V'Shar, certainly an impartial agency . . ."

"Logic isn't synonymous with impartiality."

Batanides talked over Garrett. "*Will* accompany him. If after a more formal inquiry, charges are brought, Commander Halak will be afforded representation."

"I want to be there," said Garrett, knowing her demand would fall on deaf ears. But for the same reason that she'd chosen to take the call on the bridge, she wanted her objections on record. No more cloak-and-dagger routine on *her* ship. "The regulations are clear, Commander. They *demand* the presence of Halak's commanding officer."

"Captain Garrett, those same regulations also stipulate that should said commanding officer's duties interfere, a formal statement will suffice. If it's any comfort, we've contacted *Barker* and Captain Connors is en route."

"No, I'm not comforted. Surely my testimony isn't irrelevant."

"No one's suggesting that. But we are reopening our investigation into the Ryn mission. *That* mission was and *is* none of your concern."

"Isn't Captain Connors likely to be a little prejudiced? You claim two of his crewmen were murdered."

"And you're *not* prejudiced? One of your officers is also dead."

Out of her left ear, Garrett heard Stern give a muffled curse. Swiveling on her hips, Garrett silenced the doctor with a look. Garrett faced forward again, staring at stars, talking to a woman she couldn't see. "That's not the point, and you know it."

"Captain Garrett." A little pause, as if Batanides were a disapproving schoolteacher. "Be reasonable. You have your orders. Further, Halak's shuttle is to be put under guard, and secured. The shuttle and its contents are evidence, and a team of SI agents will be dispatched to bring the shuttle back to Starfleet Headquarters for further study. As for the *Enterprise*, you are to proceed to the Draavid nebulae cluster."

"The work isn't exactly urgent. I don't expect a new star to pop into existence in the next two weeks. Surely that mission can wait," said Garrett. Privately, she was appalled. Mapping protostars was the sort of mission Command handed to junior crews—and green captains. Garrett was certain Burke had a hand in this, convincing Batanides to get them out of the way until SI's investigation was over. A trip to the Draavids would put them in a virtual communications blackout, and out of circulation, for two weeks.

"I think not," said Batanides. The woman had all the emotional reactivity of a Derellian seaslug. Garrett wondered if anything rattled the SI officer and decided, probably not. "Those are your orders, Captain Garrett. You should be receiving official confirmation any time now. Lieutenant Burke?"

Garrett heard the scrape of Burke's boots against the deck as she came to attention. "Ma'am?"

"When do you estimate arrival at Starfleet Headquarters?"

"If we leave within the next two hours—eight days, Commander."

"That's absurd," Garrett interrupted. "Sivek's warpshuttle can only make warp four. The trip will be unnecessarily long. We can cover the same distance in far less time and bring the shuttle to Headquarters without your having to send out a team. Frankly, I would think that you would be eager to . . ."

Batanides cut her off. "Thanks, but I wouldn't want to keep you from your next assignment. The time won't be wasted. We'll use it to completely decrypt the information Lieutenant Burke pulled from the shuttle log."

Garrett racked her brain for something else to say, some other avenue of protest, and could find none. She heard the unmistakable quaver of an incoming message, and looked over at Bulast, who was already turning in his seat.

"Admiral Stout's reply, Captain," he said, sotto voce. He scanned the message and read verbatim. *"Your protests noted and entered into the official record. Commander Halak to be remanded without further delay. Orders are to proceed to the Draavid nebulae cluster for astrometrical analysis.* Signed W. Stout, Admiral, Starfleet Command. Authentification code verified."

Garrett's brows met. "That's it? No other response to my inquiries?"

"No, Ma'am."

Batanides, again: "If there's nothing else, Captain?"

"Yes. I want to be informed when Commander Halak arrives."

"Don't worry, Captain. He'll get here safe and sound."

"Well, if you wouldn't *mind*," Garrett said to air, "if it's not too much *trouble*, I want to be informed, *Commander*. And I insist upon being included in the formal inquiry via subspace. I *do* have that right."

"You may ask," said Batanides, ambiguously. "Your request will be forwarded."

"Thanks." Garrett glanced at Bulast, who nodded and moved to forward the request to Stout. Despite Batanides's reassurances, Garrett wasn't taking any chances on her messages evaporating into subspace.

"Anything else?" Then, not waiting for a reply: "Very well, you have your orders, *Enterprise*. Batanides, out."

"Well," said Burke, after a moment, a *that's-that* lilt in her voice, "Captain, it sounds like we both have our orders. We should be ready to get underway shortly."

Garrett gestured irritably. "Fine. I'll have security meet you."

"No need. Sivek and I can handle the prisoner."

"Regulations demand that a security officer . . ."

"Captain," said Burke, with such good humor Garrett wanted to yank out the woman's tonsils, "I respectfully remind you that Commander Batanides specifically declined your offer for security to accompany us to Headquarters. And now if you'll excuse me."

Stern waited until Burke was off the bridge before exploding. "Captain, you're not going to let them take Halak. Not like *this!*"

Garrett turned a bleary eye on Stern. "We have our orders, Doctor."

"But it's damned irregular, it's not . . ."

"Doctor," said Garrett, mounting the two steps to her

command chair. She sat. "Please make sure Lieutenant Burke has a copy of your medical evaluation. Tyvan's, too."

"But, Captain," Stern began.

Garrett didn't even turn around. "Dismissed, Doctor." She waited until she heard the hiss of the turbolift doors open and closed. "Mr. Bulast, any follow-up orders?"

"No, ma'am."

"Excellent." Then she nodded to Castillo at the helm. "All right, Mr. Castillo, you heard the woman. Lay in a course for the Draavid nebulae cluster. I want us to be ready to get underway as soon as the *T'Pol* clears."

Castillo moved to comply. "Yes, ma'am."

Garrett swiveled her chair to face Bat-Levi's station immediately behind and to her right. "Commander, you'll continue as XO until further notice."

"Aye, Captain. Thank you, ma'am."

"Don't mention it. You've done a fine job. I want you to coordinate the astrometeorological and photoradiographic sections. Have them draw up duty rosters for around the clock shifts." *Because I've had it with that particular duty. Time to train her up and whip these people into shape. Give them something to focus on.*

Bat-Levi looked a little surprised. "Around the clock?"

"You heard me. I want those rosters ready by 0700 tomorrow."

"Right away, Captain. How far out do you want those rosters to go?"

"Mr. Bulast?"

"No specs on duration, Captain. Just orders to report before communications blackout."

"Nothing about the mission's duration?"

"None." The Atrean's eyebrows were very full and black, so that when they moved into a frown, they looked to Garrett like two furry caterpillars, mating. "That's a little odd, Captain. If you don't mind my saying."

Propping her left elbow on her chair, Garrett stroked her lower lip between her left thumb and forefinger. "Yes, it is, isn't it?"

Bulast was already preparing a channel. "Would you like me to query?"

A half-formed idea flashed in Garrett's mind. *Beg forgiveness later.* "Negative."

Bulast paused, his hand in midair over his console. "Captain?"

"You heard me, Mr. Bulast." Garrett caught the whirr of Bat-Levi's servos as her first officer stepped down from the deck and came alongside Garrett's left elbow.

"Captain," Bat-Levi's voice was low, "the duty personnel will require some idea of how long you expect to monitor the cluster. If nothing else, engineering needs to know how much power they'll have to steal from nonessential systems. The Draavids are pretty dense, and our current sensor configuration won't do the trick of piercing through the cluster's outer layers. Plus, they'll have to provide for maximal shields."

"You tell engineering that I want them ready for anything. Whether we stay five minutes or five years, I want everyone prepared for all eventualities, and I mean *all*: shields, power, sensors. Understood?"

She saw the confusion in the woman's face, but Bat-Levi just gave a quick nod. "Yes, Captain. Right away."

"Good." *And damn Batanides, anyway.* Garrett had no intention of remaining at the Draavids—and in the dark—for two weeks. Their orders hadn't specified how many protostars they should map. So, five days for Halak to get to Starfleet Command, two from them to reach the Draavids. Figure on three days, round-the-clock shifts to map four, five protostars, and they'd call it quits, get the hell out of the Draavids' radiation sink, and get Command on the horn in time for Halak's inquiry.

But why was she so interested, all of a sudden, in trying to save Halak's neck? The weight of the evidence, real and conjectural, was enough to scuttle a battle cruiser. Something was off, though. Things had gone just a little too fast, too conveniently. Maybe Halak had done everything SI claimed, or maybe he'd only done half and SI was filling in the blanks. Now these orders that would take them to hell and gone: Something was up. But why do this, and for someone she'd shown all the warmth of a Lampan icemonger? A man *she* was guilty of having juried and judged against a dead man?

Maybe, Garrett thought, because she was guilty, too, and it was as simple as that.

"Now hold on, hold on there a minute, Jo. My God, you're as twitchy as a long-tailed cat in a roomful of rockers."

"For crying out loud, Mac," said Stern, pacing back and forth like a caged leopard. "You'd be a little twitchy too, Starfleet Intelligence pulled some stunt like this on your ship."

"Well, now," said McCoy, drawing the words out in his best Georgia drawl and knowing it irked the hell out of Stern (which, she figured, was precisely why he did it). "They don't put us old coots on ships, and so I don't have any basis for comparison. Now sit down, would you? You're giving me a headache, what with you shooting back and forth like a shuttle on overdrive. Going to need the services of your own ship's psychiatrist, you're not careful. How is that boy anyway?"

"Beats me." Stern slid into a chair. "He's not a chatty guy. You know, he'd do himself a favor if he were more visible about ship. On the other hand, his plate's full, what with everything going on."

"Well, that's classic shrink behavior. All psychiatrists are a little squeamish when it comes to dealing with real people, and vice versa. I'll bet it's a tough row to . . ."

"Mac." Stern washed her face with her hands. "Forget

Tyvan for a sec. He's a big boy. Now, are you going to help, or not?"

"Jo," said McCoy, his creased and weathered features arranging themselves into a study of sincerity. "For you, anything. Just . . . I don't think there's a thing I can do on this end."

"That's crap. Snoop around. Dig up the autopsy reports on Thex and Strong. For crying out loud, you've practically been there since they laid the concrete."

"I'll overlook that reference to my age," said McCoy, though his watery blue eyes sparkled. "You know, you're about the only person I let get away with that."

"Do you good, somebody take you down a notch or two. You always have been a stubborn old coot."

"And you're one of my best firebrands. My God, I don't think there's anyone else can get my blood pressure going. Remember that case where that Andorian . . . ?"

"Mac," said Stern, loudly. "Memory Lane some other time. I need help here."

McCoy pooched his lips in a sulk. "Memory Lane's what we old-timers do best. Besides, you used to be a lot more fun. Get a couple bourbons in you and . . ."

"Would you cut it out?" Stern hated it when McCoy played the age card, something he did when he wanted things his way. True, he *did* look much older than she remembered: the wrinkles more deeply etched, that white thatch of hair a little more unruly and in need of a good combing. Well, that was only to be expected. After all, McCoy was over 100. "Mac, I have a time limit here. They're taking him out in an hour, maybe less. Then, we're heading to the Draavids, and there's no way anything you send via subspace will get through. Now, are you going to help, or what?"

"All right, all right." McCoy held his hands up in surrender, his tone letting her know that he understood he was pushing her too far. If she'd had the time and inclination, she might have played along, and not just because McCoy had been her best, and favorite, teacher. "Jo, I'll be straight with you. I've read your report—mighty fine piece of detective work there, by the way, you picking on the discrepancy in those knife wounds and dirt samples, mighty fine. Probably would have passed most of these younger folks right by."

"Thanks. But, to tell the truth, I wish I'd never thought to look at the damn stuff."

McCoy's face pruned. "Whatever for? He was caught in his own lie, far as I can see. That dirt," he made a sharp downward motion with his closed fist, "nail in the old coffin. Places him somewhere totally different."

"But that's what bothers me, Mac. On the one hand, you've got the fact that Halak lied. On the other, you've got Starfleet Intelligence conveniently making connections that rely on part-fact and part-conjecture. And just because Halak lied—well, *omitted* the first fight, the meeting with this Arava character . . ."

"Kind of a big hole there."

"It still doesn't follow he lied about Ryn III, see what I'm saying? This whole revenge theory thing, it sounds too, too . . ."

"Connect the dots?"

"Pardon?"

"Never mind." McCoy batted away the comment with a flap of his hand. "Before your time. What you're saying is you're hearing true, true, unrelated."

"Or true, *false*, unrelated. That's right."

"Okay, so you want me to do some digging around. The reports on Thex and Strong," McCoy tugged at a wattle of loose flesh under his chin, "yeah, maybe I can get to them. And how about I nose around about this Burke character, and Batanides?"

"That'd be great, Mac. We're in the dark here."

"All right, let me think on this, let me think," said McCoy, musing. His rheumy blue eyes, deep in their valley

of wrinkles, took on a faraway look, and he touched a contemplative finger to his lower lip. To her dismay, Stern saw
that he'd developed a slight palsy she didn't remember seeing before. McCoy might make jokes about his age, his surg-
eries, but he really was getting up there in years. With a
pang, she realized that she hadn't made the time for him the
last time she'd been back to Earth. She knew this was because if she spent time with McCoy, she might be tempted
to stay. She really didn't know what their relationship was.
They were colleagues, friends. Not lovers. Well, not *physi-
cally* anyway—Stern just wasn't the romantic type—but
McCoy was her closest friend, closer than Garrett. Maybe
McCoy looked at Stern the way a father did a daughter. Or
maybe they were just two lonely people who enjoyed each
other's company. Or maybe there was love there, somewhere.

"By the way," she asked, "how's the heart?"

"What?" McCoy looked up, startled out of his blue
reverie. "Oh, that. Which one?"

"Putz. The *new* one."

"Oh, I knew what you meant. And it's fine, fine." McCoy
thumped his chest with a closed fist. "Make these things better and better. You watch. I'm going to outlive a couple of
Vulcans I know. Certainly long enough to see that ship
you've abandoned me for get decommissioned. You mark my
word, Jo Stern, when that day comes, you are just going to
come *crawling* back here, begging me to take you on staff."

"Tell you what, Mac. That happens, I'll buy the drinks
and we'll get three sheets to the wind, okay?" She folded her
arms and leaned in. "Now, you going to do this?"

"My God, you'd plague a fence post. All right, here's
what I can do," said McCoy. "I know a couple people; I'll
put some feelers out, see what I get, all right?"

"*Fast.*"

"Fast."

"That's a start. Thanks, Mac. Really. I owe you."

"I already know what I want."

"What's that?"

"You take your next leave with me. We'll go on a trip. Some nice R and R."

Stern hesitated for a split second then said, "You got it."

"Good." But McCoy eyed her carefully. "You're still as nervous as a turkey around Thanksgiving. We Georgia boys have a more impolite saying, about skillets and such, but this is an unsecured channel."

"Never stopped you before." Stern chafed her arms. "Sorry. Just want to *do* something, that's all."

"You want to *do* something?" McCoy pursed his lips into a wet rosebud. "Tell me, you give Halak a clean bill of health?"

"I discharged him from sickbay three days ago. Why?"

"Oh, nothing, nothing. I was just thinking: How long that poor soul been languishing in your brig?"

"Since yesterday."

"Yesterday." McCoy's snowy white eyebrows reached for his hairline. "Over twenty-four hours without medical attention. And now he's going to spend another four, five days, no medical care, cooped up on a godforsaken Vulcan warpshuttle, no doctor to make sure he's comfortable, change his bandages." He paused. "Give him his vitamins and such."

"Vitamins." Stern's eyes slitted. "Vitamins?"

"Vitamins." McCoy's look was one of supreme innocence. "There are some powerful bugs out there, Jo, *powerful* bugs."

The silence was so complete Stern imagined McCoy heard her swallow even over subspace. "Mac," she said, "he's in the brig—in isolation. No visitors."

"Who's talking visiting? You're chief medical officer. And he's your patient."

After a moment, Stern's lips split in a broad smile. "Mac,

if my day gets any better, I may have to hire someone to help me enjoy it."

"I'll do it for free." McCoy looked supremely pleased. "That's my girl."

Two hours later, Bulast said, "*T'Pol* signals they're ready to depart, Captain."

Despite having prepared herself, Garrett experienced a stomach-twisting lurch of apprehension, the way she had when she was a little girl and someone jumped out of the shadows. She kept her voice bland. "Very well, Mr. Bulast. Wish the *T'Pol* a safe journey."

"Aye, Captain."

"Mr. Castillo?"

"Course for Draavid cluster already laid in, Ma'am."

"Very well."

Glemoor said, "The *T'Pol* is moving off, Captain."

"On screen." The main viewscreen winked, and Garrett watched as the Vulcan warpshuttle peeled away. A moment later, the stars behind the *T'Pol's* warp bubble blurred, and then the shuttle shot into warp and disappeared.

Good-bye, Halak. Garrett let out her breath in a long, slow exhalation. *Godspeed.*

She straightened. "All right, Mr. Castillo. Let's get going. Warp four. Now."

You can always tell when a ship goes to warp, thought Halak. Not that something very dramatic happened. The floors didn't shake; the bulkheads didn't rattle. If the ship and its engines were sound, you didn't feel a thing. But Halak knew. The ship just *felt* different. So he knew, without being told, when they'd left *Enterprise* behind.

His quarters were Spartan: a bunk, a square lozenge of a pillow. A chair and a small round table bolted to the floor. No companel, no replicator, no portal. The walls were gray.

They'd better make good time; else he'd go stir-crazy wondering what the hell had gone wrong with his life.

And this woman Burke: Obviously, SI hadn't briefed her about his mission to Ryn III. Well, standard intelligence procedure: No dissemination of information, for pity's sake, else everyone might know their right hand from their left. Batanides had better clear things up.

The door hissed, and Burke stepped into the room. "We're under way," Burke said. "I came to see if you were comfortable."

Halak almost laughed. "The mattress is hard."

"The mattresses are worse in prison. Mind if I sit down?" She didn't wait for his reply but took the room's only chair. Crossed her legs and clasped her hands over her left knee. "Commander, how would you like to save your career?"

It wasn't the question he'd been expecting, and he wasn't prepared for his reaction either: an overwhelming sense of relief. It was all a mistake; she was going to tell him she knew all about Ryn III and the Breen and the Cardassian connection, and it was all some horrible mistake.

"I'll take silence as a *yes*. Well, then, how much do you know about the Cardassians? Specifically," Burke gave him a look that was almost coy, "how much do you know about the Hebitians?"

Chapter 24

"Ten days," said Su Chen-Mai, pacing. His moon-shaped face was as purple as an overripe Denebian plum. "Ten days, and you haven't picked up a thing, Kaldarren. We have to nothing to show for our time, *nothing!*"

Kaldarren sat, his eyes tracking back and forth. Chen-Mai

was having another tantrum, and Kaldarren knew from experience that it was best to wait him out. It helped that after eleven hours of crawling over rubble, he was too bone-tired to argue.

They were in the biosphere's common room where they took their meals and had their arguments. The room smelled of men's sweat, sour canned air, and the apricotlike aroma of Catrayan porridge Kaldarren hadn't been able to force down because his stomach was in knots. He wanted something to drink though; he'd even settle for some of that awful bourbon Rachel liked so much. The air filters in the Cardassian biosphere were relics. The longer they stayed, coming and going and bringing more dust and debris that adhered to the electrostatic charges they built up on their suits, the more Kaldarren's mouth tasted like grit.

Chen-Mai frothed. "And what do you bring back? Just some useless artifacts." He swept a dismissive hand at a trio of sculpted stone figures. "Nothing *valuable* at all!"

Spoken like a true mercenary, not a scientist. Well, there was a saying for it, something he'd picked up from Garrett: One man's trash is another man's treasure. Kaldarren ran a finger over the rough stone of one figure. The statue was of a chimera, part lizard (*snake?*) and part woman but with the folded wings of a bat. The left edge of the stone had fractured, distorting what Kaldarren thought was the face. The figure bore some resemblance to what the Cardassians claimed were ancient Hebitian artifacts—specifically, the Hebitian god of the Underworld. As he remembered it, the Hebitian god was usually rendered as a dragon alongside the king who was portrayed as a plump, white, slumbering, bull-like Cardassian *toj'lath*.

But this figure was altogether different. For one thing, it was a woman, not a man, and for another . . . Kaldarren's finger traced the chiseled features. The stone had suffered over time, but there was the faintest suggestion of a half-mask of some sort, one that covered the face down to the nose. The mask was very odd. As far as he knew, the lore about the old Cardassian religion made no reference to masks of any kind. He wouldn't know for sure until he could study the statue under a high-resolution magnifier, and access a database to check on similar finds, if any. The Cardassians weren't known for their openness.

Kaldarren looked up at Chen-Mai. "I guess it depends on your definition of value. This *is* valuable. There's nothing like it in any collection as far as I'm aware."

Chen-Mai's black eyes sparkled like polished stones, but he didn't stop moving. "Don't play games. You know *exactly* what I'm talking about. These statues, these potsherds and other things you've found, they're not why we're here."

"I know why we're here," said Kaldarren. He swallowed, and felt his throat ball with the effort. "Chen-Mai, has it ever occurred to you that there might not be anything *to* pick up? Maybe our information is wrong."

Chen-Mai stopped his pacing long enough to fix Kaldarren with a poisonous glare. "That's not what the legends say. That's not what *you* said when you read them."

Chen-Mai had done the translation but Kaldarren decided to be charitable, and prudent. "Maybe we were wrong."

"*I* wasn't wrong, not then and not now."

"All right. You weren't wrong." Kaldarren lifted his hands in a weary, *well-what-do-you-want* gesture and let them fall to the table. One of the boys (Jase, probably, he had always been a messy eater) had left a halo of crumbs. Kaldarren pressed the pad of his right forefinger to the table, dabbing up crumbs that he rolled between his fingers.

Thinking about Jase made him tense. The boys had been very quiet at dinner that night. True, there wasn't a lot for them to talk about; no school, and both Kaldareen and Leahru-Mar were gone most of the day. But Kaldarren couldn't recall a time since they'd come to this planet when the boys had been so . . . *guarded*. Kaldarren considered the word then found it apt. Yes, they had been *guarded*, both of them. In fact, Kaldarren had been tempted to probe Jase for an instant, just to see.

So, he had. *After all my lectures about privacy.* Kaldarren was embarrassed to admit it now to himself that he *had* probed his son: a light touch, nothing more.

The surprise had come the instant a finger of his thought brushed along the contours of his son's mind. Jase had blocked him. *Blocked* him: It was as if Kaldarren stood on the other side of a pane of milky glass, unable to see through to what lay beyond in his son's mind.

How did Jase do that? How long has Jase been able to do that and me not even know? Does Jase even know, or is it reflex?

Aloud, Kaldarren said, "Maybe I was wrong. Maybe I assumed that telepathy is a constant. That was foolish, probably. We know that some species have no known telepaths, and that one species' telepathy may be far cruder than another's. It's also possible—*probable*, in fact—that there was something here once, a long time ago, but there isn't now. Time wreaks havoc on many things, Chen-Mai, not just stone statues."

"No!" Chen-Mai hurled the negative like a spear. "I presume *this* probability. You're not the right telepath for the job." Chen-Mai's upper lip curled, revealing a line of yellowed teeth. There was a gap between Chen-Mai's two front teeth, and when he spoke, Kaldarren saw the tip of the smaller man's tongue undulating, like a fat worm.

"You're not strong enough," said Chen-Mai, his tongue working against his teeth. "Maybe I need a better, stronger telepath."

"Very possibly," said Kaldarren, soberly. "Certainly that's your choice."

"Choice." Chen-Mai's features corkscrewed. "Maybe, but I don't have time, *or* money. Oh, but money doesn't mean anything to you Federation people."

"That doesn't stop us from needing resources, or pursuing a dream. Money isn't the only motivator, Chen-Mai."

"Well, it is for me. I have an employer who will be very unhappy if I don't keep my end of the bargain, and I will be very unhappy not to get my money." -

"We still have four days before the next Cardassian patrol."

"Are you saying you'll find it by then?"

Kaldarren hesitated. "Possible, but unlikely. Chen-Mai, we may have to face the fact, however unpleasant, that the translations are in error."

Chen-Mai's mouth opened in protest, but Lam Leahru-Mar stirred. "What if it were shielded in some way?" the Naxeran said. His frills trembled, and he smoothed them down with his left index finger in a slow, meditative gesture. "What if there is a portal, but there's something that blocks you from finding it? If I built something that powerful, that's what I'd do."

Chen-Mai exhaled a noisy snort. "And where's the power source?"

"There's all that magnetic disturbance in the mountains," Mar offered. "Maybe it's shielding a power source deep underground."

Chen-Mai gave the Naxeran a withering look. "If that were the case, there ought to be an energy signature. No machine is so perfect it doesn't have a signature."

Mar turned his sleek black face toward Kaldarren. "What about the ion storms? The radiation? Could they interfere?"

It was tempting to pawn off his failure on that, but Kaldarren shook his head. "It shouldn't. Honestly, I don't know."

There was, of course, one possibility none of them had voiced: Chen-Mai and Mar because they wouldn't have considered it, and he because the idea filled with him with an icy dread. What if the *portal* didn't want to be found? Or what if the portal didn't want *Kaldarren* to find it, or only wanted him to find it on its own terms? A strange way to think of a machine, but telepathy was more than intimacy. Telepathy was a form of becoming something distinctly different from what you were. When a telepath touched another mind, a little piece got left behind—like a fingerprint, or a footstep in cooling tar—and imprints, done often enough for long enough, became permanent and were not washed away. So it stood to reason that a device, one attuned to and used by enough telepaths over a long period of time, might itself become . . . selective, perhaps even sentient.

A machine with a *soul.* Kaldarren suppressed a shiver. He doubted Chen-Mai would understand *that,* so he opted to stick to the obvious. "Let's face facts. We've based this entire operation on ancient Cardassian legends. Legends aren't facts."

"But they're *something,*" said Chen-Mai. He was pacing again. "And there's something here. Why would the Cardassians bother patrolling otherwise?"

"It's disputed space. The Federation's been haggling with the Cardassians over this region for years."

Chen-Mai gave a dismissive, backhanded wave. "But the Cardassians are stretched so thin between their expansion and their conflicts with both the Federation and the Klingons, it makes no sense to worry about a region they can't legitimately lay claim to, even if they did have bases here once, like this biosphere. But they still patrol, and why? Because there's something here."

"They could just be spoiling for a fight. All Federation incursions are supposed to be cleared first." Kaldarren sighed. "Even discounting that, your *something* could be anything. Or what if they patrol because this is the way Cardassians do things?"

Mar spoke up. "Kaldarren's got a point. If there's something here, why not put a contingent on the surface instead?"

"Am I supposed to know how, or what a Cardassian thinks?" Chen-Mai raged. "Ask Kaldarren! *He's* the telepath!"

Kaldarren was tempted to point out that telepaths weren't all-powerful; Vulcans couldn't meld with Cardassians, and he couldn't read a Breen. Instead, he held up the masked statue. "Look, Chen-Mai, I can't even tell you with any certainty whether this is Hebitian, or Cardassian, or, well, take your pick. Just because these artifacts happen to be on a dead planet in disputed, possibly Cardassian, space doesn't mean that the people who used to live here are connected to Cardassia, or the Hebitians."

"That's not what the legends say."

Kaldarren made a face. "The Cardassians claim that the Hebitians *may* have been telepaths. Anyway, claims aren't proof. If true, why aren't there modern-day Cardassian telepaths? Betazoid telepaths trace their powers back in evolutionary time. Our telepathy didn't evolve *out* of us; it got *stronger.*"

Chen-Mai leaned forward on his knuckles. "Ah, but that's the key, don't you see? The Hebitians *evolved* on Cardassia. They're telepaths. Somehow, they developed a psionic portal, a gateway attuned to individual neural patterns. A properly attuned telepath activates the portal, and *poof!*" He leaned back, throwing his hands up and splaying his fingers, as if releasing birds. "Here one second, there the next. It explains *how* they got *here.*"

"*If* these ruins are Hebitian," said Kaldarren. "A big *if.* That still doesn't answer why these portals aren't on other worlds, or why Cardassians aren't telepathic."

"I don't know, and it's not my problem," said Chen-Mai. "All I know is, the Cardassians watch this planet—not just this region but *this planet*—and I think it's because they're worried somebody will find and then use the portal."

"Well, that's why we're here," Kaldarren said, his weariness settling on him now like a heavy blanket. They were arguing about a phantom. "Find this magical portal and access it, if I can? Other than the specs, what are you're going to do if we find it?"

Chen-Mai's jaw set. "You don't need to know. Your job is to find the portal. Figure out how it works. Then you get what you want, and I get what I want."

I don't know what I want anymore. "And what if I can't, Chen-Mai?" Kaldarren fixed him with a searching look. He enjoyed seeing the smaller man flinch away, worried that Kaldarren might be probing. However tempting that might be, however, Kaldarren wouldn't reach into Chen-Mai's mind unless he had no other choice. *Probably awfully slimy in there.*

"It's not a question of *can't.* You don't have that luxury, Kaldarren. You have four days. Then the Cardassians come back, and we need to be gone."

"What about your employer? What if we don't find the portal?"

"You don't have to be a mind reader for that one," said Chen-Mai.

Kaldarren left shortly after, taking the statues with him. Lam Leahru-Mar waited until the Betazoid's footsteps faded. Then he looked over at Chen-Mai.

"What if he can't do it?" The Naxeran's black skin was sweating so much he looked dipped in clear glaze. "Or what if he does, but the Cardassians catch us? We still have to rendezvous with Talma. And what are we going to do with Kaldarren and that boy of his? No witnesses, Chen-Mai, that's what Talma said."

Chen-Mai had dropped into a seat across from the Naxeran. Now he fixed Mar with a baleful look. "You let me worry about Kaldarren and the boy."

"But Mahfouz Qadir . . . Talma *said* . . ."

"Didn't I just tell you not to worry?"

"Well, I don't like it." Mar squirmed. "Kaldarren doesn't

bother me so much, but a boy? No one told me I'd have to do a boy."

"You don't have to like it because you won't have any part of it. You pilot the ship; you get around the Cardassians. I'll take care of the rest."

"All right." Mar swallowed. "Fine. But I don't want Pahl to know anything about it, you understand? He's my sister's boy, and I'm supposed to look out for him. He shouldn't even *suspect* . . ."

"When it's all over, the only thing you'll have to tell Pahl is the truth."

"And that is?"

"Accidents," said Chen-Mai. He smiled hugely, his tongue working between his teeth. "Accidents happen—all the time."

Chapter 25

The Draavids, twice as large as the Orion Nebula, were supposed to be beautiful: a maelstrom of photo-ionized gases that painted the blackness of space with brilliant violets, hot pinks, peacock greens, parrot yellows, and indigo blues. But their beauty was lost on Garrett. When they'd arrived at the Draavids two days ago, she'd spared the swirling gases and shimmering white globules that were the cluster's protostars only a cursory glance. She set to putting her crew through their paces, hoping that work would put things right with her ship. But work hadn't done squat for Garrett, because, damn it, she couldn't stop thinking about Nigel Holmes.

She couldn't sleep either, hadn't seen the inside of her eyelids for any appreciable length of time since Halak had left three days ago. She toyed with the idea of asking Stern for a sleeper but didn't because Stern would fuss. Garrett's mother was a physician, so she knew doctors could be over-protective as hell.

Garrett thought about a good stiff shot of bourbon, too. Bourbon didn't fuss and didn't talk back unless she drank too much, and it tasted pretty good. But, in the end, she decided on coffee. (Stern would've said something about that being self-defeating, but Garrett hadn't asked.)

Garrett stepped onto the bridge. The crew was an hour into gamma shift, and Glemoor was OOD, not a surprise since Naxerans didn't need sleep.

"Anything, Mr. Glemoor?"

"Not unless you're a stellar physicist, Captain. They're happy as that Earth mollusk, give me a moment . . . yes, happy as clams, especially after I shunted power from the mess and laundry to accommodate them."

"So long as the mess chief has power for breakfast. And I want clean socks. How are our communications?"

Glemoor screwed up his face. "Hash. We can't even ping the nearest Starfleet subspace beacon. If we had to, we might be able to pierce the interference locally."

"Not unless someone's planning on running out with a shuttle."

"Well, astrocartography might. Personally, I wouldn't want to be caught out in there. Those jets of ionized molecular gas generated by the protostars, those Herbig-Haro formations? Take you for quite a ride, not to mention radiation, magnetic fields. But we have found a *little* something."

"Yes?"

Glemoor moved to the science station. "If you'll excuse me, Ensign," said Glemoor to the young man staffing the station who vacated his seat and stood to one side. "We've been collating data on infrared and radio emissions."

Glemoor called up a red-grid schematic of the nebulae cluster on the science station's viewscreen. "I won't recapitulate the obvious. As you know, we're measuring the rate of star formation by studying the conformation of those Herbig-Haros, the lobes of high-velocity, high-energy molecular gas spewed along the axis of a central, accreting disk of the protostar. And we've found some unusual bursts of gamma radiation."

Garrett's lips turned in an inverted smile. "That's a problem?"

Glemoor's frills vibrated. "No, just unusual. Gamma bursts are usually associated with *neutron* stars, because of the collision of gaseous particles accelerated by the neutron star's accreting matter. But particles don't collide in a Herbig-Haro. The gas particles shoot out in narrow jets along the axis of rotation, like strings attached to both the tip and the handle of a . . . that child's toy."

"Top."

"Exactly, a top, because a right angle is the path of least resistance against the protostar's gravitational pull."

"So, if there are gamma rays, are you saying you've found a neutron star that's a gamma ray emitter?" (Garrett didn't find this very exciting, or unusual. Gamma-emitter neutron stars weren't exactly unknown.)

"No, I don't believe so."

"Why not?"

"Because some of those protostars are moving very fast. As you can see," Glemoor used the tip of his right index finger, "we're holding position on the periphery and these protostars out by us, here and here, they aren't moving that quickly, just a hundred kilometers a second, or so. But deeper into the nebulae, the protostars begin to speed up, about 700 kilometers a second. By stellar standards, that's very fast."

"Would a neutron star cause the protostars to speed up?"

Glemoor looked dubious. "It would have to be very large, Captain, and that's not possible because, beyond a certain mass, a neutron star can't hold up under its own weight. It collapses. For something to exert that much gravitational deformation of time-space *and* be a neutron star, well ... it would have to be pretty strange."

"What do you want to do?" (Garrett knew what was required but wanted to give Glemoor the choice. Hadn't her little voice chided her for not loosening up on the reins?)

"Well, one step by one step, Captain. I would like to launch a probe."

Garrett thought Glemoor meant *first of all*, and not *one step at a time*, but she didn't call the slip to his attention. "Do it. Let's see what you come up with. Nice work."

Glemoor inclined his head at the compliment and preened his frills. After a brief tour of the rest of the bridge stations—all quiet on the Western Front there—Garrett ducked into her ready room for that cup of coffee.

After the familiar blips and sounds of the bridge, the place was quiet as a tomb. She saw a good three inches of coffee still left in her pot from that morning and, after a second's hesitation, she poured a mug; added cream and two sugars; ordered her replicator to heat only, thanks; and brooded over the machine as it complied (wondering why she was being so polite to a damn machine). Then she slid into the seat behind her desk, called up reports she didn't feel like reading, and, in two seconds flat, was thinking about the very man she was trying very hard to forget: Nigel Holmes.

Garrett sipped her coffee and made a face. Despite the white and sweetener, her coffee tasted sour and burned. Old. Sighing, Garrett worried a stray bit of coffee grounds between her teeth. *She* felt old. Weighed down. She knew why. She'd been blindsided. Again.

First Nigel. Garrett picked the ground off her tongue and flicked it from her fingers. And now Halak. Garrett stared into her mug as if divining tea leaves. No answers there, not about Halak, or Nigel. She ran her thumb over the surface of her mug. The mug was black ceramic with tiny yellow and white stars: a gift from Jase for her birthday three years ago. She felt the narrow ridges of raised glaze etched around each star. She liked to hold the mug, cupping it in both hands, the way she used to cup Jase's tiny face when he'd been a baby.

Hard to hang on to the people you care about. Like hanging onto dreams when you first wake up. The dreams are so vivid you think you can't possibly forget. But you open your eyes and they evaporate, like mist from a pond under a hot sun, and the people you love are just gone.

Nigel. Those damn smugglers. Klingons, to boot. Garrett hadn't even known there *were* Klingon smugglers; she would've thought smuggling a dishonorable profession, but there were, apparently, just as many bad apples amongst Klingons as there were among humans. Her only solace was the knowledge that the Klingon High Council dealt with their own as harshly as they did outsiders. No exile to Rura Penthe for the smugglers. They'd drawn death instead, and Garrett hoped their executions had been very painful and very bloody, for a very long time.

Good old-fashioned revenge. Garrett swirled her coffee. Not an emotion fit for a starship captain, but she didn't care. Twice in her life now, she'd wanted revenge and gotten it. Nigel's death was one of those times. (The other had happened a long time ago, on Earth, when she was eighteen and her sister Sarah was nine, but she didn't like to think about it.)

Stern told her to give it up, this guilt she had about Nigel. The problem was no matter how many times she went over the scenario, she came to the same conclusion: Nigel should be alive. He wasn't, and that was because she hadn't trusted her own instincts. No, that wasn't right. Garrett's eyebrows met in a V. She'd gone by the damn book. If she hadn't, Nigel would be alive.

First rule: A ship in distress took priority over all other considerations. Everything else came second. Hell, everything else was *third.*

Reminding herself that Nigel had volunteered didn't ease the pain. So when the Klingons opened fire on the very transport ship they'd been trying to pirate, she had a choice. Rescue the transport crew, or rescue Nigel.

First rule. First duty: *A ship in distress had priority.* So the transport crew was alive because Garrett had gone by the book, and Nigel wasn't—for the same reason.

The atonal buzz at her door made her jump. Garrett checked the time: 0315. Who . . . ? "Come."

The door shushed, and Tyvan stepped through. Garrett's surprise swiftly gave way to concern. She and the psychiatrist hadn't spoken since Halak's inquiry, though Stern said she'd given her colleague a tongue-lashing: *"He didn't know anything about my autopsy findings, and you shook him up pretty good, and I said buster, you want to be in the loop, come to staff meetings and stop acting like you're on one side of a portal and we're on another, and when the captain says jump, you say how high, ma'am, that's what I said."* "Doctor? Is there something wrong?"

Tyvan crossed to stand before her desk. He carried a padd. "No, Captain. I just thought you might want my fitness report on Bat-Levi."

"Fitness report? On Bat-Levi? At *this* hour?"

"Well, you're up, I'm up," Tyvan said, proffering the padd. "Actually, I think you'll find that her performance has been exemplary, even with all the stress."

Replacing her mug on her desk, Garrett took the padd and quickly thumbed opened Tyvan's report. "I've had no complaints."

"You took a risk, asking for her."

"Before her accident, her record was good. She had a career in front of her. Very bright woman. I wanted to give her an opportunity. As for her physical limitations, well . . ." Garrett shrugged. "People make interesting choices."

"Yes, they do. All the time."

"But." Garrett tossed the padd onto her desk. The padd clattered and ticked against glass. She gathered up her mug, sipped bad coffee, swallowed. "You didn't come to discuss the obvious, though between you and me, I wish she'd get those servos fixed."

"Have you told her?"

"I hinted."

"Maybe a direct approach."

"Like an order?"

"I had a strong suggestion in mind." Tyvan's lips moved in a faint smile. "I've found that people tend to respond better to suggestions."

Sounds like you got a boot in the rear from Jo, you ask me. "Okay, I'll strongly suggest it. So, now that's settled," Garrett said, as she pushed away from her desk and crossed to the small round glass table with silvered chrome legs that squatted by her observation window. Dropping into a scallop-backed, cushioned armchair covered in mauve fabric, she waved Tyvan to a chair opposite. "There's something else on your mind, Doctor. That wasn't a question, by the way."

"But not quite an order."

Garrett's lips curled into a half-moon. "Take it as a strong suggestion."

Tyvan sank into cushions, settling his long frame, and Garrett noticed that even though he was a very thin man and his eyes were a soft cinnamon-brown and very mild, there was nothing insubstantial or weak about the El-Aurian. *Bet he's made of strong stuff, and he'd have to be to survive what happened to the* Enterprise-B *and come right back aboard her successor.*

Tyvan lifted his chin, sniffed. "What *is* that you're drinking? It smells burned."

"Day-old coffee. Want some?"

"No, thanks, I'm not that masochistic. At least it smells better than Klingon coffee."

"Never developed a taste for that stuff." Garrett didn't bother adding that she had no reason to love Klingons, or anything Klingonese. "What's on your mind?"

"Well, to be frank, Captain . . . May I speak freely?"

"Go."

"Well . . . you."

Garrett's eyebrows headed for her hairline. "Me?"

"And the crew. It's all in there," Tyvan hooked a thumb at the padd lying on Garrett's desk. "Second report after the one on Bat-Levi. Unofficial, of course."

Garrett unfolded from her slouch and, reaching forward, put her mug on the table. The ceramic clicked against glass. "What's up?"

"Actually, it's what's *down* that worries me: morale." Tyvan leaned forward and let his clasped hands hang over the points of his knees. "Morale isn't good right now. I believe the term you used with Dr. Stern was . . . in the toilet."

"I may have said something like that."

"I disagree with your assessment. I don't think what the crew's feeling right now has anything to do with depression. True, Batra's funeral was very hard, for some more than others."

Garrett wondered about Castillo but held her tongue. It wasn't her place to ask Tyvan if the young ensign had seen him, and Tyvan probably wouldn't say unless he had concerns about Castillo's job performance.

Tyvan said, "But the crew's horrified about Halak, and not necessarily because they think he's done anything. With a few exceptions, they simply don't believe Starfleet Intelligence. They . . . *we* know that our mission to the Draavids is just to get us out of the way. We know you can't refuse, but that doesn't stop us from being angry."

It was on the tip of Garrett's tongue to protest that, no, every assignment was important, but she didn't. The crew— Tyvan—was right.

"Plus, the crew's beginning to second-guess themselves, rehash things from the past, wonder whether or not they made the right decisions, whether their commanding officers know what they're doing." Tyvan gave a sheepish grin. "Me, too."

Tyvan said it all innocuously enough, but it was as if he'd read her mind. *Don't be ridiculous. He's a psychiatrist. He's a Listener, not a Betazoid.* Garrett said, "What do you suggest?"

"To be honest? Sometimes it helps to think of us like a bunch of kids."

"Doctor, some of them *are* kids."

"Okay. So if a kid falls, what happens?"

"He cries?"

"Wrong. Most of the time, if it's not serious and there's not a lot of blood, he looks to the parent first. The parent's reaction tells him how he ought to react. If the parent gets upset, so does the child. He'll cry. But if the parent stays calm . . ."

"The kid stays calm," Garrett finished, impatient now. She had a son, for crying out loud; she didn't need a tutorial in Parenting 101. "Are you suggesting that I'm not sending them . . . *you* the right message?"

"Depends on the message you want to send, doesn't it? Let me put it this way, Captain. If you weren't having second thoughts about your own abilities, or rehashing the past, you wouldn't be human. Now I know part of a captain's job is to dissect what she perceives to be her mistakes. Otherwise, you can't avoid them in the future."

"This is something peculiar only to captains? I suppose you don't rehash?"

"After you chewed me out and spat out the remainder faster than a photon torpedo?" Tyvan laughed. "I'd *better.*"

Garrett couldn't help but grin. "I didn't mean *that.* I meant, in your *work.*"

"Oh, that." Tyvan made a dismissive gesture. "All the time. Except you can't keep looking to the past when you've got to deal with the present. My patients aren't static, you know. They change from day to day, session to session. But I've learned over time that the important stuff keeps coming back up, and so I try not to worry too much about what I think I've done wrong. I figure there's almost always a second chance, a third. I'm not suggesting that a doctor, or a captain, should ignore the past. But *staying* in the past, brooding over past errors, will just get the doctor—and his patient—into a rut."

"Or a captain," said Garrett. For some inexplicable reason, she glanced at her mug of old coffee. "You think I'm in a rut?"

"*Are* you? We're both up at an ungodly hour. We're not sleeping."

"What's your excuse?"

Tyvan shrugged. "I wonder if I misread Halak all along. I brood over mistakes I make with patients, things like that. And you, you're wandering the ship, haunting the bridge. Drinking old coffee."

"I'm just minding my ship. Putting my house in order."

"Oh, that sounds like something Lieutenant Glemoor would love to store away in his stash of Earth idioms. You know, now that you mention a house . . . Freud said that whenever a house appears in a patient's dream, the house represents the dreamer. So when we say that we're putting our house in order, we're talking about us."

Garrett gave Tyvan a faint smile. "And my ship is me?"

"Why not? So, are you concerned about putting yourself in order? Not wanting to make mistakes again?"

Garrett thought of Nigel, and the choice she'd been forced to make. "You referring to something in particular?"

"Yes." Tyvan's brown eyes were steady but compassionate. "And you may believe I'm overstepping my bounds."

"Then don't," said Garrett, a nervous flutter in her throat, though she kept her anxiety out of her face . . . she hoped.

"But it's my job," said Tyvan, gently. "Captain, your sorrow for Nigel Holmes isn't a secret."

Damn that Jo. "No?" she said, forcing lightness into her tone she didn't feel.

"No, and I won't insult you by pretending I don't know. But you've lost one first officer, and you may very well lose another, and you have lost a great many other," he paused—for emphasis, it seemed to Garrett, "other *things*, all in the past year or two."

A marriage. My son. The man I loved, and may still. "And?" said Garrett. Her chest was tight, and she had to work to breathe.

"Captain, are you quite sure that you're not obsessing about a dead man and everything you *think* you did wrong in order to avoid thinking about the guilt and responsibility and sorrow you feel for all these other deaths?"

Garrett had a strange feeling then. She'd been prepared for—no, *steeled* herself against a wave of anxiety she knew was dammed up behind a fragile mental barrier. But, instead of anxiety or guilt, a wave of relief seemed to wash away the blackness tainting her mind, her perceptions. It was as if a strong wind had blown away a dense bank of clouds from her mind, and the sun begun to shine. *Yes, that's right, that's exactly it.*

But some perverse part of her—the part that didn't want to let go because old habits die hard—said, "Sometimes all your choices are bad ones. So you choose the lesser of evils."

"That's not the same as a mistake. That's just a choice you didn't like."

"Yes," said Garrett. *Uncanny, that's what Ven said a week ago? Ten days?*

"So you're brooding over your choices—good, bad, indifferent. We'll never know if they were right or wrong, or if things have worked out for the best because things will just work out, Captain. They always do. So let's not talk about ghosts. Nigel Holmes is dead, and you've lost many things, but Halak is alive. What about him?"

"I don't know. I trusted Halak . . . no, that's not right. Maybe I was trying to get there, but probably I wasn't being fair to him. And, damn it, my gut says things aren't the way SI says."

"But he *did* lie. Dr. Stern proved that, and Halak admitted to it."

"Maybe he made a bad choice." Garrett's eyes slid sideways. "Tell me something. You think he murdered those men?"

Tyvan didn't hesitate. "No. Just because he's lied about one thing doesn't mean that everything he's said is a lie. I believe Dr. Stern would say something like true, true, unrelated. True, the men are dead. True, Halak lied. But the events may be unrelated."

"But how do you know?"

"I don't *know* anything." Tyvan spread his hands. "Call it intuition."

"So, you're saying, go with my gut."

"Trust your crew, Captain, and trust yourself." Tyvan held her gaze. "Forgive yourself. And, for God's sake, get some sleep."

"Now *that's* . . ." Garrett began, but a hail shrilled. Crossing to her companel, Garrett jabbed it to silence. "Garrett."

"Glemoor, Captain. I think you should come out here."

At Glemoor's tone, Garrett became alert. "What is it?"

"A ghost, Captain. Lots and lots of ghosts."

"Sensor ghosts." Garrett was bent over a sensor displaying the probe's telemetry data. "Of what?"

"Unknown. There are also trace amounts of arkenium duranide," said Glemoor, "larger amounts of ferrocarbonite. Cohesive globules of ionized plasma."

"Well, the ionized plasma isn't a surprise." Garrett straightened and winced as a muscle in the small of her back complained. She inched her hand around to massage the muscle. "You have a theory about the rest?"

"Yes. This is data from a second probe. The first I set to scan after 600,000 kilometers. If the source was a neutron star, that should have been a good distance. But at 600,000 kilometers, the probe accelerated, and I lost it before I could program in a course change."

"Gone?" Garrett was startled, her aching back forgotten. "Just like that?"

"In the blink of an eye, Captain. So I sent out another probe, easing it in and having it come to a stop 400,000 kilometers from the ship. From there, measurements of gravitational wavefronts came out with a sphere."

"A sphere. Glemoor, the only thing that can do that is a black hole."

"A very big black hole. Not as big as our galactic black hole, of course, otherwise we wouldn't be standing here discussing it. That sphere measures over 500 kilometers around."

"That would mean it's nearly nine times more massive than a standard stellar black hole, and much too massive for a neutron star. But you said gamma rays. Your probe still sees them, and they're fluctuating. They're not constant. That would be consistent with a neutron star accreting matter at variable rates. A black hole can't emit gamma rays."

"Not in and of itself, Captain, no, especially if it's static. But I don't believe this is. I think the central mass is still spinning, very quickly. Anything falling in will release energy before reaching the event horizon. I believe that accounts for those gamma ray bursts we're reading. Plus, there's no localized magnetic field. Astronomical black holes have no magnetic fields."

"But a black hole? *Here?*"

"It would seem to be the case, Captain. There are precedents, of course. The black hole at the center of the Messier 87 galaxy, and one at the center of ours."

"But this a nebula cluster, not a galaxy."

"Technically, this is a hypernova, the end result of a chain reaction of ordinary supernovae. There's a tremendous lot of matter and gas out there."

Garrett chewed on her lower lip. "All right. Let's say that's true. Would gamma rays account for the sensor ghosts?"

"Possibly. Gamma rays combining with ionized plasma might mimic ionized plasma vented from a ship. But, Captain, nebulae contain helium. They have hydrogen. Nitrogen. Noble gases. Nebulae do not contain arkenium duranide, or ferrocarbonite. Captain, these are materials used in construction."

She'd known that, but she'd refused to believe it, hoping the readings were wrong. *Trust yourself, Captain.* "Used for plasma injectors."

"Yes, Captain, just so," said Glemoor.

"For a warp core." There was a pause as Garrett digested what she'd just said. Then she turned to look out at the fierce, stormy beauty of the Draavids.

"Oh, dear God," she said. "There's a ship out there."

Chapter 26

They'd been at yellow alert for fifteen minutes and Garrett was clenching her teeth so hard her jaw hurt. "Anything?"

Darco Bulast looked as tense as his captain. "Negative. If there's a vessel, it's not sending out a general distress, and there's no response to hails."

"Unless there's just too much interference," said Bat-Levi, looking up from her sensor display at her position alongside the science station. She blew an errant strand of her long black hair out of her eyes then hooked a lock behind her right ear. "There could be a signal, but we'd never hear it, not unless we get closer."

"What's our status?" asked Garrett. "Can we do that?"

"Right now, our shields are holding just fine, Captain. When we crossed into the nebulae cluster proper, radiation levels outside the ship jumped by a factor of five. Still within tolerance limits, presuming our shields hold. We're holding position at 35,000 kilometers from the nebulae's edge. But I'm not sure that another ship—likely disabled and running on battery power—would have the shields to last very long, not in that radioactive soup out there."

"If there even *is* a ship," said Castillo in an undertone.

Garrett's head swiveled his way. "Care to share, Mr. Castillo?"

Castillo reddened. "No disrespect intended, Captain, but there's every possibility that there was a ship but isn't now."

"Not necessarily, Ensign," Glemoor interjected from his station next to Castillo. "If we can trust our scans, there's insufficient debris, and nothing organic. If we presume a ship disintegrated, then there ought to be a debris field equivalent to the mass destroyed and some evidence of organic residua."

"Then where *are* they?" asked Bat-Levi. "For that matter, why duck into a nebula to begin with?"

"Maybe they were running away *from* someone," Castillo offered.

Garrett reflected that Castillo might need to learn to hold his tongue, but he clearly knew a good idea when he had one. "An interesting hypothesis, Ensign. But how do you account for the levels of ferrocarbonite and duranide we've found?"

"What if the core didn't breach? What if they *ejected* their warp core?"

"Why would they do that?" asked Bat-Levi. "Without a core, they don't have power for very long, and without power, they'll fry. If the gamma radiation doesn't get them, those protostars will."

"Maybe this was the only choice they had," said Castillo. "You just said it. You don't go into nebulae like this unless you're forced to, and if you're forced to, probably someone's shooting at you. So, maybe their warp core got damaged. A coolant leak, I don't know. So they have a choice. Either jettison the core, or blow up."

"So they jettison the core to buy time." Propping her right elbow on the arm of her command chair, Garrett ran the side of her right thumb along her lips in thought. "Well, a crummy choice is better than none. It's a decent hypothesis, Ensign. Very good," she said, flashing Castillo a quick smile and noting, with satisfaction, his flush of pleasure. *Trust your crew.* "Glemoor?"

"Those sensor ghosts might be distortions of the signature from a real ship. Except if Ensign Castillo is correct, then either this ship went very far into the nebula before ejecting its core . . ."

"Or they didn't, but are being dragged toward that black hole. Any way to tell for certain?"

"If there's a ship? Not without a signal of some kind. Or," Glemoor paused then said, "or we go deeper into the field ourselves."

"But we already know where to start. The first probe was, what? 600,000 kilometers in? So how about following the trail of the sensor ghosts, narrowing down our search pattern?"

Bat-Levi thought a moment. "I could extrapolate backward. Say, factor in the amount of material we've already found and then, on that basis, calculate how large the warp core would have to be in order to generate the debris field we've got. I'd have to take drift into account from the Herbig-Haro jets, though. They might have blown the debris out, not in. No matter which way you cut it, it'll take awhile."

Something about what Bat-Levi had just said niggled at

the back of Garrett's brain. She sensed an idea forming but couldn't quite put it into words. Something a ship might do if it were in trouble, in a nebula with protostars, and no way to blast free . . .

"Pardon, Captain," Ensign Castillo again, "but that's kind of inefficient. Why not narrow things down by the rate at which those gas globules are collapsing along gravitational fields? We can assume that the components left over from a warp core breach or ejection ought to follow the same path. Save time."

"Do it," said Garrett, shoving the nascent thought to the back of her brain. *Let it simmer awhile.* "Find me a focus. And, Castillo, can you move the probe in further without its being trapped in that gravitational well?"

"To gather more data? Sure, but . . ."

Garrett waved the rest of his remark away. "No, no, not more data. I want to use the probe as a proximity detector. A kind of advanced scout. With all this interference, we let that probe get out too far ahead of us, and we might as well be trying to listen to something being transmitted between two tin cans on a string."

Glemoor frowned. "Tin cans?"

"I'll explain it later. But this way, we move closer without endangering the ship without good cause. Let the probe do the searching for us. Can you do it, Castillo?"

"Sure. But, Captain, the closer the probe gets, the more its signal will be subtended and distorted by gravity. I'm not sure how accurate the signal will be."

"Understood." Garrett punched a channel for engineering. "Mr. Kodell."

"Here, Captain."

"We're heading deeper into the nebula. There may be a ship in trouble out there. How long can we stay before we get into trouble ourselves?"

"Depends. With shields at maximum, and us doing nothing but looking, probably three hours, maybe four. But if you have to expend more energy in a rescue—using the tractor beams, for example—then it depends on how far for how long. The bigger the ship, the more we'll cut into our energy reserves. We won't even talk about the engines."

"No, let's not. If we find a ship, can we use transporters instead?"

"If we can get close enough, maybe. There's a lot of interference. Personally, I wouldn't want to be the one caught in a transporter beam trying to get from A to B."

"Understood." Garrett toggled off. "Castillo, you ready?"

"Absolutely, Captain. Course?"

"That depends on Commander Bat-Levi." Garrett turned her chair to face her acting XO. "Anything?"

"Yes, Captain." Bat-Levi ineffectually brushed at her hair then seemed to give it up. "Routing information to the helm now."

"All right, Mr. Castillo, take the probe in, match course and speed to maintain a distance of 6,000 kilometers between the probe and us. Take the probe in at 1,000-kilometer increments, nice and slow. Find me a ship, if there is one."

After thirty minutes, Bulast sang out, "Proximity alarm! I've got something, Captain!"

Garrett came out of her slouch. "On speaker."

A moment later, the bridge was awash with the sizzle of static. No one spoke. Garrett listened intently, closing her eyes to block out extraneous stimulation. "I don't hear anything."

Bulast put up a cautionary finger. "Wait. Let me filter the high end."

He did and, an instant later, Garrett heard it: a steady pip, like the blipping of an ancient oscilloscope.

"Sounds like a distress beacon," said Castillo.

"But not Starfleet," said Garrett. "Bulast?"

"Matching beacon now with known Federation registry." He shook his head. "Not one of ours."

"But it's somebody," said Bat-Levi.

"Or was," said Garrett. "Anything remotely resembling a ship out there?"

"Scanning, Captain. Negative. Nothing that looks like a ship, or even pieces of one."

"Too far away," said Glemoor, more to himself than Garrett. Before she could ask, he said, "It's too far away, Captain. We found evidence of a warp core much further away. So how did the beacon get *here*, *closer* to us?"

"Maybe they launched it before they ejected the core," said Castillo.

Garrett shook her head. "That's not what I would do. Glemoor's right. Too much distance. You don't send out a distress call *before* you have an emergency."

"Unless they were in distress before they had to jettison the core," said Bat-Levi. "Maybe they were under attack, like Castillo said."

Garrett drummed the fingers of right hand on the arm of her command chair. "Then why not send out a general distress call *before* you go into the nebula? With all this interference, it'd be a miracle for anyone to pick up the signal. We didn't, and we were sitting right on the edge. No, we're missing something. Castillo, where is that beacon? How distant?"

"Six thousand," said Castillo, and stopped.

"Mr. Castillo?"

"One moment, Captain," said Castillo. His fingers recalibrated his instruments. "Captain, it *was* 6,000 kilometers distant from the probe."

"Was? It's falling toward the black hole?"

"No, ma'am." A queer half-smile played over Castillo's lips. "Reading five-nine-eight-nine kilometers. Eight-six. Eight-*three*."

"Moving *closer*," said Bat-Levi. "But how . . . ?"

"I know," Castillo blurted out. He colored as all eyes turned toward him.

"*What?*" said Garrett impatiently.

Castillo jerked his head in a quick nod. "Captain, if you found traces of warp core near the black hole, how did the beacon get way out here? Granted, the beacon probably had enough speed to go some distance, but it's got limited fuel. So there's no way a beacon could get far enough away *not* to end up falling *back* toward the event horizon. But this beacon's not even *close*, it's at a *right angle* to the event horizon, and it's getting *closer*. The only way that can happen is if something *pushed* it here and . . ."

"And something's *still* pushing it." Bat-Levi's eyes went round. "He's right."

At the same time, Garrett knew what it was she'd sensed before but not been able to put words to. "Of course! It's riding on a jet of ionized plasma, on one of those Herbig-Haros! The beacon's moving *away* from the black hole because it was launched *while* the ship rode a jet. If I'd lost my engines, or only had impulse power, that's what I would do. Ride the jet like a hawk on a thermal."

"That has to be it, Captain," said Glemoor. "Whoever was here . . . *is* here understood that the only way to avoid being sucked past the event horizon would be if he could ride a jet of ionized plasma, and that's why the beacon is moving at a right angle to the black hole."

"But where's the ship?" asked Bat-Levi.

Glemoor pulled at a frill. "Captain, we extrapolated this course on the basis of following the gravitational collapse of gas globules back into those protostars. Now, those globules are very dense, and that's why they're falling back. Well, a *ship* is much denser than a beacon, so . . ."

"So they're falling back in," said Garrett. "Not toward the black hole but right into a protostar. They won't be crushed. They'll burn up."

"Presuming they haven't already," said Glemoor.

"Anything on long-range sensors?"

Glemoor consulted his instruments. "Possibly, Captain. A moment," Glemoor's slender fingers moved to coax a better resolution from the ship's long-range sensors. "I think there's something, Captain. Deeper in the nebula."

"Is it a ship?"

Glemoor hesitated then shook his head. "Impossible to say, Captain. There's too much interference. It is, however, moving away from us."

"Falling back," murmured Bat-Levi.

"Not if we can help it," said Garrett. Her mind darted over the possibilities, though she knew there was, in the end, only one decision she could make.

"Bat-Levi, contact sickbay. Inform Dr. Stern to prepare to receive casualties. Then let Mr. Kodell know we're likely to need all the power he can spare to the shields. All right, Mr. Castillo, plot a course for those sensor ghosts, best guess."

"Aye, Captain. I'll extrapolate back from the distress beacon . . . course plotted and laid in."

"Go." Garrett's hands clutched the arms of her command chair. "Mr. Bulast, continuous hails."

"You've got them, Captain."

And now we wait. Garrett tried to think of anything she'd forgotten, and decided that she'd done everything she could. Whatever happened next depended upon time and luck. Mainly luck.

At his station, alongside Castillo, Glemoor drew in a sharp breath of surprise.

Garrett was instantly alert. "Glemoor?"

"I think I've got them, Captain." The Naxeran's normally calm voice was tight with tension.

Garrett was out of her chair and by Glemoor's side in an instant. "A ship?"

"Yes. She's in a jet all right. The problem is all that ionized plasma makes sensor readings unreliable. Boosting power to the sensors."

Garrett held her breath while Glemoor worked. She felt the muscles along her spine jump with anxiety. She didn't want to prod, then did. *"Well?"*

Glemoor's voice had reclaimed its calm, even tone. "In a moment, Captain. Yes, here. From the size and configuration, I would say that this is a small transport vessel, large enough to accommodate forty, or perhaps fifty crew. I detect no activity consistent with engine function, though there *is* evidence of warp coolant."

"A coolant leak?"

"Most likely. Assuming that they were unable to stop the leak in time, then they would have had no choice but to jettison the core. Whatever the mechanism, she's dead in space now, Captain, falling away from us and accelerating. Her captain had the right idea, but without even impulse power to help that ship along, the energy in the jet just isn't enough to counteract the gravitational pull from that protostar."

"How far away is she?"

Glemoor checked his sensors again. "Approximately ninety million kilometers from the outer heliosphere of the protostar."

"A little more than Mercury's distance from the Sun," Garrett mused. "Pretty warm."

"And likely to get much more so. At their current rate of acceleration, the ship will impact in slightly less than six hours."

Garrett waved the statistic away. "They'll burn up long before then, if they're not already dead from radiation. What about shields?"

"None, Captain. If she had them, she doesn't have them now. In fact, I read minimal energy outputs all across the board."

"Does she have life support?"

She saw the hesitation in Glemoor's eyes. Finally, he

shook his head in apology. "I can't tell. The energy outputs I read should be enough for minimal life support, but that's all. Since we have no idea even of the species we're dealing with—humanoid or not—I have no ability to forecast their survival capabilities under these conditions."

"Captain." It was Bat-Levi. "Captain, no matter who they are, without shields, the amount of time before fatal exposure to gamma radiation . . ."

"Isn't long. And we have no idea how long they've been out here. I know, Commander," said Garrett. Well, if she was going to risk her ship on a rescue, there sure as hell better be someone worth risking them for. "Glemoor, can you at least tell me if there are life signs?"

Glemoor's ebony features screwed into a grimace of concentration before he shook his head. "I can't tell. What I can say for sure is that this vessel is much too small to have lifeboats."

"So anyone who was on her when she jettisoned her core is still there—dead or alive." Garrett scrubbed her lips with her left palm in thought. She paced behind Castillo and then around the helm, staring at the angry, billowing gases and interstellar dust swirling all around them. Had they come all this way in for nothing? She refused to believe it. *Come on, come on, Garrett, think,* think! The people on the other ship couldn't leave. If they were alive, they were still on board. *If they were alive . . .* leaning back against the helm, she put her hands on her hips, studying the viewscreen. The ship wasn't visible, of course; it was much too far away. But she projected her mind into the nebulae, stabbing through the jets of ionized plasma and photo-ionized gases, searching. What would she do? Clearly, the captain of that vessel had the right idea. He or she tried to use the plasma jets for propulsion to get her ship clear, hoping against hope to build up enough momentum to carry her ship out of the nebula. Once out of the nebula, she could signal for help because

she would know by then that her distress beacon hadn't made
it out. . . .

"Where would I go?" Garrett said, out loud. She stared at
the nebula she could see, the crippled ship she couldn't. "If
I knew my life support was failing and I'd lost shields and
had no way out, where would I go to stay alive longest?"

It was Bat-Levi who answered, her voice ramping up with
excitement. "The engine room, Captain! That's where you'd
go. The engine room would be the most heavily shielded
area of the ship. Assuming the warp core's gone, you could
evacuate residual coolant and hole up there. And hope."

Garrett nodded her agreement. "As long as there's life,
there's hope. Glemoor, if we get closer, can you tell me if
there are life signs?"

Glemoor regarded her carefully. "Captain, to get us that
close, we would have to enter into the plasma jet ourselves."

"Then here's something for you to add to your collection
of idioms, Mr. Glemoor," said Garrett, though she wasn't
smiling. "Out of the frying pan into the fire. Given our current situation, that's apt, and it's the only way. Can you do it?"

"Captain, I have to remind you that long-range sensors
aren't functioning well enough to resolve into individual
life-forms. I don't know if I can tell you how many there are,
one or a hundred."

"One or a hundred, Glemoor. I don't care. We find even
one survivor, we have to go after him."

"Yes, Captain. I'll try."

"Do better than that," said Garrett. She nodded toward
Castillo. "Bring us in closer. One-half impulse power. Bring
us in into the plasma jet on a perpendicular and then aft
thrusters down, course zero mark zero so we're heading into it
face first. That way we present the least amount of surface
area to the plasma jet, make our shields last that much longer.
Then I want you to keep us on that heading until Mr. Glemoor picks up something, or I tell you to stop. Understood?"

Castillo's tongue flipped along his upper lip. "Aye, Captain."

"Bat-Levi, raise engineering. Have them increase power to the forward shields."

"Aye."

Their inertial dampers were working perfectly, and so was their artificial gravity, yet when the ship crossed the boundary of the plasma jet, Garrett felt the shudder that rippled through the floors and bulkheads as concentrated streamers of hot ionized gas and radiation pounded the hull. The bridge lights dimmed momentarily then flared back to full brilliance, and Castillo nudged the aft thrusters in short bursts until the ship was cleaving the jet head-on, like an arrow shot from a bow, slicing the jet in two.

"How are our shields, Bat-Levi?"

"Ninety percent, Captain. The energy from that jet's like getting pounded with phasers at quarter."

"Just as long as they don't buckle. How about radiation outside the hull?"

"Not good, Captain. Radiation levels jumped as soon as we hit the column and they're increasing."

"How long can we maintain shields at our current rate of energy consumption?"

"Estimate one hour, twenty minutes, Captain."

"Plenty of time," Garrett said, wondering if she believed that herself. "Stay on course, Mr. Castillo."

To Castillo's left, Garrett saw Glemoor hunched over his sensor displays. His back was to her, but she could read the intense concentration in the set of his shoulders. "Let me know the minute you've got anything, Mr. Glemoor."

Glemoor may have been tense, but his tone was as genial as if they were discussing something of no greater gravity than the weather. "That *was* my intention, Captain."

Garrett grinned at the mild jibe, and she felt her stomach unclench a smidgeon. But a few moments later, Stern

hailed from sickbay, and Garrett knew it wasn't a social call.
"You want the good news, or the bad news?" said Stern.

"How much better is the good news?"

"Not very. Listen, Captain, I'll give it to you in a nutshell.
In this radiation-dense environment, we'll last fifty minutes if
those shields fail, and not more than two hours if they drop
anywhere close to forty, fifty percent. We could probably buy
some time by moving vulnerable crew from stations along
the hull and concentrate them in engineering or sickbay,
but not much."

"Understood. Jo, I plan to have us out of here before then."

"Mmm. Well, I converted cargo bay three into a triage
and staging area. Assuming there are survivors, they're going
to need to stay somewhere, and that's as good a place as any.
We've got full decon standing by for anyone who got a good
dose of radiation. I had a couple patients in sickbay. Nothing
serious and they're pretty stable, so they got moved to the
mess hall."

"I'm sure that's made the chef's day. Good work, Jo. Let's
hope we don't have to test your team's readiness."

"Amen to that. But those shields go, and I'm going to
have more down here than I can handle."

"I'll keep that in mind." Garrett punched off at the same
moment that Glemoor looked up.

"Got it," he said.

Garrett was aware that all activity had ceased around the
bridge; all eyes were on Glemoor. "And?"

"Life signs," Glemoor said. He broke into a huge grin,
and Garrett thought he looked just exactly like the Cheshire
Cat. "A lot of them. Humanoid. I estimate forty, perhaps
sixty individuals. And they are just where Lieutenant Commander Bat-Levi said they would be: engineering."

Garrett clenched her fist in savage triumph. "Yes! Mr.
Bulast, can you hail them?"

"Trying, Captain. Once we went into the plasma jet,

things went downhill in a hurry. I can tell that this is an old ship, though. Their subspace bands are all concentrated on the low end of the spectrum. I'm amazed I can hear anything. Right now, all I'm getting is the automatic beacon from the ship itself. But I do have a place of origin. They identify themselves as Atawhean and . . ." Bulast tilted his head to one side, trying to filter meaning out of a wash of static. Then his dark eyes went wide. "It's a *colony* ship, Captain."

"Aw, hell," muttered Castillo.

"Children, Captain," said Bat-Levi. *"Families."*

Garrett punched at her companel. "Transporter room, can you get me a lock?"

"Negative," said the voice—a woman's—that issued from the speaker. "There's too much ionization effect from all that radiation. Even if I could grab a piece of them, the pattern enhancers can't compensate. I'd end up killing them for sure."

The whistle of a hail pierced the air, and Garrett jabbed her companel. "Bridge, Garrett."

"Kodell, Captain. Shields are seventy-two percent. I've robbed power from every available place on this ship without touching environmental. The next step is to evacuate crew from nonessential areas and shut down life support to those decks."

"How much power will that buy us?"

"We'll maintain status quo, Captain."

"What about if we engage tractor beams?"

There was a very long pause. Then Kodell said, "If that's what you order, Captain, I'll do the best I can."

"As I just said to Glemoor, do *better*. I want two tractor beams on that vessel, and get our shields around her. And keep those impulse engines on line. We've got to keep this ship moving, even if you have to go out and push."

"Well, I sincerely hope it doesn't come to that, Captain,"

said Kodell, though Garrett didn't detect a whiff of sarcasm. "Tractor beams on. Extending shields."

"We've got them, Captain," said Glemoor. "Barely."

"Bat-Levi, go to red alert." As the klaxons sounded and the bridge lights shaded to crimson, Garrett turned to the helm. "Castillo, get us out of the jet and then plot us a course out of here, best possible speed. Straight line, don't waste any time."

Castillo glanced back once, nodded, and then executed the command.

Now with the extra power drain, Garrett felt the ship working hard. The engines didn't grind and groan as they'd done in starships from years past, but she could tell from the vibrations coming up through the floor and into her chair that she was pushing the ship to its limit. Ironically, it was at times like this—when there was nothing to do but give orders that her crew executed and her ship strained to make good—that she felt the most superfluous, with nothing to do but wait and pray.

Come on, girl, just hold together. Just hold together long enough for us to get out of here in one piece, and then we can all take a vacation.

Her ship couldn't answer her, not in words. But she felt *Enterprise* straining to do her bidding, and for not the first time, she found herself urging her ship on, gripping the arms of her command chair as if she could infuse the very force of her will. For the briefest of instants, she believed that she and her ship were one, and she imagined it was the same way that ship captains throughout time had felt, or fighter pilots before a battle, rocketing in their planes across an azure sky. The difference, of course, was there was no sea for her and her ship to fight here, no real air in which to bank and sideslip, to roll and spiral, and no enemy dogging her tail—nothing but a howling maelstrom of supercharged particles ready to destroy them.

Come on, girl, come on. Garrett felt a thin line of sweat trickle down her right temple. *Go, go.*

As if in defiance of her prayers, the ship lurched. The lights on the bridge stuttered. She heard a circuit blow somewhere behind and to her right. "What was that?"

"Gravity wave, Captain," said Bat-Levi. Her black hair had come loose of its braid and brushed her shoulders. With an impatient gesture, she used her right hand—the good one—to push a shock out of her face. "When we weren't pulling the other ship, we didn't feel them as much. But there are gravity wavefronts emanating from those proto-stars."

Alarmed, Garrett snapped her attention to Castillo. "How's our speed?"

"Dropping. Down to one quarter impulse."

"That won't be enough, Captain," said Bat-Levi, "not to get us out. It's the additional mass. We need more speed."

"No can do, Captain," said Castillo, before Garrett could ask. "That's all I can get out of her."

A hail: Kodell again. "I know you don't have good news," said Garrett.

"No. Shields at sixty-seven percent. Our impulse engines are starting to overheat, and starboard tractor beam is down to seventy percent. It's the extra load, Captain. I can't steal enough power to keep our shields up *and* extended *and* tractors at full *and* engines." A pause. "Believe me, Captain, if it would help for me to go out and push, I would. But it won't."

"Starboard tractor beam now sixty-eight percent," reported Bat-Levi. "Port tractor beam eighty-five percent. Rate of power drop *is* accelerating."

"Captain, we're starting to lose ground. It's one or the other," said Kodell.

Garrett's jaw firmed. "Unacceptable. Now we've got them, we're not letting that ship go. You keep two tractor beams on that ship. Shut down life support on Decks 12 to 22, if you have to, but keep those tractor beams going."

"I can do that. But I can't manufacture more speed. Simple physics, Captain. We don't have the power. So, if we don't let that other ship go, we'll fall back into the star together."

"Captain." It was Glemoor. "Why not jet our way out?"

Garrett's brows met in a frown. "You mean, go *back* into the plasma jet?"

"No, create our own. There's all this gas and ionized plasma," Glemoor waved a hand toward the viewscreen, "plenty of fuel all around us. All we have to do is to detonate strategically placed charges behind the *Enterprise* and then ride the jets we create. The pressure waves will push us out."

"A good idea, Glemoor, but we can't contain the explosion. There's no way to direct the charges so we don't take out the entire region. Even if we could, our shields wouldn't hold for that other ship, and not compensate for the sheer from our tractor beams. Either they or we—or maybe both—would rip apart."

"Starboard tractor beam fifty-five percent," Bat-Levi reported. "Shields at forty-five percent. Project shield failure in twenty-point-seven minutes."

"Kodell?"

"I see it, Captain. Permission to shut down life support, Decks 12 to 22."

"Go. Bat-Levi, get me more power to that starboard tractor beam." Garrett stabbed at her intercom. "Jo, our shields . . ."

"Way ahead of you. Evacuating from the more exposed areas of the ship now. But, like I said, fifty minutes, maybe an hour, Captain. Then it won't matter if we get pulled into a protostar, or drift over to that black hole and trip over that event horizon out there, we probably won't . . ."

Tripping. Stern was still talking, but Garrett tuned her out. *Event horizon's just about as solid a thing as you can find in space and it'll be more like jumping headfirst off a cliff . . . Dammit, the thing's got a shape!*

"That's *it!*" she blurted, and she saw Castillo jump as though he'd been shot. "Gravity! We've been banging our heads trying to figure out how to beat it. But why not use it to our advantage?"

"My God," said Bat-Levi, giving a little laugh of astonishment. "Of course, the gravity well around the protostar . . ."

"It's like any other," said Castillo, his voice ramping up with excitement. "It's strong, but it's got an outer limit, an edge just like that black hole out there."

"We accelerate toward the well at a shallow enough angle, then we ought to ricochet off the gravitational field," said Garrett. "We'll rebound, like a stone skipping over a pond."

"I heard that," came Stern, who was still on speaker. "Captain, I'm just a doctor, but even I know that if there's any miscalculation, we either burn up or come apart at the seams."

Trust Stern to put a damper on things. A slingshot around a sun—now *that* would be a piece of cake compared to this.

"We'll still need the speed," said Garrett, thinking furiously. "And to do that, we'd need to make Glemoor's plan work. I don't see how we can do that without turning the immediate area into a fireball."

"Captain." It was Bat-Levi. "There *is* a way. Instead of the protostar, we go for the black hole. Like you said, Captain, it's the *shape*. The gravity well of the black hole's event horizon is spherical. Using it to our advantage will be riskier in a lot of ways. Its gravitational field will be much stronger than that of a protostar. But the pull will give us the speed we can't build up now by ourselves, and without burning us all to a cinder."

"Unless we trip over the event horizon," said Stern. "Then we just get turned to vermicelli."

"Well, look at it this way, Jo, we won't burn up," said Garrett. "But our angle's shallow enough, we skip right off."

There was a moment's silence, broken by Stern: "Why do I think we're going to try this crazy stunt?"

Garrett spun into action. "Mr. Castillo, lay in a course for that black hole. Ninety plus sixty. Keep us shallow. Kodell, divert auxiliary power to the shields. And what about my tractor beams?"

"Working."

"Beg, borrow, and steal, Kodell." Garrett watched as the nebulae swam on the viewscreen with their course change. She felt the ship lurch with a sudden acceleration as they stopped fighting gravity. It was as if the black hole had reached out and grabbed them.

"Picking up speed, Captain," said Castillo, unnecessarily. "One-half impulse!"

"Sucking us in," said Garrett. Suddenly, the ship shook, and Garrett felt her body momentarily pressed back into her chair as if a giant hand had planted itself square in her chest. Then, just as quickly, the pressure slackened, and Garrett jerked forward, almost slamming to the deck. Behind her, she heard Bat-Levi gasp, and then the stubborn squeal of her first officer's servos as they fought to hold her upright.

"Mr. Castillo!" shouted Garrett. She staggered from her chair then clutched at an arm as the ship twitched and shuddered.

"I'm sorry, Captain!" Castillo's fingers were moving desperately over his console. Another jolt nearly sent him face-first into his instruments, and he had to brace himself with his left hand as he worked with his right. "Electromagnetic turbulence is getting stronger the closer we get to the black hole. I can't hold her steady!"

Glemoor looked over from his console toward the helm and then to Garrett. "Captain, we're too steep! We won't be able to break away!"

As if to confirm his words, Garrett felt her stomach drop in free-fall as the ship took a sudden plunge, slammed from above by what felt like a solid belt of hypercharged particles and compressed gases.

"It's the gravity, Captain!" Bat-Levi shouted. The ship rocked, and the artificial gravity hiccupped enough to send her backpedaling on her heels, off-balance, and slamming into the guardrail. She wheeled around, clutching for support. "Captain, the gravity, it's sucking all the matter in this region toward the black hole! Like a column of air in a wind tunnel, only it's denser because the particles are being squeezed together."

Garrett didn't need her to spell out the rest. With the increased compression and electromagnetic winds, the ship would be slow to respond, like trying to turn on a dime in a pool of molasses.

Garrett whirled on her heel. "My ship, Mr. Castillo!"

My ship: an age-old command, one used by pilots of planes not starships, but Castillo needed no translation. He jumped to one side as Garrett leapt to the helm and activated first the starboard, then port thrusters.

"Forty degrees." Glemoor threw a quick glance at his captain then back at his instruments. "Forty-five. Hull stress increasing, Captain. Approaching tolerance limits. The closer we get . . ."

"The higher the concentration and pressure of gas and particles," said Garrett, her eyes on her controls. "I *know*, Mr. Glemoor."

"Captain, we're *close*," said Bat-Levi, and "if we pass too close to the gravity well . . ."

"Fifty!" shouted Glemoor, the Naxeran's calm breaking at last. "Impulse power at three-quarters! Hull stress at tolerance! *Captain!*"

At almost the same instant, the main computer shrieked an alarm.

"We're not going to make it," muttered Castillo, in an undertone. He stood just behind Garrett's right shoulder, and she felt a slight jolt as his hands clutched the back of the chair. "We're not going to make it."

For just the briefest of instants, Garrett wanted to spin around and shake the young ensign until his eyeballs jittered. *Later*, she thought grimly. *We live through this, then I'll give him an earful, and he'll be damned glad to hear it because it will mean we're alive.*

She grappled with the helm, trying to keep them on a steady course, feeling the ship going mushy and unresponsive and knowing that the space outside the ship was so thick with particles it was like trying to maneuver through sludge. *Like the old fighter pilots. Get her nose up, get it up!* She nudged the thrusters again and again, in short bursts. Only instead of a throttle and flaps, a shaker stick and a yoke, she had thrusters and gravity and a boiling hailstorm of superheated ionized gas and . . . heat. Garrett gasped. Hawks, gliding, and . . . *heat.*

"Glemoor!" Garrett barked. "Arm photon torpedoes two and seven!"

"Captain?"

"*Do* it! Numbers two and seven! Ten-second delay!" She fired a five-second blast from the thrusters along the ship's belly and saw the positioning gyros record the shift in the *Enterprise*'s attitude as the ship angled up, exposing more of the flat of its belly to the gravitational front of the black hole.

"Aye!" Glemoor's black skin was dripping sweat. His frills were stiff, and the yellow of his eyes had deepened to a hot gold. "Torpedoes armed! Fifty-five degrees, Captain! Fifty-six!"

Almost there. Garrett blinked sweat from her eyes and winced at the sting. *Almost there. Come on, girl, come on, don't let me down, don't quit on me now.*

But she had to protect the other ship. Her plan wouldn't do much good to them if she ended up incinerating them. "Engineering! Kodell, reinforce aft shields! Steal from us if you have to, but give that other ship every gram of protection you can!"

Suddenly, the ship dipped precipitously. To her horror, Garrett saw that they'd lost five degrees, now ten. . . .

"*Kodell!*" Gritting her teeth, Garrett brought the side of her fist down on her maneuvering thrusters and was rewarded with nothing. "Kodell, where's my power, where's my *control?*"

Kodell, on speaker: "Power drain, Captain, when I reinforced shields! Trying to stabilize now!"

"Kodell, I need *control.*" Garrett watched as the ship swung inexorably lower, being pulled into a perpendicular toward the gravity well. *We're heading nose down, no, no!* "I need it *now!*"

"Can't do it, Captain! That last surge knocked out the power couplings to the thrusters. They're offline and I can't reroute fast enough. Auxiliary power is tied up with the shields, I can't rob . . ."

Garrett didn't wait to hear the rest. Their angle was getting too steep and they were out of time. "Glemoor, launch photon torpedoes! *Now!*"

"Aye!" Glemoor stabbed at fire control. "Torpedoes *away!*"

"On main viewer!" The viewscreen swam as the angle changed, and then Garrett saw the tiny red-orange sparklers that were the torpedoes streaking away from her ship, and she imagined she could hear them sizzling across space. "Time to detonation!"

"Eight seconds!" Glemoor cried. "Seven, six!"

"Captain!" shouted Kodell. "Maneuvering thrusters nominal!"

"Four, three!"

"Thrusters!" Garret brought her fists crashing into the helm and felt the shuddering of the thrusters firing. *My ship*—she jerked her head back up to the viewscreen and saw the torpedoes fading, the violet and pink space swinging by in a dizzying arc and if it had been any other time or place, she would have marveled at how much beauty could exist in the heart of death—*my ship!*

"One!" Glemoor cried.

The viewscreen flooded with white light, and then gravity must have failed because Garrett felt her body rise out of her chair and hurtle backward to slam against the deck.

The viewscreen went black.

Chapter 27

"Just hold *still*."

"I *am*." Garrett's fingers plucked at the thin green fabric of the patient's tunic she wore. Stern and her nurse had stripped her out of her uniform when she'd been brought to sickbay—only Garrett had no memory of that, having been unconscious for a half hour after the torpedoes blew. In fact, she was a little foggy for the five minutes or so before the torpedoes went off; retro- and antegrade amnesia went with the territory when you had a concussion, Stern said. Garrett remembered giving the order to arm the torpedoes but not the order to fire.

She sighed. Her scalp itched, and her uniform was a mess from all the blood. Her eyes crawled to the soiled clothing still lying in a heap on the floor next to the biobed. Her nostrils twitched with the faint, sickly metallic aroma of wet rust.

"I'm fine," she said, not believing it but hating having to lie there and do nothing. *All doctors are overprotective.* "When can I get out of here?"

"When I'm done," came Stern's voice. Garrett could hear the frown. Garrett was on her back and facing left so Stern could work, and she couldn't see the doctor's face.

"But I'm fine."

"Uh-huh. Sure, it's every day you get knocked senseless and need stitches. Honestly, Mac was right. All captains are the galaxy's worst patients. I'm almost done."

Garrett sighed again, resigned to the fact that she wasn't
going anywhere until Stern decided she was good and ready.
She heard the steady hum of Stern's autosuture as Stern re-
paired the wound on her scalp and, outside the small treatment alcove she picked out the buzz of voices, the shuffle of
feet, the blip of monitors above biobeds. "What about the
survivors?"

"Ten cases of radiation poisoning, two serious. All of them
members of the crew, not the passengers."

"Who got it the worst?"

"The ship's engineer, and the captain. The engineer got
a double whammy when she took their mains offline. Radiation flooded the compartment, though not enough to kill
her straight off. But she knew she'd been exposed and so she
volunteered to stay on the bridge, keep their shields up as
long as she could. At least that's how the rest of the survivors
tell it. Engineer hasn't regained consciousness yet. Hell of a
brave woman."

"And the captain?"

"Stayed with his engineer. Moved the rest of his crew from
exterior portions of the ship but not to engineering; engineering could only accommodate the colonists, and so the captain
decided the colonists took priority. Damn shame, you ask me.
All those people wanted was a fresh start on a colony world,
only they get it all blasted to hell by a bunch of pirates who
chase them into the nebula and then leave them for dead."

Stern straightened, clicking off the autosuture. "I've done
all I can for the time being. The engineer and captain are
on life support. Now we wait, let nature take its course. That
ought to do it, by the way. You're done."

Stern brushed Garrett's auburn hair back over the wound
that ran from the tip of Garrett's right eyebrow and along
Garrett's scalp, ending just behind her right ear. Stepping
back, Stern cocked her head to one side, seemingly admir-
ing her handiwork.

"Not bad," she said, finally. "You're going to have a lump the size of an egg on your forehead there for awhile, nothing I can do about that. But you're lucky. The old days, you know, I would've had to shave off all that hair."

"Lucky me." Garrett blew out in exasperation. She was tired of lying flat on her back. And she hated the way they never gave out sheets or blankets in sickbay but had you lie there in your uniform or a patient tunic, and freeze your butt off.

Garrett pushed up on her elbows. "Someone bringing . . .?" She'd been about to ask if someone was bringing her a fresh uniform when a wave of nausea made her moan and roll back onto the biobed.

"That'll teach you," said Stern, the trace of a smirk on her lips. "I didn't tell you to get up yet. Just sit tight, and I'll have someone bring you a fresh change of clothes."

"Thanks." Garrett blinked, swallowed. Closed her eyes until the urge to vomit passed. She waited quietly until Stern came back. Then she asked, "Why do I feel sick?"

"Because you have a concussion, that's why. Here." Stern turned aside, replacing her instruments on their tray and then plucking up the gray tube of a hypospray. Jabbed the business end of the spray into the angle of Garrett's neck and right shoulder, and depressed the jet with her thumb. There was an audible hiss as the jet dispensed its contents into Garrett's bloodstream. "That ought to help with the nausea. You're going to have a whopper of a headache for a little while, though, and you're bound to be stiff tomorrow. Next time, pick something softer to land on than the deck of a starship. Actually, you were lucky," Stern amended, popping the empty vial of analgesic from the hypospray, "Castillo breaking your fall like that. Scared him out of a year's growth, though. Scalp wounds bleed like stink. The way he sounded when the bridge hailed, I think he thought you were dead."

Head still throbbing, Garrett eased off the biobed. The

floor was icy against her bare feet. She straightened millimeter by millimeter. Her ribs complained, and she was certain she'd be black and blue for days. "How he's doing now?"

"Castillo? Other than a knot the size of a grapefruit on the back of his head, he's fine." Stern eyed Garrett. "I just want to ask you one question. What the hell made you fire off those torpedoes?"

Garrett almost shook her head then, remembering her vertigo, thought better of it. "Just a hunch. Piloting the ship reminded me of flying in an atmosphere, and then I remembered how birds, hawks and condors, they'll ride thermals for hours. So I thought: heat. Not a thermal exactly, but I thought if I could just get us shallow enough then detonate a couple of torpedoes, part of the shock wave would be absorbed by the black hole itself and the rest ought to blast us clear. We rode an energy wave."

"Took a hell of a risk."

Garrett was about to point out that there hadn't been a lot of alternatives, but Bat-Levi hailed from the bridge. "Glad to hear you're up and around, Captain."

"Thank you, Commander." *But I'm freezing my butt off.* "As soon as I get some clothes, I'll be up. Status?"

"We've cleared the nebulae cluster. We took some minor structural damage aft. Repairs are under way. Other than that, we were lucky."

"Seems to be the word of the day. Have you been able to reach Starfleet?"

"Actually, there's a message coming in now. Commander Batanides, Starfleet Intelligence."

Likely reporting that Burke and Sivek were back at Starfleet Headquarters, with Halak in tow. With everything that had gone on, thoughts of Halak had been far from her mind. But now Garrett felt a mantle of depression drape itself over her shoulders. "Pipe it down here."

Garrett heard Bat-Levi giving orders. Then: "You're on, Captain."

Garrett straightened, even though she was on audio. She just wished she had some clothes. It was so cold in Sickbay her skin prickled with gooseflesh. Garrett chafed her bare forearms with her hands. "Garrett here."

"Captain." Batanides's voice was tense. "We've been trying to reach you for days. What's going on there?"

Briefly, Garrett went over the events of the past few days, concluding with their rescue of the Atawhean ship. "We've just gotten clear of interference from the nebula . . ."

"That's just *it*," Batanides broke in, clearly agitated. "*Why* were you there to begin with?"

That brought Garrett up short. She and Stern exchanged glances; Stern hiked her shoulders. "Those were our orders," Garrett said.

"From whom?"

"Why," said Garrett, confused, "from *you*. Don't you remember? We spoke. When Commander Halak was remanded to Lieutenant Burke's custody. I lodged a formal protest and . . ."

"Captain, I assure you," said Batanides, her voice saturated with urgency, "after our first contact about Lieutenant Burke coming aboard, you and I never spoke. And I know for a fact that Commander Halak couldn't have been remanded to Burke."

"Whaaat?" Stern drawled. "What the hell kind of game . . . ?"

Garrett cut her off with a wave of her hand. "What are you talking about, Marta?"

"I'm saying that you never received orders to proceed to the Draavids. Commander Halak never made it to Starfleet Headquarters. And I *know* now that Lieutenant Burke was in no position to be aboard your ship, taking custody of anyone."

"And why not?"

"Because, Captain Garrett," said Batanides, "Lieutenant Laura Burke is dead."

"All right, here's the situation," said Garrett, an hour later. After signing off from Batanides, she'd taken a hasty sonic shower and thrown on a clean uniform. But she still felt like hell. Ignoring the ache in her head, she leaned her forearms on the table in the briefing room next door to her ready room and eyed each of her senior officers in turn: Stern and Bat-Levi to her right, Glemoor, Bulast, and Kodell ranged along her left. And, finally, Tyvan: Garrett had debated then decided that, for better or worse, part of Tyvan's job was to take the pulse of the crew . . . and its captain. *And doing a damn good job of that.*

"Commander Batanides indicated that debris from the shuttle piloted by Lieutenant Burke—the *real* Burke—was discovered several parsecs away from Starbase 12, in an isolated section of space lousy with asteroid fields. A navigator's nightmare, which probably explains why it took so long for anyone to connect up the wreckage with Burke, or *find* it, for that matter."

"How did they know to start looking, Captain?" Tyvan asked. "Did you inquire?"

Garrett and Stern exchanged glances. "You want to answer that?" asked Garrett.

"Not really." Stern fidgeted an instant then said, "Me." She continued, a little defensively as if someone were about to take her to task for going behind her captain's back, "I got an old friend on the horn. I asked him to do some checking up on a couple of things, and he asked questions, and that got back to Batanides, and then *she* started digging around, and well," Stern's voice trailed off. She punctuated the silence with a shrug.

"Okay," said Tyvan, in the silence. He gave Stern a bland

look. "Just asking. Didn't know if I'd been making myself too scarce to have been in the loop."

"Good thing she did," said Garrett, amused despite the current situation. *Ah, Jo, someone who gives as good as he gets, how do you like them apples?* "Anyway, there's no doubt. Burke's ship was sabotaged. The recovery team found traces of divalent triceron."

"An explosive," said Glemoor. "Very powerful, highly unstable. Also illegal."

"Clearly, whoever blew up Burke's shuttle wanted to make it look like an accident, or pilot error. Starfleet Intelligence thinks the Qatala planted the bomb."

"And Burke's body?" asked Bat-Levi.

"Vaporized. Burke also had a passenger. Batanides said that Burke had been undercover for months, infiltrating the Qatala. Her mission was to make contact, gather information, and, if possible, secure a contact willing to turn on the Qatala and provide detailed information on the Qatala's drug distribution network as well as arms sales to various parties, particularly the Cardassians. Two weeks ago, the real Burke informed SI that she'd secured a contact and was on her way back."

"Any idea about the contact?"

"Not a clue. Starfleet Intelligence believes that someone caught on to Burke and alerted Qadir, who then arranged for her accident. That way, Qadir could take care of Burke and the traitor at the same time."

"I'll wager the Burke *we* saw was the real Burke's passenger," said Tyvan.

"Probably, and the person Qadir used for the job. Except she seems to have her own agenda." Garrett nodded toward Bulast. "What do you have?"

"I ran an analysis on Burke's transmission to Starfleet," said Bulast. "Remember, *she* was the one who gave me the coded frequencies. By filtering successive frequencies, I found a coned signal *inside* a real secured channel, like a hand in a glove. This coned signal rerouted the *Enterprise*'s transmissions to a subspace transceiver programmed with Starfleet authorization codes. You talked to the real Batanides at first, of course; that's how Burke was able to get aboard the ship. Thereafter, you were talking, for all practical purposes, to a computer program. If we'd been on visual, which we weren't, you'd have seen a holographic projection. The technology exists, of course; it's a variant of cloaking technology, but more primitive. When I traced the subspace transceiver signals, I found they emanated from *Enterprise*, specifically from a shielded compartment in the floor panels of that shuttle Halak brought back from Farius Prime. Burke probably planted the transceiver when she searched the shuttle. She had to have stolen the transceiver, though. It's programmed with top-secret authorization codes that SI confirms are the genuine article. Anyway, this probably explains why we were ordered to the Draavids. Burke must have known that, eventually, Starfleet would contact us with news about the real Burke, or that we might use another channel to raise Starfleet. The nebulae were insurance; it kept us in a communications blackout."

"But they—she, whoever she is—had to know we'd find the transceiver eventually," said Bat-Levi. "Why leave it behind?"

Garrett scooped her auburn hair with her hand, wincing as she tugged on her scalp wound. Gingerly, she fingered the lump on her forehead. Stern was right; the lump was the size of a small orange. "I think *eventually* is the operative term. All she needed was to get away, and she has. But I'll just bet those records Burke *found* in Halak's log and the shuttle are fakes. Bulast, any word from the V'Shar?"

"Confirmation received just before you called this briefing, Captain. Vulcan Space Central reports that the warp shuttle *T'Pol* disappeared twelve days ago. The shuttle's last known position was 30 light-years from Farius Prime. Sivek really *is* a V'Shar operative, only he's really quite *dead*: murdered. Body was found today in a cave outside Naweeth City, on Vulcan."

Bat-Levi was shaking her head. "Captain, who *are* these people? And what do they want with Commander Halak?"

Garrett weighed her response. "I think it's safe to assume that *these* people are Qadir confederates. That would explain why they know so much about Halak. Some of what they presented is, apparently, the genuine article—Halak's family, the Qatala connection, and the falsified information he gave on his Academy application."

She waited for the general shuffling as her crew absorbed that to die away before continuing. "As for *why* they want him, I don't know. Right now I don't care. Our job is to find him and worry about the rest later."

Bat-Levi gave a little laugh. "It's a big galaxy, Captain."

"A . . . what do you call it?" Glemoor frowned then brightened. "Needle in a haystack, yes?"

"Worse," muttered Kodell.

"Not necessarily." Garrett glanced at Stern. "Doctor?"

Stern crossed her arms over her chest. "I examined Halak before he left the ship, and I injected him with a nanosubcutransponder. And *no*," she glowered at Tyvan as if daring him to make an issue of it, "there was no loop, and no one ordered me to do it. Did it all on my own. Captain Garrett didn't know a thing. Just had a feeling, that's all."

There was a moment of shocked silence. A beat-pause. Garrett saw Tyvan hide a grin behind his hand. Then Bulast said, "Well, okay. All I'll need is the transponder code. You get me that, and we backtrack, I'll find him."

"But they could have gone anywhere from there. Like I said, it's a big universe," said Bat-Levi. "*Really* big."

"Well, SI's got some ideas about that," said Garrett, hoping her tone didn't betray a shred of the anxiety she felt. Then she told them.

This time the silence lasted for a good thirty seconds. Kodell broke it. "Cardassian. Space. *Cardassian?*"

"Oh, this just keeps getting better and better," said Stern.

"Well, not exactly Cardassian," said Garrett, with no more inflection than if they were talking about Halak being in orbit around Mars, or somewhere equally benign, and not somewhere in the tinderbox of disputed Cardassian space. "SI thinks. They're not sure, and they didn't really get into why they think that he's even there."

"You mean, they decided we didn't have to know," said Kodell, a man who, in Garrett's opinion, never minced words. He was prickly—downright obstinate, sometimes—but she actually liked him more because he spoke his mind.

"Maybe." And then because Garrett didn't like SI anymore than Kodell did: "Yes."

"Ah," said Glemoor, "then they want to play, how do you call it? Russian roulette. Only we are the ones pulling the trigger of our own pistol."

Bat-Levi frowned. "What's Russian roulette?" When Glemoor explained, she made a disparaging noise. "That's a stupid game. You could end up getting killed."

Kodell looked baleful. "Which is why they're sending *us* in."

Garrett eyed Kodell. "You have a problem?"

"Frankly, yes. With all due respect, Captain, we've just come through a run-in with a black hole. We're lucky there's only minor hull damage from radiation pitting, but the inertial dampers are just a little cranky, and our gravity could use some work. I'm not happy with the antimatter injectors, either. Now you're talking space that's in dispute between the Federation and the Cardassians. We all know about the Cardassians. Shoot first, and shoot later. Now, we're being asked to go in covertly. How long before the Cardassians claim we're making incursions into their territory, and do the same to us? We show up without authorization, we spark a conflict, and if we're forced into a fight, I can't vouch for the ship."

"Well then, you'll be pleased to know that our orders are *not* to fight. Our orders are not to engage the Cardassians. Our orders are to locate Commander Halak, period."

Kodell was undaunted. "You mean, evade the Cardassians, find Halak, and apprehend this Burke and Sivek, or whoever they are because if Halak's there, so are they. That's the real agenda, Captain, and that's business for Starfleet Intelligence."

"But Halak's one of us," said Bat-Levi.

"I know that," said Kodell. "I'm just pointing out the risks involved, and it's justification I'm asking about. Why doesn't Starfleet Intelligence just send their people after Burke and Sivek, retrieve Halak, and then go from there? Personally, I don't think they care one bit about Halak. All they care about is what happens to their own."

"And it comes down to that, doesn't it, Mr. Kodell?" asked Garrett. "Caring for your own people? Normally, I'd agree with you on SI cleaning up after itself. To tell the truth, I intend to file a formal protest with Starfleet Command, *after*. Batanides hasn't been on the up and up. No intelligence agency ever is. I accept that, but I move on, Mr. Kodell, because it's my *job*. Make no mistake. Until we understand the whole truth, I'm unwilling to throw a member of *my* crew on *my* ship to the wolves."

She spared Glemoor a brief admonishing glance: *Don't ask.* Now, she reasoned, was not the time to explain the vagaries of aphorisms. "This is not a debate, Mr. Kodell, nor is it a democracy. We have our orders. If it were captain's discretion, I would make the same decision. We get Halak. Then we decide what to do after that."

Kodell wasn't put off. "And the Cardassians, Captain?"

"*If* that's where Halak is, and *if* Cardassians show up, we don't fight. Period. Nothing provocative." She didn't add that she understood their presence was likely provocation enough. "We defend ourselves, if need be."

Kodell looked displeased but said nothing more. Shortly after, Garrett dismissed them with orders to rendezvous with the U.S.S. Blakely, also in that sector, and transport the survivors from the colony ship to that vessel before proceeding. Except for Stern, the rest filed out without conversation—at least, within earshot.

Stern waited until the briefing room door hissed shut. "He hit it on the head, you know."

"Please." Closing her eyes, Garrett pinched the bridge of her nose between her right thumb and index finger. Her head was raging. Concussions, she concluded, were worse than any migraine. "Not you, too. Glemoor's bad enough."

"I see we're on the same page," Stern said, straight-faced. "Isn't it nice that I don't have to explain every idiomatic expression?"

"You hanging around for a reason, or just on general principle?"

"Two things. Want the bad news, or the observation first?"

Garrett groaned. "What?"

"I told you I asked Mac to do some digging around. Damn good thing he did; it alerted Batanides to check up on Burke. But here's another thing he found: those autopsy reports on Thex and Strong."

"Halak's crewmembers from the Ryn mission. And?"

"Thex's autopsy results were consistent with death as a result of his injuries."

"Oh." Garrett blinked. "Well, that's not bad."

Stern held up a hand. "Wait. Strong's results were a little more problematic."

"No explosive decompression?"

"Oh, no, there was that." Stern made a face. "You don't tend to miss that, air-filled spaces like heads and guts and lungs popping tending to be fairly splashy."

"But?"

"*But* a more detailed analysis of Strong's intact tissues does not demonstrate persuasive evidence of a preexisting hypoxia."

"Jo, in English."

"Rachel, he wasn't suffocating. He had plenty of air. Hàlak said Strong popped his seal because he was desperate for air. Halak's story fits, *if* you're hypoxic. People do the damnedest things in those situations. But the evidence says that Strong wasn't that far gone. In fact, *Halak*'s tissues demonstrated a more severe and sustained hypoxia than Strong's, and that *does* jibe. Strong's suit *was* damaged and Halak said that he gave the lion's share of Thex's air to Strong to compensate. But the bottom line, Rachel: When Strong died, he had plenty of air. Strong had no reason to pop that seal. Absolutely. None. Burke, or whoever she is . . . she was right."

"Oh, hell." Garrett exhaled, closed her eyes. "*Hell.*"

"Told you it was bad."

"Damn it, Jo." Garrett fixed Stern with a despairing look. "Where is the truth *anywhere* here?"

"Beats the hell out of me. But that brings me to my observation. Since when did we volunteer for the espionage business?"

"When Starfleet Command volunteered us." Garrett sighed. She was so tired of lies and subterfuge. "Look, I know Kodell's got a point. I even agree: Starfleet Intelligence isn't being straight with us—not that *anyone* is, it seems. Burke and Sivek—I guess I'll just call them that until I know who they really are—they're only part of the equation. There's something else SI knows, or suspects but doesn't want to say. Something the Cardassians have, or SI *thinks* they have."

"Like?"

"Theory? The Cardassians are into expansion. We know that. So maybe they're developing a new weapons system.

Cloaking technology, maybe. I don't know. I'll tell you one thing, though." Garrett looked grim. "This isn't about drugs, not anymore."

"If it ever was," said Stern.

Garrett made a vague gesture with one hand. "Oh, Starfleet cares about the Qatala, and the Orion Syndicate, but they're much smaller headaches compared to the Cardassians. In the end, the Cardassians are a bigger threat than all the red ice the Qatala or Syndicate can deliver. Starfleet's out to prevent a war before it can start."

"Well, let's hope we don't give the Cardassians an excuse." Stern scraped her chair back and stood. "You know, Rachel, you said you didn't want to throw Halak to the wolves. I'm with you on that, if for nothing else than I want to understand what's going on once and for all. But you sure as hell didn't say anything about a lion's den."

Chapter 28

Stewing in his own juices: that's what Dalal would've said. This was apt, seeing as he hadn't showered in two days or changed his clothes. Halak had turned things over so many times in his head, his brain felt like a bruised apple. Things just didn't compute. First, Starfleet Intelligence showed up. Then they produced records. Some of them were true. Most of them weren't. They claimed Dalal never existed and that Arava was gone. And then to top it all off, after disgracing him in front of his captain and crewmates, SI wanted *him* to do *them* a favor. Actually, blackmail was more like it. They needed a fall guy, pure and simple. So they'd picked Halak, just as they'd done before.

A *fall guy*. Halak lay on his back, hands clasped behind

his head, staring at the ceiling of his tiny quarters, finding nothing of interest there and not expecting there to be anything of interest in the near, or distant future. He had nowhere to go, no place to be. Well, not yet, anyway. Soon enough: Burke said they'd come out of warp within the next five hours. Then things were bound to get dicey, and Halak probably wouldn't have time to ponder an obscure idiom that so neatly summed up his situation. Glemoor would have been pleased.

First scenario: If anything went wrong—if the Cardassians discovered him—he'd be the one who took the blame for Starfleet Intelligence. He'd be painted as a rogue officer who'd escaped while in custody and gone off on some personal vendetta.

Or second scenario: If he *didn't* run into the Cardassians but managed to end up getting himself killed in the process—by one of Qadir's men, say—Starfleet Intelligence still came up smelling like roses (an idiom even Glemoor understood without requiring an explanation). Getting himself killed would tidy things up considerably for Starfleet Intelligence, actually. It might even be preferable because it would prove SI's theory that Halak had been in on Qadir's network of operations all along.

Either way, it was win-win for SI, with Halak the loser in any scenario except one. He just might succeed.

"Are we absolutely clear on this?" Burke had asked after she'd explained what Starfleet Intelligence wanted. "Do you understand exactly what you're supposed to do?"

Halak had nodded. After recovering from the initial shock of Burke's overture, Halak had listened, very carefully, as the Starfleet Intelligence agent outlined the mission. So he understood the implications, perfectly. "No problem on the details. I think the gist is that I'm supposed to do something fairly illegal. Trespass into disputed territory, secure the specs and schematics of this intradimensional portal, or whatever you call it, then manage to get back to the *T'Pol* without getting caught by the Cardassians, or murdered by one of Qadir's men who you claim are, at this very moment, crawling all over the same area, looking for a portal that may, or may not exist. I just don't get why you think this portal exists at all. On the basis of what? A couple of legends about a race no one knows for sure existed?"

"The fact that the Qatala's financing this operation tells us something," said Burke. "Money may not mean anything to *us*, but there are many to whom it does. It comes down to this, Halak. If the Hebitians were on this planet, then they got there somehow. Ships, maybe. But a portal is much more likely given what the Cardassians believe about them. The Cardassians have never, so far as we know, found any artifacts consistent with a spacefaring race. So if they're Hebitian ruins, they got there through a portal. It's the only explanation."

"What if they were seeded?"

"By what? Some benevolent god-race? Those are just stories, Halak. Anyway, even if there isn't a portal, there may be a tomb, and if all Qadir finds is a bunch of jevonite, gold, and jewels, that's still worth his time and effort, particularly when he's not the one risking his neck."

"But Starfleet Intelligence thinks there's more."

"Absolutely. Why would the Cardassians bother patrolling a planet where there's nothing of value? Sure, the space is disputed, but they pay particular attention to that particular planet, and get very touchy if any Federation vessels request a flyby. In fact, I don't think any Federation vessel is allowed to get close."

"So, by a process of elimination, assuming it's not a research facility, you've decided that the most likely scenario is some artifact the Cardassians can't use but want to keep to themselves until they can." Halak had cocked his head to one side. "Okay. A little tautological, if you ask me."

"But I'm not asking you, Commander." Burke had given him a dry look. "I'm telling you."

"I noticed. But why me? I'm a killer, right? Murder my crewmates at the drop of a hat? Plus, I'm supposed to be in cahoots with Qadir, or want to take over, or something equally inane. Whatever I am, I'm most certainly *not* an agent, despite anything I got volunteered for in the past. Why not send trained personnel to infiltrate Qadir's network, or a couple of operatives to this planet?"

"You're an intelligent man, Commander. You tell me."

"Easy. Plausible deniability."

"Disavowal is more like it. You get caught, you were acting on your own."

"How did I get here then? Wherever *here* is."

"You overpowered SI agents escorting you to Starfleet Command. Being in Qadir's network and having recently visited Farius Prime, you knew of his plans and so decided to take it upon yourself to secure a piece of whatever it was Qadir was after."

"But, unfortunately for me, Qadir's people got the better of me, or the Cardassians caught on, and Starfleet is off the hook."

"As good a story as any."

A good story. Discounting the fact that Burke was Starfleet Intelligence (all intelligence agents were trained liars), Halak knew: Burke was a liar. Halak didn't know *how* he knew, but he did.

Staring at the ceiling, Halak felt the ship change around him and knew, without having to be told: They'd dropped out of warp. Halak pushed up on his elbows and swung his legs over the edge of his bunk. Burke would come soon. They'd go over the plan; she'd give him a chance to study the drop area and decide how he wanted to attack the problem of locating Qadir's men and the portal, if it existed.

The faintest of vibrations. Footsteps. Halak heard the

blip-blap-bleep of someone keying in the code to unlock the door to his quarters.

"I brought you something to eat," Burke said. She held a phaser in her right hand, the tray balanced on her left.

"Thanks." Without being asked, Halak jumped down and backed to the far corner as she slid the tray on to his bunk, keeping her eyes—and the phaser—trained on him the entire time. They'd gone through the same ritual twice a day for almost the last week, so Halak had it down. Odd behavior for someone who considered him a confederate, but Halak would have taken the same precautions. *After all, it's not like I volunteered.* "I could use a shower, too. A change of clothes."

"No problem." Phaser still pointed in his direction, Burke backed toward the door. "I'll have Sivek see to both."

Looking over the items on his tray, Halak made a face: same monotonous, indigestible Vulcan tripe. "May I ask you a question?"

"Sure."

"We've talked about the Cardassians and Qadir, what will happen if I get the specs on this portal for you," said Halak, still inspecting what passed for food arrayed on his tray, "but what about Arava?"

There was a pause. Then: "What about her?"

"What will happen to her? If I cooperate, that is."

"*If?*" Burke's eyes were flat. "You having second thoughts?"

"No. But it seems to me that if you know so much about me, then you might know where she is, and how important she is to me."

"And if we did? Know either? Both?"

"Can you get her off Farius Prime? Since I'm risking my life and all that, you know, for the greater good."

"You're risking your life and all that for your *career,*" said Burke. "Let me give you a suggestion. Do your job and don't worry about anything else right now. You get those specs. Then we'll talk."

"But you'll consider it," Halak pressed.

"It's not my decision."

"You could put in a word or two. I've been cooperative."

"As would anyone with the business end of a phaser pointed in his direction."

"Yeah, but that's *now*. How do you know I won't try something *later*? Warp off, or give you phony specs, or something?"

"You won't warp off because Sivek will be with you. I'm not stupid, Halak. And you stay with us, in Starfleet Intelligence's custody, until we're satisfied that the specs are genuine."

"Fair enough. But you could still ask your superiors. Ask Batanides about getting Arava off Farius Prime. Otherwise, I won't budge."

"I don't think you have many choices."

"Screw that." Halak slid back onto his bunk and crossed his arms. "And screw you. You get Arava off, or I don't work. Period."

Burke's cheeks flushed. Her phaser-hand twitched. "You *will*."

Halak laughed. "Or what? You going to shoot me? My career's over, remember? Whether you shoot me now, or I get myself killed, or I refuse and get court-martialed and put in prison, it's all the same. But if you lose me, you lose plausible deniability. So, *manus manum lavat*. One hand washes the other, in case you're not up on your Latin," said Halak, privately tickled that having Glemoor around was proving to quite advantageous. "You agree to my terms, or it's no deal."

Her brown eyes sparking, Burke stared at him a long minute. Halak returned the stare. Burke blinked first. "I'll have to take it up with Command."

"Great, you do that. Then I want to see a copy of those orders."

"That may not be possible. We're supposed to be in a communications blackout, Commander."

"Don't give me that. You've got narrow-band, secured channels. Use one. Hey," Halak gave a disingenuous smile, "this is the *mission* we're talking here. Yeah, sure, it's my career. But it's yours, too, Burke. You screw up, and I'll bet you don't get to play secret agent again any time before the next star in these parts goes nova."

The small muscles along Burke's jaw jumped. She backed up, toward the door, and Halak saw her left hand come up, the fingers move as she keyed in the combination for the lock. "I'll see what I can arrange," she said then cursed when her fingers slipped, and she botched the combination.

Good. He was making her angry, and that was good. Anger made people feel pressured, and people who were pressured made mistakes. "That's not good enough."

"It will have to do." Burke's look bordered on venomous. She jabbed at the combination again, blew out when the lock double-bleeped, and the door hissed open. "I will talk to Commander Batanides. Perhaps we can arrange to get Arava and her son, Klar, off Farius Prime, and maybe not, Commander. One damn thing at a time, all right?" Without waiting for a reply, she stepped out.

The door slid shut. Halak stood quite still, hardly daring to breathe.

Klar. She'd said *Klar.* But she couldn't *possibly* know about Arava's son, *or* his name. Halak had *never* mentioned Klar—not by name, or in any of his personal log entries. It was too dangerous. But *Burke* had known about him. Could one of Burke's sources have told her? Someone who had infiltrated Qadir's organization?

But wait. Her information was bad. She'd gotten things wrong about Arava. Yet she'd known about Klar, a boy about whom only three people, other than Arava, were in the know: Dalal, Halak . . . and Qadir. No one else knew. No one suspected. So the only way Burke could have known there even *was* a Klar was either for her to have gotten to know Arava, very well—or to have set eyes on him herself. Or both. But she'd said to Garrett, at the inquiry: *I've never been to Farius Prime, Captain.*

My God, he thought, she's lying. I knew it! She says she's never been to Farius Prime, but she let slip about Klar.

"So what else are you lying about, Burke?" Halak whispered, out loud, to thin air. "Just who, or what, *are* you?"

Putting conditions on things now, huh? Thumbing on the safety of her phaser, Lieutenant Laura Burke—whose real name was Talma Pren, a person with no rank in anyone's military—jammed the weapon into a holster hugging her hip. *Not going to do what he's told?* Talma stalked the short corridor from Halak's quarters to a gangway that led to the warpshuttle's bridge. Well, Halak wasn't making the rules. *She* made the rules, and he'd damn well do as he was told.

Check with Command, my eye. She smirked; fine, she'd check with Command.

So, Talma Pren, should we get that witch Arava off Farius Prime when her staying put is ever so much more convenient? After all, she is a little bit of a traitor now, isn't she? Oh, true, true, she's working against Qadir; that counts for something. Still, someone has to take the blame when Qadir's precious money and *portal disappear, right?*

Why, Talma Pren, I couldn't agree more.

There. Talma clambered up the short stretch of gangway to the bridge. She'd checked with Command. Now all she had to do was manufacture the forged confirmation from Starfleet Intelligence—*Dear Halak: Anything for you, darling. Love, Marta.* Thank the heavens, she'd had the foresight to know this might come up and had accessed

Batanides's personal authorization codes from the records of the real—and very dead—Laura Burke.

Tsk-tsk, Laura, how many times have I told you: Always lock your door when you go to sleep aboard ship. *You never know just who might break out of her quarters in the middle of the night and leave a nice, bright, shiny, and very sharp souvenir in your back.*

Vaavek—no, Sivek, he's Sivek for the time being—sat with perfect Vulcan poise over the pilot's console: back straight as a titanium rod, the seal-skin black of his hair gleaming in a soft white light that suffused the bridge from a bank of lighting panels recessed in the ceiling. Talma Pren paused a moment, eyes roving the bridge, her body reveling in the pristine orderliness of Vulcan engineering. She'd been on many ships in her lifetime. Some she'd stolen. (Well, actually, she'd stolen *most* of them. Maybe she'd bought one, two at the most.) She'd had Klingon shuttles, Starfleet shuttle-craft, even a Cardassian two-person trimaran liberated from a hapless Cardassian trader floating somewhere between Farius Prime and the Malfabrican Sector—and not many people living who could make that claim. (Cardassians didn't take kindly to people liberating anything.) But in terms of ships, the Vulcans won, hands down. Their ships were so much more streamlined, so functional; they eschewed luxury and favored steely blue hues and well-lit workspaces. Not as fancy as Starfleet shuttles: Starfleet loved those delicate, homey touches so pleasing to the eye but with no functional purpose. The Klingons made suffering a virtue, so their ships were not only ugly, they were no fun at all; and the shadows that fell through the grills and latticework on Cardassian ships always reminded Talma of a prison cell. But the Vulcans knew how to build ships. Surveying the bridge, Talma gave a sigh of appreciation. Play her cards right, and she could buy herself a whole damn fleet. Why, she might even buy Vulcan.

"What's our status?" she asked, slipping into the copilot's chair. Again, not luxurious but padded just enough and sensibly proportioned, with a high back and a lumbar support. (For those long space flights: absolute murder on your lower back.) "Any Cardassians around?"

Vaavek's head swiveled so smoothly it might have been oiled. "None, but I suspect that will change within the next twenty-four hours when that Cardassian scout comes through on patrol."

"What's our position?"

"On the perimeter of the system; 600,000,000 kilometers from the neutron star." Vaavek's sensitive fingers played upon his console. "Magnetic field is quite high, but one would expect that of a magnetar. Accreting gas from the remnants of this system's supernova as well as the weaker brown star of the binary are being forced to flow along field lines to the magnetic poles of the neutron star. That shouldn't pose much of a problem for us, but because the magnetic axis and rotational axis of the star aren't co-aligned, the star's an accretion-powered pulsar, with X-ray pulsations sweeping out once per rotation. Those pulsations combined with random gamma ray bursts from the star itself and a strong stellar wind from the brown star make more detailed sensor resolution quite difficult."

"Mmmm," Talma murmured, not really listening. Science always had given her a headache. She indulged in a stretch, arching her back and finishing with something very close to a purr. "Less technobabble, if you don't mind."

Vulcans were not known to smile, though they would, on occasion, give the ghost of a smirk. One touched Vaavek's lips now. "There are two stars. One's brown, and the other isn't. The one that isn't is stealing matter from the brown one. That means, there's a lot of junk floating around out there, and that makes it very hard to see anything. Right now, we're far away from the planet. At long range, our sensors and communications aren't so hot, but then again the Cardassians will be blind as Torkan cavefish, too. At best, they'll see sensor ghosts, or nothing at all. At worst, their sensors may be able to resolve a signature, but they will still have to rely upon visual."

"Why, Vaavek," said Talma. "I never knew you had a sense of humor."

"It is always advisable to know the ways of one's adversaries."

"But we're working together."

"Precisely."

Talma gave him a sidelong glance. "What about Chen-Mai?"

"He should have no idea we're here. We're early for the rendezvous. He won't even begin to look until he's ready to leave the planet's surface."

"Yes, we do want to keep that nice element of surprise."

Vaavek arched his left eyebrow (a feat Talma never could master, though all Vulcans seemed capable of it from birth). "I doubt Chen-Mai will share your enthusiasm."

"Likely not," Talma said, pulling her features into a look of mock regret. "Well, he won't live long enough to worry much about it."

Chen-Mai had been the perfect choice for her scheme. The man had been in Mahfouz Qadir's employ for the last seven years, and he'd never once been suspected of skimming. Talma knew. She'd been the one to bring him into the Qatala network. For her glowing reports to the Qatala, Chen-Mai always paid her extremely well and Talma adjusted the take she reported to Qadir accordingly. A beneficial arrangement: collateral built up against the day when Talma made her move. Today, she had decided, was as good a day as any. She had no intention of parting with whatever Chen-Mai and company had found, whether that was specs for a portal, or lots and lots of treasure. (Jevonite didn't exactly grow on trees.) Likewise, she had no intention of letting Chen-Mai—and whomever he'd been careless enough to leave alive—get a day older.

And *that*, though he didn't know it, included Vaavek. Sivek. Whatever.

"Well," she said, her tone bright and cheery, "then let's get on with it, shall we?"

Chapter 29

Nothing: nothing in his mind, on the planet, or under the rock. There was simply nothing because there was nothing to find.

Try again. Clad in his environmental suit, the sound of his breaths loud in his ears, Ven Kaldarren stood so still that he imagined anyone spying him would've thought he'd turn into a pillar of the same hard stone that formed the mountains, the land itself. *Failure is not an option. Try again.*

Yet he was going to fail. He felt it. Only a day left, and he knew. He would never find the portal. Perhaps he wasn't strong enough, or his psionic signature wasn't a match. Maybe whoever had built this fabled portal had such an individual mindprint that, like a fingerprint or DNA, there was no way for anyone else to detect, much less access, the device. Not terrifically useful then, but Chen-Mai's anonymous employer didn't seem to care about that.

Try again.

He could lie. He could say he'd picked up something faint, but they'd have to wait awhile, come back. Then, before that time came, he could take Jase and go someplace far away. Not back to Betazed: That was the first place Chen-Mai would look. But Kaldarren could take Jase to Earth, leave him with the boy's grandparents. A good thing Chen-Mai didn't know who Jase's mother was, so he'd have no way to trace the boy. As for Kaldarren, he could watch out for himself, something that was easier to do if he didn't have to worry about Jase.

And he had a lot to worry about because he'd tried to scan Chen-Mai. Doing so broke every vow he'd ever made not to misuse his gift. But this was his life they were talking about now; this was his son's life. So he'd scanned Chen-Mai—and run into a brick wall. A mind block: Kaldarren had run the fingers of his thoughts over the wall, touching it here and there, and in a way that reminded him a little of what snakes did, flicking out their tongues, tasting the air. Then he'd tried probing Mar—same wall. Same *feel* to the wall. And then Kaldarren was certain. The men were taking a neural blocking agent, probably an anti-scopolaminergic compound. The drug wouldn't inhibit their conscious cognitive processes but would render them telepathically opaque. Metaphorically speaking, he might as well have tried seeing into a room through a frosted window. Kaldarren could catch shapes now and then, vague outlines of thoughts but nothing definite.

So. The blocks and the fact that both men were taking a drug so he, Kaldarren, couldn't crack through telepathically were proof enough. Kaldarren got a certain grim satisfaction out of the knowledge that you didn't need to be a mind reader to know that a man fearful of you seeing inside *definitely* had something to hide. That both Mar *and* Chen-Mai were taking the drug told Kaldarren that both men knew the same thing, and neither could be trusted. They were going to kill him. They were going to kill Jase.

He couldn't let that happen. *Can't fail, I* can't. He thought about stealing the shuttle, or contacting Garrett. Neither was an option. There was no transmitter on the planet strong enough to pierce the interference from both the brown star's stellar wind and the neutron star's magnetic fields; and Chen-Mai had the shuttle in lockdown mode. Only Chen-Mai and Mar knew the code, and it was stupid of him not to have plucked the code from their minds while he had the chance.

Enough. Closing his eyes against the dead and rock-strewn landscape, Ven Kaldarren focused on the sound of his breathing. An old trick, one used early on in the meditation techniques that all Betazoid telepaths undertook as part of their early training.

Unbidden, thoughts—*Jase*—crept into his mind. Kaldarren frowned. Couldn't think about his son now. *Have to concentrate.* Kaldarren threw his mind out in a wide net, his thoughts like a sensitive web, ready to vibrate with the tiniest psionic disturbance.

Jase. Again. Why? Kaldarren was on the verge of dragging his mind away but didn't. If his mind kept veering to Jase, there was a good reason. Kaldarren willed the tension to leave his limbs; he opened his mind wide.

Jase. His son had seemed different in the past few days—happier, certainly, and as if he looked forward to every new day. There was Jase's ability to gray his mind; that was new, and a revelation Kaldarren hadn't spent much time deciphering, or dwelling upon. He reasoned that the action was a reflex, something the boy learned as a consequence of having to live with telepaths. Come to think of it, Kaldarren didn't have much experience with living in close quarters with *non*-telepaths. There was Rachel, of course. His mind caressed this *Rachel* thought: an image of Rachel's auburn hair fanning upon a carpet of emerald-colored grass; a burst of sunlight, and the smell of cool water from Lake Cataria. Rachel's skin. Rachel's lips.

His heart filled with grief. They'd lost so much. Until the last two rancorous years, when the marriage was dissolving, her mind had always been open. At the height of their love,

Kaldarren felt as if they shared the same mind, the same feel. . . .

Suddenly, a bolt of searing pain ripped through his brain. Kaldarren couldn't help it; he screamed. His vision dimmed, and his knees buckled. He felt the sharp bite of rock as he sagged to the ground, hands clutched at either side of his helmet. The pain came again: sharp, knifing his brain as if someone had taken an axe and driven it through his mind, cleaving it in two.

Stop. Moaning, Kaldarren tried to put up a shield, keep the intruder-thought at bay. He had to get it to stop, *stop!* Who could be doing this, who had this much *power* . . . ?

Then, through a haze of agony, Kaldarren saw an image: a shape. Indistinct, shadowy. Not humanoid. A dragon. No, not a dragon—Kaldarren tried clamping down on the pain shivering through his mind, along his limbs—not a dragon, a woman with a dragon's . . . *no*, a serpent's body, and wings, and eyes, those eyes. . . .

Dad! Dad, help! Help *us!*

"Jase," Kaldarren hissed, his mind spiraling toward blackness. "*Jase!*"

"What is it?" asked Jase. He passed his tricorder over the wall before them. The wall wasn't rock; he stared at his tricorder's readings then passed the device over the wall once more for good measure.

"It's metal," said Pahl, confirming Jase's readings. He, too, had a tricorder. "A bunch of metal. Titanium and some other stuff, I don't know what, I haven't gotten that far yet in school."

"Metal?" Jase echoed. "In a rock tunnel? And what about this?" He shoved his tricorder before his friend's faceplate. "A magnetic lock?"

"That's what it looks like."

Disgusted, Jase shook his head. "That doesn't make any sense." Looking around, he searched for a place to sit and found none. He settled for squatting, cross-legged, on the rock floor. He was tired and hungry, and now they'd run into a metal wall sealed with a magnetic lock, of all things. They'd been walking for hours, and he was sweating, not from exertion this time but anxiety.

His eyes roamed the tunnel shaft behind. He picked out the faintly phosphorescent glow of flare markers, winding round like a string of fireflies, that they'd left wedged in rock clefts along the way just in case their tricorders quit. Other than their flare markers, the tunnel was pitch black. A kilometer back they'd left a pack of supplies: spare air, more flare markers. Plus they carried tiny packs of spare air on their backs, for emergencies. He hoped he wouldn't need to use his.

Discouraged, Jase swung his head back toward the metal panel. The panel made no sense. A magnetic lock, one that was still active, on a dead planet made even less. Unless it had been left over from the time when there were people here. If true, where was the power coming from? There had to be a power source somewhere, one to power the lock and to generate the field they'd found at the tunnel mouth. But their tricorders had registered nothing, given not the slightest hint as to where this power source must be. Had to be. The only answer was that the source was shielded, or that they just didn't know what or how to look. They were just kids, after all, and neither of them were exactly in love with science.

He ought to tell Pahl to forget this whole adventure and go back. Jase was in over his head, and he knew it. Yet he felt a strange compulsion to keep going. Even as he fought the urge to go deeper and deeper, as if an invisible tether were reeling him in, Jase felt his apprehension grow. Small comfort he'd been right about the general design of the tunnel, its similarity to tombs he'd seen in Egypt. The tunnel was carved out of the mountain rock and was tall enough for a man to pass through without stooping. Unlike tombs on

Earth, however, these had no drawings on the walls, nor were the walls plastered. Instead of running straight down—under the dead lake, if their tricorders were accurate—the tunnel twisted and turned and doubled back several times in underground switchbacks, almost like a maze. Maybe now, with the metal door and the magnetic lock, this was probably just an old mine shift, and not a tomb at all. How dumb. Jase was disgusted. They'd been like little kids, thinking they were going on some great adventure when, instead, this was a mystery better left for adults who knew what they were doing, not a couple of kids armed only with dinky tricorders—not even really fancy ones—air, and flashlights.

Jase pushed against his thighs and clambered to his feet. His calves cramped, protested the unaccustomed exercise. "We should go back, tell my dad, and let him decide what to do."

But Pahl was shaking his head. "I think I can get us through this. There's a magnetic field here all right, just like at the entrance. But the field has a periodicity, like a pulsar."

"So?"

"So," said Pahl, fiddling with his tricorder, "that far in school I did get. Maybe if I match the ambient resonance frequency of the magnetic field but *reverse* it, I can open this."

"And then what? How do we know you can get us back out? We don't even know what's on the other side. Could just be another tunnel that'll go on for kilometers."

"Or it might not," said Pahl, turning his head until his ice-blue eyes and pale brown face stared down at Jase. "You and I both know there's something here, something that wants to be found. Why else put up a wall? Why lock other people out?"

He knew Pahl was right. The setup was too elaborate: the magnetic distortion field topside, the panel and its lock. "The lock could be to keep whatever it is *inside*."

"Maybe," said Pahl, turning aside and staring at the readings on his tricorder.

Jase watched in silence as Pahl's tricorder searched for a match, found it, and then began to emit a reverse polarity pulse. The tricorder pulsed red . . . red . . . red . . . green.

"Jase," Pahl began.

The metal panel slid to one side. There was no sound, though Jase imagined that there must be the whine of some mechanism scrolling the panel to one side. But Jase heard Pahl gasp and, instinctively, both boys took a step back. On cue, they glanced at one another and exhaled a peal of embarrassed laughter.

Jase shone his torch into the blackness. Almost immediately, he felt a twist of disappointment. The panel opened into a tiny, arched room that reminded Jase of the well chamber he'd been expecting. Only the walls curved and there was no shaft to catch water. The floor was smooth and level with that of the tunnel in which they stood. Opposite the panel was another door.

"Same metal," said Pahl, consulting his tricorder. "But there's no magnetic field."

"So it's not locked." Jase chewed on his lower lip. "An invitation? Like it wants us to come on in."

Pahl nodded. "There are old-fashioned laser sensors. Here and here," he gestured with his tricorder to either side of the chamber. "All along the walls. Can't see the beams, though."

"Are they weapons?"

"No, the beams aren't strong enough to burn anything. I think they're meant to trigger some sort of mechanism."

"Wait." Jase bent, scooped up a small quantity of fine-grained dirt from the tunnel floor, and tossed the dirt into the chamber. The dirt was so fine that it formed a swirling cloud, like curls of smoke. Then, so ephemeral they were like the threads of a spider's web, a network of thin, pulsing red lines appeared, crisscrossing the chamber.

"Sensors, all right. Displacement detectors, I'll bet." Jase looked over at Pahl. "And you want to go in there."

Pahl nodded. "Don't you? Can't you feel it?"

"No," Jase lied.

"Well, I do. It's almost like a voice, only not words so much. Just a feeling. It's not going to hurt us."

"Then what? What is it? And why is it talking to us? Why not my dad?"

"I don't know. Maybe your dad isn't the right person."

Jase took a step back. "I don't understand that, and I think that until you understand something . . . until somebody tells us it's okay, we ought to go back."

"Well, I'm not," said Pahl calmly. He snapped his tricorder shut and slung the carrying strap over his shoulder. "I'm going on, Jase. This is where I'm meant to be. You can go back. You know the way. Go get your dad, if that's what you want. But I'm going."

For a brief moment, Jase was tempted to do just that: to leave. The way he felt, staring at Pahl and then into the chamber, was just what he'd experienced aboard Chen-Mai's ship. There was a terrible darkness in Pahl, a void scoured out of Pahl's soul by grief and loss. This void was bottomless; Pahl's need knew no end. Once before, the Naxeran had reached out without knowing what he was doing and grabbed hold of Jase, trying to pull him down into this black whirlpool, and Jase was afraid this would happen again. Only this time, Jase was being asked to walk, willingly, into the abyss.

Yet Jase knew this was something he had to do. Something was beyond that door, calling him, tugging at his mind. It had brought him this far. Maybe it would be satisfied with Pahl. Probably would. But then Jase would have abandoned his friend.

Jase shouldered his tricorder. "Let's go."

Together they crossed the threshold and stepped into the chamber.

Chapter 30

At first, nothing happened. Then Jase heard what he thought was a faint but audible click. Impossible. He frowned. They were in vacuum. Probably all he'd heard was the pop of static that sometimes played as background on an open comm channel. Then he became aware of something else: a rushing noise, like water.

He turned to Pahl. "Do you hear that?"

"Yes." Pahl gave a slow, puzzled nod. "But how . . . ?"

Groaning, the panel before them slid right: metal scraping rock.

Sound. Jase let out his breath in a surprised exhalation. There were sounds, and if there were sounds . . . Quickly, he whipped his tricorder around, activated it. "Pahl, it's air. There's air! And it's getting warmer," Jase watched as the ambient air temperature rose: now zero degrees, ten degrees. "It's an airlock and . . . Pahl, do you see that?"

Pahl's tricorder burbled. "Yes. I read a power source, about three kilometers ahead, almost straight down. Looks nuclear. Probably a generator of some kind, only down deep where it's been shielded."

"Or maybe our tripping the airlock turned it on. Except," Jase aimed his flashlight, its beam stabbing the darkness, into the tunnel, "there's nothing. Just more tunnel."

He was disappointed because he'd expected something spectacular: a room heaped with piles of gold or jewels. Something. Why else an airlock? A metal door? The sensors, and shielding? Then he noticed something. Fanning his light over the tunnel walls, he caught a glimpse of color. Squinted. "I think there's something here. Written on the walls. Paintings, maybe."

He consulted his tricorder again: "I'm reading more tunnels, but they don't branch off here. There's . . ." He did a double take of his readings, and his disappointment evaporated. "This is really strange. There's another larger tunnel about a kilometer to the west, and then more . . . wow, at least *ten* more tunnels branching off that. But, dead ahead, there are rooms."

"How many?"

"Four." Eyes bright with excitement, Jase looked over at his friend. "You know what? I think this *is* a tomb. I think the tunnel we found was some sort of secret entrance, that the bigger tunnel I'm reading to the west is the main entrance that was probably sealed off."

"But why?"

"Grave robbers, maybe. They did that in Egypt. Sealed up the main tunnel after they moved the sarcophagus down and then left a different way, so no one would know how to get in. I'll bet that if we walked down that main tunnel, there'd be the stuff you'd find in Earth tombs: booby-traps, pits, stuff like that. But I'll bet that when we step out of here, that panel's going to slide shut, just like any airlock."

"And evacuate the air inside to equalize the pressure." Pahl's pale blue eyes looked almost silver in the glow of their flashlights.

"Yeah." Jase aimed a significant look at his friend. "Probably we can get back out. At least, there's air: oxygen, nitrogen. A little helium."

"Like someone's expecting us."

"Yeah." Jase hesitated, then reached up with both hands and thumbed the seals on his helmet. There was a hiss as the seals released. Cautiously, Jase lifted the helmet a few centimeters and sniffed. Instantly, he recoiled. "Ugh. Smells old, kind of stale. Thick. Like," he made a face then turned and spat, "tastes like something . . ."

He stopped as he recognized the stench of death. And what else was he expecting? *It's a tomb, you jerk.* Jase worked out another mouthful of foul-tasting spit. *Of course, there's something dead.*

"Come on," Jase said, clipping his helmet to his waist. He hoped he would get used to the smell. Otherwise, he would be forced to put his helmet back on; the smell of decay was that strong.

As Jase predicted, the panel slid shut behind them when they stepped away. Through the metal, they heard the swoosh and hiss of air being evacuated.

As they walked through the tunnel, Jase swung his light over the paintings on the wall. They were done over what looked like plaster, almost exactly the way he remembered tomb paintings from the Valley of the Kings, but the plaster here was very different: textured so that the images were arranged within outlines that were diamonds and trapezoids. Many of the patterns overlapped and intersected along diagonals, like—Jase groped for a comparison—like glass that had been shattered into a spider's web of individual panels but not fallen out its frame. The paintings were probably of gods, Jase thought, or demons. He recognized one animal: a plump, ashen-white bull with long, pointed horns. He couldn't quite place it; the name was on the tip of his tongue, and he knew he'd seen the painting before, someplace with his dad, some collection. He just couldn't remember where.

There was one recurrent image: a great woman-snake, or maybe it was a dragon, Jase couldn't tell. The thing had green scales, curved talons, and batlike wings; her eyes were set within ridges of scales and the same rhomboid- and diamond-shaped scales ran down the sides of her neck. Her neck wasn't exactly straight either; it flared, so her shoulders and neck inscribed an arc, not an angle. In some of the paintings, the woman-snake hovered over figures that were clearly worshippers; Jase spotted humanoid figures carrying baskets of offerings—jewels, coins, food—and other figures that played upon piped instruments or harps. But in other paintings, the woman-snake formed the background for a figure that Jase thought must be the king: a jeweled diadem nestled on his forehead.

Playing his light over the walls and ceiling of the tunnel, Jase saw irregular, glittery white streaks of calcite, the end result of water having seeped through the rock over time. *Probably from that big, dead lake.* And he noticed something else. At first, it seemed a trick of the way the light from his torch spilled along the walls. But, no—he blinked—the tunnel was getting brighter.

He tapped Pahl on the arm. "Do you . . .?"

Pahl nodded and stared at his tricorder. "There's light. Just ahead."

The tunnel dipped left then right, took a last turn, and there was an arc of light straight ahead: the end of the tunnel. They hesitated an instant just beneath an arch, and then they crossed the threshold into a room.

In the room was a man with golden skin. Staring at them.

Jase flinched back with a cry. His heart thumped against his ribs, and his legs went watery with fear, and then he made himself look again. Almost at once, he wanted to kick himself for being so stupid. *No, jerk. It's not a man. It's a statue. Jeez.*

The statue was gold, its features inlaid with colored stones: rubies for the lips, coal-black obsidian eyes outlined in some dark blue gem, black crystals for nostrils. A green faceted stone (an emerald?) centered on the forehead: the king's diadem. The statue stood before a stone altar that was a triangle three meters high; each side was flanked by a flight of three stone steps. Chiseled carvings of chimeras roiled along the altar's three stone faces.

Everything in threes. Jase took a few steps toward the statue, and then turned to inspect the rest of the chamber. Jase saw that the tunnel they'd traveled came in from the side of the chamber, at a diagonal. The room was a rhomboid and studded at equal intervals with three curving stone pillars that arced from floor to ceiling. In each of the chamber's four walls were three arched niches spaced at equal intervals, and within each were gold statues of women with peculiar diamond-shaped scales that ridged their eyes and long hair that spilled over their shoulders and breasts.

"An altar," said Jase. He knelt on a step and his gloved fingers played over white smooth humps of material clinging to the rock. "Melted wax, like from candles. They probably did something religious here, prayers or something, before they left."

"This way," said Pahl, indicating a small passageway to the right of one statue. "There's another room, much bigger."

Once in the room, which was lit with a dim glow that seemed to have no source, they stood for several seconds, mouths open. Just staring.

"Oh," said Jase, releasing his breath in an astonished gasp. His gaze traveled along the vaulted ceiling. The ceiling was painted a rich, dark blue and studded with glittering yellow stars. *Like the sky at night, and there are two bigger than the rest, probably those binary stars.* He saw at once that the paintings on the walls of the elliptical room—a dizzying array of red, blacks, and greens—were divided into three registers, with figures contained within intersecting rhomboids and trapezoids. *Probably telling a story.* Yet the story didn't unfold in a straight line; the mural swirled along the walls. Jase spotted serpents, jagged bolts crashing through skies studded with blazing stars, the arcs of arrows curving in the air. The paintings felt organic and alive but suspended in time, in that instant between life and death every child knows but does not remember: the moment before he draws its first breath. Instinctively, Jase understood that the mural told a story of the hours of a single night. The story seemed to end with an image of huge golden disc at the far side of the room.

Jase took another step into the chamber. That disc had to be a depiction of the rising sun—maybe the neutron star before it had *become* a neutron star. Just beneath the disc, he saw the woman-snake again, with its angry blood-red eyes, its shimmering green-scaled reptilian body. Those black wings.

He felt Pahl touch his arm. "Look," said Pahl, pointing toward the center of the room.

Jase's gaze followed. A red-stone, rhomboid slab stood in the center of the ellipse. Unlike the stone altar in the other room, however, this was carved with scrolls of ivy twisting around arcing columns incised out of the rock. Scattered on the floor were heaps of gold; dark wooden chests with latinum inlay and the rich green of jevonite; the crumbling remains of candles long since burned to nothing. And there was a body.

Jase and Pahl exchanged glances, and Jase saw Pahl's throat work in a hard swallow. Without a word, they crept toward the slab and fanned their lights over the body. The skin of the dead man—and it had been a man, Jase saw (*the king!*)—was drawn tight as old black leather. As the skin had mummified, it curled and drew back; the lips were parted in a horrible rictus, the teeth startlingly white. As the soft tissues had decayed, the face had fallen in, and Jase stared into black, eyeless sockets. The cheeks were so taut the bones of the skull had torn through. Gold rings hung loosely on bone fingers; jeweled pendants and latinum chains dangled in the clefts between the dead man's ribs where the flesh had rotted away, and the rich robes were reduced to shredded tatters. A deep, forest-green emerald glittered in the center of the dead king's forehead.

So this is what his dad had been searching for. But was *this* what he and Pahl had been meant to find? No. Jase felt as if there was still more . . .

"Over there," said Pahl, echoing his thoughts. He nodded toward the far end of the chamber. "Through that arch."

Unlike the burial chamber, this next room was pitch dark. The boys teetered on the threshold, and then stepped together into a thick, inky blackness. As if by unspoken agreement, they left their flashlights off for a moment and just absorbed the feel of the room. This room felt smaller, more dense. Jase had the impression of a diamond-shaped room, and his tricorder agreed. But the air was thick. Jase sniffed. Not musty but *crowded*, almost as if the darkness were filled with people jostling one another.

He felt Pahl at his elbow, searched for his friend's eyes in the glow of their tricorders. "Do you feel it?"

Pahl nodded. "They're here."

They're here. Without warning, all the hackles along the back of Jase's neck rose. He shivered. Something was watching. Quickly, he flicked on his light; the blue-white halogen beam punched through the darkness. Jase whirled about on his heel, trying to catch whatever was there in the light. His beam cut the blackness. Stone walls. No paintings. Nothing else. No one.

No, thought Jase, there *was* something—someone— there. He felt it. Jase took a step back and then another, and then his heel caught. Crying out, Jase threw his arms up. His flashlight cartwheeled through the air. Jase fell back, hit something that rustled and chattered like icicles dangling from bare branches after an ice storm. Gasping, he rolled to one side, away from the sound, just as his nostrils were assailed with the musty odor of dust and decay.

Pahl's torch flared to life, stabbed through the black, and Jase turned. Screamed.

The desiccated, mummified corpse of a boy slid out of the darkness.

Eyes bulging with horror, Jase scuttled away like a crab. He'd touched it; he'd fallen against it! And that clattering sound, his bones, the boy's *bones!* Jase rolled to his knees, gasping. His skin was clammy with icy sweat.

Calm down, he's dead, he can't hurt you. Jase tried corralling his addled wits. Now that he was further away, he saw the body was slumped against a wooden triangular stand of some kind. Jase stood slowly, gulping air, heart hammering in his chest. There was movement by his elbow, and he almost screamed.

Pahl handed Jase the flashlight he'd dropped. "Look at his *face*," Pahl whispered.

Despite his fright, Jase leaned forward. He frowned. "What *is* that?"

Pahl knelt by the dead boy's side. He reached forward, his fingers trailing along the contours of something that glinted and shone. "It's a *mask*."

"Don't touch it!" Jase cried. Instinctively, he knew: *danger*. "Leave it alone!"

"Why?" Pahl continued to caress the mask. His movements were slow, languid. "It's harmless. It's . . ." Without warning, Pahl plucked the mask from the corpse's face.

"No!" Jase cried, too late.

Suddenly, the room was suffused with a soft, silver light. There was a hum, a sense of expectancy. *No, no, what now, what's happening?* Jase jerked open his tricorder.

"Pahl's, something switched on. Another power source. Somewhere, outside this room, I don't know, and now there's an energy surge." Jase jerked his head up. "Pahl, Pahl, let's just go now. We've seen enough, we've seen . . ."

His voice died in his throat. He felt the same thick congestion in the air, only more now than before. *Like the bodies of people all pressed together in a small room, all breathing the same air. The energy surge*—Jase stared at his readings—*like a door opening somewhere, letting something out, and it started when Pahl touched the mask, when he took the* mask. Jase stared wildly into the silvery glow. The air was thick, and as he stared, the air changed colors. The air trembled and writhed, and then the air uncoiled, coalescing into shapes, things that lashed the air like dragons. Like snakes.

"Pahl!" Jase's voice came in a thin, high whisper. "Pahl, Pahl, do you see them? Do you see?"

"Yes." But not a word: more like the hiss of some serpent. Pahl's ice-blue eyes started from his skull, but he wasn't looking at Jase. He was staring into the roiling air. "Yessss, yesssss."

And then, before Jase could move, Pahl placed the mask over his own features.

"*No!*" Jase cried, starting forward. "Pahl, stop!"

Pahl opened his mouth and let out a long, loud wail. Jase couldn't help it; he was so frightened, a cry jerked from his throat, too. Pahl's scream echoed like the cry of a bat flinging itself from one dark corner to the next. His scream was inarticulate, formless: a never-ending wave of sound that went on and on, crashing through the darkness.

Jase's mind gabbled in panic: *no, no,* no! He had to get that mask off Pahl's face; he had to get them *out* of there!

"Pahl!" Lunging forward, Jase clawed at Pahl's face. His fingers grazed the silvery metal, and it was like he'd touched a live circuit. A sudden, hard shock rippled down his hand and shivered through his arm. He flew back, his body twisting through the crowded, thick air. He crashed against the wooden stand, and the ancient wood, rotted with age and time, erupted, exploded from within, rising in a cloud of dust and debris. Jase felt the patter of wood against his skin, heard it rain upon the rock like hail. A brackish taste filled his mouth, and he spat out a gob of saliva and blood. He groaned. Every nerve ending of his body felt on fire. He tried moving, and electric shocks tingled through his limbs.

He shouldn't have left the biosphere; he should have listened to his dad. *Dad, help us, please help us!*

"Pahl," he moaned. His fingers scrabbled uselessly over cool red stone and bits of decayed wood. "Pahl."

But Pahl was quiet now. Shuddering, Jase lay with his cheek pressed against rock, felt the bite of grit against his skin. He saw that Pahl was shaking; his friend's hands were twisted, claw-like. No. Jase felt the weight of the air heavy along his body, pressing him into the stone until he couldn't breathe. *No, no, nonononono . . .*

And now, in the gathering darkness, he heard them: their voices shrill and greedy: *Ours, our time, our time, ours, ours!*

"Pahl," he said, his voice a dry croak. "Pahl, help me!"

Slowly, Pahl turned, and then Jase saw Pahl's eyes shining and luminous, glowing with all the hard, cold beauty of two blue stars. Fear gripped Jase by the throat. His voice came out in a strangled squeak of a whisper. "Pahl?"

"No." Pahl's voice was stony, the tone flat. Alien. "I'm not Pahl. Not now."

Horror washed through Jase and left him weak. "Please," he said, "please." And in his mind: *Dad, Dad, help us!*

"Are you afraid?" Pahl—*It*—took a step then two toward Jase. The air coiled around Pahl—*It*. The air gathered, bunched. "*Are* you?"

"Yes," Jase wailed. *Dad, Dad!* "Yes, yes, yesyesyes!"

"Yes," It said, an echo, that serpent's hiss. "Yesssyessss-yesss." A pause. "You should be."

And, a second later, Jase Garrett began to scream.

Chapter 31

"An *alarm?*" Chen-Mai asked. "Are you *sure?*"

"Positive," said Leahru-Mar, disliking the way the other man crowded him. "I missed it on standard scans. You'd just never think to look."

"Why did *you?*"

"There was a faint distortion of the magnetic field local-ized to an area around that old lake, and after I saw the power emanations, I tried to figure out what *that* meant. I read that there's a power source that's been switched on, and an alarm that's gone off. The alarm's weak, on a very narrow band. In fact, it's much closer to old infrared or laser-propagation waves than subspace channels."

"*Infrared?*" Chen-Mai scowled. "That's not old, that's ancient."

"Well, whatever it is, someone's tripped an alarm. Either that, or someone's broadcasting a signal, probably automated."

"A signal. To whom?"

Mar's frills canted at a right angle to his nose before settling back down. "I'm not a communications expert; I just pilot ships. If that *is* a signal, I'm not sure it will pierce the magnetic interference blanketing the planet. Probably not."

"But if it does get through, then the Cardassians will know we're here," Chen-Mai fumed. "The Cardassians will be all *over* this planet!"

Mar waited him out. Privately, he thought the alarm wasn't a huge concern. Likely the Cardassian patrols wouldn't pick up a thing until they swung back through the system. If the Cardassians stuck to their schedule, they were a little under a day away. By then, they—he, Pahl, and Chen-Mai (the Betazoid and his boy were on their own)—planned to be very gone.

"Well, how long has the power signature been there?" asked Chen-Mai.

"An hour, maybe a little longer. The sensor grid showed red about two hours ago, but when I tried to reconfirm, the signal vanished. I didn't think any more about it. Besides, it read a little like a magma disturbance, about two kilometers down."

"Except this planet's dead, Mar. It hasn't been geologically active for centuries."

"There's always some residua," said Mar, defensively. "Even with dead moons, there are subterranean shifts."

The cast of Chen-Mai's skin was always sallow, but now the blood rushed to his face, mottling his skin with ugly splotches, like bruises on a yellow pear. "But that doesn't explain how you could miss a signal that indicates periodicity, and a power source!"

Indignant, frills twitching, Mar drew himself up. He might be a Leahru, clan of the Weaker Brother, but he wasn't an Efram, or *anyone*'s Naxeran punching bag. "*You* try sitting here, hour after hour and day after day, sifting through sensor *garbage!* I don't know how I missed it. You can bully me all you want, but the simple fact remains that I found it now, and we've got to decide what to do!"

"What to do?" Chen-Mai's jaws clamped down so hard, Mar heard the click of his teeth. "It's obvious, isn't it?" He pushed his way forward again and jabbed his finger square upon a pulsating green blip on the sensor display. "*That* is a power signature. It means that Kaldarren's found the portal!"

"Well," said Mar, slightly mollified now that Chen-Mai was concentrating his wrath on the Betazoid, "that would explain the alarm, certainly. Except for something reportedly so invaluable, to arm it with an alarm that's essentially a laser-propagation wave doesn't make sense."

"It's old. It's ancient. We're talking thousands of years. Maybe this passed as state of the art back then. Or maybe the Cardassians didn't have anything better, or don't know about it," said Chen-Mai. "*I* don't know. But I do know this. There's a source powering something, and now there's a signal that might be strong enough to pierce the magnetic blanket that's all over the wretched planet, and to think that it's been there, right there, under our noses the whole time!"

"Well," said Mar, trying to temporize, "not exactly under our *noses* . . ."

"Shut up, Mar. You puling Naxerans are all alike. Just shut up and let me think."

Mar lapsed into silence. He didn't distrust Ven Kaldarren the way Chen-Mai did. The xenoarchaeologist was just naïve. Well, actually, he was *stupid*. Kaldarren trusted Chen-Mai to keep his part of the bargain: share and share alike.

.Stupid. Well, the Betazoid had no one to blame but himself. *He* certainly wasn't going to charge to Kaldarren's rescue. Mar wasn't the kind of man who would voluntarily jump into the fray. But, puling Naxeran, eh? True, he *was* Leahru; G'Doks had all the power. As Leahru, Mar knew all about the fine art of treading lightly around people in power. The equation was simple. Chen-Mai had the power; Mar did not. All right, so maybe that made him puling in Chen-Mai's calculus.

And Kaldarren? If he'd been Naxeran, Kaldarren would've been Efram: a member of the servant class. If Kaldarren were stupid enough to trust Chen-Mai, he'd have probably wound up getting himself killed sooner or later—if not by Chen-Mai then by someone equally vile. Briefly, Mar debated about whether or not he might be able to do something for Kaldarren's son, and then decided he couldn't. Actually, *shouldn't*: It wasn't as if the boy could be counted on to keep his mouth shut, and what would they do with him afterward anyway?

Which left him with another problem. Mar's sulfurous eyes slid sideways. Chen-Mai was pacing and muttering. If Chen-Mai had always intended to eliminate Kaldarren, he'd most certainly have decided that sharing whatever booty there was with *him* wasn't very desirable either. Chen-Mai was a good enough pilot; he'd be able to get the shuttle off this rock. Maneuvering around Cardassians was another matter, and maybe Chen-Mai wouldn't want to take that much of a risk. On the other hand, he *might*—if the rewards were big enough. Now that an alarm had sounded, Mar thought the rewards would be very big indeed. Otherwise, why bother with an alarm? So his problem: Who would get to whom first?

Chen-Mai broke into Mar's thoughts. "All right. Here's what we do. We're going to assume the Cardassians will pick up that signal sooner rather than later. Now, Kaldarren took one skimmer, right? Well, we'll take the other. If Kaldarren's

found the portal—and I'll just bet he has—we assume he's
found a tomb, too. There'll be so much treasure we'll need
two skimmers. And don't forget a tricorder. We want to make
sure to download the specs on the portal, assuming Kaldarren hasn't already done us the favor. Phasers, too."

"Phasers are a given. And if Kaldarren objects?"

"Two skimmers, two pilots. Two phasers. Do the math,
Mar."

"All right, then. Let's talk math." Mar tapped the sensor
display. "There're *three* life signs down there. What about
the boys? No." He put a finger to his lips and felt the fine
tips of his frills brush his skin. "I misspoke. There's no question about Pahl. So about the other boy?"

Chen-Mai shrugged. "What about him?"

Kaldarren's fingers were shaking so badly he had trouble
keying in the correct sequence to reverse polarity on his tricorder. After that first wrenching mind-scream, Kaldarren
had been so disoriented he hadn't known which way to go.
Finally, he remembered his tricorder and then he'd seen
them: two life-forms beneath the surface. *The boys.* Then
he'd seen the power signature, and Kaldarren knew. The
boys had found the portal—or something.

But the mind-scream—Kaldarren had stumbled over rock
until he found the tunnel—how had Jase managed that? The
echoes were still there, and there was something else, too,
something that was neither Jase, nor Pahl. Something alien.

Oh, Jase. Kaldarren's pulse throbbed in his temples. His
mind was still bruised from the assault, and he willed a par-
tial shield, knowing he'd be of little help to his son if he
were incapacitated. *Jase, Jase, Jase, where are you?*

Getting down the tunnel was difficult; Kaldarren didn't
have a light, and so he let his tricorder, the boys' flare-
markers, and his mind lead the way. Now, standing in front
of the metal panel, Kaldarren felt rivers of sweat running

down his back. His breath fogged against his faceplate and he forced himself to slow down, try to stay calm, and he found himself wishing, fervently and for the first time in years, that Rachel were there.

She'd know what to do. Kaldarren's fingers slipped over the tricorder controls; the indicators went red, and his tricorder blatted an error message. Oh, how stupid! He wanted to scream, smash the instrument against the rocks. *Damn her, damn her, I've seen her about as frightened as a person can be and still live, and she'd know how to handle this, what to do, Rachel, Rachel . . .*

Stop. Kaldarren clamped his shaking lips together. He couldn't panic. If he did, he couldn't help his son. Steeling himself, Kaldarren tried again.

The tricorder went red . . . red . . . red . . . double green. The panel slid to one side. Another room. Small. Dark.

Go. Kaldarren hesitated, all his senses screaming in protest. If there was nothing on the other side, if the panel didn't open, he'd be trapped in there and Jase, he wouldn't be able to get to Jase. But, no: His eyes scoured the readings on his tricorder, and he adjusted its range and gain. Beyond that second panel, there was air, warmth. Jase.

Go. Kaldarren squared his shoulders. *Go!*

Kaldarren stepped into the darkness.

"I see it," said Talma. They had moved to within sensor range of the planet, and now she found that she wanted to break something. But Halak was standing right beside her, so she couldn't. Instead, she drew a deep breath. *Appearances.*

"Sivek?" She almost said *Vaavek.* "Are you absolutely sure?"

The Vulcan threw her a glance that, on a human, might have been describing as withering. "There is no mistake. Granted, the magnetic interference coupled with ionized plasma contrails makes sensor readings difficult. But difficult is not a synonym for impossible, and I had rerouted auxiliary power to my sensors to compensate. Therefore, *that*," he nodded at one grid upon his sensor display, "is a signature consistent with a landskimmer. And that," the Vulcan enhanced another area of his scans, "or should I say *those* are life-forms, humanoid, three. Two are in close proximity, perhaps in a room. The third is heading in their general direction."

"And that?" Halak reached past the Vulcan to point out a pulsating resonance signature deep in the planet's surface. "That's much further down. It's not geological?"

The Vulcan pursed his lips. "I had considered that as a possibility and discarded it. The signature has periodicity; it appears to be artificial and is likely an energy source. There is also a secondary energy signature that I have never seen before."

"Do you know what it is?"

"I believe I just said, I've never seen it before. Therefore, I can only describe, not tell you what it is. It is neuromagnetic."

Halak frowned. "Brain waves? Sivek, you've got to be wrong. How . . . ?"

"Commander, I just said . . ."

"All right, boys," Talma intervened. "Zip 'em away for now. And no," she said before the Vulcan could ask, "I'm not explaining that."

"All right." Halak folded his arms over his chest. "We've got a power source and some archaic laser-propagation wave, and now we've got a location, the place this portal of yours most likely is. As I recall, the plan was *not* to have a run-in with whomever Qadir's got down there, and you can bet that propagation wave's going to be picked up by someone soon, and that someone's likely to be a Cardassian, and probably more than one."

"Not necessarily. You heard Sivek. It's so weak we're lucky to have seen it, and we're still fairly far out, not even in orbit yet. Right?" Talma addressed this to the Vulcan. "It looked like a magnetic burst, right?"

"Correct. Most ships would pass it off as being inconsequential." Vaavek paused. "Unless it happens again."

"See?" said Talma to Halak. "Nothing to worry about on that score. That thing's so weak, it would take a miracle for anyone to see it."

"What if it's a distress call?"

Talma shifted impatiently. "If it is, then that's all the more reason to get down there. Now I'm certain those energy fluctuations come from that portal. We can't beam down because of all that radiation and stellar wind. Better you and Sivek go down in a pod."

"So Sivek can keep an eye on me," said Halak, his tone sour. Talma suppressed a tight smile. She'd produced the orders with assurances about rescuing Arava he'd requested, so there was no question now that he'd follow through. "As if I'll get very far in a pod. What's it make, Sivek? Warp one?"

"One-point-five. Under optimal conditions."

"Uh-huh." Halak turned to Talma/Burke. "And what about you?"

"I will stay onboard the *T'Pol* and nudge her into lunar stationary orbit on the far side of the planet's larger moon, out of sight. From there I can monitor the space immediately around the planet. Don't worry," she said, reading Halak's expression. "I'll let you know the instant any Cardassian scouts arrive. Remember, Starfleet has no more interest in the Cardassians finding us than you do."

"With that signal, they'll be in this sector . . ."

"They *won't*, but the longer we stand around arguing, the greater the likelihood they will. Now you know what to do?"

Halak sighed. "Locate and secure the portal. Take detailed sensor readings on the construction and operation. Try not to get myself killed. Anything else?"

"No." Talma's eyes slid to Vaavek. "You?"

"A moment alone, if you please."

"Right," said Halak, backing out of the *T'Pol's* bridge toward the gangway. "I'll just stand over here while you two whisper."

"No," said Talma. "Stay right where you are. Anything you have to say, *Sivek*, you can say in front of the commander."

The Vulcan didn't look convinced. "Why are *you* remaining aboard? It's a Vulcan ship. *You* are Starfleet Intelligence. This is not the V'Shar's mission."

"But you're a Vulcan," said Talma easily. "And a Vulcan male at that. Far better equipped to deal with Commander Halak than I am." She looked over at Halak. "Isn't that right?"

Halak put his hands on his hips. "Maybe. We could certainly go one-on-one right now, see what happens."

"You would not enjoy it, Commander," said Vaavek. "If, however, you are someone who thrives on experiential learning, I am willing to accommodate you."

"Down, boys." She returned her gaze to Vaavek. "That's the plan. Okay?"

"Not entirely," said Vaavek.

"Good, I'm glad that's settled. Now, we're wasting time. You and Halak get down there. And Sivek, don't forget a phaser."

"Wait a minute," Halak protested. "If he gets one, I want one."

Talma slid into the pilot's chair and swiveled around until her back was to the commander. "No."

"I get it. I get to take care of whomever's down there, but then Sivek gets to take care of me."

Talma plotted her course for the planet's moon. "Only if you misbehave, Commander."

"You know that won't happen."

"Well," now Talma pulled her head around and gave

Halak a sweet smile, "let's hope not, for your sake—and for Arava's."

"*My* sake?" Halak's face darkened with an angry rush of blood. "The only reason I'm doing this is for Arava. I don't have anything left to lose except her."

"Then I'm quite fortunate," said Talma, turning aside once more. "Because they say that the most dangerous man is the one who's got nothing left to lose. Good luck, Commander."

"I believe in making my own luck, thanks."

"Then I suggest you make a lot of it, Commander." *Because you can bet*—Talma listened to Halak's angry footsteps fade away as he clambered down to the waiting pod—*that if you and Vaavek fail, I'll be making mine.*

"*Twice?*" Garrett leaned over Bulast's shoulder and stared at his communications display. "Are you sure?"

"There's no mistake, Captain," said Bulast. "See, these time indices, here and here? Two distinct signals: a blip on and then off, and now one that's continuous."

"Oh, good," said Stern, who'd been hovering around Garrett's command chair for the last hour. "Now we've got alarms. We lose Halak's transponder signal in all that radioactive slush out there, but we get alarms."

Garrett ignored her. "So you're saying it's like a door."

Bulast nodded. "Like a door that opened and closed. Twice. Only the second time, someone left it open."

"Careless," said Stern.

"Or maybe," said Bat-Levi, who'd been studying the same signal at her station, "maybe it's not that the door's been left *open*, but that the alarm hasn't properly been turned on, or off, to begin with. Captain, I remember my parents had an alarm for their house. Even if your retinal scan matched, the thing let off a little bleep. It was a redundant system. Retinal scan outside, voice print inside. But here was the real catch. If someone, an intruder, were to somehow fake the retinal scan but made a mistake along the way—bungled the match before getting it right, let's say—the system let him in. But then it sent out a silent alarm, and the alarm stayed on."

"So as not to alert the intruder." Garrett looked over at Bulast. "Could that be it? Is it a distress call?"

"Captain, there's no way of knowing. The first signal reads just like the commander said, as if someone opened the door, maybe tripped an alarm doing it but then *disarmed* it. Closed the door correctly, maybe, I don't know. The second reads as if they didn't bother closing it, or maybe didn't know they had to. But here's the other thing that's peculiar. That signal reads like a general distress only the band is narrow, closer to infrared. So the technology is ancient. Mid-twenty-first century stuff."

"Damn." Sighing, Garrett resumed her pacing. She'd been pacing for two hours, too keyed up to sit in her command chair. *Probably wearing a groove in the deck.* "Damn, why did this have to happen now?"

"Captain," said Glemoor, "in terms of probabilistic . . ."

"I think that was an expression, Glemoor," said Stern. To Garrett: "What do you want to do?"

"What I *want* and what I *have* to do might be mutually exclusive. What about Halak? Any luck getting his signal back?"

"No," said Bulast. "We lost him as soon as the *T'Pol* dropped out of warp."

"But we've still got the *T'Pol*."

"Not really," said Glemoor. "We've picked up remnants of a warp signature consistent with a Vulcan warpshuttle in this sector. But those remnants are decaying fast in the strong magnetic field of that binary star system out there. Old or new, I have no way of knowing. They could have left this sector and we wouldn't be able to tell."

"But they were heading in this general direction," Stern pointed out. "And there's nothing leading *away* from here. So they're still around."

"Unless the ship backtracked and exited the system at a point too distant for us to see, perhaps subtending its signal behind the neutron star. If the *T'Pol* elected to swing close to the neutron star, any warp signature would have been distorted, almost like a cloaking device."

"*Could* the alarm be coming from Halak?" asked Stern.

Bulast spoke up. "Negative on that, not unless he's jury-rigged something. If he has, you'd assume he'd try to target us, not just blare a general distress."

"Maybe he didn't have a choice," said Stern.

"And risk alerting the Cardassians?" said Garrett. She ran a hand over her forehead. "I don't think so. And speaking of Cardassians, any sign of them?"

"Not yet," said Bat-Levi. She didn't say that might change in the very near future. She didn't have to.

"What about origination point?" Garrett looked over at Glemoor who was seated at his console to Castillo's left. "Where's that alarm coming from?"

"Origination point of the propagation wave appears to be the fourth planet, Captain. I read power emanations and a periodicity that's different from the general background wash of gamma rays from that neutron star."

"What type of power is it?"

"That is what is so unusual, Captain. I wasn't certain of my findings initially, but Commander Bat-Levi has verified. There are actually two signatures: one is something very close to fusion power. But the other is neither nuclear nor thermal. It is not *electro*magnetic, but it appears to be a highly charged *neuro*magnetic plasma interface."

"Neuromagnetic?" Garrett glanced over at Stern, who only shook her head. "You're saying brain waves?"

"In a manner of speaking. It's more like a plasma cloud of ionized particles, only in this instance the driving force is neuromagnetic, and not radioactive. Both emanate from deep beneath the planet's surface. And there's something else."

"What? Another power source?"

"Not exactly." The Naxeran screwed up his face in a way that reminded Garrett of an inquisitive cat. "There's a biosphere, Captain. That is, I believe there is. We're still at the extreme limits of sensors."

"A biosphere?" Garrett was at Glemoor's station in two strides. "Are there life signs? Did *they* send the signal?"

"Negative. The alarm appears to have originated underground."

"Near that neuromagnetic power source?" And when Glemoor nodded, Garrett continued, "What about ships?"

"At this distance, I can not say for certain if there are ships. Certainly, there are none orbiting the planet. The planet does possess two moons, however."

"So a ship could hiding behind one."

"That is a possibility. With all the radiation in the area, it is also just as possible that there is a ship we cannot see."

Bat-Levi said, "Captain, we have to assume that the alarm's genuine until we know otherwise. The *T'Pol* could be anywhere, and we have no way of knowing exactly where, or whether she's moved off. But distress calls take precedence."

"Rachel," said Stern, "you *can't* . . ."

"Doctor," said Garrett, in a peremptory tone that brooked no debate. "Much as I might like it to be otherwise, Bat-Levi's right. If that's a distress call, we have to answer."

Stern was undeterred. "And if it isn't? What if it's some old hunk of junk that's malfunctioned, or something? You going to gamble Halak's life on a lousy *machine*?"

"We don't know that it *is* junk, and we don't have the luxury of assuming anything." Garrett blew out a long sigh. "All right, everyone, listen up. This is what we're going to do."

Chapter 32

Air. Kaldarren jogged down the tunnel, his helmet banging his right thigh. The air was warm but smelled old and was thick with decay. Kaldarren saw light just ahead. He squinted at his tricorder. *Reading an entryway, and this tunnel's been carved, it's artificial, there's plaster on the stone, and that long tunnel to the west, those branch points, this has to be a* tomb . . .

For an instant—when he turned into the main burial chamber, with its vaulted ceiling, and saw the dead king and all that wealth spilling over the stone floor and the fabulous mural—Kaldarren forgot everything: Chen-Mai, the portal. Even Jase. Kaldarren let out his breath in a sigh of wonder. It was all here. He'd been right. A xenoarchaeologist's dream, the find of a lifetime. And the writing on the walls: Hebitian, but with archaic variations different from the script he'd seen, the one officially touted by the Cardassians as proof positive of their descent from the ancient race. But the Hebitians had *been* here, Kaldarren knew now. The Hebitians had been on *this* planet, thousands of years ago.

Then Kaldarren remembered the mind-scream. They were *still* here.

Jase. Kaldarren's eyes jerked to an opening diagonally across the main burial chamber. *In there.*

He felt them before he saw them or knew what they were: a strange, insistent tugging at the back of his mind, like fingers scrambling around the seam of a door, searching for a way to pry into his mind. Their touch was cold, malevolent. Kaldarren shivered. Evil.

And for a split second, Kaldarren felt fear. But he had to stay calm. More than that: He knew, beyond the shadow of a doubt, that if he was going to get Jase out, he'd have to open his mind and let these things inside, so he understood what he was dealing with and how to fight them—but not just yet.

Oh, Rachel. Kaldarren thought her name as if it was a type of prayer. He wasn't sure why he thought of Garrett just then, but perhaps it was because of the darkness of the things skittering around the edges of his mind. Their evil filled him with fear and such foreboding... Kaldarren closed his eyes, as if doing so would block out his fear. Oh, there were so many things he'd never told her, and other things he wished he'd left unsaid. How they'd hurt one another, and now it was too late to tell her how sorry he was. *Good-bye, Rachel.*

And then, before he could change his mind, Kaldarren hurried into the next room.

The room was small and close, suffused with a silver glow that reminded Kaldarren of light globes, though none were visible. He saw Pahl, standing beside a pile of dark rubble. The boy's back was to him, and as Kaldarren stepped forward, the boy pivoted on his heel until Kaldarren saw the ice-blue eyes, the silver mask.

"Pahl," Kaldarren said, his heart sinking. "Pahl, where...?"

"Dad!" Jase's voice, on the edge of hysteria, and then in the next instant, Jase had darted from a far corner and launched himself into Kaldarren's arms. "Dad, *Dad!*"

"Jase." Kaldarren's throat constricted with emotion as he hugged his son tight against his chest. Then he gripped his son by his shoulders. "Jase, what's wrong with Pahl?"

"They're here," whispered Jase. His lips trembled, and Kaldarren saw that the boy's skin was so pale it was almost translucent. "They're here, Dad, they're here, don't you see them? They're all around, and now they've got Pahl. Only It's not Pahl, It only looks like Pahl, but It's not Pahl."

"How?"

"He... Pahl picked up this mask. He picked it up and he put it on. I couldn't stop him! And then they were everywhere, coming out the walls, can't you see them, can't you..."

"*Jase.*" Kaldarren's fingers dug into Jase's shoulders, and he held his son at arm's length. He would've touched the boy's mind, but he was still wary of dropping his guard. *Can't let them in all at once, or I'm lost. I need to be the one to control the contact, not the other way around.* Instead, Kaldarren searched the boy's face and saw his terror. "Who are they?"

And then Kaldarren felt a stab of fear. "Did *they . . . ?*"

"No, they didn't hurt me. They didn't get inside. They tried. But I'm not right, I can't . . . I don't think they can get inside me. I don't understand it all, only I know they took Pahl and they wanted to take me, but they can't. But, Dad, they're *here,*" Jase looked behind Kaldarren, eyes darting from side to side, "they're all around. Can't you see them? Can't *you see?*"

No, he couldn't see. Kaldarren kept his mind closed. He wouldn't let them in, not yet. But the air was thick and he *felt* those icy fingers again, tapping at the opaqueness of his mind, like leafless branches tapping at windowpanes on a winter's day.

But his tricorder saw them. Kaldarren scanned the data. Highly cohesive fields of psionic energy held together the way that high-energy particles were contained in a magnetic field. Energy that had form but was not matter: there, and not there, as if they—whoever they were—trembled on the threshold between dimensions. Had they been there all along? If so, why hadn't he sensed them? They flitted about the periphery of his mind *now.* Why not earlier? All the hours he'd spent searching in vain for beings that now his tricorder registered as a matter of routine.

Or maybe it was something the boys had done. That mask, for instance. Kaldarren studied Pahl's face, the mask. An image flashed in his brain: that small, chipped stone figure he'd found a few days ago. It had a mask. Come to think of it, the mask Pahl wore was very similar to ones he'd heard about but never seen. An obscure Cardassian religion, one that the government didn't endorse but which survived in small pockets here and there. What was it? Kaldarren searched his memory. Yes, the Oralian Way, that was it. If he remembered rightly, certain Oralians used what they called a recitation mask as part of their religious ritual. They claimed that the mask was a conduit, connecting them to a higher spiritual power. The Oralians who wore the mask did not claim that they spoke the words of a god. Rather, the mask served to augment powers they already had.

And now Pahl wore a mask, and Kaldarren knew, unequivocally, that the boy had somehow opened the door through which a being that was pure thought had managed to slip, invading the boy's mind. What if this was the original mask upon which the Oralian recitation mask was based? The mask could be a device attuned to the psionic signature of a certain select few.

Kaldarren looked down at his son. "I can't see them, Jase. I can't . . . let myself just yet. No time to explain, Jase. But tell me: What do they look like?"

"Animals." Jase licked his lips. "Like from those old stories you showed me. Egypt, Greece, early Betazoid mythology."

"Like the statues in the other room?" said Kaldarren. "The murals?"

"Yes, but there are also people, and they look like . . ." Jase's eyes slid to a spot behind Kaldarren.

Turning, Kaldarren spied the corpse of the boy. He studied the dead boy's facial features. Even with decay and mummification, Kaldarren could see that the boy had raised periorbital ridges. Pre-Cardassian?

"Dad," said Jase, "you have to help Pahl."

"I don't think I can, son."

"But we can't leave him here. How do you know? You haven't even tried!"

Kaldarren licked his lips. "Jase, I'm a telepath, but there

are limits. I couldn't find this place, remember? You and Pahl did. Whoever's there, in Pahl, allowed the two of you in, not me."

"But you're here now. *They're* here. They let you come, and you found me because I knew you would, because I need you. Dad, you have to try!"

"Son, there's nothing . . ." He stopped when he saw Jase's face change. "Son . . ."

"You're afraid," said Jase. His voice was hard-edged, bitter. "That's what it is. You're afraid to try. Mom would be afraid, but *she'd* try."

Kaldarren felt a lump swell and lodge in his throat. He *was* afraid. Maybe that's why he'd not been able to find the portal *(is this a portal?)* and why he couldn't see what his son said was there. He was afraid, as he'd always been afraid. Rachel had been the stronger one. That's why he'd been attracted to her. The only risk Kaldarren had ever taken in his entire life was to marry Rachel Garrett. In the end, he'd let her walk out of his life; he'd lost her without a fight.

And he didn't have to fight now. He could walk away, with Jase, and he didn't think these beings would stop him. They had Pahl, and perhaps that was enough. Besides, Pahl wasn't his responsibility.

But Kaldarren also knew that if he did that, if he succumbed to fear, he'd lose Jase the way he'd lost Rachel. Oh, Jase would still be alive, but his soul would be closed off to Kaldarren forever and Kaldarren would lose his son just as surely as if Jase's mind had been taken over by one of these beings.

"All right," said Kaldarren, even as his instinct for self-preservation screamed that this was anything *but* all right. "I'll try."

Jase's face was pinched with apprehension. His eyes were wide, dark. He gave his father a slight nod. Took a tiny step back.

Kaldarren turned to Pahl. The boy hadn't moved or spoken. With exquisite care, Kaldarren opened his mind, just a bit: like cracking a window to let in a whisper of fresh air. He probed the boy's mind, first touching the surface the way a blind person traces the contours of a stranger's face. Instantly, Kaldarren felt the presence of the Other. Formless and cold. Dark, as if it dwelled in the deep caverns of the mind.

Kaldarren flinched away even before he knew he had, and then he was orbiting the periphery of the boy's mind, his own mind safe and unscathed. In the next instant, hot shame flowed through his veins. *Stop, don't let fear control you!* He was acutely aware of his son's intense gaze; of the closeness of the air, thick with these beings; of the stink of his own sweat.

I must. Kaldarren gathered himself. *I must.* He loosed part of his mental shield, as if shedding a piece of clothing, and then he waded into the black ocean of Pahl's mind . . . and there was the Other, in the shallows—a woman, not a woman, and thoughts that twined and writhed like a serpent's tail.

Jase caught at his hand. "Dad?" He squeezed Kaldarren's chill fingers. "*Dad?*"

"Quiet, son," said Kaldarren, his voice strange, halting. "I have to concentrate, I have to . . ." He broke off, redirected his focus toward the Other. *Who are you?*

Dithparu. The word floated, tenuous as the silver strand of a spider's web. *Dithparu.*

Night Spirit, Kaldarren translated. Kaldarren always found it easier to imagine his own thoughts as a voice and he thought his voice now. "Do you have a name?"

"Uramtali"—her thought-voice, like a sigh on the wind— "They called me Uramtali."

"What do you want, Uramtali? Why do you hold this boy?"

The *dithparu,* like the dry rasp of leaves upon dead

branches: "He has a hole in his heart. There is Night in his soul. The other, he is Night but not enough."

Night. Kaldarren's mind held the word, examined it. Uramtali said *Night,* but she—It—meant something different. What?

Uramtali was speaking again. "This one is a boy of Night, like the Night Kings before him. Bred to the purpose."

Kaldarren didn't understand. He closed his eyes. He knew vaguely that Jase still held his hand, but Kaldarren's mind was further from shore now, and he drifted, opening more of the shielded, secret places of his mind. *Think it to me.*

Instantly, a blizzard of strange images streamed through his consciousness. There were so many, Kaldarren couldn't put names to any of them and he merely held his mind open, letting the images impress themselves into his brain like red-hot brands upon exposed flesh. The aroma of incense was full in his nostrils; he heard the voices of a people crying out their grief; he saw a glittering processional of mourners, light globes floating in the air above their heads, as they snaked their way through mountain passes—

Uramtali's thought-voice in his head: *the light globes floating in the air above their heads, as they snaked their way through mountain passes to this place, these mountains with their strange magnetic fields, trapping us here.*

Then he understood. The *dithparus:* fantastically old, the remnants of a powerful civilization predating the Vulcans, the Bajorans, even the Organians and the Metrons, and so ancient that they no longer remembered where they had come from, what their true names were, what their own bodies had once looked like, or that they'd even had bodies. They knew only that they were the *dithparus,* the name given to them by the people on this planet, who worshiped them as gods.

In exile—Uramtali's thought-voice, so sad—*in exile.*

Exiled to a parallel dimensional plane. Trapped.

Imprisoned. Brothers, they were our brothers, but they

said that we were evil, darkness, the night side of their own souls.

The Brothers of Light: beings that thought it crueler to kill the Night Spirits than to place them here, unable to cross over, to make the transition from one phase to another, unless there was a suitable container. A waiting vessel.

And willing—Uramtali pushed that thought home—*we are not all-powerful, the vessel must welcome us, must want our minds.*

And so the tradition had built up among the people of this planet: the Night Kings.

The Night Kings, bred for the purpose.

For something very much like a phase change—Kaldarren's own thoughts went, of their own volition, to a physical analogy—*like the phase change that occurs when water goes to steam, or ice. Whatever the form, it's still water.* But the conditions for the transition, whether of water to ice, or a *dithparu* to a form capable of inhabiting a living being, had to be ideal, or else the phase change wouldn't occur. The container—no, thought Kaldarren, not the container, the *mind*—had to be flexible enough to accommodate and adapt to the *dithparu's* psionic patterns.

Maybe that's why the *dithparu* was able to use Pahl. The boy was young, his powers still raw and his control not as finely tuned as Kaldarren's. His mind was malleable; he didn't have the ability to shield himself the way Kaldarren did. Kaldarren doubted the boy even knew he was a telepath.

Kaldarren knew now that there was no portal, not in the way Chen-Mai or Kaldarren had imagined. The place was more like an incubator.

A prison, they hold us here, but they are gone, long ago, and we are forgotten.

A storage container: the magnetic field designed to keep these *dithparus* trapped here until they could exchange places with a telepath bred to the purpose, like being granted a parole by an unseen jailer. This explained the elaborate rituals, the texts on the walls that spoke of exchanging the king's spirit for another, because the Night Kings had been bred, perhaps even genetically modified, to serve as the containers in which a *dithparu* could live for a span of time outside this place, this prison.

Tend the machines. But we have no knowledge, no science; we can be nothing more than we have been.

Yes, Kaldarren understood it now. When the Night King died, his body was laid to rest in these mountains, and his heir was brought here to serve as a container for another *dithparu*. It was, Kaldarren thought, a primitive yet effective way of keeping the *dithparus* in check, letting one out at a time. That one *dithparu* lived out a mortal span, tending to the machines it knew how to access *(that power source, probably the last of many)*, but never expanding further than the accumulated sum of the knowledge of the *dithparus* that had come before. They didn't even know how to set themselves free.

And then something had gone wrong. (Kaldarren felt the *dithparus* clamoring in his mind: *Yes, yes, yes!*) Either the line of kings had died out, or there had been war, or some calamity.

All three. They broke the cycle, one named Nartal, a prince, a coward.

Prince Nartal, who left before the transfer could take place, and so a *dithparu* had taken what it could find: the boy, Ishep, now dead at his feet. But Ishep didn't know how to get out of the tomb. Only Nartal had, and the *dithparu*'s powers were limited. So they had been trapped here for thousands of years, waiting for someone to find and free them while, above, the planet had died because Nartal did not know how to tend the machines, or even that they required this.

The mask, use the mask.

The mask was an amplifier, channeling the flow of psychic energy into the new host. And that was why they needed Pahl.

Still, to Kaldarren, it made no sense. Yes, they might lure

Pahl here and inhabit his body, as Uramtali did now. But
that being done, why keep Jase? Jase was no telepath. True,
he called out; Kaldarren caught that mind-scream and followed it here, but was that *Jase*? Or had the *dithparus*, had
Uramtali *amplified* Jase's cry?

Kaldarren felt weak and dizzy. He was aware now that he
was trembling from the effort, his mind reeling from the images that pummeled his mind. Why keep Jase? No, no—
Kaldarren's mind labored over the question—that was wrong,
he was asking the wrong question. This wasn't just about
keeping Jase; that mind-scream had been Jase calling for him,
but Jase shouldn't have been able to do that, not without help

Help us, please help us.

Such an innocent request: *Help us, please.* Kaldarren
very nearly responded, but something—that instinct for self-
preservation again—stopped the thought, cold. Something
about what the *dithparu* had thought at him niggled at his
brain, and Kaldarren thought back now over what the Night
Spirit had said.

Willing. Yes, that was it. The container, the new host,
had to be *willing*, had to *want* the *dithparu* to slip inside and
take over.

Kaldarren felt cold beads of perspiration speckling his
brow. This wasn't about keeping Jase, or even Pahl. This
wasn't about Jase at all. It was about finding . . .

You.

"But why?" Kaldarren cried, out loud now, his voice ripping the air. "Why?"

"Dad?" Frightened, Jase jerked at Kaldarren's hand. His
father's eyes bulged, unseeing. "Dad, what is it?"

"Why did you need to find me?" Kaldarren's anguished
cry banged off stone. "Why have you hidden yourselves until
now?"

No. The word shivered through his mind. *You have hidden yourself from us.*

Of course, Kaldarren thought, that was right. They'd sensed Pahl in orbit and tried to reach him through a dream, and then when Pahl had been most vulnerable, flinging his tortured thoughts so widely that Kaldarren had detected them for the first time, they'd sensed *him*. But the contact had been so brutal—*the pain, I remember that searing pain*—that his mental shields had snapped into place, and he'd automatically shut them out, a response so reflexive he wasn't aware he'd done it. After that, he hadn't been able to find them; with his shields in place, they couldn't touch him. How ironic: He'd thought at that retreating contact not to be afraid, and yet *he* was the one who'd felt fear. Wanting without wanting. Searching for the portal, but with his mind veiled, protected.

It was, he considered, the way he'd lived his life: the same way he'd kept himself hidden from Rachel; the hurt they'd caused one another making him withdraw, close off to so many things. The *dithparus* must have sensed him long ago, but Kaldarren was—*strong, you are strong*—stronger than he imagined, or had wanted to believe, and so his mind had been hidden—*afraid of us, of yourself, of her*—resistant to their pleas. *Not open to us, or to her, dwelling on your hurt.*

So they'd done the next best thing. They'd fixed upon Jase and especially upon Pahl, who was young, untrained. Defenseless.

Cold fury blossomed in Kaldarren's chest. They'd used Pahl, and then they'd used Jase, as bait. They'd tried to take his son, his *son!* And even if they had Kaldarren, would they stop? *Could* they be stopped? Or could *he* hold them, in place, inside where they couldn't get at Jase, or anyone? Because he was strong: stronger than he'd imagined, or dared to believe.

For you, my son, Kaldarren thought. *I would do this for you. For us all.*

The twin poles of anger—grief and resolve—blazed in his

heart. He turned away from Pahl's face, expressionless beneath
its silver mask, and his voice boomed through the chamber.

"Well, I'm here now!" he roared. Kaldarren struck his
chest with his clenched fist. "My mind is open now, and I'm
here, I'm here, you have what you want, so let them go and
take me, take *me!*"

"Dad!" Jase shouted. "Dad, *no!*"

Open your mind.

"All right, come on, I'm waiting!" And then, just before
he dropped the last of his defenses, he thought at Jase: *Son,
when it happens, run, run!*

Jase gasped. "Dad, no, I won't, *no!*"

Jase, you must! Then, without waiting for his son's reply,
Kaldarren unveiled his mind. "Do it," he cried, "*do it!*"

Yes—the *dithparus* gathered themselves—*yes.*

"*Dad!* No, stay with me, please! Dad!" Jase shrieked.
"*No!*"

Suddenly, the air in the chamber was bright and it
whirled, rushing with the force of a gathering storm. Pahl
stiffened, screamed; then the boy crumpled to the stone
floor. The light in the chamber spasmed then contracted
and gathered around Kaldarren, looping tighter and tighter
and tighter.

"Dad, no!" Jase shouted. His face was wet. "*Don't!*"

"Jase!" Kaldarren gnashed at his lips and tasted fresh
blood. "Son, run! Run! I don't know how long . . . I
don't . . . !"

He broke off, clutched at his head, his soul spilling between his fingers like water. "Son, please, run, while there's
still time, *run*, Jase, ru . . ."

And then Ven Kaldarren's mind burst in two. He gave a
long, agonized scream as his soul was torn out and the others poured in, choking him, crowding into his mind. Dimly,
he heard his son crying out for the man Kaldarren no longer
was, but there was nothing Kaldarren could do for Jase now

because his mind was hurtling toward darkness, toward oblivion. Kaldarren felt his strength leave him, and then the bite of stone through his suit, against his knees. And then he was on his back, his vision darkening.

"Rachel," Kaldarren choked, his throat raw and bloody. "*Rachel.*"

Chapter 33

"*What?*" Garrett looked over at Stern, who was glowering over her tricorder. "What did you say?"

"I didn't say anything," said Stern, her voice slightly tinny and attenuated over her environmental suit's comm unit.

"I could have sworn."

"Not me," said Stern, and then she looked up. "Although with all the distortion from the magnetic field here, maybe your comchannel caught a glitch."

"Maybe," said Garrett, though she was doubtful. Her fingers found her comm unit controls, and she double-checked the frequency and found that it was right where she'd set it before they left the shuttlecraft, a short distance from two landskimmers they'd spied from the air, and started down this tunnel.

Odd. She knew she'd heard something, someone. Familiar voice, too. Someone on the same channel? Maybe the *Enterprise?* No, then Stern should have heard it. Garrett cocked her head, listened. She was aware of how dark the tunnel was around them, how deep underground they were, and how far they still had to go. She wasn't claustrophobic, and the dark didn't bother her, but the space around her felt strange. Crowded and close: the same way she felt in a turbolift when too many people crammed into too small a space. *Don't get spooked.* Her eyes roved over the red-hued rock and noted where tools had bitten into the hard stone. Dead planet, empty biosphere—well, not quite empty, it was clear that someone had been there, and not too long ago, from the looks of the place. She and Stern had reconnoitered the biosphere just long enough to take note of a medium-range shuttle, and the general disarray. As if whoever had been there had left in a hurry.

After another few moments of listening, Garrett gave up and nodded toward Stern's tricorder. "You still reading atmosphere in there?"

"Yup, *and* heat, plus some sort of organized energy signature. And that neuromagnetic field, it's still there. Stronger than we read on the ship."

"What about life signs?"

"Now *that*." Stern grunted. "Reads like a convention down there."

"How many?"

"A lot. Five humanoid and, oh, *hell*." Stern jiggled her tricorder then smacked it with the side of her gloved hand. "Damn thing."

"Very high tech."

"Whatever works," said Stern. She squinted. "Sorry, Rachel, they're not all resolving. Like I said, I read at least five humanoids. Can't tell you what they are either, what species. And there's a whole bunch of other readings."

"Define bunch. Are they life-forms?"

Stern made a piffling sound with her lips. "Life-forms. It's a damn big galaxy, Rachel. I'm reading high-energy, almost like ionized plasma. But they're contained, cohesive. I'm just not sure. I'll tell you something, though. They remind me of something I read once. Mac talked about them in his seminars on xenobiology. You remember the Organians?"

"Who doesn't? Organian Peace Treaty, 2267," Garrett recited, "imposed by the Organians to prevent war between the Klingons and the Federation. Are you saying that these are Organians?"

"Not quite. The Organians were noncorporeal life forms, though: pure energy, pure thought. Mac was there, you know. Well, his captain was, anyway, Kirk, and his first officer, Spock. Anyway, they encountered a similar class of beings, two years later. Zetarians, they were called. Same deal: highly cohesive noncorporeal life-forms."

"Are you telling me that's what you're reading here?"

"No, but it's close. I'd have to get further in, I think, past all this damned interference, but there's energy in there, and a lot of it. Neuromagnetic, for sure."

Garrett was tempted to try to decipher the readings herself but doubted she'd have any more luck than Stern. "We saw two skimmers. Could whatever you're reading have come from the biosphere?"

"I doubt it. That biosphere was made to handle *our* kind, not," Stern held her tricorder up, gave it a waggle, "this."

"Okay," said Garrett, though it wasn't. "What about this panel? You sure about its being the source?"

"Absolutely, and I'll tell you something else. This thing's been opened three times now."

Garrett was startled. *"Three?* But we only saw two alarms."

"On the *Enterprise.* I know." Stern gave her captain a significant look. "I don't make these things up. You'd never catch it if you weren't looking for it; the resonance band's only slightly above that for Halak's transponder, which was the reason we caught it the first time around. Only the *second* time, whoever opened it made a mistake. See here?" Stern pointed to a magnetic variance signature on her tricorder. "The first time, whoever did this got it right on the money. The second time, though, someone keyed in the wrong sequence to reverse polarity going in. Botched it."

"And that set off the alarm."

Stern nodded. "Then they seemed to have gotten it right. But the third time, well, here, look for yourself."

Garrett thumbed through the entries. "Ionized debris, trace ferrous . . . Jo, this reads like a phaser blast. Recent, too."

"Like within the last hour."

"But then why isn't the panel damaged? Or the surrounding rock?"

"Beats me. All I can tell you, whoever did this doesn't have a hell of a lot of finesse, or patience. Not that hard to figure out, you know; this isn't exactly twenty-fourth century state of the art technology here. But whoever was here just didn't care, and that's why the alarm has read continuous, only at a higher frequency. You could go in and out a hundred times now, and the alarm wouldn't be any different."

"Well, we ought to be able to do the same trick, minus the phaser."

"But that's weird. Phaser blast ought to have taken that thing right out of commission. From the looks of it, though, all it did was ramp up the alarm, only silently."

"Your point?"

"Hell, I don't know if I *have* a point. But I'll tell you, this is one of the few times I wish we could just beam in, do our rescue, presuming whoever's down there wants to be rescued, and then beam the heck back out."

"We went over that. Too much . . ."

"Right, right," Stern interrupted impatiently, "too much interference from the magnetic field. Don't forget, I was there when you hatched this cockamamie plan. And I'll tell you something right now. You can bet whoever's out there listening won't be far off. One blip, you can ignore. But not when it's screaming. I don't think we have a lot of time."

"Noted." Handing Stern back her tricorder, Garrett ran her eyes over the seam of the panel. "What's immediately beyond this?"

"Another door. Passage beyond that. Tunnels. Beyond

them, looks like a maze of tunnels, like an anthill. But, for my money, this is a kind of antiquated airlock."

"So no explosive decompression," said Garrett, pulling out her phaser. "Well, if someone's coming, I guess we'd better get our asses in gear, don't you think?"

"I was afraid you'd say that," said Stern. She keyed in the sequence to open the panel: red . . . red . . . red . . . double green. Watched as her tricorder read air evacuating from the lock. The door slid open. Stern slung her tricorder over her shoulder. "Fools go gladly."

"Where angels fear to tread." Garrett thumbed her phaser to setting two. "No one ever accused me of being an angel."

"What do you mean, boy?" Chen-Mai felt so much blood choking his face, he thought he probably looked as purple as a bruised plum. He glared down at Jase, who knelt by Ven Kaldarren. "What's wrong with your father? Speak sense!"

"But I'm *trying* to tell you," Jase said, desperation in his voice. He held his father's head in his lap. Kaldarren grimaced, moaned. His face was stained with sweat and blood; his shoulder-length black hair clung in wet tendrils to his neck. Every few seconds, a tremor shuddered through his body. "They're *here*, and they've *got* him! Don't you see them? They're all over the place!"

"*Who?* All I see is you, that boy," he jerked his head toward the prostrate figure of Pahl, "and your father."

Kaldarren. Chen-Mai had to restrain himself from giving Kaldarren a swift kick in the kidneys. After Chen-Mai had blasted that panel blocking their way into the tunnel (*and then that panel just slid open, who built such a stupid mechanism?*), he and Mar had crept down the tunnel, half-expecting Kaldarren to ambush them at any second. What they were not prepared for was a treasure trove. Jevonite, gold, platinum, fabulous gems: The sheer amount of treasure spilling out of rock crystal chests and heaped in piles around the red stone floor was simply dazzling. There was little doubt that they were a hair's breadth away from being rich beyond their wildest dreams. Both he and Mar had been so awestruck they hadn't budged until they heard Jase's frantic cries mingled with Kaldarren's screams.

Well, the Betazoid *did* look bad. He watched as Kaldarren writhed, the cords of Kaldarren's muscles standing out along his neck. And his screams, Chen-Mai thought, they were loud enough to wake the dead.

But he didn't understand any of this. Chen-Mai's look took in the chamber. Pahl, slumped in his uncle's lap. That silver mask. Chen-Mai plucked it up between two fingers and held it up in a soft silver light that washed over the chamber from somewhere high above. (Recessed light panels, Chen-Mai thought absently.) His eyes traveled over the simple contours of what was otherwise an unremarkable piece of what? Art?

"Don't," said Jase. He was staring at the mask, a wild expression on his face. "Don't put it on!"

"And why would I do *that?*" Chen-Mai exhaled a harsh laugh, flipped the mask with a short, quick movement. (*It doesn't look that valuable, not worth bothering over, just one of Kaldarren's useless artifacts.*) The metal clattered against stone: a dull, clicking sound. "But he found something, right? Your father? How else do you explain what's going on here?"

"Leave the boy alone."

Chen-Mai swung his head toward Mar, who cradled Pahl in his arms. "What?"

"You heard me," said Mar. "Pahl's hurt, and any fool can see the Betazoid's sick. Leave the boy alone, can't you? We've got the money. Let's get out, now."

"But I want to know," said Chen-Mai. He hooked a thumb at Kaldarren. "I want to know what he's found out!"

"Well, I don't." Mar gave Kaldarren a long look before his

golden eyes flipped up to Chen-Mai. "And you shouldn't either, if you've got any brains. Look at him. You want to end up like that?"

"The boy hasn't."

"But Pahl *has.*" Mar cupped the unconscious boy's cheek, smooth as cold wax, in one hand. "Look, there's no portal. You see any portal? Whatever's going on here, it's for these telepaths, it's stuff we don't understand! I say we just leave, now. We take some of the jevonite back there, to show that we mean what we say, and we get out. We rendezvous with Talma, and then she can send someone back to collect the rest. We take our money and be thankful."

"No," said Jase, his face streaked and shiny with tears. "No, please, don't leave us here, don't!"

Kaldarren moaned. "No . . . *no!*"

"No what?" Chen-Mai squatted down on his haunches. "No, we don't leave your kid? No, we don't take the money? What? What did you find, Betazoid?"

Kaldarren's eyelids fluttered, his eyes roving wildly from side to side. "No good," Kaldarren managed at last. "No *good.*"

Those simple words seemed to cost him. He sagged back again, panting.

"No good?" Chen-Mai repeated. He reached out with one hand and gave Kaldarren a hard poke in the ribs. Kaldarren gave a short cry. "No good about *what?*"

"Stop!" Jase pleaded. "Stop, please!"

"Shut up." And to Kaldarren: "No good about what? *What?*"

Kaldarren's chest heaved. "No good to *you,*" Kaldarren managed, his breath hitching in the back of his throat. "No portal. But they're here, they're *here.*"

"They?" Chen-Mai frowned. "What, the same ghosts your kid . . .?"

"Get *out.*" Kaldarren moved his head the way a feverish

man does in a delirium. "Get . . . *out*, get out before it's too . . . too *late* . . . I can't hold them, I can't . . ."

"Please," said Jase again, clutching his father's hand. "Please, you've got to *help* him! Take us with you, *please!*"

Chen-Mai stared down at Kaldarren's flushed, sweat-soaked face for a long moment. Then his lip curled and, cursing, he pushed himself to his feet.

"I'll help him," said Chen-Mai, jerking his phaser free. "I'll help him right now."

Jase screamed. "No!"

"Wait," cried Mar. "Chen-Mai, stop!"

"No, no!" Uncoiling, Jase launched himself at the stocky man. Chen-Mai staggered back then cut Jase a vicious blow across the face. Jase cried out, reeling back before collapsing against a wall. Blood gushed from his mouth.

"Chen-Mai!" Mar shouted, horrified. He started to his feet. "What are you *doing?*"

"Shut up!" Chen-Mai threw the words over his shoulder. He leveled his phaser at Jase. "They're trouble, don't you understand? They're nothing but trouble!"

"But he's a kid!"

"So what? What, you're going to save him?"

"No," said Mar, faltering. He turned away, ashamed. "It's just . . ."

"Then shut up, Mar!" Chen-Mai flicked his phaser to kill. "If you've got nothing to add, then shut the hell up!"

"Please," Jase sobbed, blood drooling from his lips, "please, don't hurt my dad, *please.*"

"Look at it this way," said Chen-Mai, leveling his phaser at Jase. "I do you first, you won't have to watch."

"*Freeze!*" The command cut through the air like a knife. "Right there! Don't move, don't so much as goddamn *breathe!*"

Mar froze. Chen-Mai flinched then whirled on his heel, weapon hand coming up for a shot.

There was a high-pitched whine, a flash of light, and the phaser blast caught his weapon hand. Shrieking, Chen-Mai spun around; his phaser clattered to the stone floor.

"I said," Garrett readied her phaser for another blast, "don't goddamn *move*."

"Mom?" Jase tried pushing himself from the stone floor. "*Mom?*"

At the sound of her son's voice, Garrett started, blinked as if she'd been struck. An instant later, the color drained from her face. Her eyes flicked over to the far wall then down to Kaldarren.

"Jase?" she whispered in disbelief. She took a step forward. "*Ven?*"

"Oh, Lord," said Stern. She stood at Garret's elbow, her own phaser out and ready. "What the *hell?*"

"*Ven,*" Garrett said again, starting forward. "Jase, what's wrong with your father? Ven, I don't understand, what . . .?"

It was the only opening Chen-Mai needed. In a blur of movement, he had swept up his phaser with his good hand and come up behind Jase, locking the boy's neck in a stranglehold with his forearm.

"All right," said Chen-Mai, jamming the muzzle of his phaser against Jase's temple. "Everyone, drop your phasers. Nice and easy."

Chapter 34

"A *shuttlepod?*" Servos protesting, Bat-Levi crossed to stand behind Glemoor at his station next to Castillo. "Are you *sure?*"

"Positive, Commander. Sensors indicate a Vulcan shuttlepod heading for the planet's surface, and Commander Halak's transponder signal indicates that he is on board."

Glemoor twisted his head around to look up at Bat-Levi. "Those shuttlepods are short-range vessels."

"I know. I think it's safe to assume they didn't give him a ship for his own amusement. Who's with him?"

"Life signs read Vulcan."

"So Fake Burke is still aboard the *T'Pol*, and that means she's nearby. Where?"

"Unfortunately, I can't be precise."

Bat-Levi gave the Naxeran a dry look. "Guess."

Glemoor blinked. "Well, I *guess* the *T'Pol*'s hidden behind the planet's moon, or the planet itself."

"Yeah, that's what I would do." Bat-Levi watched the course of the small green blip of the shuttlepod as it angled in toward the surface. "The fact that the shuttlepod's headed down also means they don't know we're here."

"Very likely. A Vulcan warpshuttle would have limited sensor capabilities. The question is what do we do now?"

Bat-Levi debated. She rejected as useless any speculation as to why the *T'Pol* was in the vicinity. They had no way of knowing, and this wasn't her primary concern at the moment. Safeguarding the crew was. Bat-Levi wanted to try hailing Garrett but knew not only that their signal was unlikely to pierce through the interference, but this risked revealing their position. Not that she worried about *T'Pol*'s firepower: *Enterprise* won that particular argument, hands down. The Cardassians, however, were a different matter.

Bat-Levi looked over at Castillo. "Helm, I want you to take us into the transition region of that brown star."

Castillo looked startled. "That's awfully close, Commander. Even with shields at max, we'll cook."

But Glemoor was shaking his head. "No, Ensign, it's a good strategy, an *excellent* move. By definition, the brown star is cooler than, say, your Sol."

"And since the star itself is cooler, the temperature will

be low enough for us not to be in any danger but just high enough to obscure our plasma trail," said Bat-Levi. "We won't cook, not if we don't stay too long."

"Permission to give a suggestion, Commander?" asked Castillo. At her nod, he continued, "We have no way of knowing how long we'll have to stay. It's much less risky if we adopt the same strategy as the *T'Pol*. Keep the planet and its moon in front of us as a natural barrier. The stellar winds ought to obscure our plasma trail, and you said yourself that the warpshuttle's sensors can't read very far."

Bat-Levi and Glemoor exchanged glances. Then Bat-Levi put her good hand on Castillo's shoulder.

"It's not the *T'Pol* I'm worried about," she said, gently.

Jase, all that blood, what are you doing here, what's happening? And Ven, Ven, what's wrong with you? Garrett swallowed back her panic. "Jase?"

"I'm okay, Mom. But, Dad, you've got . . ." His voice ended in a choked gargle as Chen-Mai tightened his stranglehold around the boy's neck.

"I said, be quiet!" Chen-Mai peered at Garrett over Jase's right shoulder. "*You,* drop your weapon! Do it now! The other woman, too! In front of you where I can see them!"

"Fine." Garrett held up her hands, palms out, and let her phaser clatter to the rock. Stern hesitated then followed suit. "No problem," said Garrett. "Just take it easy."

"I am *very* easy! Now, kick them out of the way . . . good. Now back up."

The women did as they were told. Garrett's gaze dropped to Kaldarren, who lay crumpled on his side. "Ven," she called. She saw his eyelids flutter then open. "*Ven!*"

"Rachel." Kaldarren's face was a mask of pain. "Rachel, I knew you'd come if I called, I *knew* . . ."

He gave a sharp cry as Chen-Mai aimed a vicious kick at his back. "Quiet!" screamed Chen-Mai.

"Stop!" cried Garrett. She balled her fists in frustration and grief. "Let us *help* him!"

"Not until I get some answers." Chen-Mai rammed the point of his phaser into Jase's temple. "Now, mind telling me how you got here?"

"Mom," Jase began again, "Mom, I . . ."

"Enough!" Chen-Mai tightened his grip.

"Jase." Garrett gritted her teeth. It was all she could do to keep from leaping across the room and throttling the man. "Jase, don't say any more. Just be quiet."

"Well," said Chen-Mai, his black eyes swiveling to take in Jase, Garrett, and then Kaldarren. "A family reunion. What're the odds on that, huh? When did you and Kaldarren hatch up this little scheme?"

"I don't know what you're talking about," said Garrett.

Chen-Mai snorted. "Let's see, we've got the kid and his father, and now his mother conveniently shows up at just the right moment. Did Kaldarren set this up? I didn't think he was that smart."

Garrett wet her lips. "Listen to me. I don't know what's going on here, but . . ."

"Captain, I think I do," Stern interrupted, her tone low and urgent. "Those energy signatures I read at the tunnel entrance. They're *here*."

"Captain?" Chen-Mai was instantly alert. "What do you mean, *Captain*?"

Ignoring him, Garrett glanced back over her shoulder. "That neuromagnetic plasma you read?"

"What do you mean, *Captain*?" Chen-Mai shouted. "What do you *mean*? *Who* are you?"

Garrett turned, teeth bared. "I am Captain Rachel Garrett of the Federation Starship *Enterprise*. *This* is my ship's doctor. *That* is my son, and *that's* his father. Okay?"

"Not okay." Chen-Mai's eyes narrowed. "What are you doing here?"

"We answered a distress call."

"Distress call . . . we didn't send out any distress call."

"That's because you tripped an alarm, you moron." Stern's voice dripped with contempt. "At the tunnel entrance. Let me guess, you're the one with the ham handed approach to opening doors, right? Phaser, right? Idiot, you tripped an alarm."

Chen-Mai gaped, his mouth opening and closing like a fish. "The mechanism was jammed, it was . . ."

Stern made a horsey sound. "Jammed, my eye. You fired your damn phaser and set off a silent alarm beacon. We picked it up aboard our ship. And you can bet we're not the only ones."

Garrett said, "We had to investigate; we had no way of distinguishing an alarm from a distress call. We found the biosphere then picked up your life signs and followed them until we came here. I had no idea that either my son or my . . . husband was here." She looked past Chen-Mai at Jase. "Jase, what happened here, son?"

Jase's eyes slid sideways as if to gauge whether or not he was about to be choked again. "I," he began, "Pahl and I, we found the tunnel a couple of days ago. Then Pahl, he put on that mask, and then one of those things, it took him over."

"The mask?" Chen-Mai searched the floor until his eyes caught a glint of silver. "You mean, that? That's *important*?"

"You bet your sweet ass, it is," said Stern. "I think I get it, Captain. It's all here. There are hundreds of signatures in this room. Here and not here, almost as if they're," she studied her tricorder readings then shook her head in bewilderment, "as if they're cloaked in some way. But the energy is neural. Captain, they're minds. Or spirits, ghosts. And a lot of them . . ." she inclined her head toward Kaldarren, but didn't finish the sentence.

"They're inside?" Garrett paled. She closed her eyes for a moment, steeling herself. "Oh, dear God. Can you help him?"

"I don't know," said Stern, starting forward. "I need to do . . ."

"Don't move, don't move!" Chen-Mai shouted. "You, the doctor, put that down, put it *down!*"

"Oh, give it a rest," Stern growled. She dropped to her knees by Kaldarren and ran her medical tricorder over the length of his body. "I'm a doctor and this man's hurt. So either shoot me or shut up." When Chen-Mai didn't respond, Stern continued, "Wising up, right? Look, some of those things are *inside* him. For all I know, some more are inside that boy over there."

"What?" Mar started, stared down at his nephew's still, waxen features. "*In Pahl?*"

"No," said Jase, "no, it's not. It's gone. When Dad talked to It, It left Pahl and went into Dad."

It, thought Garrett, like a name. "Talked to It. Telepathically, Jase?"

Jase nodded, and she saw his eyes pool. "I couldn't hear it. I felt it, though. I knew they were here, that they *are* here."

"Makes sense," Stern murmured.

"I knew it," said Chen-Mai. His lips trembled with suppressed excitement. "I knew it, I knew it! He found a portal."

"No," said Jase, the tears spilling down his cheeks. "There's no door, or anything like that. Pahl used the mask, but Dad didn't."

Stern grunted. "Mind transference, Captain, same principle as the Vulcan mind-meld, or any true telepathic contact. But that mask, I'll bet my bottom dollar that it's a device that focuses or collimates neural energy. Like a lens focuses diffuse light to a single point: The lens doesn't *make* the light. It's simply a conduit for allowing certain properties of light to be exaggerated, or used."

"What do you mean?" Chen-Mai raged. "Speak sense! Can that be used, or not?"

"Probably not by you." Stern's look spoke volumes. "Or

me, for that matter, but not because I'm the least bit like you, thank God. That thing just makes it easier for an energy exchange to take place. True telepaths wouldn't require it."

"But empaths would?" asked Garrett.

Stern hesitated, gave Jase a quick glance. "Sure," she said, then with added emphasis, "or people with fledgling telepathic abilities."

"That can't be," said Mar. "Pahl is not a telepath."

"But he's Naxeran, and from his complexion, one of his parents was a Weyrie, right?" When Mar nodded, Stern looked over at Garrett. "The Weyries are the only class of Naxerans who dream, Captain. They also have a fairly high prevalence of psychiatric problems. Hallucination, delusions."

"Telepathic equivalents?"

"Maybe for the Naxerans."

"Glemoor's never mentioned it."

"The Naxerans may not know, Captain. As I recall, the Weyries don't tend to live very long. They're also pretty reclusive; I don't think other Naxerans have much to do with them."

"The Weyries," said Mar, his frills trembling, "very strange, very odd . . ."

"Weyries," Chen-Mai interrupted. "Empaths, telepaths! Enough of this talk. What matters now is that you *are* here."

"Don't you get it?" Stern asked. "We wouldn't *be* here if you hadn't been so helpful with your phaser on that airlock. And you can bet your bottom dollar that if we caught that signal, so will the Cardassians. They're probably on their way now."

Garrett looked over at Mar. Of the two men, she thought that the Naxeran would be the most reasonable. "Look, I don't know why you're here. Frankly, I don't care. Right now, I care about getting out of here before the Cardassians show up.

Now the best thing for everyone is for you to come with us. We've got a shuttle. We can take care of your boy on the ship."

Mar hesitated, glanced over at Chen-Mai, then nodded.

"No!" Chen-Mai shouted. "No, are you *crazy*? You want to leave all this behind?"

"But if they're right and the Cardassians are coming, what good will it do us if we're dead?" asked Mar.

"They're just making it up," said Chen-Mai. "The boy's father and his mother, they're both in on this."

"Oh, that's intelligence for you," said Stern.

"Jo!" Garrett snapped. And to Chen-Mai: "If we don't leave now, we'll be stranded here. Our ship has orders to leave the system if they so much as sniff a Cardassian ship. We have to go now!"

But Chen-Mai was shaking his head and, to Garrett's dismay, he began backing up, using Jase as a shield. "Oh, no. Your ship might leave, and you might be right, but I'll be taking my own ship, thanks. Now I want what's my due. I didn't take all these risks to be left with nothing. All that money in that other room there, I'm not leaving it behind. And just to make sure your ship doesn't fire on me on my way out of the system, the boy's coming with me."

"Mom," said Jase, his eyes wide with fright. "Mom!"

"Wait a minute." Mar started to his feet. "What about me? What about Pahl? You're not leaving us behind!"

"*No one* has to be left behind!" Garrett said sharply. "Look, I give you my word, we'll let you go. You won't be charged. Come with us; you don't have to do this!"

Chen-Mai's face was hard. "I don't believe you. I'm leaving and I'm taking the boy. You, Mar, if you're coming, leave the boy and come now!"

"No." Mar spread out his hands in a helpless gesture. "I can't do that. I can't leave Pahl. Please, Chen-Mai, at least let the doctor . . ."

"There's no *time*!"

Mar's jaw firmed. "I won't leave."

"Fine," said Chen-Mai. His phaser flicked away from Jase's temple. "Then stay."

"No!" cried Garrett, too late.

There was a brilliant flash as the phaser beam lanced across the chamber. Mar screamed as the beam struck the side of his head, and collapsed in a heap to the stone. Before Garrett could move, Chen-Mai had his phaser trained on Jase's head once more.

Stern rushed to Mar's side, ran her medical tricorder over his body. Shook her head.

Choking back her fury, Garrett turned on Chen-Mai. "There was no reason for that, *none!*"

Of all things, Chen-Mai grinned, showing the gap between his teeth, the pink nub of his tongue working. "One thing you learn in my business: People do what they're told. Otherwise, things go wrong. I don't like it when things go wrong."

"You didn't have to kill him. There's no reason that anyone else has to die here."

But Chen-Mai was backing out, pulling Jase with him. "You come after me, I'll kill him, you understand?"

"Mom!" Jase began to struggle. "Mom, don't let him!"

"Shut up!" Chen-Mai cuffed the boy across the temple with the butt of his phaser.

Jase gasped, staggered. Then, roaring with anger, Jase brought the heel of his foot down, hard, on the man's instep.

"Jase!" Garrett shouted.

Chen-Mai choked out a scream. Jase tore away and dove for the floor just as Chen-Mai let loose a blast from his phaser. But his aim was off, and the beam sizzled wide, skirting the boy's head. The beam was so close that Garrett heard the sputter-crack of the phaser as the beam gouged a hole in the red stone floor. The floor twitched with the force of the blast, and Jase tripped, tried scrambling to his feet, but then Garrett was diving for him, knocking him left as the phaser licked the stone to her right. Garrett banged into the hard rock floor; the impact knocked her breath away and left her gasping. There was a high whine and then the red rock erupted in a spray of pulverized and superheated stone, showering her with debris that pattered down upon her head and bit at her cheeks.

"Go!" Garrett choked, gulping down air. Reaching down, she detached her helmet from her waist and rolled into a crouch. "Move, Jase, *move!*"

Jase darted left, and as Chen-Mai brought his phaser around for another shot, Garrett sprang, flying across the room, slinging her fist around in a roundhouse swing. She caught Chen-Mai on the point of his chin with an audible crack. The man went down in a heap, his phaser whirling from his hand. Garrett knew her own weapon was too far away and she lunged for Chen-Mai's. At the last second, he reached up and grabbed her ankle, sent her crashing to the floor.

"Jase!" she yelled to her son who was crouched in a far corner. "Get the phaser, get the *phaser!*"

Jase started for the weapon, but, somehow, Chen-Mai staggered to his feet and scooped up the phaser, juggling the weapon from his left to his right hand.

"You're too much trouble," he said, backing away, chest heaving, blood trickling from the corner of his mouth. Turning his head to one side, he spat out a gob of rust-colored saliva. His teeth were orange with blood. He took aim at Garrett. "Too much damn trouble."

Suddenly, there was a shout from the arched doorway just behind, the one that led to the main burial chamber. Garrett twisted her head around in time to see Sivek stumbling through the opening, off-balance, his arms out and windmilling for a support that wasn't there.

At the sound, Chen-Mai jerked his weapon up and fired.

The blast burned through the Vulcan's suit, through his flesh, and into his lungs, and the force sent Sivek hurtling against the far wall. The Vulcan never had a chance to shout, not that it mattered. He slammed against the wall with a solid thud and collapsed, his body slithering down the wall.

In the next instant, Halak leapt through the entrance, Sivek's phaser in his hand.

"Watch it, Halak!" Garrett shouted, her shock turning to urgency. "He's got a phaser!"

Without breaking stride, Halak dove for cover behind a boulder, firing as he went. His phaser shot lanced across the cavern, exploding into the rock above Chen-Mai's head, sending down a rain of gravel and pulverized stone. Turning, Chen-Mai fired once, a wild shot, and then bolted for the corridor at the far end of the chamber. Jase threw himself forward, but the stocky man was much stronger and threw the boy aside like a rag doll before disappearing down the corridor.

Garrett pushed to her feet. "Let him go!" she said to Halak, who had started after.

"You picked a hell of a good time to play cavalry," Stern observed. She was still squatting by Kaldarren but hooked a thumb toward Sivek's body. "How did you figure it out?"

"Later," said Halak. He trotted over to Garrett. "Captain?"

"I'm fine," said Garrett, pushing her hair from her face. She looked around wildly. "But, Jase, where's Jase?"

Jase dodged around Halak. "Mom," Jase said, throwing himself into her so forcefully that Garrett staggered back. Halak caught her by the elbow and steadied her.

"Oh, Mom," Jase said, "Mom!"

Garrett gave him a fierce hug, held her son's face between her hands, and said shakily, "If you weren't too old . . ."

"Rachel." Garrett turned around. Stern was running her tricorder over Kaldarren's prostrate form, but when she raised her eyes to Garrett, her face was grim.

Heart sinking, Garrett knelt by Kaldarren. "Ven," she said. She swallowed hard and ran her hand, still gloved, along his brow. "Ven, can you hear me?"

She had to call his name twice more before he responded. "Rachel," Kaldarren said, his voice breaking. The muscles of his face twitched and danced. "Rachel, you have to leave . . . you have to take Jase away . . . away from here."

"Sshh," said Garrett, blinking back sudden tears. In an instant, the years of hurt and disappointments, all the acrimony and recriminations, were erased, and she saw only the man she had once loved with all her heart: the man who had been her lover, her steadfast friend, her most ardent critic. The father of the son they both loved. "Ven, let us try to help you, let us . . ."

"You can't." Kaldarren's head rolled back and forth in weak protest. "You . . . can't. They're *in* me and I can't *break* away, I can't . . ."

"Don't talk. We'll get you aboard the ship."

"Rachel." Stern reached out and gripped Garrett's wrist. "Rachel, I'm sorry, but I can't let you do that."

"What?" Jase cried.

Halak put a hand on the boy's shoulder, but Jase didn't seem to notice. His face was a mask of anguish and disbelief. "You have to help him!" Jase cried. "He's my *dad!*"

"Tell me, Jo," said Garrett, her heart swelling with dread. "Just tell me."

Stern exhaled her breath in a long sigh. "I'm sorry. God, I'd give anything to tell you differently, Rachel, but the fact is I don't even know where to start. His brain wave patterns are changing; these things are like a wave propagating on itself and getting stronger and stronger by the minute. His cortical activity has jumped threefold; the levels of serotonin, epinephrine, GABA, PGBC, they're going through the roof. He's fighting, but these other *things* are just getting stronger, chipping away at his mental defenses. Who knows where this will end, or how strong he'll . . . *they'll* be at the end. Or what he'll become."

"So what are you saying?"

"You know already. You can't bring this aboard the ship."

Garrett could only gape. "*Leave* him here? But you said that only telepaths were affected."

"Only telepaths can *host* whatever this is. But you have no idea how powerful he'll be when the transformation is complete. For that matter, you don't know that they won't find someone more compatible aboard *Enterprise*."

"Mom." Garrett twisted around to see Jase, the tears streaming down his face unchecked. "Mom, don't let her do it! Don't *let* her!"

"Son," said Halak, reaching for Jase's shoulder. "Don't make this harder for your mother than it already is."

"What do *you* know?" Jase batted Halak's hand away. "How do you know what's hard?" he shouted, his face contorted with his grief and fury. "How do you know?"

"I know," said Halak. "Sometimes love means making hard choices because that's all there are."

Halak's eyes drifted to Garrett's then back to Jase. "Mourn your dad. Grieve for him. But take a good hard look at your father and then tell me that your mother's wrong."

"No, no," Jase moaning, his chest convulsing with sobs, "he's not dead, I'm not ready, I'm not ready for this, I don't want to *see* this. It's not fair." Jase turned aside and buried his face in Halak's chest. Jase began to cry in that open-mouthed despairing way of young children when their heart is breaking. "It's not fair, I'm not ready, I'm not *ready!*"

"It's all right," said Halak, wrapping his arms around Jase's shoulders. He held the boy. "It's all right."

Garrett's vision blurred with tears. She felt Kaldarren's fingers scrabbling at her wrist. She turned back; Kaldarren's dark eyes were fixed on hers.

"Listen to your doctor," he said, his voice hitching. A spasm of pain made his face twist. "She's right. If I go aboard your ship . . . if they find . . . a more compatible match, they will . . . will hop. Rachel, they can't die, and they are more of them here, they'll bring others, they'll . . . *force* them, and I'm not sure how . . . how much longer I can . . . I can . . ."

"Don't talk," said Garrett, hot tears tracking down her cheeks. She clutched his hand to her chest. "Ven, please, please, don't talk."

"No," Kaldarren hissed. "You have to listen. My data . . . my *data*." He subsided, took a deep breath, and seemed to gather the last of his strength. "Tricorder has it all. Take that with you. Don't let this be . . . be for nothing. Don't . . ." His back arched, and his teeth clenched in a sudden spasm. "Don't!"

"Ven!" cried Garrett desperately. To Stern: "*Do* something! *Anything!*"

Face set, Stern fitted a hypo and jetted the solution into the angle of Kaldarren's neck. Almost instantly, Kaldarren's muscles relaxed; his head lolled to one side.

Garrett looked up, apprehension etched into her features. "Did you . . .?" The words died on her lips, but her meaning was clear: *Did you kill him?*

They had known each other so long Stern read Garrett perfectly. "Not my call to make, Rachel. That was just a strong painkiller."

Stern replaced her hypospray, then pushed up and bent over Pahl. There was an atonal whirling sound as she ran her tricorder over the boy. "This one, we can help. Jase was right; there's nothing here. Far as I can tell, his brain's shut down, that's all. Traumatic withdrawal. The sooner we get him aboard, the less psychological damage there'll be." When Garrett didn't respond, Stern continued, "Rachel, we don't have much time."

"What do you mean?" asked Halak. Jase had quieted, but he still held the boy in his arms. "What's going on, Captain?"

"One word," said Stern, pushing to her feet. She winced as her knees cracked. "Cardassians."

The color drained from Halak's face. The face he turned to Garrett was grave. "Captain?"

Without looking up, Garrett nodded. "In a minute. Jase."

Halak felt Jase stir, and in another moment, the boy lifted his face from the hollow of Halak's chest. Jase's face was splotchy and swollen from crying, but his eyes were dry now, his tears spent. Without another word, he disengaged himself from Halak's arms, and Halak let him go.

Jase dropped to his knees. Put his arms around his father's neck. "I love you, Dad," he whispered into Kaldarren's ear. "I'll always love you."

There was no indication that Kaldarren heard, and after a few seconds, Jase kissed his father's cheek and stood. He backed away until he stood a few inches from Halak.

Halak didn't touch him. He said only, "It's hard, son."

The boy nodded but didn't turn around. Wordlessly, they watched Garrett.

Still kneeling by Kaldarren's side, Garrett pulled first her right then her left hand from their respective gloves and let her bare fingers trail over Kaldarren's features. She closed her eyes. *This is what it's like to be blind and so you memorize the face of the person you love and you pour all your love into a single touch.*

Garrett touched Kaldarren's face again and again: tracing his broad forehead, that fine nose, his high cheekbones. And something extraordinary happened. With every pass of her hand, Kaldarren's face softened beneath her fingers; the deep lines etched on his face smoothed; and she heard his breathing grow less labored and more like sleep. At last, Kaldarren exhaled a long, deep sigh.

It's his soul. Garrett knew this was absurd, but the thought sprang to her mind anyway. *He's letting go, but I'm here, I have him, and I'll carry his soul like memory.*

Finally, Garrett ceased. She opened her eyes, sat back on her heels, and let her hands rest on her thighs. She stared down at Kaldarren for a long moment.

Good-bye, my love. Kaldarren's face wavered in her vision, and the hot burn of tears pricked her eyes. *Good-bye.*

She stood then, her heart full of grief, her will stronger than steel. "I'm ready," she said, cupping Jase's hot cheek with her right hand. Their eyes met, and for an instant, she imagined that their minds joined, and that Jase knew what his parents had shared. Or maybe it was just an illusion.

Then Garrett pulled on her gloves and retrieved her helmet. She clipped her helmet to her waist, and the snap was crisp and sharp. "Let's get the hell out of here."

Chapter 35

The problem with a stationary orbit, lunar or otherwise, is that it's very boring. Same scenery, same bunch of coordinates. Same old, same old. Talma yawned. Well, at least, she was comfortably bored.

Only one real glitch so far: an odd signature about an hour ago. At first, she'd thought nothing of it. It had been a simple variance in the far end of the electromagnetic spectrum—there briefly and then, just as quickly, gone. Hunkered down behind the planet's larger moon, she had no way to study the blip further. Sure, it could have been a ship, but then where had it gone? Her mind drifted to the Cardassian scouts she was sure were only hours away, if that. But a Cardassian scout ship would have continued its sweep, and she would have seen the ship on sensors as it came out of her blind spot. So, probably just a glitch and this was understandable, what with all the *junk* in this system. Talma smiled. How apt.

And speaking of Vaavek: Talma rechecked the ship's chronometer, saw that it was only five minutes later than when she'd last checked, and cursed. He was late.

Why? Two possibilities: Either Vaavek had found the portal and was simply delayed, or he hadn't. Following from those conclusions, if Vaavek had found the portal, Halak was dead. If he hadn't, Halak was still alive but wouldn't be for long. Ditto for Vaavek, actually. (Her mother always said she never *had* learned to share.)

Of course, if she was planning on vaporizing Vaavek, likely the Vulcan had worked out a way to do the same to her. She'd have to be careful around him—doubly so if he'd found the portal.

She'd manage. That was the problem with Vulcans; they could exaggerate, but they weren't devious. So Talma doubted that Vaavek had bothered to sabotage the *T'Pol*'s engines the way she'd sabotaged the shuttlepod. If they hadn't found the portal and Halak was still alive—something she could ascertain in a flash before the shuttlepod even got close—all that would be required was one phaser hit in just the right spot . . .

Her concentration was broken by a shrill bleat from the *T'Pol*'s comm. Talma started, her heart ramping up a beat or two as a squirt of adrenaline coursed through her veins. The bleat came again, and Talma confirmed: Vaavek's signal, all right. Set on a prearranged frequency, piggybacking onto the periodic signal emitted by the neutron star. Any ship in the vicinity (a Cardassian scout, say) wouldn't hear or suspect a thing, not unless it knew what to look for. Vaavek was on his way back, with the goods.

A signal within a signal: again, simple. Elegant. Clean. Just the way she'd done with the *Enterprise*, coning her signal inside another signal. A grin tugged at the corners of her lips. Those dopes. Out-thunk by a dirt-poor kid from one of the roughest planets in the galaxy.

The signal came again.

Engaging her sensors at maximum—*the better to avoid unpleasant surprises in Cardassian trappings, my dear*—

Talma nudged *T'Pol* from lunar stationary orbit. She was delighted that the scenery was about to change.

"Got something," said Glemoor.

Bat-Levi, who was seated in the captain's command chair, leaned forward. "What?"

"Movement," said Glemoor, and he was reminded of his perusal of old Earth history: literature of submarine battles and then of classic Starfleet maneuvers. James T. Kirk, as he remembered rightly: a splendid warrior, Glemoor decided, and superb tactician. Kirk's first run-in with Romulans, for example: a classic and required reading for any tactical officer interested in the principles of stealth warfare.

"Movement?" Bat-Levi echoed. She stepped down from the command chair and hovered behind Glemoor's left shoulder. "What? A warp signature? Impulse engines?"

"No," said Glemoor. "I mean, *movement*."

Castillo, who had called up the same display on his station, shook his head. "I don't see anything."

Bat-Levi's eyebrows mated as she bent to study Glemoor's readings. "He's right. There's nothing there."

"No, there is. It's simply that you don't know what you're looking at." Glemoor's tone wasn't smug; he was just imparting facts. "There's too much interference in this general vicinity to distinguish easily between true vessel signatures, or plasma trails and ambient ionized plasma. So, in addition to my usual sensor scans, I've calibrated the sensors to detect changes in the wave particle fronts surrounding both the planet and its moon, on the theory that a ship might be hiding there."

In response to Bat-Levi's quizzical expression, Glemoor added, "Think of it as trying to scoop up a cracker from a bowl of thick soup. If you chase your cracker, you set up a displacement of the soup itself."

Castillo brightened. "I get it. There's so much stellar soup out there you looked for compression of wave fronts."

"All right, I'm impressed," said Bat-Levi. "So, is it the *T'Pol*? Or a Cardassian?"

"The *T'Pol*, I think. The degree of displacement is too small for a Cardassian."

"Shall I plot course for intercept?" asked Castillo.

"What about that, Glemoor?"

"Nothing from the planet's surface yet, Commander."

"But there must be something," said Bat-Levi, "otherwise, the *T'Pol* wouldn't be moving out." She glanced over her shoulder at communications. "Bulast?"

The Atrean shook his head. "Nothing."

Bat-Levi pursed her lips. "Then why is she moving? There's got to be something . . ."

"Wait," said Bulast, suddenly. His fingers stroked the controls at his console. "Got it. Same trick she used before. Coned inside the periodic bursts from that neutron star. A signal."

Glemoor cut in. "Something else, Commander."

"The captain?"

"No," Glemoor said. "On long-range sensors. Company, closing fast."

Seated in the pilot's chair of her shuttlecraft, Garrett opened a channel to Halak in the Vulcan shuttlepod. "Think she got it?"

"Positive." Halak's voice was marred by pops and crackles of static. "She ought to be moving out from behind the larger moon any minute now."

"Let's hope." Garrett looked over at Stern who sat in the co-pilot's chair. "Well?"

"Too much damned interference," Stern muttered, twiddling with the shuttle's sensors, "like pea soup, I don't see how you expect me to look for Cardassian scouts, they'd . . . ah! Got 'em."

"How many?"

"Two. Closing fast. They've got a bug up their thrusters, all right."

"That bug would be us," said Garrett, bringing the engines on-line. "Or the *T'Pol*. Let's hope it's the latter. What about the *Enterprise?*"

"Still nothing. She's gone, all right." Stern gave Garrett a narrow look. "You sure you don't want to just sit this one out?"

"We've got a much better chance if we're moving. Hunker down here, and we might as well hand out invitations for those Cardassians to take potshots."

"We're not exactly fast, you know. And our range . . ."

"Let me worry about that. Besides," Garrett plotted a course out of the system, "there are two of us. With the *T'Pol*, that makes three. If I were those Cardassians, I'd go for the bigger ship because I'd know there's no way a smaller ship would get far."

"Oh, that's comforting. Let's hope the *Enterprise* isn't too far away."

Otherwise, we're on our own. Stern didn't say it, but Garrett thought she might as well have. It had been Garrett's call: getting the *Enterprise* out of harm's way if the Cardassians showed up (as they just had). If Bat-Levi had followed her orders, the *Enterprise* had left the system at the first sign of the Cardassian scouts. So that meant her ship would be heading for the rendezvous coordinates: seven light years away.

She glanced back over her shoulder at Jase who huddled on a chair just behind her station. "Buckle up. I want to see that restraining harness on."

"Sure." Jase managed a wan grin. They'd bundled Pahl into restraints on a makeshift hassock aft. It would have made Garrett feel better if Jase were with his friend; Jase would be that much closer to an environmental suit if they had to evacuate. But Jase had refused, and Garrett hadn't the heart to press it. They'd just take their chances together. On reflection, Garrett thought that was probably the way things were meant to be.

She watched as her son reached over his shoulders with both hands, grabbed the buckles of his restraining harness, and tugged them down. "Snug it. And hang on now, okay? It might get rough."

"Promises, promises," Stern grumbled, shrugging into her own harness.

"If we're lucky, they'll go after the *T'Pol* and leave us be." Garrett punched up the Vulcan shuttlepod. "On my mark, Halak."

"Ready, Captain."

"On three, two, one. Mark!" Garrett punched up her engines. There was a perceptible jolt, the rush of a red-hued landscape, and then the blackness of space, stars.

As one, the two ships rocketed up from the planet.

The way was dark as pitch. Chen-Mai blundered along, rebounding off rock walls, the round hump of his helmet banging against stone. He might as well be blind.

He was dead. Chen-Mai felt a bubble of panic pushing at the back of his throat and his chest heaved, trying to pull in air. Or as good as dead: He'd die down here if he couldn't find his way back. My God, but the air was so close! He ran his naked hands along the rough stone; he'd pulled off his gloves because the fingers were too padded and once the light went, he needed to have more feeling. The walls, they were closing in, he couldn't breathe! Chen-Mai's chest was tight, and he struggled to breathe, breathe, *breathe. . . .*

Hyperventilating. He was getting dizzy. The sour taste of bile filled his mouth, and Chen-Mai doubled over, vomited until his stomach was empty and all he could do was hack dry heaves. Sagged back against stone.

Calm, he had to be calm. Chen-Mai pressed the back of his left hand against his forehead. Sweating like a pig. Hot, so hot in here, the air so close. He had half a mind to get out of this infernal suit, then maybe strip Kaldarren or Mar—yes, Mar, because Kaldarren had something wrong with him, and Chen-Mai wouldn't touch him, wouldn't take the chance—yes, he could strip Mar of his suit when he found the room again because he would find the room, he would.

But he might not. Chen-Mai turned his head aside and hawked up foul-tasting spit. There was more than way out of here, there had to be. So he had to keep his wits about him. But which way was out? He had a sense that he was heading down deeper, and that was wrong. That turn he'd taken a while back: He shouldn't have done that. But he'd been certain he was circling back, to the chamber where he'd been, where that Kaldarren had tricked him. . . .

He tripped over something—a rock lip, a stone perhaps—staggered. Pitched forward into the darkness. He managed to get his hands out in front and caught himself, but the tunnel floor was uneven and dropped a half-meter. Then the heels of his hands banged into the hard rock, and he heard something snap in his right wrist.

Chen-Mai screamed and then he screamed again. His scream bounced off the low walls and reverberated in the darkness. Rolling onto his left side, Chen-Mai cradled his shattered right wrist against his chest. He couldn't see his wrist, wasn't sure he wanted to, but he knew that it was broken.

Now, something else: something wet, warm on his fingertips, the fingertips of his left hand. And an odd smell, like wet metal, damp rust. Cautiously, he wormed the fingers of his left hand around his right wrist. Grazed against something sharp, and then moist fabric. Odd. Maybe he'd torn his suit and . . .

Bone. Chen-Mai's eyes bulged in the darkness. The jagged ends of bone that had torn through his skin.

Chen-Mai threw his head back and howled.

At just about the same time that Talma spotted both the shuttle and shuttlepod—and before she had a chance to even wonder about why a Starfleet shuttlecraft was in the vicinity much in the less in the company of Vaavek's shuttlepod—she also saw the Cardassians, barreling her way.

"Hunnh!" Her breath rushed out of her lungs in surprise. For a brief instant, she was absolutely frozen in place, her mind slamming on the brakes. She watched the Cardassian scouts get larger and larger, closer and closer . . .

She snapped out of her shock and tried to get her mind working. The Cardassians were here, now, *early*. But how?

Her forehead crinkled. Could it be the signal, the one Vaavek had sent, that alerted them? But no—as quickly as she had that thought, she dismissed it—the signal had come first, then the Cardassians appeared, and then . . .

Her eyes went round. *Then* Vaavek had lifted off the surface and *in* the company of the shuttlecraft. Too far away for her to figure out where the shuttlecraft had come from, which ship, though she had a fair idea.

Garrett. The *Enterprise*. By God! Her fist slammed onto the console. But how had Garrett figured it out? *When?*

And no matter that: The order was wrong. She should've spotted it right away, but she'd let her greed get the better of her. The order was *wrong*. Vaavek *should* have lifted off first *then* activated the signal. He—or Garrett—was counting on her moving out from behind the moon.

A decoy. Talma's brown eyes slitted. Yes, that was it. Vaavek had sent the signal. He knew, somehow, that the Cardassians were there. Using that cold Vulcan calculus she'd come to appreciate, Vaavek would gamble that the scouts would either ignore the tinier shuttlepod completely, or lose it in the confusion of weapons' fire. How he knew didn't matter at the moment. Nothing mattered anymore except that Talma was a sitting duck. The Cardassians were faster, more maneuverable than the Vulcan warpshuttle.

Now her mind raced over her options. They were diminishingly few. It was either run, or run.

All right. Bringing the ship's navigational computer back on-line, she barked out a command as her hands flew over the T'Pol's weapons' systems. All right, two could play at this game. They wanted a decoy? Talma's lips split in a savagely triumphant smile. She'd give them a decoy.

She picked out the shuttlepod's port nacelle, targeting manually as the computer chittered to itself in Vulcan, spitting out coordinates for taking the ship toward the neutron star. Talma listened with half an ear; her Vulcan was impeccable and she was confident the computer knew what it was doing.

She didn't bring the weapons on-line. Not just yet. Lock on, and the shuttlepod might see, veer off. Or that shuttlecraft might warn Vaavek. Talma tracked the blip that was the Vulcan shuttlepod. One shot, she figured, then the Cardassians would be on her—*unless* she gave them something *infinitely* more interesting to look at.

"Come on," she urged under her breath, watching as the Cardassians sped toward them. The shuttlepod was nearly in range. "*Come on.*"

Five, four . . . the shuttlepod drew closer, closer and she saw that its shields weren't up and that was very, very good . . . three, two.

"Now!" Talma shouted. "Computer, *nu-at, weedawa! Nave-zehlek, klamacha thes!* Dooohchat!

And because Talma's Vulcan *was* impeccable, the T'Pol's shields snapped into place, her phasers locked on target, and the computer fired phasers. Full power.

And, at that exact moment, the shuttlepod accelerated straight for her on a collision course.

Chicken. Halak barreled toward the *T'Pol*. He'd just play chicken and see which of them blinked first.

"Because I don't trust you, Burke," he said, his smile vicious and just this side of truly malevolent. "Because I think you're going to try to blow me out of the quadrant before the Cardassians do. Because that's what *I* would do."

An alarm screamed, and Halak's eyes jerked left. Cardassian scouts and, damn, they were *fast!*

"Captain, here they come, here they come!" Halak shouted. At the same instant, he saw the phaser lock from the *T'Pol*. Read that her shields had snapped into place.

"Halak!" It was Garrett. "She's got a lock! Get your shields up, get them up!"

"Shields! Taking evasive maneuvers!" Halak slammed his palm down upon his shield control as he brought the ship around in a tight, spiraling turn, port and aft. If there had been air, he imagined that he would hear it screaming past his window, feel the force of his acceleration flattening him into his seat, squeezing his chest. But his gravity was holding and so he felt nothing: saw only the dizzying stirring of the stars and ionized gases outside his window, the flickering beams of phasers licking past the ship.

Missed. But she'd fired again. Halak slid the shuttlepod Z-plus 50. Climbing, climbing . . . and where was she, where was the *T'Pol*? Halak's eyes scrambled over his sensor displays. She ought to becoming around for another pass, leaping after him like a hound chasing a rabbit.

But *no.* Halak gawked. Scrubbed at his eyes to be sure. No, the *T'Pol* was headed in the opposite direction, toward the neutron star. Not after him, or the shuttlecraft. Probably thinking she could hide in the magnetic well, wait things out.

Then he saw something that made him bang his fists

down upon his console in frustration. One Cardassian on T'Pol's tail, but the other Cardassian was letting her go, at least for the moment.

Because you were so helpful, Burke, pointing us out. Halak punched in a channel. "Captain! The brown star! Make a run for it! Go, go, *go!*"

Without waiting to see what Garrett did, Halak jerked the shuttlepod around and bore down on the remaining Cardassian. *Same game*—his hand hovered over his phaser controls—*we play the same damn game and let's see if this Cardassian even* knows *what a chicken is.*

He managed to evade the first disruptor blast but not the second. For a split instant, the shuttlepod's artificial gravity wavered, and Halak pitched forward, banging the point of his chin against the edge of his pilot's console. Pain exploded along his jaw and shivered into his teeth. Blood filled his mouth, trickled down his throat, and he gagged. There was a sensation of spinning; the tiny craft whirling like a top . . .

I'm dead, thought Halak. The centrifugal force had him pinned in his chair, and he couldn't move, but he didn't think there was anything he could do anyway. *I'm dead.*

Then the gravity clicked back and Halak lurched forward, coughed out a spray of blood. Alarms screamed. With a vicious swipe, he silenced them. He knew how bad things were.

"Halak!" Garrett's voice sizzled through static. Halak heard the thin high whine of a phaser discharge, then looked out his window and saw the space bloom around the Cardassian scout, watched as one of the Cardassian's forward shields flared orange from a phaser hit. Instead of making a run for the brown star, Garrett had circled around and was trying to draw the Cardassians away from his ship. "Halak, answer me, damn it!"

"Here, Captain." Halak coughed again, sponged blood

from his jaw. The skin over his chin was split wide open and he was bleeding so much he could feel it pooling at his neck.

He toggled up his displays. "Shields fifty percent. And there's something wrong with my engines. They've kicked out. I don't understand, the disruptor blast wasn't that bad, it wasn't . . ."

Burke. Halak felt himself go cold. The way she hadn't come after him. Somehow she'd rigged the engines so a phaser blast or a disruptor hit would take them off-line, would finish him. That's why she'd only fired once.

But he had no time. He ground his teeth together. The Cardassians out there, angling around for another run, they'd finish him off, and he was out of time, there was no time, no *time!*

"Captain!" Halak grappled to bring the ship around. The shuttlepod was sluggish, the controls mushy, and Halak had the insane thought that he'd probably be better off getting out and pushing for all the maneuverability he had. "Captain, can you hear me? My navigational control's shot! I've got nothing here! Do you copy? Captain? *Captain?*"

"Dead in space," said Glemoor, his eyes taking in the scene from the bridge's main viewscreen. He looked back at Bat-Levi. "Whoever's on board that shuttlepod still has shields, but he won't last another two, three passes."

"Life signs? One of us?"

"We're too far away. Too much interference."

"So, nothing to lock onto, and no way to beam them out even if we could, what with that mess out there." Bat-Levi's jaw set. "Well, at least, we have an idea where the captain is. How's the shuttlecraft?"

"I read minor damage to the aft hull. Shields are holding. The shock waves from those disruptor blasts are going to be tricky for the captain in terms of maneuverability, but as long as her axial stabilizers are functional she ought to be able to dodge them. She appears to be on course directly for us. She's fine, for the moment."

"Dammit, how *fine* can you be with a Cardassian disruptor pointed down your throat?" said Castillo.

"Anything, Mr. Bulast?" asked Bat-Levi, judging Castillo's question to be rhetorical.

"Nothing, Commander. She's not hailing, so she must believe we've left the area. Castillo's right. If the Cardassian can't see us, then she can't either. Even if she knew we were here, I can't imagine that she'd alert the Cardassian to our presence."

"Well, we've got to do *something!*" Castillo blurted. His face was getting pink. "That's the *captain* out there! Look, she's trying to make a run for the star. Well, we're *here*. What, we're just going to wait and congratulate her if she makes it? We can't just stand around and do *nothing!*"

Kodell had come to the bridge as soon as Glemoor had sighted the Cardassian bearing down on the fourth planet. (Bat-Levi thought it curious for him to be on the bridge at all; Kodell could just as easily handle his duties down below. But she found his presence reassuring, and then wondered if that's what he'd had in mind.) Now he turned from his station and favored the ensign with a cool glance. "I'm sure the commander doesn't require *you* to remind *her* that something needs to be done, Ensign."

Bat-Levi held up a hand—her bad one, as it happened, but she wasn't feeling self-conscious at the moment. "No, it's all right," she murmured, her eyes scanning the main viewer and watching how the space around the shuttlecraft and Vulcan shuttlepod erupted in fiery blossoms of ignited gas and plasma. "I'm just trying to figure out how many orders I want to disobey in one day."

There was movement behind her left shoulder, and then she heard Kodell's voice, low, pitched for her ears only: "But you *do* need to do something."

That made her mad, but she kept her voice down. "Thanks for the reminder. You know damn well I can't fire on the Cardassian scout, without raising all kinds of hell. We're in disputed space and we're here because of a breach in Starfleet security, remember?"

"The captain's turning!" Castillo sang. "Heading back toward the shuttlepod!"

"What?" Bat-Levi didn't want to say it, but she thought that this bordered on suicidal.

"May I remind you," Kodell continued, as if nothing had happened, "that if that Cardassian *does* see us and lives to tell about it, the end result will be the same? All they have to do is report back to their Central Command, and we'll still have an incident on our hands. There are, however, creative ways to bend the rules, without you having to fire one *direct* shot."

Kodell nodded toward the viewscreen, and Bat-Levi turned in time to see another piece of space around the shuttlecraft flare. "That's a lot of plasma out there," said Kodell. "A lot of very *volatile* plasma."

Her anger evaporated. Bat-Levi looked from Kodell to the viewscreen and then to Kodell again.

"Oh," she said, showing her teeth in a savage grin, "you are *good*."

"He'll blow," Stern warned. "No way Halak's going to last they keep firing at him like that."

"He's not the only one. Can you raise him?" Garrett spun the shuttle port and down thirty, but not soon enough. The shuttle lurched and bucked, and she heard Stern curse.

"Crap," Stern rapped. Then: "No. We're too far away. Too much damned interference."

"Any closer, and we might as well charge admission," said Garrett, trying to force the shuttle into a turn by dint of her will. She felt the vessel turn, turn, turn . . . then slam into a shock wave. Garrett gasped, felt her stomach bottom out as gravity failed for an instant then came back.

Those damn disruptors, they're touching off plasma explosions left and right, shock waves from all sides . . .

Clearly, they were trying to stop her from making a run for the brown star. Succeeding, too. She understood the Cardassians' strategy. If they couldn't get her with a direct shot, they could ignite the space around her. Like having a whole bunch of phasers. No, better than that: mines. Garrett pushed a shock of hair out of her eyes and tried to think. Either her shields would fail, or the ship would simply buckle and break apart from the shock waves, all that radiation and charged particles slamming into their hull. She couldn't fault the Cardassian on his tactics either. She'd have done the same thing herself if she had enough firepower.

She watched Halak's shuttlepod flounder through space. Somehow, miraculously, the commander had managed to eke out some power from a maneuvering thruster and he'd avoided the Cardassian so far. Not for long, though: She watched the Cardassian scout peel off and bear down on Halak's vessel. As the Cardassian ramped up his speed, she saw a brief pink flare erupt then disappear as the Cardassian's vented plasma ignited a swirl of ionized gas.

Enough firepower. Garrett's breath caught. *My God, of course!*

"Hang on!" Garrett slammed the shuttle into a reverse turn, pivoting the vessel on its long axis and bringing it around. She punched the shuttle to max acceleration, and the vessel leapt toward the Vulcan shuttlepod.

"What are you *doing*?" Stern shouted. Grabbing onto her console, she braced herself. "Are you trying to end this *sooner* rather than later?"

Garrett didn't answer. She punched up Halak's comchannel. "Commander!"

A wash of static, then: "Here."

"Do you still have phasers?"

"Affirmative."

"What about shields?"

"Twenty percent, max. But . . ."

"That will have to do. Listen. I want to try something. Two words: Kolvoord Starburst."

An instant's silence. "Captain, I don't have the maneuverability. There's no way I'll be able to cross your flight path and ignite my plasma trail without ramming into . . ."

"You and I won't have to get that close. Listen. It's the same principle, but instead of us crossing each other's flight paths, I want us to pull closer to the Cardassian and concentrate . . ." It took her five seconds to explain, and two for him to agree.

"My God." Stern was shaking her head as Garrett dropped the ship at Z-minus-70 and brought the shuttle around. "You're both certifiable. You are going to get us barbecued."

"Not if I can barbecue them first." Rushing toward the Cardassian scout, Garrett targeted the space behind the vessel. She brought her phasers on line, full power. "Shields at maximum. Commander, on my mark, in three, two, one, *fire!*"

Garrett's phaser beams sizzled across space. The energy from Halak's phaser joined hers. There was a split second where absolutely nothing happened—when Garrett watched the Cardassian plowing through plasma whorls and ionized gas toward Halak's shuttlepod. Then there was a blinding flash, so bright and quick that the automatic polarizing filters didn't have a chance to snap into place and Garrett winced, threw her hand up to shield her eyes. Then she watched as the space ignited behind the Cardassian, streaming up the Cardassian's vented plasma trail the way fire licks along a stream of kerosene. The space behind and around the Cardassian exploded in a fireball, and the scout disappeared in an orange-yellow maelstrom of ionized gas and ignited plasma.

"Shock waves!" Stern cried.

A wall of ionizing radiation crashed against the shuttle like water barreling through a broken dam. Something shorted just behind Garrett's head; she smelled ozone and scorched metal.

"Jase!" she shouted, battling for control of the ship. She watched, helplessly, as her port maneuvering thruster went out, and her starboard thruster flickered.

But her son was already out of his seat. "I got it!" he cried, grabbing for an extinguisher. Wrenching it free of the bulkhead, he thumbed the extinguisher on and opened up with a short burst once, twice. He staggered back as the shuttle rolled then canted on its short axis.

"I'm losing her, I'm losing her!" Garrett shouted. She tried slowing the ship's spin, but she had no thruster control.

The hull began to vibrate, the consoles to rattle. "Shields and phasers off-line!" Stern reported, shouting above the din. "Rachel, your inertial dampers are failing."

Garrett's teeth gritted. "You need to *tell* me this?" she grunted, wrestling with the controls. "We're going to break apart."

Then she heard Stern gasp. "Oh, my Lord."

Garrett looked up. "Oh, God," she said, going numb with horror. "Oh, my God."

There, like some phoenix arising from the ashes, was the Cardassian. The scout barreled though the firewall and, although Garrett thought it couldn't possibly *not* be damaged in some way—for God's sake, that was the equivalent of several thousands of megatons going off—the Cardassian wasn't hurt enough.

She felt Jase's hand on her shoulder. Garrett slid her arm around her son and pulled him tight. "I'm sorry, son," she said.

Jase's face was pale but calm. "It's okay, Mom."

Garrett pulled Jase's head down to her chest. "Don't look, baby. Don't look."

The Cardassian filled space until that was all Garrett saw.

Dear God. Garrett uttered a silent prayer. *Make it quick, make it . . .*

In the next instant, there was a bright flash, and then space blew apart. And then the Cardassian was spinning out of control.

"Phasers, *fire!*" Bat-Levi shouted.

"Aye!" Glemoor's voice was gleeful.

They watched as the *Enterprise*'s phasers lapped at the space around the Cardassian, setting off another plasma burst.

"*Report!*"

"*That* got their attention!" Glemoor's voice was taut with excitement. "Breaking off pursuit, coming around. Impulse engines only! I read that their axial stabilizers are down fifty percent."

"Those impulse engines," Kodell said from his station, "they're fluctuating."

"Damage?"

"Very likely."

"Mr. Glemoor, are they still with us?"

"On our tail!"

"I like this better and better," said Bat-Levi. She took the command chair. "Bulast, hail the captain—and try to raise the *T'Pol*. Mr. Castillo, bring us about. Head directly for the brown star."

"*For* it?" Castillo twisted his chair around. "Commander, with all due respect, don't you want to lead them away . . ."

Bat-Levi silenced him with a look. "Full. Impulse. Now. Kodell, reinforce those aft shields, those Cardassians are likely . . ." She was interrupted as the ship vibrated. "Likely to fire," she finished wryly. "Damage report, Mr. Glemoor."

"Disruptor cannon fire. Aft shields at ninety percent. Minor hull damage, Decks 15 and 18."

"Order evacuation of all personnel away from the outer hull areas. Kodell?"

"Already doing it," said Kodell. "Reinforcing aft shields. The problem is, it goes both ways. We try to burn up space around them . . ."

"And they try to do the same to us," Bat-Levi said. "Understood. Steal me power and buy me time, Kodell. Mr. Bulast, they getting off any distress calls?"

"Not that I read, but I've got the captain."

Bat-Levi spared Kodell a quick glance. "On audio."

Garrett's voice sputtered through static. "*Enterprise*, just what the hell are you doing?"

"Disobeying orders, Captain." Bat-Levi couldn't help it; she grinned, insanely, and wondered what Tyvan would say about *that* as a manifestation of her anxiety.

"You are *not* to engage the Cardassians! I repeat you are *not* to engage!"

Bat-Levi raised her voice. "I'm sorry, Captain, you're breaking up. What's your status?"

"They're firing again!" Glemoor shouted.

"Evasive maneuvers! Hold your fire, Mr. Glemoor!"

The ship rattled and lurched. "Keep those stabilizers online!" Bat-Levi ordered.

"Switching to backup systems," Kodell reported, "firming up." Then he shook his head. "Stabilizers read nominal but those aft shields, they're at eighty percent. It's not the Cardassian himself; it's what he can do with the plasma. Hull breach reported on Decks 23 and 24. Force fields up, damage control parties en route."

Then Garrett's voice came back. "I heard that." There was a moment of dead silence, and Bat-Levi thought they really *had* lost contact. She was about to order Bulast to get Garrett back when Garrett continued. "You get this, Commander, loud and clear. You are *not* to engage. Do you copy?"

Garrett's tone was ominous, her meaning crystal clear. Bat-Levi swallowed. "Perfectly. And I promise: I won't fire a shot at them. Now, please, what's your status?"

Garrett rattled off her damage. "And my maneuvering thrusters are gone. Shields were too, but we've managed to coax fifteen percent. Life support's fine, for all the good it does."

Kodell spoke up. "Captain, if you shut down life support and get into your suits, you can steal power to reinforce your shields."

"Will I need them?"

He and Bat-Levi exchanged glances. "I'd recommend it for the time being," he said. "Can you relay to the commander?"

"Yes." Another pause. "Bat-Levi, tell me you have a plan."

"Yes, Captain, and . . ." Bat-Levi laid the plan out. She waited in an agony of suspense then, her lips dry, her heart racing. If the captain didn't agree, Bat-Levi wouldn't do it—even if the captain said great, fine, do it, but forget that near-warp transport stuff, are you crazy—because, quite simply, she wasn't about to kill her captain.

After a few seconds that seemed like days, Garrett's voice, tinged with static, came on. "Take care of my ship, Bat-Levi. Anything happens to her, I swear that when I get back aboard, I'll bust you down so fast you'll think you've been greased."

Bat-Levi didn't even have time to feel relief. "Aye. *Enterprise* out. Mr. Bulast, any response from *T'Pol?*"

"Negative, Commander. She's receiving, but she's ignoring us."

"Damn. Keep trying; we've got to get her to talk to us." Bat-Levi spun the command chair back toward the helm. "Mr. Castillo, distance from Cardassian scout."

"Seven thousand kilometers, and closing. Shall I accelerate?"

Bat-Levi breathed in deep. "Negative. Cut speed to one-half."

Castillo's back stiffened, but he complied without a word of protest. "One-half impulse, aye."

Bat-Levi punched at the command companel. "Transporter room, reroute transporter control to the bridge." She looked back at Kodell. "You can handle both ships? All three, if we raise *T'Pol?*"

"The captain and Halak do their job," said Kodell, his hands flying over his controls, bringing the transporter on-line, "I'll do mine. Like you said, I'm good."

"Excellent." She turned away as Kodell ordered a medical team to the transporter room. "Bulast?"

"Still nothing from *T'Pol.*"

Bat-Levi debated a half second. "It can't be helped. We don't have the time to waste. Mr. Kodell?"

"Vent tubes five, seven, and eight at maximal capacity."

"Stand by to vent. All available power to the shields, Mr. Kodell, I don't want them to so much as burp. Glemoor, arm photon torpedoes one and four. Proximity detonation."

If the Naxeran had any reservations, he didn't show them. His movements were quick, economical. "Photon torpedoes armed. Three-second delay."

"Mr. Castillo, on my mark, bring the ship about, hard starboard, reverse course, and accelerate to warp two. Take us right down their throat, Mr. Castillo."

She saw Glemoor nudge Castillo and wink. "Hold onto your hat," Glemoor said.

"Uh-huh," said Castillo, his tone clearly indicating that, perhaps, he ought to kiss his ass good-bye instead.

On the viewscreen, Bat-Levi saw the brown star loom closer and closer. The plasma streamers, the ones created by the tug of the neutron star, unfurled like the thick bodies of twin serpents.

"Almost," she said, and her good hand gripped the arm of

her command chair. She felt the hard edge of plastic polymers bite into her skin, but the pain was good.

"Cardassian's closing," said Glemoor. "Six thousand five hundred kilometers. Six-three."

The ship bobbled, righted. "Passing into gravity well," said Glemoor. "Cardassian right behind, four thousand nine hundred kilometers, taking the bait, pushing his speed up! Three-eight, two-nine . . . he's close enough for a shot! One thousand kilometers!"

"*Now!*" Bat-Levi was on her feet. "Kodell, vent tubes five, seven, eight! Drop shields!"

"Venting! Dropping shields!"

"Bulast, signal the captain and Commander Halak! Glemoor, fire photon torpedoes, proximity detonation!"

"Torpedoes away!"

Bat-Levi's teeth were bared. "Kodell, activate transporter! Mr. Castillo, hard starboard, go to warp two . . . *now!*"

"Aye, hard starboard!" Castillo reflexively grabbed onto his console. "Reversing course! Warp *two!*"

The space around the ship elongated then compressed upon itself as the warp bubble initialized. And then everything happened quickly and precisely the way Bat-Levi had imagined. The *Enterprise* hurtled starboard, its nascent warp field intensifying, expanding the gravity well of the brown star, and then the *Enterprise* wheeled about, shooting past the Cardassian and literally dragging gravity with it. The expanding wavefront slammed into the Cardassian; Bat-Levi watched the scout shimmy, stagger. And then, the coup de grace: The *Enterprise*'s photon torpedoes detonated. The plasma streamers whirling off the brown star ignited into a fury of red plasma flame that propagated forward and back. The brown star flared and bulged and began to break apart.

The Cardassian's hull sheered, split—and then the Cardassian scout imploded.

"Yes!" Castillo cried, pumping his fists like a maniac. "Yes!"

It was the cue everyone on the bridge had been waiting for. The bridge erupted in relieved laughter, Bat-Levi's included. Glemoor preened his frills over and over, and Castillo kept whooping, "Yes! Yes!"

But Kodell—Bat-Levi suddenly froze—he hadn't said . . . the *captain* . . .

"Kodell," Bat-Levi said, urgently, turning so quickly her servos squalled, and she almost lost her balance. "Kodell, report! Did we get them?"

"Commander." Kodell was standing, hands clasped behind his back and quiet triumph written on his face. "Confirm transport, five individuals—alive and well."

Oh, thank you, God. Bat-Levi felt weak and she backed up, groping blindly for the command chair, swiveling the chair so she could sit. With the smallest of sighs, Bat-Levi slid back, and her servos, for once, didn't make a sound. She felt eyes on her, and she looked up—and into Kodell's smiling face.

"Well done, Commander," he said. "And all without firing a shot—more or less."

Gaining. Talma had pushed the *T'Pol* engines into the red but still the distance between her and the Cardassian scout was dwindling by the minute. Gaining—she ground her teeth together—the Cardassian was *gaining!*

Just ahead, she saw the great dense ball of the nebula cloud, its pink and purple colors more intense, the entire cloud more substantial now so close to the neutron star whirling at its heart, being fed by plasma streamers coursing from the brown star.

The *Enterprise* hailed again, but Talma ignored them. She'd listened to their twaddle: something about her dropping shields the instant they went to warp so they could beam her aboard. She'd cut off the transmission, finally. What, did they think she was that gullible? Probably blow her out of space the moment her shields were down.

Well, she'd take care of herself, thanks. Talma found every spare ounce of auxiliary power and re-routed to the engines. *If I can just get inside that nebula, I'll lose that Cardassian, and to hell with Garrett's ship.* She wouldn't have a lot in the way of sensors and her tactical would be fried, but the trade-off would be worth it. The Cardassian would be blind; and then she'd hang there and bide her time.

T'Pol edged past the outer fringes of the nebula; minute particles of dust and debris scoured her hull. The computer warned, in polite Vulcan, that the radiation level outside the ship would reach lethal levels in sixty minutes. Talma told it to shut the hell up then gave a more refined command, in Vulcan. She watched the random flashes of energy radiating through the nebula like the flow of neural energy through a network of nerves and dendrites. *Almost there*—her eyes fixed on the screen, as if willing the nebula closer would make it so—*just a few more seconds, and I'm safe.*

And because she'd told the computer to can it, and because her gaze was riveted upon her viewscreen, Talma didn't see the other Cardassian scout disintegrate; she didn't know that the *Enterprise* had gone to warp; and she most definitely did not register the flow of ignited plasma rippling from the exploding brown star and propagating itself along the plasma streamers being pulled toward the neutron star until the nebula was a ball of plasma flame—and that was much too late.

All she could do then was scream, and even that was lost as *T'Pol* flashed, vaporized, and was gone.

She would have taken some comfort in knowing that, a split second later, the Cardassian found that it was much too close indeed.

* * *

The wall of fire expanded. It tore through one planet. Then two. A few minutes later, the third planet shuddered and convulsed and died.

And on to the fourth.

His throat was so dry he could barely draw a breath. Chen-Mai's broken wrist throbbed, and he'd tucked it into his suit. But every step jolted bone against bone, and once he'd fainted, fallen. Awakened to find that he'd gashed open his forehead so that he had to blink blood out of his eyes. Still he dragged himself through the maze of tunnels and blind alleys, going by feel, groping along the walls with his good hand. And then, because he was so frightened, he started running, fell, clawed his way to his feet as his wrist screamed in pain, and then fell again. This time, he couldn't get to his feet, because the ground was moving.

What was happening? The ground was alive; Chen-Mai felt the rock jolt, ripple as if composed of something liquid, not solid. An earthquake. No—Chen-Mai tried to get his mind to work rationally—*not possible, the planet was dead, it was dead, the planet was dead!*

Something sharp bit his cheek. Chen-Mai flinched, turned his face toward the arched ceiling of the tunnel. He heard the sharp pop and ping of compressed rock splintering, and then a long, loud roar as the mountain began to tear itself apart.

High above, the shock waves from the neutron star coupled with those from the brown star, and rolled over the fourth planet. In a few seconds, the landscape was flattened, the mountains collapsing in, falling toward the planet's dead core.

And, deep underground, the rock groaned, opened beneath Chen-Mai's feet. Screaming, he tumbled into the abyss.

And on to the fifth planet.
And, finally, into empty space.

Chapter 36

"I can't imagine what you expect of me," said Mahfouz Qadir, in an oily tenor. He tweezed a tiny porcelain cup rimmed with gold from an equally fragile saucer and took a delicate sip of strong, sweet coffee. "You can't expect that I keep track of every nursemaid, housemaid, and slut on Farius Prime."

Halak's swarthy features darkened with a rush of angry blood. "Dalal isn't a slut, Qadir, and you know it. Now Dalal and Arava are gone, and I want to know where they are."

"Or what?" Qadir replaced his cup upon its saucer with a soft click of china against china. He squared the saucer on a low carved wood table inlaid with a mosaic of jewels before inclining his head up at Halak who towered over him. "Supposing that I knew and was unwilling to tell you, then what? Eh? Are you threatening me, Samir? You," Qadir's bright, black eyes flicked right, "and this pretty Starfleet?"

Oh, brother, thought Garrett. "You could say that." She folded her arms across her chest. "About Starfleet, that is. Pretty, I couldn't care less. This isn't an official visit, though."

"No? Then those uniforms, they don't mean anything? The fact that your starship, bristling with armament, is parked in orbit, its weapons trained upon my home, this means nothing? You bring weapons to my house, weapons I must confiscate to ensure my safety, and then you make demands, and this is not official, not a threat from Starfleet? How am I to take this then? How would you, a reasonable woman, take this?"

Garrett wasn't in the mood. "Don't count on my being very reasonable. Frankly, you can take it any way you like, but the fact remains that one of your operatives posed as a Starfleet Intelligence officer, kidnapped my first officer, and endangered the lives of my crew. And you're right; you're damned lucky I don't order my ship to vaporize this house of yours. Don't think I'm not tempted."

"You see?" Qadir slapped a palm against his thigh. "Threats. Where are your manners, Captain? You make wild accusations and demand information." Qadir took up a silver tray of sweets and sugared dates that sat beside his coffee cup. "Captain, be reasonable," he said, stirring pastries with one finger then plucking up a triangular date-filled pastry scented with rosewater. "I'm a businessman. Try to understand from my point of view. The first rule of business is quite simple. Nothing is free." He popped the mamoul into his mouth and chewed with an air of supreme satisfaction. "Everything is for profit," he said, around sweet date filling. "So I ask you: What do you offer in return?"

Ah. Garrett thought they'd get to it eventually. What was she willing to trade? "Information," she said. "Pure and simple."

Still chewing, Qadir replaced the tray of cakes. Swallowed. "What sort of information?"

"The Orion Syndicate." She caught the flash of excitement in Qadir's eyes and knew she had his attention.

"What of them?"

Garrett gave a faint smile, and she lifted a finger in admonishment. "No, no. This is the way it will go. *You* answer questions first. Then *I* give *you* information. Take it or leave it."

"Hmmm." Qadir considered. "What if I leave it?"

"Then I'll make sure Starfleet sends patrols through this part of space on a regular basis. Be bad for business, all those official-looking ships out there."

"They have no jurisdiction. They have no, what do you call it? Probable cause."

"No one's talking about a search. This is out-and-out harassment."

"You can't do that."

"Sure we can. It's free space, right? You're not Federation, thank God, so who are you going to complain to? So, do we have a deal?"

Qadir settled back upon his pillows and considered. A wise move, Garrett thought, because the man had a lot to lose. Mahfouz Qadir's house, with its grilled screened windows and lush tapestries and thick marble walls, was located on a black basalt promontory that jutted out into the Galldean Sea. Qadir's riyad—his garden where they were now—was tucked in an open courtyard that was shaded by orange, cypress, and lemon trees. In the center, squatting beneath the shade of a vaulted Earth-style Moroccan gazebo, was a low divan of green silk with a carved bloodwood frame so dark it was almost black, and on the divan, tucked amongst pillows of gold and iridescent peacock blue, sprawled Mahfouz Qadir.

He was not, Garrett had decided, an attractive man. His skin was sallow, and he had too much flesh on a frame that was much too small. She thought it likely that the man hadn't seen his own feet for over a decade. His face was very round, with jowls that substituted for a neck, and his lips were small, with a pronounced cupid's bow. But if he had the face of fat cherub, his eyes were those of a Donoor rat: like shiny black marbles.

Those eyes gave her a shrewd look. "Very well," Qadir announced. "I accept. But I want a retainer. How else am I to judge that my information is worth the price?"

"All right. Two words." She held up first one finger, then a second. "Talma Pren."

Qadir's rat's eyes narrowed. "Done."

"Where's Dalal?" Halak said.

Qadir steepled his pudgy fingers together. "As I said, I am not responsible for every woman on the planet, but," he held up a hand, palm out, as Halak took a step forward, "it so happens that I do know of a case very similar to what you have described. I am afraid, however, that the woman in question is dead."

Halak's voice came as an astonished whisper. "Dead?"

"Yes. It appears that someone broke into her home and murdered her. The apartment was ransacked, some valuables taken, the perpetrators not apprehended," he waved a hand, and his jeweled rings sparkled, "and that is all."

For a moment, Halak didn't move. Then he started forward. "That's all? That's *all?*"

"Commander!" Garrett put a restraining hand on Halak's arm. Halak's arm was stiff and rigid as iron beneath her hand, but she felt him tremble, and she heard the harsh rasp of his breath. "Back down, mister."

Halak gave her a quick nod then looked back at Qadir. Hatred blazed in his eyes. "What about Arava?" Halak asked, his voice thick with emotion. "Where is Arava? Where is Klar? Are they dead, too?"

Qadir, who hadn't flinched a muscle during all of this, gazed up with an expression of calm serenity. "No. They're safe."

"I don't believe you. I can't find them."

"I said they were safe. I did not say that they were easily located."

"Where are they?"

Qadir inhaled deeply, sighed. In the silence, Garrett heard the lazy drone of a fly.

"A question," said Qadir and then, in a quick aside to Garrett, "Just one."

Garrett gave a miniscule nod. Qadir trained his gaze on Halak. "If I tell you, what will you do?"

"I take her as far away from here as I can, as quickly as I can."

"And she does not come back, correct?" Qadir zeroed in on Halak. "More importantly, *you* do not return, yes?"

"Not in a million years."

"You relinquish all claims?"

Halak's eyes slid quickly to Garret then back to Qadir. "Whatever deals you made, you made with my father. I am not my father's son, not in that way."

"Yes," said Qadir, his oily tone faintly derisive, "you're reborn, in Starfleet now. Found yourself a new family, eh? Cleaner? More to your liking?"

When Halak didn't answer, Qadir's pink lips puckered. "Well, I suspect that once Starfleet knows everything there is to know about you, they might not *want* you for a son. Every family exacts its own price for loyalty."

"But that's my problem, isn't it? Not yours. Now, I've answered your questions. You answer mine."

Qadir studied Halak for another brief moment. Then he gave a backhanded wave of dismissal. "I'll have her brought here. Take her, and welcome to her."

"And the boy."

"Yes, of course, of course. But, you," Qadir flicked a jeweled index finger at Garrett, "she won't be as useful as you think. Her information is obsolete."

"That's not for me to decide, and I really don't care," said Garrett.

"Then we both don't." Qadir gave a good-natured shrug. "And now, information, yes?"

Garrett turned to Halak. "Wait outside." When he hesitated, she said, "Go. I'll be right with you."

Qadir's eyes followed Halak as he walked out of the courtyard and disappeared into the house. "A difficult man. You'll have your hands full, Captain, presuming he's allowed to remain on duty, eh? Assuming he's not court-martialed, sent to prison?"

"Stop fishing." Garrett did not return the smile. "Whatever happens, I'm sure you'll be one of the first to know."

"Eyes and ears, Captain," said Qadir. "You know, there's

a fascinating bit of Earth history I learned the other day. Did you know that Queen Elizabeth I had a most advanced spy network? Sir Francis Walsingham ran it, and legend has it that his network was so extensive and advanced it was the envy of its day. And everyone knew it, you see, that he was Elizabeth's eyes and ears; that someone was always listening for her, watching. So when some court painter did Elizabeth's portrait, he incorporated the most ingenious thing, a bit of code. She wears a beautiful orange mantle and if you look very carefully, you see that he's painted tiny embroidered eyes and ears all over the cloak. Eyes and ears, Captain," Qadir touched a finger to the corner of one of his bright, black eyes and then to the lobe of his ear, "eyes and ears."

"Then let's talk about one of *your* spies, shall we? Talma Pren."

Qadir reclined on his gold and peacock blue pillows, like a child settling in for a good story. "Yes, what of Talma? Do you know I can't find that girl anywhere? You can be sure, I'm going to give her a talking to."

"That's going to be a little hard. She's dead," said Garrett, and saw the genuine surprise in Qadir's eyes. *Gotcha.* "Incinerated in a stolen Vulcan warpshuttle. Would you like to know how and why?"

"Please."

"It goes like this, Qadir. Talma worked for you, a middleman I'm guessing, someone who ran interference between your mercenaries and the organization itself. So she'd be privy to a lot of information, know about your distribution corridors, where you're getting arms and to whom you're selling them, how you network red ice, things like that."

"I run a legitimate business, dealing in antiques and archaeological oddities. I have no idea what you're talking about."

Garrett lifted an eyebrow. "I'm not bugged, if that's what you're worried about. Besides, you said it: The Federation has no jurisdiction here. Anyway, I'll bet you that Talma Pren looked around at all this," she motioned to include Qadir's house, the riyad, "and wanted more. As you said, every family has its price, and I guess you weren't paying her enough. Then along comes Laura Burke . . ."

"Burke, Laura Burke," Qadir said, a pudgy finger to his lips. "Who is this Burke?"

"Save it." Garrett tone was caustic. "You have eyes and ears; don't tell me you didn't know."

"And what if I did?"

"You're a businessman, Qadir. You know what would happen if word got out that, somehow, you let a Starfleet Intelligence operative into your organization. So you sent Talma, whom you trusted implicitly, to get rid of her. Only Talma outfoxed you, and she did a number on Starfleet Intelligence, too. She rigged the explosion on Burke's shuttle, but then she assumed Burke's identity. Only *you* would know that Talma had been with Burke, and so you'd assume Talma was dead. It was perfect because when Talma, posing as Burke, showed up again, you'd naturally assume that Talma's plan had failed and Burke had, somehow, gotten away."

"But for what reason?"

"Talma knew you were after the portal. Hell, she probably arranged it for you," said Garrett, knowing that Qadir had no way of knowing that the portal did not exist, nor what they'd found beneath the surface of that dead planet. "She knew what was going down. So after Halak showed up and provided a very convenient cover, she knew that all she had to do was pose as an intelligence agent, take Halak, and use *him* as a middleman. She'd never be directly implicated; Talma Pren's dead, after all. So she'd get the portal and whatever else your mercenaries found—they'd all die, by the

434 Ilsa J. Bick

way—and it's likely that you'd believe the expedition was a failure, and she'd walk away, probably with more than a small fortune."

Qadir picked up his gold-rimmed coffee cup, studied its contents for a moment then replaced it without drinking. "That's a very nice story. But you're overlooked one thing. Of what possible use would the portal be for Talma? Talma runs . . . ran nothing."

"In *your* organization. It's so obvious even you must see it, Qadir. Talma worked for the Orion Syndicate, and that's how she managed to convince Burke that she'd be as good a contact as Arava, except Arava passed information to Starfleet, and Talma played both sides." She didn't add that this was the only way Talma Pren could have known about Halak and his forged documentation. Halak's brother Baatin had given these documents to Halak, and used Orion Syndicate contacts to arrange for Halak's disappearance.

"When she was posing as Burke, she mentioned that Orion Syndicate operatives are scattered throughout your organization. I just didn't put it together until later that she was talking about herself, too." Garrett gave Qadir a look of mock sympathy. "You're going to have a really tough time knowing who to trust from now on." (She didn't add that Starfleet Intelligence would be all over Qadir's case like Xanarian fleas.)

Two high spots of color burned on Qadir's fleshy cheeks. "A very interesting story," he said, finally. "Too bad Talma's dead, and we can't have a little chat."

"Yes, isn't it?" Garrett turned to go then stopped. She bent from the waist until her eyes were level with Qadir's. "Look, I don't care about you," she said. "All I care about is my crew. So listen, very carefully. Stay away from Halak. Stay away from my crew."

"Or?"

"You need me to spell it out?" When Qadir didn't reply,

Garrett nodded. "Good, I'm glad we understand each other."

She straightened. "Eyes and ears, Qadir, eyes and ears. Someone will be watching. Someone will be listening. So will I. Don't cross me."

She walked away without another word.

They'd flown in silence for a few moments when Garrett said, "Mind if I ask you something? What really happened at Ryn III?"

Halak shot a quick glance over his shoulder at Arava, who was seated just behind Garrett, and a young boy whose hand she held. "Arava, why don't you take Klar aft, get him something to eat? There's a little replicator further back, and we've got another forty-five minutes before we get to the ship. He must be hungry."

"I'm not hungry," said Klar. He had Arava's dark eyes, but his jaw was square, like Halak's. "Please, Uncle, can't I stay up here with you?"

"Now, come on," said Arava, unbuckling her harness. "You heard your uncle. He's a busy man, a Starfleet officer, and that's his captain there, wants to have a word with him. You'll have plenty of time to spend with your uncle later on. Come on," she gave the protesting boy a little push, "let's go exploring."

"It's just a ship," Klar said, "and it's a *little* ship."

Garrett watched them go then turned back to Halak. "Good-looking boy. He's got her eyes."

"And Baatin's face."

"Yours too. Do you think your sister-in-law knew what Talma was up to?"

"That Talma would kill Burke?" Halak frowned. "Absolutely not. The way she told it, Talma argued that she had more information to give Starfleet than Arava. Talma had worked for the Orion Syndicate and Baatin, and Arava trusted her. So I guess Arava convinced Burke that Talma would be a better witness. Plus, Arava had Klar to worry about. Anyway, the next thing Arava knew, Burke never returned and she didn't hear from Talma. I don't know why Qadir let Arava live. Maybe he was playing both sides against the middle—funneling useless information to the Syndicate, and vice versa." Halak blew out, scrubbed his hands on his thighs. "I don't think she has anything useful for Starfleet."

"We'll let SI decide that. Now, what about you? Ryn III? I want to know."

Halak licked his lips, blew out again. He stared out of the main shuttle window, but Garrett could tell from the look in his eyes that he was staring at a memory.

"Everything happened the way I said," Halak began. "Those scouts fired on us. We had to abandon ship. A desperate thing to do, but it was better than nothing . . ."

"Ten hours," said Strong, his face glistening with sweat. His breathing was labored, although he had more air than Halak and his supply wasn't dwindling as quickly. But fear also ate oxygen. "It's been ten hours."

"Stop . . . talking," Halak panted. "Using up . . . your . . . air." He gulped, his lungs trying to wring more oxygen from air that didn't have it. The air inside his suit was thick, and he had a roaring headache. Carbon dioxide poisoning, he thought. Headaches, diaphoresis, dyspnea. But not unconsciousness, not the nice quiet exit one would get from carbon monoxide poisoning. They'd pass out eventually, but only after they'd had convulsions, vomiting. So maybe he'd choke on his vomit and suffocate that way. He wasn't sure which was better.

Strong gave a weak laugh. "Doesn't matter. Both of us going to end up like Thex."

Halak didn't have to strength to glance over at the lifeless body of the Andorian. Thex had died within an hour of their beam-out. They'd bled the Andorian's air, Halak giving Strong most of it because of the damage to Strong's suit.

"Still got time," said Halak. He checked his automatic distress beacon, but the readout was blurry and he had to shake his head to clear it. "Maybe the *Barker* . . ."

"They'll never hear it." Strong spoke in a hopeless monotone. "Too far away."

They hung in space, neither one of them speaking. Then Halak stirred. "Have to," he worked at forming the words, "have to ask you something."

Strong's eyes had been closed, but now he pulled them open. "Chest hurts."

"Carbon dioxide, and . . . and you're scared. But, *listen*," said Halak. He moved, too abruptly, and had to fight back a wave of nausea. *No, no, please, God.* When the urge to vomit passed, he said, "Thex said there was a signal. Said it was coming from us. 'Member?"

Strong grunted. Halak took that as assent. "Why did you fire?"

"Told you. I thought they were pow . . . powering up . . ."

"No, no, the two readings, they're not even close." Halak had to stop a moment and gulp air. "You can't mistake them."

Then he said, without knowing that this is what he thought until the words were out of his mouth, "You're with the Syndicate."

" 'S crazy," Strong moved his head back and forth. " 'S crazy."

"No, no." Halak was so dizzy that Strong's face swam in his vision. "Those were Syndicate ships, not . . . not Ryn scouts. You led them to us with a homing beacon . . . that signal, that signal Thex saw."

"S'crazy . . ."

"Stop." Halak grabbed at Strong's shoulders. Strong's

hands scrabbled at Halak's, but Halak hung on and gave him a weak shake. "Stop, we're going to die out here . . ."

"Get away." Strong batted at Halak's helmet, tried pushing him away, although the irony of it was, they were tethered together. "Get away."

"No, no. I have to know . . . I have to know wh . . . *why*." Then Halak ran out of breath, and he felt himself sinking under a wave of dizziness. "Coward," he gasped, releasing Strong, "you . . . you're a *coward*. You've killed us, and you don't have the guts . . . the guts to own up . . . up to what you've done."

He heard Strong's rasping breaths over his comchannel but nothing else. Halak felt a surge of anger and revulsion. He could accept death when it finally came, but to die like this, not knowing what he was dying *for* . . . Maybe it was good Strong had more air. Then Halak could die first, and then Strong could hang here and rot, for all Halak cared.

He fumbled at his comchannel and was about to switch off when Strong said, "Yes."

Halak stopped, his fingers frozen above his comcontrols. "What?"

"I said yes. Yes, what you said. I . . . did that. I did it."

"Why?" Halak was too astonished now to feel anger. "Why, in God's name?"

"Wasn't the plan to . . . *kill* anybody. Plan was to capture the shuttle."

"Capture the shuttle?" Halak said. "That . . . that was all?"

"Embarrass Starfleet." Strong licked his lips, took a deep gulp of air. "But then . . . they started firing and, see, I knew . . . I knew they were going to kill us."

"Because the results," Halak panted, "they'd be the . . . the same."

"Same questions, if we're dead as if we're alive. Only killing us, no witnesses."

"No *you*." Halak dragged in air. "You were the ... dangerous one. Loose ... loose cannon. So you killed them first."

"Backfired, huh?" Strong doubled over in a coughing fit.

Halak made no move to help. When Strong had caught his breath, Halak said, "Why?"

"Do it?" Strong rasped. "I don't know. Stupid reasons. I wanted to be in charge ... charge of something. Turned down on promotion last month, so I knew it was a matter of time before I'd get the boot, probably leave Starfleet ..." Then, in a pitiful whine: "I ... I never meant for anyone to get hurt."

At that moment, Halak felt the dam of his self-control break. *Not get hurt, not get* hurt! A hundred awful scenarios crowded his vision: cracking Strong's helmet, venting the man's air, ripping open his suit ...

"Didn't *mean* it?" Halak rasped, choked with rage and lack of air. "Thex is *dead!* You killed the men ... the men in those ships! And us, you've ... you've killed ... you've *killed* ..."

Shaking with fury and dizziness, Halak spun away, not trusting himself any longer. Since they were weightless, the movement propelled him out in a whirling pirouette until his tether ran out and the line went taut. They hung there, twirling through space—Halak, Strong, and the lifeless Thex—each at the end of a tether, the grotesque points of a fractured star.

There was a sound then. At first, Halak thought that Strong was starting to cry; he heard the wheeze of air, a hitch in Strong's breathing. Then the tether around Halak's waist went limp and he turned in time to see Strong's body hurtling toward him. For an instant, Halak was frozen in place. Then he threw up his hands to ward off the blow he thought inevitable, when he realized that Strong was coming at him much too fast, faster than he could possibly have managed by pulling on the tether and letting momentum do the rest.

That hissing sound. Halak's eyes widened. Strong was purging his air.

"No," Halak said. "Strong, stop!"

Too late, he saw the white jet of Strong's air shooting out to hang in a fog of frozen water and gas, like a veil. Strong plowed into him, and then Halak saw Strong fumbling with the seals on his helmet.

"No, stop! Why are you doing this?" Halak shouted, knowing that the other man wouldn't be able to hear in another moment because there would be no air to carry the sound of his voice, no air for him to breathe. Knowing what Strong's face would look like in less than three seconds because that's all the time it would take for Strong to pop his helmet. Watching as the seals opened, and Strong yanked off his helmet.

"Why?" Halak shouted, watching as the horror unfolded. "*Why?*"

He never got an answer.

Garrett let the silence go for a long moment. "Why do you think?"

Halak turned from his vision of the memory. "Captain, I've asked myself that every day since it happened. He could've killed me, but he didn't, and I don't know why. I guess Strong figured he was dead either way, or maybe there was some last vestige of pride in there, his wanting to make things right, I don't know. Anyway, he knew that either we ran out of air, or the *Barker* got there, and I turned him in. Because I *would've* turned him in."

"Why didn't you tell the truth?"

"Orders, those damn orders. I wasn't supposed to be making contact with the Syndicate, remember? SI played that line, hard. No matter who asks, or what happens, stick to the official story. So I did, figuring that SI would watch my ass. That's why I didn't say anything when Burke . . . when Talma was here. I couldn't, and I didn't know what she knew, or how this would play out. And then there was Strong, his family. When all was said and done, I couldn't see how the truth helped. What was the point? The man was already dead. So I let it go."

Garrett nodded, and they fell into a silence that Halak broke.

"What will happen now?"

"I have to remand you back to Starfleet Command," said Garrett, as evenly as she could. She kept her gaze fixed on some distant point in space. "There's the issue about your lying about your past, and your initial report on Batra. You'll have to answer for all that. At best, you'll get off with a reprimand, maybe another transfer. At worst . . ."

"I'll be court-martialed."

"Yes."

"And what do you want, Captain?"

"I don't know," Garrett said truthfully. She looked over at Halak. Reached out and clapped a hand on his arm. "Let's just see what happens, Commander. What is it Glemoor says? One step by one step."

Epilogue

"Darya, I'm so sorry I'm late," said Tyvan, as he hustled into his office and tossed a pile of datadisks onto his desk before dropping into his chair. "I just couldn't tear myself away from medical. It's good luck we put in for repairs at Starbase 12 because there's a child trauma specialist here working with that Naxeran boy, Pahl. So I stayed on, watched her work a bit and time passed and . . . why are you laughing?"

"Because it's nice that even psychiatrists have problems. Anyway, it's fine."

"Then I'll stop apologizing. You're looking good, by the way."

In the past, Bat-Levi would've felt self-conscious, as if Tyvan were trying to compensate in some oblique way for the very obvious fact that she didn't *look* very good at all. But now Bat-Levi smiled. "Thanks. I *feel* good. I think I know why."

"Oh?"

"It was having to come front and center. When the captain made me XO, I didn't have the luxury of worrying about what how I looked or what people thought every time I gave an order, or had to make a decision."

"To put it bluntly, all eyes were on you."

"And then some." Bat-Levi exhaled a half-laugh. "It's very strange how you said I wanted people to notice me but in a negative way. I was so angry with you, but you were right. I kept telling myself that I just wanted to be left alone, but the way I am . . ." She made a helpless gesture. "I can't help but attract notice."

"Do you know why?"

"Yeah. I think it's something like, as bad as you feel, I feel ten times worse. And I just dare you to make something of it."

Tyvan folded his hands over his lap. "And now?"

The left side of Bat-Levi's mouth tugged into a wry grimace. "There are a lot of times I'd still rather hide in a closet than get out there and be with people. But when push comes to shove, it seems that *here*, at least . . ." She used her left hand—the one without nails—to gesture in an all-inclusive way. "On *this* ship, with *this* captain and *this* crew, it doesn't matter what I look like. What matters is that I do my job, and if I fail or succeed, it will be because of the way and how well, or poorly I do that job. How I look has nothing to do with it."

"And when did you come to this conclusion?"

"Honestly?" and then Bat-Levi laughed again. "That's dumb. Like I'm going to lie, right? When I was on the bridge, and the captain asked me what the hell I was doing, and when Kodell pissed me off."

"Kodell was provocative?"

"Sort of. Not overtly, but he nagged me, and that made me mad. In retrospect, I understand now that he was pushing me to take a chance . . . hell, to do something downright dangerous." Bat-Levi's gaze skittered away, to a spot on the floor. "Kind of a dare, like, come on, it's up to you, are you up for it, or not?"

"So you took the dare. Why?"

Because I like him, a lot. Aware, suddenly, that she felt uncharacteristically warm, Bat-Levi shook her head, shrugged. Gave a small, embarrassed laugh. She directed her answer to the floor. "I don't know."

"I don't believe you."

He might as well have said he'd caught her out. She knew she was blushing—*really* blushing—but this time she met those brown eyes square on. "There are some things I want to keep private for now, even—or maybe especially—from you. It's not that I'm angry, but . . . remember when you're a kid and you discover something for the first time? Part of you is just busting with wanting to tell someone, but another private part wants to keep the secret either because you don't quite believe it, or it just feels good to have something that's totally yours and doesn't belong to anyone else."

"A delicious secret."

Relieved, she nodded. "So we'll just leave it at that about Kodell, okay?"

"Fair enough." Tyvan laced his fingers over his middle, slouched down, and put out his long, slender legs. "And what about the captain? What happened with her?"

Bat-Levi smiled at the memory. "She got on the horn, told me to back off."

"And you didn't."

"I knew I was right. No, that's not quite true. I *thought* I was right, and the rest of the bridge crew—even Castillo, who probably thought I was certifiable—they did what I said."

"Well, you could say they're just professionals doing their jobs."

"Which they wouldn't if they didn't have faith," said Bat-Levi, "especially if the XO didn't have faith in herself. You're on the bridge, you can tell these things. So I was right there, up front where Kodell essentially told me I had to be. We make it, we don't—it's my call. No place to hide, no one else to blame and . . ."

Bat-Levi halted then. A wave of sadness washed over her, and she half-expected Tyvan to ask her what she was thinking, but he let the silence go. Bat-Levi shifted, crossed her right leg over her left, kept her eyes averted. (Another part of her mind remarked on the fact that Tyvan hadn't commented on the obvious, but she ignored it for the time being. Maybe he'd notice, maybe he wouldn't.)

Then Bat-Levi said, as if she hadn't fallen silent, "And then I realized that I didn't make Joshua's choices for him. He'd made them. I told him not to go down into the pod, but he did it anyway and it was the wrong decision to make, and he died."

Now her eyes sought Tyvan's. Held. "Just like the captain and me. She argued, and then she got behind me, and I did what I thought was right. Kodell told me I had to make a decision, and I did. It was my decision, not his. Mine. If I made a mistake, there wouldn't be anyone to blame but me. Oh, the captain might blame herself for putting me in charge, but she had faith that I'd make the right decisions. I just had to have faith in me."

Tyvan gave her a frank look. "There's only one thing I take issue with. You said Joshua made the *wrong* decision, but it's like I've always said. We have choices, but sometimes we don't like the ones we have. So Joshua made *a* decision, Darya. You'll never know if it was the wrong one because you'll never know the alternative. Perhaps, in the end, his choice was best for you."

Bat-Levi was silent. What could she say when she knew he was right? In the quiet, she heard the tick-tock of the pendulum clock, and she suddenly realized something.

"It's been five sessions," she said. "You're supposed to make a recommendation now, aren't you? About my being on probation?"

"I already have. In fact, I've given it to the captain, though I doubt she's had much time to read it."

She felt an unpleasant jolt of surprise and then wariness. My God, she'd been absolutely *awful* to the man for the majority of their time together: a basket case, she thought grimly, and then considered that would be an expression she ought to quiz Glemoor about, if she got the chance. She watched as Tyvan twisted around in his chair, rummaged around a pile of datadisks, and then tweezed out one between his thumb and forefinger.

He offered it to Bat-Levi. "Would you like to read it?"

Her anxiety fluttered in her throat, like a trapped bird. "Why don't you just tell me?"

"All right. I've recommended no further treatment or evaluation, and I've recommended that you stay on."

Shock made Bat-Levi's mouth drop. "But, but I missed sessions, I *yelled* . . ."

Tyvan held up a hand. "First of all, we've been kind of busy. Second, you made a choice. You took responsibility, and you told me where to get off. Good for you. I don't need you to agree with me, Darya. I'm glad you feel better, but I don't *need* you to feel better, nor do I need you to have an operation, fix your scars, get a new face, pony up for the latest prostheses, or do anything you don't want to do. All I want is for you to know *what* you're doing, and *why*, and the rest is up to you, because it's your life, Darya, not mine."

She sat a moment, absorbing this. "So I don't have to come back?"

"Not unless you want to."

"Well," she said. "I might, from time to time. Things come up. But you know something?"

"What?"

"Sometimes, I talk to you. In my head," she added hastily. "I mean, I'm not nuts, I don't hear voices. But sometimes, lately, I hear you making comments and, sometimes," she gave him a lopsided smile, "I just tell you where to go."

"Does this bother you?"

"It should, but it doesn't. I've been arguing so much with myself for so long, it's kind of nice to have someone new in there."

Tyvan gave a delighted laugh. "I'll probably go away eventually, when my opinion stops mattering so much."

"Probably." She paused, head cocked. "Does becoming obsolete bother you?"

"No. I'm not a crutch. My job is to become obsolete."

They shared a brief moment of comfortable silence. Then Bat-Levi smiled, rose, and moved for the door.

"Okay then, thanks. But I'd better get dressed. The captain will have our hides if we're late." She hesitated then said, "By the way, you haven't said anything."

Tyvan's brow furrowed. "About?"

In reply, Bat-Levi extended and flexed her left arm. Did it again, twice. Then she saw the confusion on Tyvan's face clear.

"Wait," he said. "Your servos. There's no noise."

Bat-Levi laughed hugely. "The ship's not the only thing that needed repairs."

"My God," McCoy complained peevishly, "you're as twitchy as a long-tailed cat in a roomful of rockers."

"Mac," Stern flung over her shoulder as she palmed open her closet, "I told you before. I have to get moving, or I'm going to be *late*."

"Making me dizzy, what you flitting back and forth like a bumblebee."

"Then use audio next time, you don't like the view," said Stern, pawing first through her collection of uniforms, and then an array of more casual slacks and a few skirts. She made disgusted sounds. "Now where I did put that thing?"

"You could be better organized."

"I'm a doctor," she grumbled, "not a chambermaid. I could've sworn I put . . . ah!" Stern yanked out her dress tunic then dove back for her dress slacks. "Now if I can just find my boots . . ."

"My God, woman." McCoy craned his neck as if he could see around the corner of the viewscreen, which he couldn't. "Are you getting *disrobed*?"

"Listen to you." Stern's fingers fumbled with her belt

buckle. "It's not as if you haven't seen this sort of thing before."

"Only in an official capacity. But if you're offering, come over here where . . ."

Stern stripped off her uniform tunic. "Watch it, Mac."

"I'm not the one doing a striptease. Anyway, I thought you'd be interested."

"I *am*. You just pick the damnedest times, that's all."

"Then why not hop on over, and we can visit? You owe me bourbon."

"Mac, I'm at a starbase about a gazillion light years away. It's not as if I'm next door. I'll get back to Earth soon enough and then we can visit, have a couple drinks."

"Don't forget, you owe me an R and R. I aim to collect."

"I haven't, and you will."

"Promises, promises." McCoy still sounded miffed. "When are you shipping out?"

"Tomorrow." Stern stepped first her right then her left foot into her dress uniform trousers and pulled. "Repairs are just about done. All we're waiting on is that transfer shuttle."

McCoy *mmm*ed. "By the way, I heard a rumor that someone on your ship slipped a subcu transponder into that Halak fellow."

Now it was Stern's turn to *mmm*. She did so as she pulled her hair free of her standard ponytail and began pulling a brush through. Her hair crackled with static electricity and she made a mental note to talk to environmental engineering about adjusting the humidity in her quarters. Too damn dry. "That's what they say."

"You wouldn't happen . . ."

"Mac," Stern paused, brush in hand, "open channel."

"Ah. Well, I hope our little talk about vitamins was helpful."

Stern grinned at her mirror image. "Very. So what were you so hot to tell me?"

"Oh, nothing much. Only that the data your captain forwarded on to the folks here at Command? From that old tomb site? Looks mighty old. More than ancient: We're talking thousands of years."

"Wait a minute." Stern turned until she was looking at McCoy, properly. "You're a doctor, not a xenoarchaeologist. Why are you even involved with this?"

McCoy held up a hand. "Hold your horses; it'll all come clear. Like I said, this place was old. We're talking either pre-Hebitian, or the Hebitians are a hell of a lot older than even the Cardassians know."

"Or claim." Turning back to her holomirror, Stern touched the controls. The mirror shimmered, and then she was looking at the back of her head. She gathered her hair together in her left hand while her right stirred through an array of elastics. "They're not exactly forthcoming. So you're saying that the natives were Hebitians?"

"No, and we're not entirely sure we're talking Hebitian either, but that's the working hypothesis. Anyway, this is where it gets pretty interesting. It looks like the natives were an entirely different species. Tomb drawings show two distinct types of people: the ones that were descendents of those Night Kings, and everybody else. So probably there was an indigenous population on the planet, but one that was very primitive by Hebitian standards. Now there's always been a suspicion that at least some of the Hebitians were telepaths. Even the Cardassian legends talk about that a little. But I don't think that, on the basis of what you and your captain saw, we can say that every Hebitian telepath was all sweetness and light."

"Amen to that." Stern smoothed stray hairs back then keyed in for her holomirror to show alternate views: back, front, each side of her head. She twiddled with her ponytail, centering it snugly against the nape of her neck. "Rogue telepaths, right?"

"Or just common criminals. So how do you control a telepath gone sour? You can either kill him, and that doesn't seem to have been the Hebitian style, or you can exile him somehow, put him on ice, like stasis only telepath-style. Here, they reduced their neural patterns somehow and put them into a containment field."

"Like a genie in a bottle."

"Only these genies got out. Probably an accident: one of these rogues figuring out that a person with a certain genetic makeup could act as a receptacle. So breed a select line of those people but make it mystical, like a state religion, and these rogues get their chance, now and again, to go free. Except you'd dilute the stock over time; happens when there's a large population. And genetics is funny business. Too much inbreeding, you make the stock weak, and too much mixing with the rest of the gene pool and your chances of getting exactly what you want go down."

"Makes sense." Stern replaced her brush and then popped open another drawer and began affixing her pips to her uniform collar. "It would explain the need for the mask."

"Yup. So here's the kicker and where you have to use your imagination, take a couple leaps of faith here. Now, for the sake of argument, let's say that these rogues were Hebitian and the Hebitians, as a species, were telepaths. Some were good; some were bad. The Cardassians say they're descendants of the Hebitians. But Vulcans can't mind-meld with Cardassians and there are no Cardassian telepaths. None. Zip. Not a one. Okay, your turn."

"Oh, Mac, that's a gimme." Stern turned and ticked off her conclusions on her fingers. "It's obvious. The Cardassians *aren't* descendants of the Hebitians, but they may have evolved *parallel* to the Hebitians. Only the Hebitians were the stronger, master race. The Cardassians revered the Hebitians, maybe not like gods, but they build up this religion around access to a higher spiritual Oversoul, Overmind, whatever you want to call it. You know those murals they have around Lakarian City?"

"That thing with wings and a Cardassian face, the one with tentacles?"

"That's it. First of all, that creature hovers above the planet, like a sun god, just like what we saw. Second, those tentacles radiate down to the people on the planet and then through the people *into* the planet. I think the official interpretation is that this refers to this Overmind, or something, binding the people together, anchoring them to the planet. Only what if that's a reference to the Hebitians? To something down deep, in the planet, like what we found?"

"Interesting idea." McCoy pulled thoughtfully at a wattle of flesh beneath his chin. "Can't prove it, can't disprove it, but it would answer why the Cardassians look on the Hebitians as gods. Go on."

"Mac, don't you get it? Those tentacles, they're metaphorical references to the Hebitians' telepathic capabilities. Over time, the Cardassians develop resistance to psi influence. The Hebitians lose control, and then, like all gods, they fall. Except for the Cardassians, it's a disaster because the planet's in chaos, and they're still rebuilding, getting stronger. But here's the real mystery." Stern leaned on her knuckles and eyed McCoy through her viewscreen. "Mac, those telepaths on that planet, how did the hell did they get there? Who was smart enough to know how to capture their neural signatures in a magnetic containment field?"

McCoy pooched out his lips. "The Hebitians themselves?"

Stern ducked her head in agreement. "Or somebody equally, if not more advanced. And they had to be a spacefaring species, Mac. So who were they?"

"Beats me. Like all mysteries, just opens up more questions, stuff we can argue about over drinks. So." He clapped his hands together, gave them a good scrub. "When you going to happen back my way?"

"Soon." Stern straightened, tugged down on her tunic.

"Sooner, if you give me a good mystery. You know I love a good mystery."

"Will do." Then McCoy pulled his face closer, squinted. "My God, woman, are you wearing lipstick?"

Stern laughed out loud. "Mac, I *told* you. It's a *party.*"

The doors opened to the ship's arboretum, and Garrett stepped into the soft, sweet scent of roses and Asian lilies. The air of the arboretum was damper than the rest of the ship, and Garrett listened to the splash of water cascading over a tiny rock waterfall to a pool where the green discs of lily pads and Denebian watertrumpets floated. The sound of the water reminded her of Qadir's riyad, and that made her think of Halak, and she wondered where he might be at the very moment.

Not now. With an effort, she tore her thoughts away from Halak. Later—she checked the time because she'd wanted everyone convened at 1900 on the dot—she had plenty of time to think about Halak later. Right now, she had to find Jase.

That didn't take long. She wandered down a path that began with the spiny, squat desert *wahmlats* that studded Vulcan's arid plateaus and ended in a small grotto of tropicals—bromeliads and orchids—native to Earth.

Jase slouched on a slate stone bench next to a tiny pool stippled with the stalks of musk-scented butterfly wands. He held a drawing pad in one hand, a pencil in another because, as he told his mother, he was a purist. A collection of Matrayan blueglows ducked and weaved over a profusion of wide, splayed petals of hot pink and deep purple.

"Can I sit down?" she asked.

Jase nodded without looking up. Garrett slid onto the stone bench, feeling how cool the rock was beneath her thighs. She cocked her head to study Jase's drawing: the half-finished portrait of a man. Her heart squeezed. There was no mistaking the high cheekbones, the fall of that raven-colored hair.

She touched a finger to the drawing. "It's beautiful."

"It's not done," said Jase. His voice was thick with unshed tears. "It's only been two weeks, but I can't remember his eyes. I try, but the more I try, the more he gets blurry, like I'm looking through fog."

Garrett wanted to point out that they had pictures; there were archives and records. But she held her tongue. She was always in such a rush to fix things, provide false reassurances that everything would be all right. Sometimes the best thing was to allow space for pain. God knew she'd had her share of grieving before, and after the divorce. But at that last moment, when she'd knelt beside Ven Kaldarren, her grief had crashed through the barrier she thought she'd erected. Grief was still fresh in her heart, with anger at her own stupidity— her own stubbornness—not far behind.

She knew, too, that Jase had lost something infinitely precious: his father. Conceivably—though she couldn't imagine it—she might come to love again. But Jase would never have another father, and there were experiences Jase had with Ven Kaldarren that Garrett wouldn't ever be a part of because she simply hadn't been there.

She ached to brush the boy's hair from his forehead, but she wasn't sure she should touch him just yet. In the two years since the divorce, how he'd grown. No longer a little boy but teetering on the brink of adolescence.

Time's tricky that way. You've got your memories, but time flows all around you and you're always thinking you have so much more time than you really have. Really, all you have, in the end, is time for regret.

That niggling little voice of conscience? Or was it her, accepting herself? Maybe, she conceded, it was both.

Jase traced the angle of his father's jaw with one gray-smudged finger. "Do you remember what he looks like?"

Garrett inhaled the scent of wet earth and damp leaves. "Sometimes . . . no. And then sometimes, like here," she nodded at the pond, the flowers, the blueglows, "I'll smell something and then I'll remember a picnic by Lake Cataria, what I wore, how your father made a joke and I spilled a glass of Potroian punch all over his shirt because I was laughing so hard." *And, so, why do I feel like crying?*

"I can't do that," said Jase miserably. "I can't think about him much without remembering what happened and how he looked when those things . . ."

Jase's eyes pooled, but no tears came. "Why? Why didn't they take me? Why Pahl and Dad? I felt them; I *saw* them."

Acting on impulse, Garrett put her arm around her son. She felt him stiffen, and for an insane moment, she thought that he was going to scream at her to get away; that she could never be like his father; that she'd left them both behind for her ship and people she loved better. She almost pulled away.

Stop running. You ran from Ven, and now you're trying to run from him. You're so ready to be rejected you'll do the rejecting first.

She squeezed his shoulder. "I don't know," she said. She thought back to the mind-cry she'd heard—Ven, calling—how strong that momentary connection had been. Fading now. Receding into memory.

"All I *do* know is that, for a brief instant, I heard your dad calling. Up here." She tapped her left temple. "Inside."

"Yeah," said Jase. "Me, too. Only it went both ways. Dad never talked to me that way. Said I needed my privacy. But sometimes he leaked."

"Leaked. Thoughts?"

"Yeah. Sometimes I could hear him and Nan yelling, only not in words. You know? The air got," he cupped his hands, "heavy. So I figured out how to make my head go gray. Like the way the sky looks just before it rains."

An empath . . . or something more. Garrett felt an electric thrill tingle through her limbs. She wasn't sure if it was from apprehension or excitement, and then decided it was a little of both. She'd always known Jase might inherit some of his father's abilities. But what Jase described was so eerily close to telepathy, she wondered if she should have Stern, or maybe Tyvan, spend some time with Jase, maybe test him.

No. She reined in her natural desire to try to find an answer, close a loop. She had to let this go for now. The important thing now was to be here for her son, to be with him, and to let him talk about his father, and what would happen next.

"What's going to happen next?" asked Jase, suddenly.

"What?" Garrett felt the way she had when her mother caught her climbing on the roof when Garrett was a little girl (and wasn't *that* a whole other story). "Well, I've talked to your Nan on Betazed. We all think it would be better for you to live there."

Jase looked solemn. "Does it matter what I think?"

"Yes."

"Then I'd like to stay here. I know I can't," he added quickly, "but I'd like to. I love you, Mom."

Garrett put both arms around her son. No resistance this time. She felt the tension melt from his limbs as if he were flowing into her and becoming one. It was the way she remembered he'd been as a baby: a little ball of fury until she'd taken him in her arms and soothed him back to sleep.

"Oh, Mom." He pressed his hot face against her neck and she felt the wet of his tears on her skin. "Mom, I'm sorry, I'm sorry, I'm . . ."

"No, quiet," she whispered, tears burning on her cheeks. "It's all right; it's all right for you to have been angry. I understand. I love you, Jase. I'll always love you. And who knows? Maybe, someday, I'll be able to take you with me, and we'll live together on a starship and travel to places so far away that the light of where we've been won't have time to catch up."

She hugged him close. "Someday," she said, and believed it.

* * *

In the turbolift, Castillo glanced at his chronometer, saw the time, and knew that Garrett was going to eat him for breakfast. He was going to be so late it wasn't even funny. (Not that Castillo understood the origin of that expression. Where was the humor in being late? Maybe Glemoor could explain it.) It wasn't his fault, either: the people over at transfer, the ones from Starfleet Command, *they* were the ones insisting on forms being voice-printed three times over. Chain of custody, they called it. Figured. The first time the captain wanted Castillo at an official function—had specifically *requested* he show up, in dress uniform, *on time*—and here he was going to be late, and there wasn't a damn thing he could do about it.

Other than a few pleasantries, they'd exchanged not two paragraphs on the ride over in the shuttlecraft. And now the turbolift seemed to be taking forever. Castillo fidgeted, staring in that blank, abstracted way at the flashing indicators just above the doors that he always did when riding in a turbolift with a complete stranger. Only he wasn't with a stranger. They simply didn't know to what to say to one another.

Then Halak spoke. "Any idea why they wanted the inquiry on Starbase 12 rather than the *Enterprise*?"

Careful. He'd been briefed on what to say. Castillo spoke to the indicator lights. "They don't tell me why they do anything."

"Mmm-hmmm." A pause. "But you'll be there."

"Why do you say that?"

"You're in dress. So I figured you were going to sit in. Observe?"

Castillo hiked one shoulder. "Maybe." Then because he couldn't stand the feeling he was having—the way he heard Tyvan's voice in his head, telling him he couldn't keep running from himself forever and would have to have more courage than he thought he possessed—Castillo said, "Stop."

The turbolift jerked to a halt.

Halak turned, eyebrows raised. "Ensign? Is there something wrong?"

"No," said Castillo. He licked his lips. Tyvan's voice again: *Getting started will be the hard part.* "Yes."

He filled his lungs, blew out. "Commander, I have to tell you something."

"About what?"

Castillo was already regretting this (*go away, Tyvan, just go away!*), but he pushed on. "About what happened with Ani. Everything that happened, it was my fault."

Halak's brow creased. "*Your* fault. How?"

"I . . . well, you know, we were close. Before you came." When Halak just nodded, he continued, "And then you showed up and I could tell that Ani, she'd fallen hard. I was jealous, but I got over that. At least, I thought I had. People change their minds all the time, and . . ."

Castillo looked away for a moment, dreading what he knew he had to say. Sucked in a breath and continued. "Anyway, I would watch the two of you, and she looked so damned happy, I couldn't stand it. I thought all kinds of things. Crazy stuff now that I look back on it, but pretty awful stuff."

"I can imagine." Halak's voice was quiet. "You're not the only one who's ever been jealous."

"Yeah, well, I thought I'd gotten past that. And then Ani came to talk to me. This was about a week before she died. We were still close after she took up with you, and we'd talk. We were friends." Castillo wondered if he sounded too defensive then thought to hell with it.

"I know that. I never held it against you." Halak paused. "What did she say?"

"She said she was having second thoughts. I wasn't sure what about; she'd gone to see Stern. She wouldn't tell me what Stern said, but whatever it was, she was pretty upset."

"Well, it doesn't matter anymore, Ensign. Ani's dead, and . . . we'll just never know. Dr. Stern won't tell us, and it's more than likely that, after the inquiry today . . ."

Halak broke off, and Castillo thought he'd just let this pass, but Halak squared his shoulders and said, "After the inquiry today, I doubt very much that I'll ever serve with Dr. Stern, or anyone else from the *Enterprise*, ever again."

Castillo knew something about that but judged that now was not the time. He had to finish this.

"Ani talked about wanting to break it off with you." Castillo closed his eyes, remembering the surge of elation he'd felt, the sheer joy that maybe Anisar Batra might be his after all. "But then you took off, and she was beside herself. Whatever was bothering her, she didn't want to wait until the two of you got to Betazed."

"All right," said Halak, puzzled. "But I still don't understand . . ."

"I told her where you'd gone," Castillo blurted. "I told her that you were on your way to Farius Prime."

Halak was stunned. "*You?* But how did *you* know?"

This was the hard part, Castillo knew. Best just to admit it and go on. What had Tyvan said? *He can't hate you anymore than you loathe yourself.* "I was on the bridge when Bulast patched that call through to you. I used my bridge access code to break into his communications archives and pull up the message. Then I gave the information to Ani. If I hadn't, she wouldn't have gone, and she'd still be alive."

For a moment, Halak said nothing. Then he let out a very soft breath, almost a sigh. "Yes, that's true, isn't it? I guess it also means that I'd be dead instead."

"Sir?"

"There'd have been no one there to save my life, twice over. Ensign, why did you do it?" Halak's voice trembled, and Castillo thought that although the commander appeared calm, he probably wasn't.

I sure wouldn't be; I'd be aching to take a swing.

"It's obvious, isn't it?" Castillo heard his shame and pushed on. "I wanted her to break it off with you, and I was willing to do just about anything to speed that along. So I told her, and now she's dead, and that wasn't supposed to happen." Castillo closed his eyes. Had to steel himself before he could look Halak in the eye again. "There was a time when I wanted you dead, Commander. I didn't care how—a shuttle accident, a transporter failure. Anything. So when everyone blamed you for Ani's death, I did, too. I was happy to. And when they took you away, part of me was glad because I wanted revenge, and part of me was ashamed that I was glad because the only revenge I ended up taking was on myself, really. And on Ani: She was a victim, too. I know now that I was wrong, not just because of everything that's happened since but because I spent a lot of time thinking about how I'd let my jealousy turn me into the type of man who didn't deserve the love of a woman like Ani."

There. Castillo stopped talking, stood his ground, and waited. He'd done it. He didn't feel good exactly. Relieved just a little. Sick with shame, too. That would take time to go away, Tyvan had said. The important thing was that Castillo had admitted his culpability to a man he'd hated but didn't any longer because Castillo understood that his hatred had merely been the mirror image of his hurt and anger. When he'd gone to see Tyvan, he'd known the doctor wouldn't turn him in—couldn't because Castillo had seen him in a professional capacity, patient to doctor. But now he'd revealed his secret to someone who could take action, and very likely would.

"Why have you told me this?" Halak asked then. "Why are you telling me this?"

Castillo searched Halak's face and saw no anger there. Only sadness. Resignation. "Because you had to know," Castillo said. "Because we'll . . . because you needed to know going forward."

"Going forward." Halak gave a mirthless laugh. "Ensign, the only place I'm going right now is to a formal inquiry. *Again*. And," he tapped his wrist, "we're late."

They didn't speak again until they stood before the doors leading into the Starbase 12, Level 7 conference room.

Halak took a deep breath. "Before we walk through those doors, Ensign, I just wanted to say . . . thanks. I know that was hard for you. It took courage."

Castillo's gaze was unwavering. "It would have taken more courage to live with my feelings. To learn that things can't always go my way."

"We all learn, Ensign," said Halak, and then his lips turned in a slight smile. "One step by one step."

They walked through the doors.

A waiter came her way with a tray laden with Maltran sea-scallops marinated in a Kefarian apple-orange sauce, but Garrett waved her away. She taken special care with the menu, though she didn't exactly enjoy that duty. My God, when was the last time she'd arranged a reception? She sipped at an amber liquid in a squat glass tumbler, smelled the spicy aroma of bourbon. The *Carthage*, that reception for the Klingons and Cardassians—*Cardassians*, for crying out loud. Garrett swallowed, felt the bourbon burn its way down her gullet before exploding in a ball of heat in the pit of her stomach. What a headache *that* was. Garrett gave a soft, private laugh of amazement, shook her head. Trying to figure out what Cardassians would eat, and then having to find those bizarre *taspar* eggs, getting the mess chef to cook them just the right way so they weren't still raw and *looking* at you . . . Garrett shuddered. Everything had gone off all right, though she'd drunk a fair amount of bourbon that night, enough to kill the pain. She'd made sure there was plenty to drink, for everyone, including Ian Troi who was practically addicted to Betazoid *allira* punch.

Poor kid. She smiled at the memory. Fresh off his honeymoon, and wishing he could go back to Betazed and his new wife Lwaxana, but itching to have his adventures, pursue his career; she could sympathize. She'd known exactly how he felt because that was how she'd been torn between Ven and *her* career. Only the Trois had made it work. Ian was still serving on the *Carthage*, still happily married; from what Garrett heard, they'd just had a second child.

Oh, Ven. Her eyes glazed with tears. She turned aside; she was glad now that she'd chosen to take up a station next to a viewing window that looked out at the stars and her ship. She took another pull from her drink (*easy, girl, don't get weepy on me*), composed herself. Waited until the burn of tears pricking her eyelids faded.

Time for this later, in private. She turned back, let her gaze wander over the room, her crew. She spotted Tyvan right away; he was so tall it was hard not to. She saw that he was talking to two science techs, and good for him. Coming out of his shell. Glemoor was shooing Bulast away from the servers readying the food at the buffet, no surprise there.

Then she spotted Kodell and Bat-Levi at a small round table, their heads bent toward one another in that earnest way of two people who are, for the moment, seeing only one another, and that *was* a bit of a surprise. Kodell said something to Bat-Levi, and Bat-Levi laughed, hooking that star-white streak of hair, so startling in that otherwise full head of black, behind her right ear. Bat-Levi was wearing her hair down this evening—still tucked up in some ingenious way as to be within regulations, because she was in full dress—but Garrett thought that the effect of that river of black spilling around her shoulders very attractive.

Something there. Garrett saw how Bat-Levi brushed her fingers against Kodell's forearm. *Something's going to happen for those two.*

She thought about Ven again, and that made her immensely sad, but she couldn't help it. *And maybe that's the way I will have to be for a while.* Garrett swirled her bourbon, watched the amber fluid catch and refract and break the light. Her thoughts spiraled, like the liquid: *Maybe that's the way it should be. Maybe I haven't let myself be sad, only angry that I couldn't fix it, or that loving Ven wasn't enough when it should have been enough and now it's too late . . .*

"A penny for your thoughts," a voice said from over her right shoulder.

Grateful for the interruption, Garrett turned. "Don't forget to clue Glemoor in," she said, lightly, covering. "You look very nice, Doctor. Is that make-up?"

"Don't be mean." Stern raised a flute half-filled with pale yellow champagne. "And Glemoor knows that one, I'm sure. You're not mingling, Captain."

Garrett gave a disparaging half-shrug. Swirled her drink. "Just thinking."

"Wait a minute, wait a minute." Plucking Garrett's bourbon from her hand before Garrett could protest, Stern snagged champagne from a passing waiter and handed the flute to Garrett. "Bourbon's for good cries, and smoky bars on rainy nights. Or sickbay, when there's just the two of us. You want to talk about it?"

The flute was chill against her fingers, a nice feeling. Garrett took a tiny sip. After the bourbon, the champagne tasted icy and crisp and fizzed in her mouth. "Not really. But . . . thanks."

"My pleasure."

Garrett changed the subject. "They're late."

"Think there was a screw-up somewhere?"

"Maybe. You never can tell with Command."

"Amen to that. Relax. If it was really serious, we would've heard." Stern nudged Garrett, lifted her chin toward the waiter who'd been circulating with the sea-scallops. "Ten to one, I have to put Darco on another diet."

Garrett followed Stern's gaze and saw her communications officer busily plucking scallops and crackers from the hapless waiter who stood, tray proffered, a study in patience. Glemoor stood alongside Bulast, gazing mournfully at the rotund Atrean.

"Know any pithy idioms about weight?" Stern asked.

"Penny wise, pound foolish?" Garrett saw Stern's expression and wrinkled her nose. "I guess not."

"Not that old saw. But you and me, we'll think of something." Stern slipped an arm around Garrett's waist and gave it a quick squeeze. "Come on, you're so *serious!* This is a party! Relax!"

"Can't help it. It's been rocky, these past few weeks—Batra, Halak." *Ven.* Garrett gave a rueful smile, a little laugh. "Everything. Tyvan would say I'm brooding about past mistakes."

"And he'd be right. You've got a good crew, and they've got a great captain." Stern raised her flute in a toast. "The best damn ship in Starfleet. To the future, Captain."

Garrett smiled. "To the fu . . ." But then the doors hissed, and Garrett turned in time to see Castillo walk in.

And Halak.

The room went dead. Halak stood absolutely rigid, a look of utter shock frozen on his face.

Then, Castillo blurted, "I couldn't *help* it! They gave me the runaround when I took custody!"

"What?" Halak found his voice. He turned first to Castillo then to the rest of crew, and then his eyes came to rest on Garrett and Stern. *"What?"*

"Oh, for God's sake," said Stern, exasperated. "If no one's going to say it, I will. *Surprise.*"

The room erupted in a swell of laughter and applause. Someone shoved a glass of champagne into Halak's hand, and then Halak disappeared from view as his fellow crew members converged, deluging him with handshakes and pats on the back. Garrett hung back and waited, letting the rest of the crew have at Halak, allowing Halak to revel in the moment.

When the noise level in the room had finally settled down to a manageable roar, Garrett lifted her champagne and raised her voice above the din. "A toast!"

She waited as everyone in the room raised their glasses. She glanced at Stern, gave her friend a wink then turned her smile to her family—her crew.

"To us," she said, simply. "To the future. Welcome back, Commander. Welcome home."

ACKNOWLEDGMENTS

There are a few people without whom this book wouldn't have seen the light of day, and they deserve recognition and special thanks.

First and foremost, my most profound thanks and gratitude go to Marco Palmieri, an editor who took a chance on an unknown because, as he put it, sometimes you just gotta roll the dice. Marco has been the most patient, encouraging, and available of mentors, and his invaluable comments and insights into the manuscript, from proposal to outline to finished product, made my work—already enjoyable—an invaluable learning experience as well. Thanks, Marco: let's hope you rolled a lucky seven. I know I did; other newbies should be so fortunate.

My thanks go to Keith DeCandido, writer and editor, who went over this manuscript with a fine-toothed comb, provided copious and exhaustive notes, and dinged me, gently, on the craft of telling a story well—and dang, if he wasn't right about those point-of-view shifts. Thanks also to Paula Block at Paramount, who gave my outline the go-ahead.

There is one person who deserves my very special thanks: the editor who gave me my first break. Since 1999, Dean Wesley Smith has been a teacher to whom I have turned repeatedly for help and advice. Dean is not only a great writer;

he is also an unselfish and experienced teacher of a craft he truly loves and champions. Dean has been encouraging when I've been discouraged; he's listened to rants; he's wisely chosen not to respond to self-pity; and he's not been above giving me a nice supportive boot in the pants when I've needed it (thank God, not often). Above all, Dean and his wife, the equally impassioned and accomplished writer Kristine Kathryn Rusch, have taught me that, barring the sun going nova, I really am responsible for my own career. Dean, I am indebted more than I can say, or possibly express.

Finally, my tally wouldn't be complete if I didn't thank my husband, David. Seven years ago, David was the one who dared to voice what I could only half-acknowledge: that writing is what I've always wanted to do. Since then, David's enthusiasm, support, and love have made it possible for me *to* write, and while I don't think that he or my two girls, Carolyn and Sarah, suffered too terribly much, I know that he had to put up with his share of what he's come to call my "writing frenzies." Wisely, he knows when to phone Domino's and keep the children at bay.

ABOUT THE AUTHOR

Ilsa J. Bick is a child, adolescent, and forensic psychiatrist and has written extensively on psychoanalysis and cinema. One day, her husband insisted that what she really wanted to do was chuck all that psychoanalytic stuff and write stories. After staring at acoustical tile in her analyst's office for two–three years, she decided he knew her pretty darn well and since then, she's done okay. Her story "A Ribbon for Rosie" won Grand Prize in *Star Trek: Strange New Worlds II*, and "Shadows, in the Dark" took Second Prize in *Vol. IV*. Her novelette "The Quality of Wetness" (Second Prize) appeared in *Writers of the Future, Vol. XVI*. Her work has appeared, among other places, in *SCIFI.COM*, *Challenging Destiny*, and *Talebones*. Her short story "Strawberry Fields" appeared in *Beyond the Last Star* (edited by Sherwood Smith) and her story "Alice, on the Edge of Night" was published in *Star Trek: New Frontier: No Limits* (edited by Peter David). This is her first published novel. She lives in Wisconsin, with her husband, two children, three cats, and other assorted vermin.